To Adina,

this book edition wouldn't have happened without you. Thanks for the great work of extracting us out of trouble

Ron Dahill

Thanks Adina.

Danny Who?

Four Decades in Irish Music

*****

The Fortunes and Misfortunes of a Hapless Irish American Musician who was Born in St. Paul, and during a Life of continu'd Variety for Four Decades, in which are included excursions into The Oilfields of Louisiana, the Industry of Commercial Fishing, the Joys of Jack Pine Savagery, as well as Encounters with the Supernatural & the Worlds of Structural and Personal Rehab, Poverty, Yachting and Irish Country Living, was Three Times a Husband, at Times a Thief, Three Months a Felon in the Workhouse, at last grew Rich (in Experience) and liv'd Honest.

Written from his Own (We Trust) not Faulty Memories.

Published by Gwenwst Books

St. Paul, Minnesota, U.S.A.

First Gwenwst Books Edition 2017

ISBN 97809914423-6-2

Dedication

To My Old Masters

Patrick Hill 1900-1979

Patrick Flanagan 1914-2001

Terence P. Teahan 1905-1989

And to All of Those

Who Play for the Honor and Glory of Ireland.

Author's Foreward

Back when used cars were cheap and long distance phone calls expensive, writing letters was a common and enjoyable practice. The words seemed to flow as if the pen had a mind more acute than the writer's. Telling the tales in restaurants, pubs and speeding cars was entirely different. The stream of words was usually interrupted by the arrival of the food, the direction of the conversation or the direction of the vehicle. As the years went by the stories and experiences piled up and holding on to the memories was becoming a job in itself. One night at the Dubliner Pub in St. Paul I had a conversation with Matt Dahl, a writer himself, who suggested that it might be a good idea to put some of the stories down on paper while I still could. The time wasn't right, but the seed was planted. A few years later I was asked, first, to act as the storyteller in a stage production, and then to contribute an article to a publication. Those two events caused the seed to germinate and it grew into this book.

With a pen in hand once again, filling three spiral bound notebooks took about three months. That was the easy part. Putting the stories onto a computer was completely beyond me since I didn't own one. That job fell to Ginny Johnson, my partner for the past eleven years. Ginny sat at the table with the computer, and I parked myself in an easy chair with the notebooks. Together we worked editing and re-editing, filing off the many rough edges and axing the stories too rough to include. Now I don't have to remember not to forget the people that filled my life with music and stories.

Any lies are unintentional. I tried to tell the true story without triggering any new indictments. No names have been changed to protect the guilty, but a few have been left out. I'm chalking up any mistakes of fact to "artistic license." I fully realize that my perceptions of the past will not necessarily match up with others' recollections. I've enjoyed the privilege of being allowed to tell my tale and hope that more Irish musicians of the last half century will be encouraged to write their own memoirs.

Table of Contents

Tom, on his way

Prologue
Galway City, Ireland
1973

I'm sitting at the crowded bar in Cullen's' Pub near the train station. There are jigs and reels being played. It's a smoky little place. I am listening to a local, an older fellow who, when he hears that I enjoy music and singing, starts a recitation that is unfamiliar to me. I'm always on the hunt for songs and stories. It seems he has a good one. He gives me the first line.

"There is not in this wide world a vision so sweet"

There is a guy dressed up like a cowboy with a ten gallon hat and a big silver belt buckle. His arrival distracts the man with the recitation. I feel like giving the guy a wallop, but being that it is my first time in Ireland I am on my best behavior.

So I call for two pints. I take a gulp. He mentions the proper way to drink a pint.

"Drink it down to the thumb on the first pull."

We drink. He's getting ready with the rest of his poem. I buy another round to keep him in the mood.

"There is not in this wide world a vision so sweet,
As a plate of red cabbage...."

"Time please," the barman calls.

The music is out of this world. There is just time to buy another round. Pints are only seventeen pence, about a quarter of an American dollar.

Before we leave the pub, he intones something about, "Red cabbage and pigs feet" and mumbles about a bus to Salt Hill, and a hotel that he knows will be open.

We chat on the bus going to the Banba Hotel, named after a local pagan goddess.

At the hotel I buy a couple more rounds. The old fella has run out of money after buying cigarettes. He's generous with the cigarettes.

A few hours later I am back on the bus alone, seven or eight pints poorer, repeating over and over, being sure to remember....

"There is not in this wide world a vision so sweet,
As a plate of red cabbage and plate of pig's feet,
And Sir Thomas Moore, had he not an arse in his britches,
Nor a penny in his pocket,
He wouldn't give a shite for where the waters meet,
He'd be headin' straight for Kilkenny!"

Part One

Chapter 1
Wake Up the Old Man

We were up on stage at the Sword in the Stone Coffeehouse in Boston, performing some of our own songs. I was singing and playing a twelve string guitar and Barbara was playing the flute. The coffee drinkers were going out often to smoke. Although tobacco smoking was allowed indoors in those days, what they were smoking wasn't. The coffeehouse was part of the folk scene in Boston and there was music most nights. People in the early seventies had heard plenty of original music. I was starting to realize that, just because our music was original, it didn't mean that it was going to be popular. Although the crowd was a polite one, about halfway through our set, a young fellow shouted out, "Don't you sing any Irish songs?"

I thought back to some of the songs that the nuns used to have us sing around St. Patrick's Day in St. Paul and said "How about Molly Malone?"

"Let's hear it," he said. Off we went and that song got more response than anything we had done that night. "How about another one?"

I dredged up "The Whistling Gypsy" and "Over in Killarney", reaching the bottom of the barrel very quickly, but thankful that my parents owned all of the Bing Crosby records.

"How about 'The Wild Colonial Boy' or 'Whiskey in the Jar'? No? Come on, let's wake up the old man, he'll teach 'em to you! Come on!"

So we followed these guys home and indeed did wake up the old man. We were all about twenty and the old man was maybe forty. We opened some beers and had a sing song in the house that night although I am sure the poor man had to be up for work in the morning. I was surprised these kids considered Irish music cool because I thought that Irish music was for some of the older people I had grown up around. When I heard "The Moonshiner" and "Finnegan's Wake", I suddenly realized that these songs were not only simple to play but suited me to a "t" because they were about the things that I loved best - drinking, courting and the occasional brawl.

Barbara's uncle had given us some Clancy Brothers albums right before we left Minnesota and between the two of us, we had quite a few folk music records. We started looking through them the next day, searching for any Irish songs that we might be able to learn.

We were living on the second floor of a three-story tenement on Rockvale Circle in Jamaica Plain, an old suburb of Boston next to Dorchester. It was one block long with a circle of six three-story flats. Almost no men lived there, mostly mothers with lots of kids. The fathers or boyfriends who stopped by late at night had the bad habit of breaking the bottles of whatever they were drinking on their way into or out of the buildings. There were lots of beatings, black eyes and tears. It was a pretty sad neighborhood at the time, but the rent was cheap.

Our landlord kept fifty-five gallon drums of flammable liquid on the wooden fire escapes of his buildings with a promise to burn them down if the rents weren't paid. Behind our building and up a steep slope was a section of Franklin Park known as "The Wilderness." At night you could hear the gunshots, screams, fights and police sirens coming from the park and be glad not to be up there.

It was a hot summer, 1971. The buildings were sweltering and we had a big fan in the window to keep us from cooking. I would go to the liquor store every morning and in an attempt to keep myself cool, buy a $1.99 gallon of S.S. Pierce Hearty Burgundy with an ID that gave my name as Ray Lama. I had copied a driver's license which had been left behind in a St. Paul bowling alley and used colored pencils to make the governmental stamps look real. I accidently cut off the last two letters of the name when I was trimming the plastic I had used to encase the thing. As bad as it looked, that ID had served me well for years. Nearly any ID worked back then.

I'd pour the burgundy over ice in a big tumbler and I drank it like Kool Aid. I would work away at songwriting, still thinking I had a vocation, and by four or five in the afternoon, the gallon of wine would have disappeared. I would have a song or two written, complete with harmonies and perhaps a new Irish song memorized.

Back then, I wrote down the music for Barbara, which was easy for me to do even though, oddly enough, I was not able to read music easily myself. I also had to write one letter a week to my probation officer, Vito Marascuillio, back in St. Paul. When I left for Boston, I had just started three years of probation and I was trying hard to stay out of trouble. In spite of my intentions, when the battery died on the black van that was our only form of transportation, I found myself pulling a battery out of a company truck down on the corner, having jumped a ten foot fence before I even realized what I was doing. I kicked myself afterward. It took time to break bad habits.

Dad and Tom in Rowley, Mass.

There was a street dog in the neighborhood named Jimmy, a big black and brown collie-shepherd mix. He would follow me around when I was out and about and jump into the van if we drove off anywhere. The three of us went for a drive up the North Shore of Massachusetts one day and on the outskirts of the town of Rowley, we saw an old farm that had a sign out front that said, "Apartment for Rent". The red barn had been turned into a dinner theater and the old farmhouse, also painted red, had three apartments and the office of Claude Grisell, who went by the name Pierre for professional reasons. He had a striking resemblance to Napoleon Bonaparte and was the man who owned the premises.

We stopped in and rented the apartment for a hundred dollars a month. Jimmy the dog ran around and liked the little town of about 3,000. It was September in New England and Rowley and the surrounding countryside were beautiful. The town was about five miles from Ipswich and near Newburyport and all those little Yankee towns that dated back to before the American Revolution.

We went back to Boston because we had a month or so before we could move out and Rockvale Circle looked as grim as ever. I was still writing letters to my P.O., Vito, and in the next letter I told him about the new apartment in Rowley. I had developed the habit of writing everything in rhyme which Vito didn't mind. He gave us the OK to move.

Even as a kid, I tended to remember where I was when I first heard a new song. The tendency was reinforced when I started playing in a rock and roll band in high school and we were constantly on the lookout for good songs to learn. It was at Jack's, a typical college bar we were playing near Harvard Square in Cambridge that I first heard Rod Stewart singing Maggie Mae on the juke box. I remember saying at the time, "He'll ruin his voice singing like that. The poor guy will never last."

At Jack's we were doing a mix of original songs and covers from my days in rock-and-roll and were starting to throw in a few Irish songs. Someone at Jack's told us about a great little Irish pub on Massachusetts Avenue. I had just turned twenty-one, so

I retired my phony IDs, saying good-bye to Ray Lama and to Victor Crumb, another of my aliases for all those years. We headed down to the Plough and Stars.

The Plough and Stars, also in Cambridge, had Guinness on tap, a rare find in those days even in the Boston area. Better still, the Plough and Stars was where many Irish musicians and singers hung out and played. Declan Hunt, Clive Collins, Sean Tyrrell and Jack Geary were regulars. Maggie Barry, Pecker Dunne and many others stopped in when they passed through. Jigs, reels and all the old rebel songs of Ireland were in vogue. There was a great buzz of Irish music all over town and we found ourselves being drawn into it.

Everything Barbara and I owned fit into the van and we moved to Rowley in one trip. Jimmy the dog decided to join us and jumped into the van as we were getting ready to leave. We thought that since he didn't belong to anybody, he might as well come with us. We settled into the upstairs of the farmhouse. The farmer who lived in the house before it had been converted had hanged himself in the barn and there were occasional sightings of him in The Chanticleer Dinner Theater next door. The restaurant employees refused to work alone at night. I never saw him, but in our apartment in the old house I did notice that the trap door to the attic in the bedroom ceiling was always ajar. I would close it, but within a day or two it would be out of place again.

I had done a stint in the workhouse in Minnesota before heading to Boston. After I had been out a year, I received a letter from Vito saying that I was being let off probation early. The judge decided that in spite of the conviction, I was probably innocent of the charge because I had passed a lie detector test twice before going to trial. What the judge didn't know was that I passed because I thought I was innocent until my day in court. When I saw the detective who had been working undercover on the night in question, I recognized his face instantly and only then remembered the truth of what happened. Oh, well, everyone makes mistakes and some make more than others. Since I hadn't been caught at anything new I was off the paper. I just wanted to play music and so was doing my best to stay out of trouble.

Money was tight and it was tempting to get a job. I'd had jobs in a couple of factories between dropping out of college and the workhouse, and knew from experience that an eight or ten hour shift was exhausting. If I had a job, I was pretty sure I wouldn't have the time or energy to play music the way I wanted to play it. Poverty, hunger, (and thirst) were wonderful motivators that inspired both of us to throw ourselves headlong into the life of professional musicians.

*****

Jan and Ron Nilan lived in the apartment below us in Rowley. Jan worked at the Chanticleer and Ron was a bartender and professional gambler, whatever that meant. Jan had worked with a girl at the restaurant who had been a violinist, but had been in a bad car accident. She had gone through the windshield into the woods and bounced off a couple of trees. She broke a lot of bones and the doctor said that if she hadn't been drunk, she would have been dead. I had mentioned in passing to Jan that I wanted to try playing the fiddle. When Jan told the girl about my interest, she gave her violin to me.

I became instantly addicted to practicing the fiddle. I practiced all day and night. Any tune I had in my head I would try. I had no teacher, but would ask for and get pointers from any fiddler that I met. In spite of that effort, my fiddling was pretty screechy. I think it was about this time that Jimmy the dog disappeared. We looked all over, but he was gone. I hoped that he hadn't been hit by a car. I felt guilty for bringing him up out of Boston and for not being a better fiddler. I couldn't really blame Jimmy for disappearing. The music was much better in Boston.

A Pub in Haverhill Massachusetts, The Cork and Kerry, hired Barbara and me to play Irish music. I only knew about twenty-five Irish songs at the time, but we got the gig. When we showed up, the bar was empty except for one older fellow who asked us, "Have you ever had a White Russian?"

We answered, "No."

"Come on, they don't make them here, but I know a place that does."

Well, when we finally arrived back at the Cork and Kerry, it was full of people waiting for music and they were mad... at us. I started singing but forgot the words, broke a string, and started laughing. Eventually, we pulled it together enough to get through the night. Afterwards, a lady whose name I later found out was Marie Eason said, "We really hated you until you started laughing and smiling. Never forget to smile!"

"The Ox" Calling

In the crowd that night, there was a big Irish mafia guy called "The Ox" McCarthy. He owned a pub in Springfield Massachusetts and wanted us to play there on St. Patrick's Day. He also hired us for a concert at the Paramount Theater beforehand. We showed up at the theater after a lot of van trouble, little sleep and no food to discover a huge crowd and a great line up of musicians, all from Ireland except for Barbara and me.

Butch Moore and Maeve Mulvaney headlined. They had each been stars in their own right on television in Ireland. Butch had a popular show band and had represented Ireland in the Eurovision Song Contest. Maeve was known as "Ireland's Queen of Ballads." They got together, married and came to America. As was popular at the time, Maeve wore her black hair big. I would even go so far as to call it gigantic. Her stage costume ran to mini-skirts, almost transparent blouses, big false eye lashes and go-go boots. Even with inch long fingernails, she played fiddle with flair. She could drink any man under the table and often did. Butch was the more conservative looking of the two. He was always humorous and looked bemused when on stage. Jesse Owens and James Keane were also on the bill under the name "Jesse and James." Backstage the whiskey bottles were handed about and everyone was having a ball. We played the pub later, and I was told that we were good.

The next morning I woke up out of a dead sleep to the sound of a phone ringing. It was the Ox telling me to get down to The Keg Room right away. He was outraged at something I had done. I had no idea what it was, and he wouldn't tell me over the phone.

When we arrived at the pub, he roared at me for a while but still didn't tell me what I had done. Barbara didn't seem to know either. I never did find out what the trouble was. He must have been able to tell that I was used to being in trouble when he realized that his words were having little educational effect. He stopped yelling and forgave me for my offense, whatever it was. Then he and Big Aggie, his head bar matron discussed their next steps as if we were not in the room. They decided that they wouldn't damage me in such a way that I would never be able to work again and instead would clean us up and turn us into the next Butch and Maeve. The Ox took me into his office and demanded, "What is your Irish name? I know you have Irish in you."

I said, "Dahill."

"OK, from now on you are Tom Dahill."

I spelled Dayhill for the Ox with a "y" because I didn't know what he was up to, and I didn't want to sully the Dahill name. I also wasn't sure how my father would feel about me using his mother's family name.

The Ox pointed to a map of Ireland and said, "Put your finger on the map. What does it say?"

I read, "Ballyduff, County Waterford."

"From now on, if anybody asks, you're Tom Dayhill from Ballyduff, County Waterford." Then he and Big Aggie took us out and bought us several nice new outfits for the stage.

I once told someone that I was from Ireland, but it didn't feel right so I never did it again. In one of those strange coincidences, though, I found out a few years later that my great grandfather, James Dahill, was born in Ballyduff, County Waterford.

When I told my dad that I was going by Tom Dahill, he was happy. I had been in a lot of trouble as Tom Suess and this was a fresh start. Tom Dahill hadn't been in the workhouse. My dad's maternal uncle, who had been Chief of Police in St. Paul, was Tom Dahill and I had been named after him because he had always been good to my dad. With my father's approval, I dropped the "y" and have been going by Dahill ever since. "Dayhill" looked better in a band name, so we kept the "y" for the band.

Whenever we were on the road, we brought the portable turntable with us to listen to our records, old and new. In Springfield Massachusetts we heard the "The Long and Winding Road" on the new Beatles album. I teared up because it reminded me of Jimmy the Dog.

A few weeks later, we were down in Boston for a session at the Plough and Stars and decided to swing by Rockvale Circle just to say "Hi." Who should we meet but Jimmy the Dog. He had apparently walked the fifty miles home and was again living house to house. At least I think he walked. He might have hitch-hiked the long and winding road from Rowley.

During this time we were meeting a lot of musicians from Ireland and the people who loved their music. We had come along at the right time. There were very few non-Irish born people playing and the musicians we met were willing to help a couple of kids from St. Paul, Minnesota learn the Art even though most of them didn't know where Minnesota was and had never heard of St. Paul.

Ron Nilan, the bartender from downstairs, liked to hunt geese. He would bring a couple of cases of Heineken home from work and we would stay up until we got the "Heineken stay-awakes." Then we would load up the car with his shot guns and Irish Setters, Dylan and Fall, and head for Newburyport, cross over the bridge to Plum Island, drive the twelve miles to the end and climb the sand dune bluffs. I was working on memorizing "The Foggy Dew" at the time and while we waited for the morning light, I would go over the words in my head. After a while, we would hear the geese coming through the dawn mist over the Atlantic. Then, suddenly, they were right above us.

We only shot a few, but it was nice to have an excuse to be there. The dogs would retrieve a bit but were not all that successful. Perhaps they had the "Heineken stay-awakes" too. When Dylan and Fall later had puppies, Jan asked us if we wanted one of them. Of course we did, and we chose Daniel, who was a little gentleman and learned fast. He could sit, lie down and always came when we called.

One day a curly-haired teenager came by the house because he had heard that I played guitar and he wanted to know if I would teach him how to play some Led Zeppelin. His name was Kevin McElroy and he lived in town. I said, "How would you like to play some Irish music?"

We gave it a try. He loved it and started coming over every few days for more music and laughs.

Bob Hardy was the town's Chief of Police. He was a big, round-faced, happy-go-lucky kind of fella who was very friendly to everyone, even us. We were hippy-types and not used to cops who would joke around with us. Bob actually liked us. Even though he was a Republican, he asked us one day if we were registered to vote. When we said no, he told us how and where to register although he knew we wouldn't vote his way.

Once he told us a story about discovering a body in the woods that had been there a few months. Bob and a crew of town employees had to pick it up and, for obvious reasons, were all wearing rubber gloves. After that unpleasant task, they all stopped at The Clam Box in Ipswich. Bob went in, ordered the fried clams and while he was at it, he washed his hands and put on a clean pair of rubber gloves. Then he brought the clams to the people waiting outside and started handing them out. When they noticed he was still wearing gloves, they looked horrified. Bob looked down at his hands and said, "Damn, I forgot to take 'em off."

One afternoon we were walking along the road in Rowley when a semi-truck came barreling around a bend. Daniel was out in the road. We whistled and called to him. He almost responded, but then he saw the truck and froze. The truck hit him and he was mangled. Bob Hardy came by and had to shoot him. It was a sad day for us. Later that same day, Bob was driving "Old Nancy" the town squad car out on Hwy 1 and got hit head on by a guy driving 110 miles an hour. We were asked to play a benefit memorial for Bob at the Chanticleer Restaurant. It was tough to play for others when we felt so bad ourselves. That was the first of the many wakes and funerals that I have played.

For the benefit, Pierre had about 50 cases of Miller High Life delivered to The Chanticleer. Most of the beer didn't get drunk that night. For the next few months, Pierre would sell it to me at two dollars a case. I would sometimes feel sick from it and would joke that I had a bad case of the High Life.

That fall we were playing at a place called P. J.'s Pub in West Andover, Massachusetts and met a nice young couple who loved the music. They invited us to the nearby town of Lawrence for dinner at the woman's apartment. The guy lived in Boston and was married to someone else. The girlfriend was very friendly and had a seven-year-old daughter even though she was only about twenty-two. We drove over to her place a few nights later, as arranged. Apparently expecting someone else, she answered the door in a short, see-through negligee. Seeing that it was us, she invited us in and fixed dinner. She told us that her boyfriend, Jack, was down in Boston that night where he had a job as a social worker. After we finished eating, we were sitting around her kitchen table talking when a uniformed policeman from Boston showed up to get a package from her. She seemed to be running several "businesses" out of her apartment. She said that we should all get together the following Saturday to run around Boston and that we should bring our instruments. We arranged to meet at P. J.'s, and from there we would all head down to the city. It sounded like fun.

On Saturday around noon, we were sitting at P.J.'s having a few beers before leaving for Boston. The little pub was busy with people coming and going. One fellow passed by on his way to the toilet in the back. He took a hard look at Jack and his girlfriend as he went by our booth. As we got up to go, Jack said, "I'll be right with you."

We walked out to the parking lot. Jack joined us, we all piled into the car and headed for Jack's neighborhood in South Boston. He had a bunch of talkative and energetic friends who met us at the first pub we hit. Most of them were wearing pork pie hats and clean sleeveless white undershirts. They seemed to know everyone. Many of them worked for the city. Besides Jack the social worker, there were a couple of teachers, a psychologist and a cop. We were a jolly lot.

When they asked us to play and sing some Irish songs, a couple of them removed their pork pies, and wove through the crowd collecting donations for us. Amazingly, the hats filled up fast. After the first pub, we had a couple hundred dollars! These were workingman bars and we were impressed by the generosity and good taste in music that these South Boston people showed. We hit another pub, and then another with the same result. Our friends were popping a lot of speed, chewing gum like crazy and were very enthusiastic about the music. I'm not sure what we sounded like, but we soon had close to a thousand dollars.

Jack and his friends decided that we should go to the Holiday Inn. They booked a number of rooms, including one for us. When the gang gathered in the bar after check-in, all the other customers slipped out leaving us alone with a small staff. Shortly after we were served our first round, Jack and a couple of the other guys stepped out.

Barbara and I started putting two and two together, when the remaining crew took out the concealed guns they were wearing and showed them to us with pride. Then they proceeded to discuss truck high-jackings, dope deals, extortion, murder .... and the joy of it all. We waited for our friend Jack and the others to return. Barbara and I were relieved when a few hours later they arrived.

Then Jack dumped $87,000 on the table and divided it up among his gang. For the rest of the evening, we played Irish music when asked to, including all of their many requests, and wondered just how scared the "contributors" in those bars must have been when they dropped their "donations" into the pork pie hats. Everyone in the hotel bar that night loved us and treated us like royalty, but I was looking forward to returning to Sweet Raul, Kevin McElroy's pet name for Rowley.

In the morning Jack drove us back to P.J.'s Pub to pick up our van. He told us how he had become the leader of his gang. Jack had been the body guard for the former leader until he was assassinated. Jack let us know that it had been an "inside" job. Over the next year, twenty-eight South Boston gang members were killed in a turf war. I never saw Jack again, and couldn't help thinking that he might have been one of those twenty-eight.

When Jack drove away, Barbara and I entered the pub, glad to be on safer ground. The owner came up and asked, "Who was that you were with on Saturday?"

"Oh, just some guy we met."

He said, "Right after you left, we had to send a man to the hospital. We found him in the toilet. Someone had stabbed him about fifty times with a pen-knife."

We were never asked to play P.J.'s Pub again.

Chapter 2
Boston in the Rare Old Times

Newburyport was becoming a base for Irish musicians. Declan Hunt, Jack Geary, Sean Tyrrell and quite a few others had migrated up there from Boston. It was an old harbor town much the same size as an Irish town and was within striking distance of Irish pubs in Danvers, Lawrence, Lowell, Manchester, Portsmouth and a dozen other towns. Within a fifty or sixty miles radius there was plenty of work for Irish musicians.

However, Irish musicians weren't the only ones travelling the Pub Circuit. There was a gigantic, greyish beast which would appear at, for instance, Poor Richard's in Newburyport, where the patrons would buy him a bowl of his favorite drink, Guinness. He would next be seen a few hours later at the Cork and Kerry in Haverhill about twenty miles away, again lapping up Guinness. He was an Irish wolfhound named Brian that travelled fast and far. He was very sociable but never lost sight of his dignity.

Joe and Joan McGrath, known as The Rapparees had been playing together in America for a long time. They gave us some good advice when we ran into them at the "Ox" McCarthy's place. They told us that it was best to build up your own rooms. When you are the first to bring live music to a place that hasn't had it and you do it well, you can always come back when you want to. We got a gig at the Dunphy's Sheraton Hotel in Lexington, Massachusetts. It was a good, steady job in a nice restaurant. The manager not only paid us, he fed us and best of all it was a venue that we had started. We were a "house band" for the first time.

At the Sheraton we met many of the illustrious Dunphy family. They had started with a clam stand on Hampton Beach in New Hampshire. Led by the widowed mother of twelve, the Dunphys had parlayed their holdings into a large chain of luxury hotels that operated all over New England. Several of the girls in the

Dunphy family were nuns and one of them asked us to play at a school where she taught. We played "Full Fathom Five" and "The Willow Song" from Shakespeare and some Irish songs that date back to Elizabethan times.

That spring we were asked to play the Parker House in Boston, the oldest hotel in New England which was currently owned by the Dunphys and was a very posh place indeed. The occasion was a reception for a book release. Kenneth O'Donnell and David Powers had been aides to JFK and were the authors of the book *Johnny We Hardly Knew Ye* about the man. Senator Tip O'Neill, former Speaker of the House John McCormick and plenty of other politicians were there. When we took the stage, the first request was for the song "Johnny We Hardly Knew Ye". The waiters, who wore white gloves, were serving gin and tonics off of silver trays. They stopped by the stage and offered us a couple when we finished the song, which we gladly accepted. After a second song, another request came in for .... "Johnny We Hardly Knew Ye", so we sang it again.

The waiters stopped by with more gin and tonics. There were also lovely trays of shrimp and oysters going around, but it's hard to sing songs or play the flute with your mouth full so we didn't have any. We started to sing something else. I think it might have been "The Wild Colonial Boy", but a very distinguished looking big-wig came up and requested "Johnny We Hardly Knew Ye", so we sang it again. Those waiters at the Parker House were very diligent and they kept the gin and tonics coming. The white gloves, friendly demeanors and encouraging gestures of the waiters, combined with the hearty response to our songs, especially "Johnny We Hardly Knew Ye", turned the soiree into a blur of faces made familiar by the evening news. Every toast or speech was followed by another "Johnny We Hardly Knew Ye" and more gin and tonics.

After about twenty renditions of "Johnny We Hardly Knew Ye" the party finally ended and we had to drive to Maynard, Massachusetts to play Doran's Pub until 1 a.m. From there it was another fifty miles back home to Rowley. Because I used to have trouble staying awake with all the travelling, I would drive just as fast as the van would go so that I wouldn't fall asleep. It made sense to me at the time.

Meanwhile, life in quiet old Rowley was pleasant. Most mornings we would walk down to the drugstore in town for a cup of coffee and a chat with the owner John MacDonald, his son the pharmacist, and Opal Stone, the jolly lady who ran the soda fountain. They were all from old local families. At that time there weren't many non-New Englanders around Rowley. They liked to listen to tales of far off Minnesota and enjoyed hearing of our travels around Massachusetts. I suppose Barbara and I had a different take on things. We got as much of a kick out of their "odd" accents as they got out of ours. Old John and his son liked to go fish for "floundah" and tell stories about the old "clammahs" around town. Opal was good to us and gave us day-old pastries saying, "We were just going to throw them out anyway."

A local known as Old Man Bishop would often be there. He had grown up in a big house in town and had been a dandy in his day. He used to drive a large 1930s touring car that still sat in the garage. His sweetheart had died young and soon after her death his parents passed away. Mr. Bishop left the house, car and property just as it was when his loved ones were alive and time had taken its toll. The suit he always wore when sitting at the drugstore counter had once been very fine, but like the house had seen better days. He was pleasant to us but didn't talk much. Nobody bothered him. Help had probably been offered over the years and refused until eventually people just left him alone to become the town eccentric.

Old Man Bishop did have some competition for the role of town eccentric. I was working on memorizing "The Rocky Road to Dublin" and other tongue-twistery songs. As I walked from place to place, I sang out loud and sometimes startled people as they came out doors or around corners.

We had taken to visiting Patrick Quirke, a psychiatrist from County Kerry, who lived in Georgetown, the next town over. We would get together at his house which was across the road from the Baldpate Psychiatric Hospital where Patrick was the director. People thought the hospital was named after Patrick because he had a particularity large bald pate himself. In truth, the hospital was named for the hill on which it stood. The hilltop was devoid of trees. The early European settlers thought that the Indian Tribes in the area had probably burned the forest off and used the cleared hilltop for growing crops.

Patrick's wife knew Marie Eason who had heard us at The Cork and Kerry on the night of the White Russians and had told them about us. We'd been in Rowley a few months before we actually met. Patrick was a "good old shkin" and we had a lot of laughs and tunes together. He was about seventy when we met him, which meant that he had been a young man during the Irish War of Independence and the Civil War that followed.

After a few visits Patrick told us, "This is an Irish house. You don't have to call before you come. Just drop in when you want to."

Pat was the one who had first suggested that we get Bunting's Collection of harp tunes from 1792 and his recommendations didn't stop there. He told us to find the Joyce and Petrie Collection and to obtain a copy of O'Neill's Collection.

Patrick would play the accordion reading out of his copy of O'Neill's book and we spent plenty of time discussing the music as well as playing it. One time I told him that I had read *The Hidden Ireland* by Daniel Corkery when I was in the workhouse. He was pleased that I had read it and surprised that the St. Paul workhouse had provided a volume of Gaelic poetry from the eighteenth century for the enlightenment of the prisoners. Pat thought that the more we knew about Ireland the better our music would be, so he recommended Eugene O'Curry's *Manners and Customs of the Ancient Irish* and for lighter fare Seumas MacManus' *The Story of the Irish Race.*

Patrick was fond of the card game Forty-Five and tried to teach it to us. Sometimes it was just Barbara and me, and sometimes other friends and family members were in the game as well. With all the tricks, trumps and reneging, I never did get the hang of the game, but I did get a hold of the books he recommended and read them. Patrick's ideas about the connection between Irish music, history and culture helped put into more substantial form something that I felt but hadn't yet had the time to explore, that underlying the pub songs and shenanigans of entertainment there was a deeper more serious element to the music.

When we were at home in Rowley, we spent most of our time working on tunes out of *O'Neill's 1001 Irish Dance Tunes* and Bunting's Collection, on which we had splurged. We were also able to get the Joyce and Petrie Collection. We spent whatever we scraped up on books and records. We were finding some gigs in Irish pubs and I had been losing interest in writing my own songs since discovering that the Irish songs were so much more fascinating. Time had worn away the rough edges of the words like a river tumbles stones until they were smooth, easy to remember and rolled off the tongue.

*****

One citizen of Rowley got very interested in waste disposal and set up the region's first recycling system at the town dump. The system consisted of a series of labelled bins for various kinds of waste. At the grand opening he wanted us to sing a composition for the dignitaries that would be attending the innovative facility. The song was called "Pollution Pete and Ecology Sue", which he had written to the tune of "Turkey in the Straw". Assistant District Attorney John Kerry attended this auspicious event and seemed to enjoy it.

Sean Tyrrell and Jack Geary had been playing all up and down the East Coast. Barbara and I would go up and listen to them in Manchester, New Hampshire. Over time we became good friends. As The Gingermen, Sean and Jack, who had grown up together in Galway, were a fantastic duo. One of the things that made them stand out from the rest, besides their great musicianship and fine singing, was the three-piece tweed suits brought over from Ireland that they wore when performing. They both had long black hair and Sean wore a mustache. Sean went on to be known and respected as a researcher and singer of deep, introspective songs, but in those days he was one of the best singers of comic songs that I ever heard. I learned a couple of music hall songs "Cushy Butterfield" and "The Night the Old Dun Cow Caught Fire" as well as dozens of others from him.

Sean once told Barbara and me a story about his difficulty juggling his various engagements. He had a gig on a Friday night and stayed out late afterwards. The next morning he was supposed to play a wedding in another city. He woke up late with a terrible hangover, but he jumped into his car anyway, determined to make it to the wedding on time. His head was still pounding when he was pulled over on the Mass Turnpike. As the state trooper approached his window, Sean began to apologize for his speed and to explain why he was in such a hurry. The trooper held up his hand to stop him and said, "Son, I'm pulling you over for going twenty-five on the Turnpike."

I stopped by Jack Geary's apartment in Newburyport one afternoon where he lived with his wife, Terry, who at the time was affectionately referred to as Ratzo by Jack. There were a number of other musicians who had also dropped in. Finbar and Eddie Furey's new record, "The Lonesome Boatman" was playing on the turn-table. When I heard the first note of the second part of the title tune, it hit me wrong and I said loudly, "That's the worst note ever recorded! " Everyone just turned and stared at me. That tune went on to become one of the most popular Irish melodies composed in the last fifty years. That showed what I knew. I had a lot to learn and people like Sean and Jack were generous with their time and music.

I brought the fiddle over to Sean's apartment. He showed me on his mandolin how to play triplets and grace notes and how to rock between the strings and play double stops. He also showed me how he held the pick when playing the mandolin or tenor banjo, keeping the thumb and forefinger very flexible. Holding the pick this way gave him better control and speed when playing tunes or backing up singing. Up until that time I had been using finger picks playing a twelve-string guitar. I began using a flat pick and I made up my mind to keep my eyes open for a mandolin and a tenor banjo. In those days it wasn't hard to find old instruments, and I was soon in possession of a 1916 Gibson mandolin and a 1929 Leedy tenor banjo.

Looking back I think I picked up most of what I know from comments I heard from musicians and knowledgeable listeners who talked about "The Greats" of Irish music past and present, what they said, and how they played. Sean told me that one of his heroes, Joe Cooley had asked Jack Geary and him up on stage at Harrington's in San Francisco. Sean decided to tear into Cooley's Reel like a race horse out of the gate. Joe stopped him and in a gentle voice said, "Nice and stately, Sean." Later, possibly from one of the Chicago musicians I met, I heard that to set the right pace before starting a reel at Hanley's House of Happiness, Cooley would call out, "Alright lads, nice and tough now."

There were lots of memorable stories about the musicians coming and going in Boston. Maggie Barry, the Travelling street singer from Cork, was playing at a session at the Plough and Stars in Cambridge. That evening she broke a string on her banjo. Several other musicians started digging into their cases to find a new string to replace her broken one. Maggie refused all offers and set about to repair the string. She took off the broken string, unwrapped the brass wire from the two ends, bent the ends and hooked them together, carefully rewrapped it with the brass wire, put it back on the banjo and tuned it. She said, "I wouldn't want to change my luck by changing a string."

Maggie met a man named Peter who was promoting folk music concerts in Boston. He was the son of a very wealthy family but had to appear once a year before an uncle in the corporate office and show that his teeth were brushed and his fingernails were clean. He would then and only then be granted his allowance for the year. Even though Maggie was about thirty years his senior, when she let on that she was in need of a green card Peter promptly proposed to her and they eloped. They had to go into hiding in New York, not so much because of his family but because of hers. She was a sort of queen among the Travelers and her people were the ones who had objections to this marriage of convenience. The Travelers cornered them in the apartment in New York and they barely got away by climbing down the fire escape. I never heard what happened after that.

Pecker Dunne was another Traveler banjo player and singer who came through Boston. Sean told me that on one of his U.S. tours Pecker played The Old Shieling in Queens, New York. Sean drove down with some friends to listen to him. While Pecker was on break the bartender, a friend from Galway, asked Sean to play a few tunes and kept at him until, "being young and foolish", he agreed. Sean tried to get his tuning on Pecker's instrument with disastrous consequences and blushing to high heaven got off the stage and hid somewhere in the back of the room.

Pecker, whose given name was Patrick was a huge man with a fierce face and a drooping Poncho Villa mustache. He had wild black hair and sometimes wore a sombrero to accentuate his resemblance to the Mexican revolutionary. He had a massive hairy chest sticking out of his shirt that was unbuttoned halfway down in the fashion of the day. Pecker returned to the stage, picked up the banjo and announced into the microphone that someone had been "mickey mousin" with it and broke a string.

Sean's prayer to be swallowed up by the earth went unanswered so when Pecker finished the set Sean screwed up his courage and followed him into the toilet to admit to being the mickey mouser. Sean was just a few words into his confession when Pecker started apologizing profusely to Sean for commenting into the microphone. In spite of his imposing appearance Pecker Dunne was actually a gentle giant who would never knowingly hurt another musician and that night was the beginning of a long, long friendship that lasted until the day Pecker died.

I had heard the word "rake" being tossed around and I asked a woman at The Plough and Stars what the word meant. She pointed to Declan Hunt and said, "There's a rake." Declan Hunt was someone who, once met, would never be forgotten. He dressed well in bright-colored, wide-collared patterned shirts and three-piece suits with no tie. He had long flowing hair like a lot of musicians and always had a big smile on his face. All the girls were crazy about him, his rebel songs and his guitar. They would lend him cars which he frequently destroyed, but he always managed to show up driving another sporty model. The album he made with his band, The Battering Ram, was one of the first produced by Rounder Records in Boston. On the strength of that album Rounder became a successful label and Deckie was able to earn a little money. He was also a good handyman and builder. He made himself useful around the girlfriends' houses, even if he was hard on their automobiles. Like Sean, Declan crossed paths with Pecker Dunne while in Boston and the friendship continued back home in Ireland.

Barbara and I played the "Ox" McCarthy's bar in Springfield fairly regularly. There was a restaurant on the main floor, but the music was in The Keg Room, the pub in the cellar. It was a dark place with a lot of red in the décor. Just above the door was a sign that read, "There are no strangers here, only friends you haven't met."

A big round-faced patrolman named Jimmy McAleer from Kerry worked the downtown Springfield beat on foot. His beat included the Keg Room, so he would stop in regularly to have a look around and sometimes sing a song. His favorite was the 1798 ballad "Kelly, The Boy from Killanne". When we asked him, Jimmy would jump up on the stage in full uniform with his hat on, his police radio blaring, his Billy club and gun flapping up and down while he hopped around the stage wearing a big grin, putting everything he had into his party piece.

The real stars of the Keg Room were Butch and Maeve. We thought of them as seasoned veterans although Maeve was only five years older than us. Their act was warm and they convinced the audience that they cared about them. They were able to do this because they really did care about whomever they met. They were as friendly off stage as they were on the stage and were free with their advice, often suggesting places that Barbara and I might pick up a gig.

We were playing four or five nights a week when the stars were aligned and often crossed paths with Joe and Joan McGrath, The Rapparees. Joe was a stocky man from the North of Ireland who sang and played the banjo. Joan, from Clare, played guitar and sang. They were very good entertainers, but also took the music seriously. Once they were on stage when a table full of construction workers in front started mocking Joan's rather high voice. Without missing a beat, Joe stepped off the stage, laid out the main culprit with his banjo, stepped back up on stage and finished the song with Joan while the bartender dragged the downed fellow out the door by his feet. Joe was good natured. He played the "leprechaun's harmonica", an instrument so small that he could hide it in his mouth and play tunes on it. We shared information about where the jobs were, first in the Boston area and later in St. Paul, Chicago and Kansas City.

I was not only learning songs and tunes from the musicians I met. I was also learning how to be an entertainer by watching and listening. Seamus Kennedy from Belfast was a hard working musician and one of the funniest. He lived in Newburyport and played with Tommy Carroll, a banjo player from Dublin. They were a great act together, and were known as The Beggarmen. Seamus was outrageous. He would make things up off the top of his head and somehow manage to get away with it no matter how off the beam. Later Seamus went on to have an illustrious solo career in Washington D.C.

Toby Lynch was another singer/entertainer whom we met in Massachusetts. He was one of the few non-Irish who played in the pubs. He was a tall, curly-haired Lithuanian known in the area as the "Tom Jones" of Irish music. He looked and dressed like the Welsh singer and had all his moves, which he managed to work into the drinking and rebel songs that he performed. Toby was a big help to us. He lent us a little P.A. system and insisted that we take a big pile of Irish records that he wanted us to keep and listen to. Very importantly, he made a list for us of the "fifty survival songs" that he thought we needed to play Irish pubs.

Kevin McElroy, of the large ginger afro.

Kevin McElroy had given up on playing Led Zeppelin and had been going up to Newburyport to hang out with the Irish musicians. He was really coming along in the music and played his first gig with us at Tammany Hall in Worchester, owned and run by a former boxer Boom-Boom O'Sullivan and had a bunch of regulars from Holy Cross College.

Things went well, so Kevin joined us at Doran's Pub in Maynard, or Maynid as he called it. Doran's was owned by Ronnie Doran, another former boxer. It was a good place to play because friends from Springfield, Holyoke and the Lawrence/Lowell area could meet up with us there. In all the places we played, drink was free for the musicians. Ronnie one night said to me, "You guys don't tip enough."

I fired back, “You don’t drink enough.” Then I said, “We don’t want your drink.”

For the rest of the weekend engagement we spent our breaks in the parking lot. We encouraged the crowd to come out with us and patronize a nearby package liquor store. We were all surprised at how much cheaper the beer was. Soon people were buying the beer at the store and bringing it into the bar.

Ronnie was right, of course, and I was wrong. Even if the beer next door was cheaper, it wasn’t as cheap as getting it for free. I was young and dumb enough not to tip much and not to admit when I was wrong. Once we finished Saturday night’s performance we never worked for Mr. Doran again. I have always tipped as well as I could since that gig.

Three friends from Holyoke, Donny, Sean and Curley were up to hear us that Saturday at Doran’s. They were planning to spend the night at our place in Rowley and when the gig was over, Barbara, Kevin and I piled into the van and they, into their car, and we had a race back to town. Rowley was about fifty miles away by backroads. We drove like hell and halfway there we all pulled over to answer nature’s call, then jumped back in our vehicles and continued the race. When we reached the Chanticleer, the boys from Holyoke were ahead of us and swung into the parking lot. Seeing that they were about to beat us, I drove over the lawn with Kevin and Barbara hanging on for dear life, pulling in just ahead of them. We stayed up late.

The next morning, Pierre, my French landlord, caught me when I came out the door and said, “What is thees? You drive over my lawn?” I looked at the van and noticed the dirt and vegetation piled on the bumper. I said, “No, I was driving in a cornfield last night.” There were no cornfields around there, but being from Minnesota, it was the best I could come up with on short notice. Then I saw the deep tire tracks going across the grass in front of the house. Up until that time I had always gotten along well with Pierre, but I was becoming a little too wild. Although I never admitted my guilt, we fixed up the lawn and cleaned up the grass and mud. Like I said earlier, I was young and dumb and thought I could talk smart.

Somehow, around this time we acquired an Afghan hound, Pat the Dog. He was a wild thing. Sometimes I thought he was half dog and half monkey. Pierre was disgusted with him because he actually tore holes in the plaster and lathe walls trying to escape the apartment. The other recently acquired lodger in the house was a bit better behaved. Kevin McElroy had moved into an attic space on the second floor. Barbara and I replaced the black van with an aqua blue Dodge van for $350.00. It soon became apparent that it was not the step up that we had been hoping for.

The word was out that Irish music was catching on, so all kinds of people and places were trying to cash in on the trend. We got a gig in Waterville, Maine at an “Irish Pub” in the basement of a Chinese restaurant. There wasn’t much to the gig and only a few people came in. Orrin Shiro was the owner of the building and had grown up there. Once it had been a hotel/bar and the rooms upstairs were formerly part of a brothel. Orrin had a bald head that he said he got from all the bottles bouncing off of it when he was a kid. We stayed in the rooms upstairs which were supposed to be haunted. We were there for three nights and thought we heard women weeping occasionally. It did seem creepy.

Our turn-table was with us in our room as usual and we were listening to Na Fili, the great traditional trio that had recently put out their first recording. I was trying to pick out “The College Groves”, a nice reel that I thought I should know since I hadn’t given college much of a try. It was a tricky tune and out of desperation I flipped the speed down to 16 2/3 rpms instead of the usual 33 1/3 making the reel play at half speed and one octave lower. I could play along that way and I could also hear that all of the triplets, rolls, grace notes and crans were played perfectly. I was amazed that they were able to execute these details when playing full speed. It was a revelation and I realized just how intricate the Irish music was when played by the best musicians. Since then it is the small details of the tunes that I am listening for and I am still trying to put the nice touches into the music to this day.

I started to get interested in piping. Besides listening to the playing of Tomas O'Canainn from Na Fili, I listened to Paddy Maloney of the Chieftains and Liam O'Flynn of Prosperous, later to become Planxty. The first time I heard the Uilleann pipes

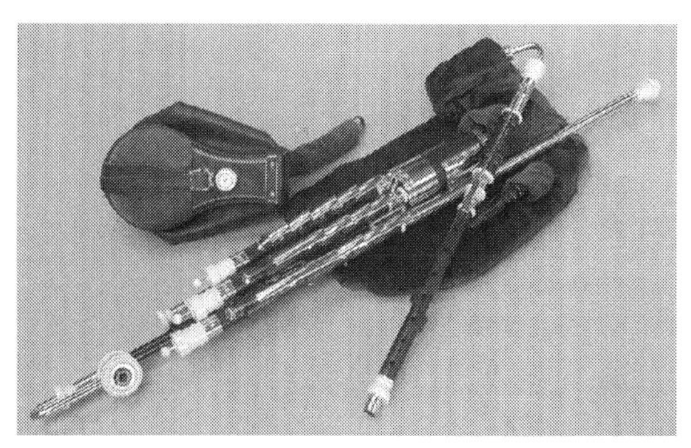

I loved the sound. My impression was that the music was coming from underwater. That was how my head interpreted the bubbling, popping, droning and odd harmonics that issued from the instrument and when I first saw a picture of the pipes, they did resemble an octopus.

I decided to make a list of Uilleann pipers in America. There were only ten or twelve when I made the list. Today there are hundreds. Some of the world's best pipe makers are building sets in America. There are teachers, workshops and pipers' clubs creating opportunities to play what was, in '72, a very rare instrument.

*****

Conditions were tough in Ireland in the sixties and seventies. Jobs were hard to find and many young people came to America in search of work. Some of those who played music found enough work in bars to keep the wolves at bay and ended up becoming professional musicians almost by accident. Some married in America and some bounced back and forth. I knew musicians who were homesick, but more or less had to stay on because they wouldn't be able to return if they left the US. Then the "troubles" worsened in Ireland making life there harder than ever.

We were sharing the stage with a fellow from Belfast, taking turns playing sets in the Keg Room from six until one. A waitress came by and handed him a note while he was performing. He read it and his face turned white. It was a message from Ireland that his brother had been shot and killed on the street back home in Belfast. That was the first time that I felt the troubles over here. The rebel songs were a big part of all of our repertoires, but that glimpse of tragedy made them more real to me.

I have to give a lot of credit here to the lovers of Irish music in America who came out and filled the pubs. They spent their money and supported the musicians by buying records and tapes back in those heady days. They often had parties, put up performers, drove them around, fed them and bailed them out of the difficulties brought on by the life style that seemed a prerequisite of the profession. The crowds kept growing, led by the stalwarts who understood the culture. These folks would be out to hear the music night after night back when gigs were often five nights a week for a month. Irish music was featured in scores of pubs around the country. People were drawn in by the happy throngs who showed up wherever there was live Irish music.

Many of the musicians we met would become quite well known in later years, but back then we were all just starting out. It was a great time to be young and free to follow the music.

Chapter 3
The Sweet Smell of Goat

In the early seventies, you could play any kind of Irish music in the pubs. Rebel songs, comic songs, recitations, and plenty of jigs, reels and harp tunes were being played. I remember one tough kid from Dublin at the Harp and Bard in Danvers, who was wearing a military bandolier draped across his chest while on stage. Instead of bullets, the bandolier was full of tin whistles in every key. Each band had its own personality back then. The band he played with did political recitations as well as a full range of Irish music. The common characteristic was that they were all performing their very best material. But the Irish music scene was changing.

After we had been in the Boston area a few years, the "Formula" took over. A bunch of the pub owners and musicians had a meeting and decided that only half of what was played should be Irish and the rest should be American pop songs like "American Pie", "Charlie on the MTA" or "Country Roads", along with plenty of Pat and Mike type jokes. Recitations were forbidden. Harp tunes went by the wayside.

Musicians who were on opposite sides about the "Formula" had fist fights over it. When I called Irish pubs to book gigs they would ask, "Do you play the 'Formula'?" I would reply that we didn't and the response was, "We only hire the "Formula." If you wouldn't play the "Formula", you didn't get much work in the Boston area. We wouldn't play the "Formula" and it was time to leave.

In the early spring of '73 the aqua van left Boston with me behind the wheel, Barbara the wife riding shotgun and Kevin McElroy of the large ginger afro and Patrick the Afghan Hound in the back. Sean Tyrrell who wouldn't play the "Formula" either came with us. In fact, he inspired the trip. Our ultimate goal was California. We were headed there because Sean had told us about Joe Cooley from County Galway, "THE GREATEST IRISH BOX PLAYER OF THEM ALL!" who was living in San Francisco.

At first we pulled out our instruments and tried busking along the way for gas money and tires. We went to college campuses but soon realized that college students didn't have any money either. We were reduced to picking up coins at every toll booth. Kevin, Barbara and Sean would all jump out and search for quarters to put in the kitty while I stayed behind the wheel. It was a good thing that it was turnpike or toll road all the way to Wisconsin. It was also a good thing that people had such poor aim when they threw their change into the baskets. We usually ended up with a dollar or two at each booth and sometimes even more.

We stopped in my home town of St. Paul, it being nearly halfway to California and there we met a box player from County Roscommon, Martin McHugh, standing at the bar in O'Gara's. He was forty-two at the time, a stocky, pugnacious looking man with black hair worn in a kind of pompadour and long sideburns. He was wearing a black leather jacket. When we introduced ourselves, the first thing he wanted to know about us was whether we played "The Lark in the Morning". Musicians from Ireland often seemed to have tunes that they used as a test to discover what kind of musicians they were dealing with. We brought in our instruments from the van and played the jig. During a chat afterwards he told us about some older musicians in town that we should meet. We told Marty we would look him up the next time we came through and over the years we have become fast friends.

While we were in St. Paul, Ann Heymann, a harpist and at that time successful horse trainer, put us up at her place west of town. She was a friend of Barbara's and had sent us some money to help us get out of Boston. She was renting a converted chicken coop just out of town. Her hospitality when we were there was abundant and for the next few years, whenever we passed through St. Paul, we stayed with Ann. She had automatic overdraft protection on her checking account and didn't mind running it up when we were in town. The sessions we had at the chicken coop often lasted until long after dawn. On that visit, we stayed about a week, but when Pat the Dog peed on Ann's foot we took it as a signal that it was time to move on.

As we careened westward in the aqua van with worn out shocks and springs, we would stop in any small town that had a bar with an Irish name and ask if we could play. They often said yes. We found out that people enjoyed whatever we played which was a relief after dealing with the "Formula" in the east. The proprietors of the little bars and pubs didn't have preconceived ideas about Irish music and were open to whatever we wanted to play.

Pat the Dog was excellent theft protection for the instruments when we had to leave the van. He would lie in the van very quietly until someone came too close. Then he would jump up, beat on the windows with his paws and start up an ungodly yowling. The unfortunate passerby would move away quickly.

Although he was good theft protection he couldn't resist Kevin's goat skin bodhran. Being an Afghan, the scent of goat was probably irresistible. Not much love was lost between Kevin and Pat after the drum-eating incident.

It was the beginning of the disco era and none of us were inspired by what was played on the radio. We thought traditional music was more exciting and the speeding van was a perfect place to practice. We played a lot of music as we rolled and bounced along gazing at the vast Western landscape.

When we reached San Francisco, we looked up a man Sean knew named Harry Harrington. He was a friend of Joe Cooley's and had a bar in the financial district. Harry was famous in San Francisco Irish circles and known as “the nicest guy in town”. He received a letter once from Australia, addressed simply, “Harry Harrington, San Francisco, USA.”

We drove up to Harry’s house around sunrise and Sean jumped out roaring that we had arrived. When that didn’t wake Harry, he had the rest of us join in the shouting. Even Pat the Dog contributed with barks and howls. Harry came out and told us that our timing was bad. We had just missed Cooley. He had been living in San Francisco since he left Chicago about a dozen years before. He taught many young people in the area to play Irish music. He didn’t limit himself to strictly Irish venues. He would play his box for anyone who enjoyed wild music with a great beat. Rumor has it that Joe played with Mother Machree’s Uptown Jug Champions, the group that later became The Grateful Dead and taught the hippies how to dance the Haymakers’ Jig.

Cooley was now very ill and had returned to Ireland suspecting that he did not have much time left. Harry told us that he had been diagnosed with cancer and that we had just missed him by a few days. In fact, his wife had not yet left and was still in California according to Harry. I never did get a chance to see Cooley. He died within a year of returning home but managed to get around to the pubs of Galway and Clare to play first. I do have a record of Cooley’s that was his only commercial recording put together shortly after his death. I still listen to the record frequently, as well worn as it is.

We did get a chance to meet Kevin Keegan, one of Joe’s best friends and a great box player. When he first saw Sean, Kevin, Barbara and me playing some tunes in the corner of a Parish Hall during an Irish get-together, he walked over and smiled at us, as scraggily as we were, and said, “Great craic in America”. He then joined us for a few tunes. Later when he was called to the stage, he asked us to join him.

We slept on the floor of an apartment just off of Haight Street rented by an Irish musician whom Sean had met on a previous trip to San Francisco. Over the few weeks we were there, maybe thirty other people came and went. A lot of Irish music was played in the apartment, traditional as well as experimental and Sean decided to stay in San Francisco for a while. The rest of us busked in Union Square and at Fisherman's Wharf until we had earned enough money to head for LA where we had been promised a gig.

When we arrived in LA, the gig had already been filled. That put us in a fix. The van had barely survived the trip. It was belching black smoke and needed a valve job. We didn't dare drive it any further, so we parked it in a lot behind the bar in Burbank and lived in it for a few days.

Des Regan, a friend of the bar owner, was an accordion player and a humanitarian who owned an Irish Dance Hall about six blocks away. When he heard of our plight he arranged an audition for another gig, as much to remove us from his friend's parking lot as anything else. The gig was at Molly Malone's on Fairfax Avenue on the Miracle Mile in Hollywood.

At Molly Malone's, we were supposed to get room and board, and play every night for six weeks. The bar was owned by a Dublin woman who agreed to put us up in her house. The conditions were not quite what we were expecting. There were no beds available, so we again slept on the floor. As for the "board", after the first day or two there was no more food in the fridge. These inconveniences were to be expected. What we didn't expect was the demented soap opera that was playing out in the residence. There were numerous fights in the house between the bar owner and her bartender who was over constantly, her husband being in Japan. The front door of the house made a terrible noise when it opened or closed and the owner's teenage children liked to sneak in and out at night. Sometimes the mother made nighttime excursions as well. Since it was impossible to leave quietly by the door, the method of choice to enter or leave the house at night was the living room window. Unfortunately we slept under the living room window.

In spite of all that, Molly Malone's was an interesting place to play. Because of its location in Hollywood, the regulars wore costumes every night hoping to be discovered and put in the movies. There were cowboys, Indians, soldiers and spies. People dressed as nuns and priests made out in the corners. All of them were enjoying the Irish music. Many of them thought that we were only playing the music so that we could become movie stars too.

James Cagney was a regular and came in several times while we were there. I learned that he had played the Uilleann pipes for a while. Cagney always had six or eight people with him but the last time I saw him, the bar threw his party out because one girl in the group was underage. There was another regular, Scotty from Scotland, whose pastime was to sit at the bar and start a conversation with some guy wearing glasses. He would put his arm around his victim's shoulder and then give him a head butt. The victim's glasses would be embedded in his face and they would hang there sometimes for ten seconds or more. Scotty did this on a regular basis, but they never threw him out. It was that kind of a place.

On one of the last nights we were playing Molly Malone's a huge Mexican fellow punched his girlfriend on the dance floor. Before anyone else had time to react, Kevin went into action. He set down his guitar, pulled off his belt, wrapped it around his fist, dove off the stage onto the guy's back and started giving him some solid wallops to the head. Kevin was only half the size of the man whose back he rode and a hippy to boot, but the man could not get Kevin off him. He tried to reach around to hit Kevin, but he couldn't connect. When the bouncer stepped in, Kevin hopped off and climbed back on the stage none the worse for wear after his wild and slightly comical ride. He picked up his guitar and joined in on the next chorus. The bouncer, with the help of a few of the regulars, hustled the Mexican out the door.

Finally, the six weeks were up and the van was repaired. We couldn't wait to leave LA and neither could Pat the Dog. My older sister had an apartment in Denver, so that was where we headed, driving right past the bright lights of Las Vegas. We didn't want to be side-tracked. We were on a different trip altogether.

When we reached Denver we moved into my sister's apartment and again slept on the floor. Anita had been living in Denver for a few years and was working as a nurse. In general, she handled the band invasion with a good nature, but my obsession with playing the fiddle seemed to overwhelm her at times. Some days she would come home from work, and sit down in the middle of the living room floor with her headphones on, blasting her music at top volume. I took the hint and would take my fiddle into the bathroom, shut the door, and practice in there.

Denver was full of transplanted hippies who had fled to Colorado fearing the predicted earthquakes in California. Many of them were planning to move up to the mountains, but very few actually managed to leave town. Most of them apparently decided that Denver was "high enough". A lot of folk music clubs and a few Irish bars offered opportunities to play. We played at the Oxford Hotel on Wazee Avenue or, as Flannel Grimes referred to the street in song, down on the Avenue de' Crabbe, as well as at the Folklore Center on Colfax and at Shannon's in Boulder. The Irish crowd who showed up wore suits, ties and dresses but still mixed easily with the hippies in their colorful dashikis, bell bottoms and headbands. They taught the exotic newcomers some Irish dances and got a big kick out of how high these mountain hippies could leap when they all danced together.

It was at Shannon's that we met Pat Flanagan, the One-Handed Upside Down Box Player from County Mayo. Pat, or Packie as he was called by friends, was the first of the old musicians who took me under his wing and passed on as much of the music as I could hold. He was not really one-handed, but he played the accordion upside down using just his left hand because of a bout with polio as a boy. He had played the fiddle until the polio struck when he was eleven or twelve. It left him with a withered right arm and he switched to accordion and made it work. He had a gigantic repertoire of jigs, reels and hornpipes and played for step dancers. His copy of O'Neill's *Dance Music of Ireland* was annotated with every variation that he had ever heard played and the name of the player. They sometimes called him "The Professor".

Pat Flanagan, County Mayo

Flanagan had lived in London and Chicago and then moved to Denver for his wife Mary's health. Pat and Mary had three kids who were all into the music as well. Johnny played fiddle and bagpipes, Maura was a step dancer and Jimmy played the whistle. The Flanagans had a house party every Sunday and many of the Irish families like the Murrays, Connells, and Hayes would be there. Pat and Mary invited us to join them for the gathering the first night we met.

When we got to the house, Pat greeted us at the door. He was a man of medium height with a head of thick curly reddish hair that was turning white by the time we met him. He was wearing a white dress shirt buttoned to the top. In all the time that I knew him, I never saw him dressed down. He wore a shirt, tie and jacket when he was out and the white shirt, always neatly buttoned, when we saw him at home whether for the Sunday house parties or on the nights that Kevin, Barbara and I were invited for tunes. His thick glasses caught the light as he turned to usher us in that first night.

Singers were taking turns with their party pieces and everyone danced. Anyone who wanted to play was welcome. Mary loved the music and never tired of it. Though she did not play herself she knew all the tunes by name. The Flanagans served pork, chicken, beef, spuds, veggies, fruit salad and anything you wanted to drink. The failte was amazing.

The Flanagans opened their home and their hearts to us because we had devoted ourselves to travelling around and playing the Irish music. When we told Pat that we had decided to head for Chicago, he said, "Why don't you stay here a while and I'll teach you the tunes you'll need to play for the Irish immigrant crowd there."

We took him up on his kind offer and stayed in Denver for a couple of months. Pat drilled us three or four nights a week when he came home from work. He gave us hundreds of tunes with variations that are still some of the best I have ever heard. At ten o'clock sharp we were politely but firmly sent on our way. Pat and Mary both had to work the next day.

We left Denver early that summer. On the way to Chicago, we stopped in St. Paul to drop off Pat the Dog with Ann. She had forgiven Pat for his indiscretion on the previous visit and had a Great Dane named Goth that needed company. If you have never seen a Great Dane and an Afghan hound playing together in a small house, it is a sight to behold. Pat was able to jump nearly four feet straight up in the air. He would hurdle Goth and then the Great Dane would chase Pat around the room. Ann got Pat the Dog a good gig with an Afghan breeder somewhere out of state.

When we hit Chicago, the first thing we did was contact Barbara's brother who owned New Orleans Records which specialized in traditional New Orleans Jazz. He had a one bedroom apartment on Marshfield Street. We were veterans at sleeping on the floor by this time and that is what we did in his third floor flat. We called Barbara's brother Jack Reid when he came out to hear us in the Irish bars. Reid was his mother's maiden name. We were playing a lot of the tougher kind of Irish bars in Chicago and he felt safer with the alias. His true name was Paige VanVorst.

The name he chose to go by didn't really matter because he had a personality that was appreciated wherever he happened to be. He was an eccentric who was not very tall and wore thick glasses. He had an encyclopedic knowledge of anything having to do with New Orleans Jazz. He had another passion as well. He kept a scanner in his kitchen that monitored all the calls to the Chicago Fire Department and was a member of the Five-Eleven Club. The Club would go to the site of fires and bring donuts and coffee for the firefighters. For the next seven years, whenever we stayed in Chicago, Jack let us room with him. He got married, bought a house and had a couple of kids in those seven years, but even though his living situation changed, his door was always open to us.

In cities that had large immigrant populations, the Irish import stores were the places to go to find out what was going on. In Boston the place was O'Byrne DeWitt. In Chicago it was Shamrock Imports and the heart of Shamrock Imports was proprietor Maureen O'Looney, from Bahola, Co. Mayo.

Maureen O'Looney, Co. Mayo.

When we first walked into Shamrock Imports, Maureen was instantly in a flutter. She wanted to know who we were, where we had been and who we knew in Chicago. She invited us into the back room which served as her parlour. She put tea and soda bread in front of us, all the while chatting away fiercely about all the Irish doings in Chicago. She was a small woman with red hair, in her forties at the time and she had her finger on the pulse of all things Irish in town. Whenever the bell on the door rang Maureen dashed out front, never pausing for a breath. Everyone who came in the door was given the big welcome.

That first afternoon in just a few hours she had introduced us to many of the people who were involved in the various Irish organizations in Chicago. Anyone that came through the door of the shop who she thought we should know was ushered into the back room to meet us. This was the beginning of many of our friendships. When Maureen realized that Pat Flanagan, who was also from Co. Mayo and whom she knew well when he lived in Chicago, had taught us, she made a phone call and got us set up to play in a concert. When we left the shop we had half a dozen record albums that Maureen decided we needed. We had a box of Barry's Tea, a loaf of soda bread, a couple of Irish newspapers and a bag of Taytos. Most importantly we had a guide to the ins and outs of Irish society in Chicago.

The concert we were to play was hosted by The Irish Musicians' Association of the South Side and was held at Bogan High School. We were one of many acts on the bill that night. The auditorium was full of South Side Irish, mostly immigrants and their families. When we arrived we were directed to a classroom behind the stage where all the musicians and dancers waited to be called up. There was drink available, but no food. Smoking was permitted because that's the way it was back then even in schools. There were maybe thirty performers there who seemed pleased to see young American-born musicians interested in Irish music. They made us feel welcome.

When our turn came we played some of the tunes that Flanagan had said we had to have if we were going to play for this very crowd. I remember playing "The Three Little Drummers" and "The Rose in the Heather" as well as some reels. We sang a couple of rebel songs. As best as we could, we played the tunes the way Flanagan had given them to us. As we were coming off the stage someone called out, "Good gimp on those tunes, lads."

Before we performed, everyone had been polite and welcoming, but afterwards the musicians came up and introduced themselves to us. Some of the musicians that we met that night were Johnny McGreevy, Seamus Cooley, Frank and Jimmy

Thornton, Albert and Eleanor Neary, Kevin Henry, Noel Rice, Joe Shea, and Frank Burke. Pat Cloonan, a box player from Connemara, County Galway commented, “I don’t know where they got it, but they got something.”

We got that “something” from Pat Flanagan.

A man from Kerry gave me his number and told me that he lived on the North Side. He said, “Next time you are in Chicago, give me a call, Cuz.” I had just met Terence P. Teahan.

We were soon playing regularly at several bars. Tom McCauley’s place The Emerald Isle, a fantastic pub downtown on Rush Street, was one of them. We were also asked to play on quite a few of the Irish Radio hours, of which there were many in Chicago. The hosts would interview local Irish bands and the musicians visiting from out of town. The musicians would play a little bit and let people know where they could be heard that week. Maureen hosted a radio show every week. Another host was Pat Roach, of County Clare, a veteran of the Irish War of Independence, a dance master, a former boxer and an instructor to some of the best Irish dancers in Chicago at the time. Jack Haggerty and Mike O’Connor both had programs as well.

Doing promo spots on the radio hours was a good way to meet fellow musicians. Things got busy fast. We sometimes were asked to play for benefits in addition to our pub gigs and this made us feel like part of the community.

O’Hare Airport was close enough to Jack’s place for us to see and hear the planes flying over when we walked around the neighborhood. Aer Lingus had direct flights to Ireland nightly. We finally had money in our pockets. We saw our chance and took it buying return tickets to Ireland that were good for six months. Jack Reid dropped us off at the airport and we were soon on our way. It was late July of 1973.

Chapter 4
A Vision So Sweet

It had been quite a party on the way over. The plane was full of people singing, smoking, drinking and visiting as they wandered up and down the aisles. We made the approach to Shannon through the clouds and caught glimpses of the legendary gem of an island below us. We saw green fields, stone walls and sometimes the remains of what we found out later were ancient ring forts scattered about in the fields. When the plane landed everyone applauded. We picked up all our gear and waited in the rain for a bus to Galway. Across the road I noticed a small man wearing a three piece suit and Wellingtons coming out of a field and climbing over a stone wall. He was smoking a pipe with the bowl facing down and didn't seem to notice that it was pouring. I thought, "I guess we're in Ireland now."

When the bus started up the road to Galway, we had a chance to look around. The countryside was of course very green, but what struck me was how old the buildings were. The road was narrow and winding with stone walls on either side. Looking out the windows from high up in the bus, it was hard to tell how traffic could get past us. The driver was driving on the left and that added to the feeling that everything here was different. In the fields and sometimes on the road there were cattle and sheep. We saw lots of horses and occasionally donkeys pulling carts. Bicycles were everywhere, ridden by the young as well as the very old. We drove through every small town between Shannon and Galway. Most of them had a castle either in town or just outside. There were also ruins of much older castles and churches, many of them standing alone in fields sometimes with ancient cemeteries beside them. There were thatched cottages both inhabited and in various states of ruin. The rain would stop, and then pour out of the heavens again, but the sun would break through the rapidly moving clouds and mist. The bus rattled and swayed all the way to Galway.

We arrived at the train station and walked a half block to the right into O'Reilly's on Forrester Street. We were able to get a room on the top floor for a few Irish pounds or "punts" as they were usually referred to. It was an unfinished attic with no heat, but the price was right, and there was a pub downstairs. Barbara and Kevin were jet lagged and fell asleep as soon as we settled in. There was no music in the pub below that night, so I crossed the street to Cullen's. There I met a pub poet and I had a long night of it.

Our attic room had real beds. I hadn't slept in one in quite a while and when I woke up the next morning, I didn't want to leave it. The windows were open and as I lay there, I could smell the ocean and the turf smoke carried in on the breeze. I could hear the seagulls and the sounds of an old country that was new to me. I heard the voices of older women complaining about the "binmin" and the noise they made earlier and earlier each morning and the gonging of the Guinness barrels being rolled and tossed about behind O'Reilly's. I rolled over and slept late.

That night we met Mairtin O'Connor who was playing in the pub downstairs with a fiddler named Fahey who sold insurance. Mairtin was fifteen or sixteen and a sensational box player even then. It was, I think, Mairtin that told us about the All Ireland Fleadh Cheoil in Listowel. I did not yet know what a Fleadh Cheoil was, but I knew we had to go.

We spent a day or two knocking around Galway and then boarded a bus to Kerry. In Limerick we changed buses and our new bus was packed full of Dubs singing, "Stop the Bus, I Want to Wee-Wee" to the tune of "I've Been Working on the Railroad." A person could smoke and drink on the bus in Ireland in those days, so we did. When we reached Listowel in the Kingdom of Kerry and saw the huge crowds, we knew that this was paradise for music lovers. There were fiddlers and box players, flutes and banjos in every sheltered spot. They played in doorways, recessed windows and sheds. The pubs were packed. Music mad people were squeezed into every available space to hear some of the greatest musicians in Ireland. By this time I had figured out that a Fleadh Cheoil was a music competition.

We needed a place to sleep, so we went out to a cow pasture that had a sign saying "Camping" and we put up our "tent", two rubber ponchos that snapped together. We found two sticks, whittled a few pegs, and used our boot laces to tie the thing down. All three of us piled in along with the guitar, fiddle, flute and whatever gear we had. The wind blew and it poured, the snaps holding our ponchos together flew apart and we had to beat a slippery retreat through the watery cow pies to a hedge where we took shelter.

At dawn the next morning we were back on the town square, sitting on the circular wall around the church playing tunes. Some older musicians came by with big bottles of Guinness, banjos and fiddles. They sat down with us and started playing. They were Travelers, the Dunnes from Limerick I think. We were all having a good time and RTE, Irish National Television, came by and filmed us.

Young Cathal McConnell was the talk of the town with his flute playing and his vast repertoire of tunes and songs from the North. We managed to get in close enough to hear him in a pub. I don't think we saw even one competition because the venues were so crowded, but there was plenty of music all over town, so we didn't miss them.

At the end of the festival, we found a hay barn a little way out of town and had a snooze. Then we caught a bus to Ballybunion because the buses heading anywhere else were full. We found a B & B in Ballybunion, but had an awful time with the landlady who didn't want three in a room, even though Barbara and I were married. We finally convinced her that if Kevin tried anything I would kill him. She relented and let us have the room. Apparently, she preferred murder to fornication.

Since that first night in Galway with the pub poet, I had a yearning to taste pigs' feet. In Ballybunion I ordered crubeens, as they are called in Ireland, and they were pretty good, but I wouldn't write a poem about them. As we walked through Ballybunion, I stepped out into the street looking over my left shoulder instead of my right. A car driving on the left ran over the tip of my boot, just missing my big toe. I have been careful to look the correct way when crossing the road in Ireland ever since.

When we returned to Galway we headed to Lower Salt Hill and Philomena Helly who ran a B & B. We had gotten her name from Sheila O'Leary, one of the Irish immigrants that we knew in Chicago. Philomena and Frank Helly were very good to us. Frank was a postman and knew Galway like the back of his hand. They filled us in about all the goings on around town and we stayed for a few weeks. We spent a lot of time at a pub nearby called The Thatch, where Kevin Keegan's brother played. It stayed open late.

The old part of Galway is a medieval walled city, nearly a thousand years old. Parts of the wall are still visible here and there. We would walk in from Salt Hill to the Cellar Bar on Shop Street, just off of Eyre Square, which was a haven for students and musicians our own age. The students mostly attended University College Galway. Some of them were acquainted with the Irish musicians that we had met in Boston, so we had mutual friends. We met Eugene Lambe, the flute player and piper, Padraig O'Carra who played old harp tunes on a zither and Seamus and Manus McGuire, fiddle playing brothers among others.

It was there that we met Mickey Finn, the wild and brilliant fiddler. The last time I saw Mickey, he was on the bonnet of a car carrying a bride and groom off on their honeymoon. They were in front of the Cellar Bar and Mickey was demonstrating, on the hood of the car, how to conduct the honeymoon. He had a fiddle in one hand and was humping the car, while his bottler was shouting, "Ladies and Gentlemen. Mickey Finn, the Greatest Fiddler in All of Ireland."

Everyone in the street was roaring with laughter, including the blushing groom and bride. The bottler's job, after rounding up an impromptu audience, was to pass through the crowd and collect money, saying things like, "Come on now people, dig down deep and come up decent." There was, and still is, plenty of busking going on in the streets of Galway. We often played ourselves on Shop Street and it helped keep us going.

Clive Collins from The Battering Ram, an acquaintance from the Boston days, was another fiddler who played on the street. He favored striped suits and a bowler hat. When I saw Clive a few years ago in Galway, he was very, very thin and was just back from seeing a doctor. He told me that the doctor, after examining him, said, "I'm sorry sir. According to my instruments, you are already dead."

Clive Collins and Mickey Finn have both passed on. They left their friends with many fond memories.

One beautiful morning we walked out of Helly's over towards the Prom, the footpath that ran along the bay from Salt Hill to the Claddagh and Galway. We noticed a lovely horse in some vacant land across the street with a caravan nearby. A man shouted, "Com'ere."

We had made eye contact and it was too late to walk away, so we ambled over and met a Traveler, who had a very nice style of shaking us down for coins. It was good luck anyway to give a coin or two to Travelers, especially the older ladies who sat in doorways here and there around town. They usually had Holy cards attached to the little cardboard boxes that they held in their laps. They would always say, "God bless you", when you dropped a coin or two. You would often hear the Traveler kids singing "The Rocks of Bawn" or "Spancil Hill" with big voices and their brothers and sisters doing the bottling for them.

We went to a couple of cinemas, which we really enjoyed. There were ashtrays built into the seats and the crowd would comment out loud on the film. I remember watching one Clint Eastwood movie and for a little while everyone was quiet, watching closely. Suddenly a girl blurted out in a loud whisper, "He's a ghost." Then we heard, "Yes! He's a ghost," or "No, I don't think... Well, maybe."

The American dollar went far in Ireland in 1973. You could go to the Cheap Jack's shops which were second hand stores that sold used clothes and purchase whatever you needed for very little money. You could stop into a shop that sold food and buy nice bread and cheese or some soup for not very much, or you could go into a restaurant and order a full meal including desert for about five American dollars.

Sheila O'Leary, our Chicago friend who had told us about the Hellys, was originally from Co. Offaly. She had recommended that we travel to Birr where Stephen Tierney, a friend of hers from childhood, owned a place called The Palace Bar, so we did. Stephen and his wife loved music and we enjoyed some good nights there. Before we left Galway, we had talked to some of the musicians in the Cellar Bar and picked up a few leads on some pubs in the Midlands that we might be able to play. With the Tierneys' help, we booked a little tour.

We had a hired car, a rough one, from a fly-by-night outfit in Galway and were up in Moate for a Sunday morning session that started right after Mass. We were playing away and it was the custom for everyone to buy a round for the musicians. Soon there were twenty or thirty drinks on the table and we were putting them away as best we could. The Holy Hour started at noon and everyone had to leave except the staff and the musicians. They made sandwiches for Barbara, Kevin and me. We had nearly cleared the table of the excess drinks when the doors reopened and the crowd piled back in. There was plenty more music and drink, not necessarily in that order. Around six o'clock the three of us made it outside into the hired car and headed back to Birr.

I was behind the wheel when we sideswiped another car with a family in it. Both cars pulled over and I thought we were in big trouble, but the driver said, "Not to worry. My car is a bit banged up already."

The hired car didn't look too bad so the man just said "Good luck" and we drove off, this time in another direction.

I was mad at myself and something came over me. I stopped the car, jumped out, ran across the road and disappeared into the hills and fields, heading west. Kevin and Barbara drove off, I guess, and I just kept running, jumping walls, chasing cattle, roaring and singing. I chased a small herd of cattle over a hill and suddenly saw the gigantic full moon in front of me. I stopped and regained my senses, saying to myself, "No wonder I'm going mad. It's the full moon!"

I walked back to Moate, entered a pub, sat at the bar and ordered a pint. I wouldn't talk to or look at anyone until Kevin and Barbara came in and we went to a hotel nearby to get a room. The man behind the desk took one look at us and said we couldn't stay there so, as we were leaving, Kevin took a fancy barometer off the wall. We climbed into the car and headed south to Wexford town on the coast. If we had known how to read the barometer, we might have realized that a hurricane was coming in.

We pulled into town at about two in the morning and knocked on a hotel door. No one answered so we started shouting in the street for someone to let us in. The roar of the storm was drowning out our voices. We drove out a few miles into the country and pulled off the road into a field. We slept, or tried to sleep, in the little car. The guitar case was on top of Barbara and me in the back seat. Kevin had the front seat with the fiddle and the rest of the gear. The car was rocking with the wind. There were torrents of rain. We woke up the next morning with massive hangovers and a very nice looking barometer.

On the radio we heard that several ships had been lost and people had died in that storm. There was flooding and trees down. We just wanted to get back to Galway. We returned the car as soon as we arrived and walked up to Phil Helly's.

Walking around town one day we heard the Rabbitte brothers busking on the street. They were older fellas and I think one or both of them might have been blind. I was much taken with their music.

Not long afterwards I was thinking about the Rabbittes as I sat in a thatched house at a party thrown by some college students. We were smoking weed that had been grown by some of the marine biology students at the Carna Research Station. I mentioned how lucky they were in Ireland to have so many great old musicians. One of the students took issue with my comment and said, "The old people here don't know anything about music!"

I was surprised and was actually angry with the guy for years. Later I realized that I didn't think much of the music that my father listened to either. It was only when I grew older that I could start to appreciate the musicianship of my father's music, even if I still didn't want to listen to it. It could be that the young guy that I was talking to, like many young people the world over, didn't like anything he associated with his parents' generation and put all of traditional music in that category.

The Cellar Bar had two rooms. The first was actually in the cellar. It was more of a club and a venue for bands playing all sorts of music. The room on the ground floor was a pub and restaurant and it was there that we went to meet people our own age while we got a bite to eat and a pint.

When we walked through the doorway, we could usually spot Maggie sitting in a booth against the far wall taking in the goings on. Maggie was an American girl from the East Coast who lived in Galway. She was a year or two older than us with curly reddish hair and was a little bit like a big sister. She would listen to tales of our travels and adventures. As there weren't many Yanks around, we would have long chats about what was happening in America. The Viet Nam War was winding down and there was plenty to talk about socially and politically. Even though Maggie loved Galway and knew most of the Cellar crowd, our conversations may have helped with the inevitable loneliness that comes, at times, when living abroad.

Around that time she met Charlie Piggott, a banjo player who became a founding member of De Danann, and they later married. Maggie died young of an illness. Had she lived, she would have been a great help to me remembering the stories of what was happening in Galway at the time. She was a great listener and everyone talked to her. She was one of the nicest people I've ever met.

After a few weeks of carousing, we asked Phil Helly what we owed. To our dismay we found out that instead of one punt seventy-five per night for the rooms, it was one punt seventy-five per night per person. We counted our money and realized that, once we paid the bill, we would be stone broke.

We couldn't even afford to pay for the phone calls to cancel the gigs we had booked in the Midlands. Making a phone call from a public phone in Ireland in those days was a long, expensive, and frustrating experience. The process involved standing in a small booth with a pocket full of change and telling the operator where you wanted to call. Then you waited for the operator to find the number and connect you, while continually feeding change into the coin slot to keep the line open. If you were lucky, the call was connected before you ran out of coins and you would have thirty seconds or so to talk to the other party. The whole process often resulted in damage to the public phone. We had to leave

Ireland and return to America immediately, so we hitchhiked to Shannon and waited around for a flight back to the States. I had no idea at that time how soon I would back, and how often I would return over the next four decades.

Chapter 5
On A Roll

Back in America, we didn't stop long in Chicago, but scurried back to St. Paul, where we again stayed in Ann Heymann's chicken coop and looked for places to play. We met John and Leah Curtin at O'Gara's through Martin McHugh. They asked us to play a dance to raise money for Irish Northern Aid at the Commercial Club on Snelling Avenue near University. The Irish Northern Aid Dance was an instant hit. Hundreds showed up for the music and dance and to show support for the victims of injustice. Josie Vaughan from Dublin and her husband Andy from Clare taught the ceili and set dances to the younger crowd that showed up with the help of Bernie and Tommy Roe from Mayo and Roscommon. Martin McHugh's brother, the genial Mike McHugh, his wife Kathleen and his sister Kathleen formed the core of the experienced dancers. Mike Whelan, a St. Paul boy took to the dancing right away and soon could organize a Siege of Ennis or a Haymaker's Jig like a native. As it was in Denver, the colorfully dressed and free form hippy dancers joined in with the more formal Irish crowd and these benefit dances soon became a regular occurrence in St. Paul. Irish Northern Aid had been quick to catch on to the ceili dance potential and at that time the benefit dances were spreading all across the country. The scoffers sometimes called such a dance a "Gun Runners' Ball." There were many investigations, but as far as I know, the money went where it was supposed to go, to the families of those who were jailed without trial in Northern Ireland.

Barbara, Kevin and I started meeting Martin McHugh up at O'Gara's on Sunday evenings to play tunes. It turned into a session when Mary MacEachron showed up with her fiddle. Soon Laura MacKenzie with her flute, Sam Dillon, a beekeeper at the time and later a journalist, with his fiddle and Jamie Gans also with a fiddle became regulars. The Devaneys from Galway, the Scanlons from Limerick, the Roes, the Vaughans, and the Tipperary and Kerry crowds all started showing up to enjoy the sessions. The bartenders were grumpy about the session. They had been enjoying nice quiet Sunday nights. O'Gara's was a very small bar at the time and the musicians would all crowd into the corner of a small side room to the right of the bar to make a place for all those who came to listen. This side room, which was very tight quarters to play in, has since been turned into a good sized toilet.

Because we were drawing crowds at the ceilis and sessions, our group, The Dayhills, was asked to play at the Commodore Hotel, a landmark in St. Paul with a beautiful ballroom next to an Art Deco bar. F. Scott Fitzgerald, a native son of St Paul and his wife, Zelda, had been living and tippling there in the roaring twenties. In the thirties, Ma Barker and her boys were rumored to have frequented the place as well.

The occasion was St. Patrick's Day and some of the Irish-American upper crust, including judges, attorneys, doctors, clergy and even the mayor, those who did not often go to little neighborhood Irish pubs or Northern Aid dances, came to the celebration at the Commodore and heard us play. The dance floor was full the whole evening.

About a half mile away on Grand Avenue, was another Art Deco restaurant and bar, Fran O'Connell's. When Steve O'Connell, Fran's son, saw the big crowd enjoying the Irish music at the Commodore, he asked us to play their back room, which, being rather small, was easy to pack. It had a tiny dance floor and became one of our regular places to play whenever we were in town.

Kevin, Barbara and I were on a roll, and it was easier to keep working when we changed cities every few months, so that was what we were doing. We wanted to go to Denver to see Pat and Mary Flanagan, so we called Harry Tuft at the Folklore Center there and he booked us for a concert. When we rolled into Denver, we learned that Mary Flanagan was in the hospital. She had contracted tuberculosis in Ireland when she was young and had been in a sanitarium there. She still suffered frequent lung trouble and that was why the Flanagans had moved to Denver from Chicago. They hadn't wanted to leave and missed the large community of Irish immigrants there, but they gathered together the Irish in Denver and helped form the Irish Fellowship Club.

My parents had been in the habit of visiting relatives who were hospitalized and always brought us children with them. Later, after I had started playing the fiddle, I would bring it along when I visited people. I particularly remember playing for two great aunts in the nursing homes where they lived. One aunt, Aggie Roach, lived to be 102. Her husband, John, had been an Irish fiddler. The other, Helen Dahill, lived to be 103. When I would play for Aunt Helen, she always had me adjust the door so that those outside couldn't see into the room, but could hear that someone had come in to play Irish music just for her.

We were saddened that Mary's health had taken a turn for the worse and visited her in her hospital room bringing the fiddle and the flute. She brightened right up when she heard the music. She asked for her favorite jigs and reels by name and the ones that we didn't have we vowed to learn.

The Folklore Center was a regular stop for us, and although they did not serve drink, they were always shocked at the number of empty bottles left on the floor after we gave a concert. The Oxford Hotel, on Wazee near the Denver train station, had a big music hall called The Press Room that was run as a folk club and had acts like The Nitty Gritty Dirt Band, Hot Rize, John Hartford and Bonnie Raitt. The room was booked by Graham Lewis, who, because he loved Irish music, scheduled us on a fairly regular basis. He would give us rooms in the hotel and let us stay on sometimes for a week or more after we had finished the engagement.

Pueblo, Colorado isn't a town where one would expect to find an Irish pub, but there was one there for several years in an old hotel downtown. The hospitality there was so good that I can't remember the owner's name, but he had seen us in Denver and invited us down to play. The rooms in the hotel were very small, no more than eight by ten and from the stories we had heard, the place had a notorious history dating from the Wild West era. We would practice all day in our rooms, then come downstairs in the evening, have a meal and play four nights a week for a couple weeks at a time. The main characters that I remember from that gig were Tiny and his crew. They were gigantic, averaging about six foot four and three hundred fifty pounds each. There were six of these young fellas who all worked together. They discovered that they loved Irish music and would sit in a row right in front of the stage singing along and drinking their beer out of pitchers that looked like beer mugs in their huge hands. I have never seen such guzzling and gulping in all my life, but they were very polite and enthusiastic, which is a rare combination. I think between the six of them, they spent enough to cover the band's salary.

When we returned to Denver, Mary Flanagan was back home and again hosting the Sunday afternoon soirees. The Flanagan house was actually in Littleton, a suburb just south of Denver. Mary worked in the cafeteria of the town's high school, Columbine. Columbine High School was the site of a tragedy years later. Pat had worked as a mechanical engineer for most of his life and was nearing retirement. After he retired, he finally got around to taking, and passing, the test to get his license just to show that he could do it.

Pat had gotten to know us better. He continued helping us learn the tunes with the right variations and rhythms, but he also now felt free when he heard me singing, to correct me on my pronunciation of the Gaelic phrases and place names that were in the songs. Pat was a native Irish speaker, and I generally followed his advice. However, when I sang "The Leaving of Liverpool" and he said, "No Tom. It's the 'Laving' of Liverpool", I decided, that for me, a Yank, that was going a little bit too far.

In Flanagan's basement one Sunday, Sean Sheehan from Limerick sang a comic song that he called "The Kilkenny Flays" about Kilkenny and fleas. I thought it was hilarious.

Sean asked, "You don't have that one?"

"No."

"Give me a pen 'til I write it down for you."

That was perhaps the first time I realized how open people were to sharing their party pieces. "The Kilkenny Fleas" was one of the first songs I collected. People gave me hundreds more over the years.

Somehow we ended up being asked to play at Adolph's in Winter Park, a ski resort up in the Rocky Mountains. We made our way up there, still in the trusty, rusty aqua van. It was absolutely beautiful in the mountains with windy roads, towering pines and plenty of snow. When we walked into the bar, there was a big fire roaring in the fire place and the crowd was roaring too. We looked up and saw why. A girl was about halfway up a rope attached to the ceiling, which was about thirty feet high. It turns out that the patrons were taking turns climbing to the top to win a free drink. We found the owner who was named Keith. I asked him if he thought Irish music would go over with this crowd. He said, "Let's give it a try."

The crowd danced to it just like they would dance to rock and roll. After hours, Keith did recitations, like "The Cremation of Sam McGee" or "Dangerous Dan McGrew" for the benefit of the staff and the band mostly. Those Robert Service poems were great favorites as party pieces and I had heard them both before at The Palace Bar in Offaly when we were in Ireland.

We slept right in the bar, under the stage which had about four feet of headroom. One night we heard the sound of breaking glass, as if the stray bottles or ashtrays left on the tables at closing were being thrown on the floor. No one was around.

There was no sound of footsteps, only the sound of the breaking glass. The next day we asked Keith what was going on. He said, "Oh, that's just Adolph. He gets mad when we don't clean up properly at the end of the night."

Adolph, the man who built the place, had been dead for years. We heard Adolph several more times over the course of the engagement.

We went down the road one night to another bar. We sat around a table near the dance floor where a band was setting up. When the band began to play, a crowd of young, fit skiers came out onto the floor and started dancing. Then a girl stopped for a second or two and took off her leg. She then returned to the floor dancing on one leg. A minute later, a guy took off an arm and threw it into a corner. Kevin, Barbara and I looked on in amazement, as more legs and arms were being removed and stacked off to the side while their owners kept dancing. The waitress, noticing our gaping mouths explained to us that the dancers were members of a ski team that was competing in a Handicapped Olympics event in Winter Park that weekend. They were a happy bunch and all smiles. We didn't stay long, but we were mightily impressed with them.

Keith gave me a free tow ticket, so I tried skiing in the mountains. I had made a pair of skis out of staves knocked out of an old wooden barrel when I was a kid. I sawed and whittled the staves down to a point in the front and back, then sandpapered and varnished them and attached leather straps. I could ski backward or forward on them. In the winter, I would use them on my newspaper route. I later got a pair of WWII era army surplus skis that were made to use for both cross-country and downhill skiing. I used those, doctored up with paint to look a little fancier, at local ski hills, so I had a bit of practice going downhill. I discovered that, for me, the trick to having a good time skiing is being able to turn, slow down, and stop. Falling when speeding down a big mountain the few times I tried it didn't add anything to the experience.

We played a half dozen more ski resorts over the next few years in Colorado and Utah and I really enjoyed being way up there on those beautiful mountains and coming down slow and easy, watching the other skiers and the gorgeous scenery. I was surprised that so many of the jetsetters on their winter ski vacations liked Irish music. It was really sinking in that Irish music had appeal even to those who had never heard it before.

*****

We eventually left Colorado and headed for Massachusetts where we had a gig booked at a new place in Newburyport called Timmy Meehan's. Since we had a few weeks before we were due in Newburyport, we stopped in Chicago along the way and played at Pat's Pub on Kedzie. It was owned by Paddy Hirst from County Mayo. At the time there was another Paddy Hearst in the papers. This Paddy Hirst looked entirely different. He was a big tall athletic looking fellow with black hair combed strait down over his forehead and worn short on the sides. His skin was very white and covered with freckles. The crowd in his pub was nearly all Galway and Mayo. After he closed, at 2:00 a.m., we would go play at Bill Bailey's on Montrose 'til 5 a.m., and most of the crowd would stay with us. There were lots of singers and a few box drivers who would get up and play a few numbers with us.

Paddy Hirst asked us to go on a Northern Aid bus tour of the South Side pubs. We played half a dozen bars full of Irish immigrants in the neighborhood of 63rd and California. There was The Kerryman's, Hoban's, Hanley's House of Happiness and the 6511 Club on Kedzie which later became one of our favorite places to play. Paddy had sound advice for us when we played for him in the pub. We were receiving requests for country and rock and roll songs. I asked Paddy if he wanted us to mix it up.

"Keep it traditional, lads," he answered and so we did.

We rolled into Newburyport at about three o'clock in the morning and decided to drive by Timmy Meehan's new pub to have a look at the place we would be playing five nights a week for the next month. When we drove into the lot, we saw that it was a fine, big place with plenty of parking. We got out of the van to look through the windows. There was a sign on the door that said, "Closed." That didn't bother me, but the sign next to it did. It said, "Out of Business." The next morning I called Timmy and asked him what was up.

"They shut me down," said Timmy.

I didn't bother asking him why. I said, "That's too bad Timmy, but we drove out all the way from Chicago to play. Can you help us out at all?"

He replied, "I'd love to, Tommy, but I can't. I don't have any money."

I didn't press him. It sounded like he was in as much of a state of shock as we were, if not more.

Since the gig fell through, Barbara and I headed for Rowley with Kevin and we stayed at his parents' house. We decided to pick up the books and records that had been left at our old apartment next to the Chanticleer. When we took off for California, I hadn't realized that we were basically moving out and I hadn't talked to Pierre in over a year. He was a bit upset with us. We had to settle up in court.

We rustled up a gig at the Village Coach House in Brookline, near Boston. It was owned by Henry Varrian, a man from Cork. Henry was a musician himself and a gentleman. He gave us quite a few nights in the short time we were there. It was at a session at the Coach House that Henry introduced us to Seamus Connelly, the legendary fiddle master from East Clare. That afternoon, Seamus taught me "The Cuckoo Hornpipe" which wasn't very well known at the time. He said, "Take that one to Chicago and play it for the lads on the South Side."

At the Coach House, on our last night, a crowd of Dahill women from South Boston showed up and wanted to meet me. My father had stayed with them when he was in the army in WWII. It was nice to meet some relatives, and, very much like my relatives back in St. Paul, they were big, hearty and full of fun.

Kevin didn't return to Chicago with us. He stayed in Rowley where he kept playing the guitar, but eventually gravitated to the fiddle. He got involved in restoring old Colonial houses that were built with pegs rather than nails. He also started collecting and repairing vintage violins.

I didn't see him again for twenty-five years. Then I received a call. He had married and his wife Kate was one of the Butlers, a prominent St. Paul family. They were in town visiting her people. I was playing a wedding that night and invited him to play with me. He met me at the University Club on Summit Avenue. Because we had both "kept it traditional", we could still play together as if no time had passed at all.

I saw him again a few years later at Willie Clancy Week in Miltown Malbay, County Clare, where his daughters were signed up for classes. He lives in Freeport, Maine now and often gets together with Seamus Connelly and piper Kieran O'Hare. He visits St. Paul more often now that his kids are leaving the nest and drops in for a tune when he can.

Chapter 6
Chi-Town Frolics

"Hello. Terry Teahan?"

"Hello Cuz, how are you? Who is this?" He sounded very weak.

"Tom Dahill. I met you at Bogan High School on the South Side and you told me to call."

We chatted for a while. Terry Teahan was in the habit of calling everyone Cuz. He told me that he came to Chicago in 1929, on Black Tuesday, the day of the stock market crash.

Terrance P. Teahan (Cuz),Co. Kerry

When he arrived he looked for a job and finally found one with the Illinois Central Railroad. Over the years, when relatives or friends from Castleisland, County Kerry came over looking for work, Cuz would advise them to apply at the Illinois Central. When they were asked for a reference he told them to put down Terence P. Teahan, relationship, cousin. Cuz soon had nearly thirty "cousins" employed by the Illinois Central. Whenever they saw him they would call out "Hello Cuz". Their families would all be "cousins" as well. Soon, the entire town was calling him Cuz. He told me that he had just retired from the railroad job.

When I invited him over, Cuz told me he had recently had an operation and he wasn't feeling too well. I told him that Barbara and I could pick him up in the van. He asked if I had a tape recorder. I told him that I had a small cassette player.

"Good. There's some tunes that I want you to have, Cuz."

We said that we would be right over and picked him up at his house on Agatite just off of Milwaukee Avenue. When we arrived at his house, Cuz came out, moving pretty slowly. He had a bowling bag containing his concertina. He said, "I'm leaving Big Liz here, Cuz, she's too much for me to handle."

He was referring to his big white melodeon, a Baldoni with eight reeds to each note. It was a fancy box that he had custom made with two flags, Irish and American and his name emblazoned on the front in rhinestones and more rhinestone decorations encrusting the fingerboard and ends.

I settled him in the passenger seat and we drove back to Barbara's brother's apartment on Marshfield. Cuz never stopped talking the entire way to our neighborhood. He told us all about Castleisland where he was raised. He had been a student and neighbor of Padraig O'Keefe. He said that his mother had played the concertina. All his conversation centered around the music and the people he had known when he was growing up. I asked him if he knew Pat Flanagan and he said, "I did, Cuz. We often played together when he was in Chicago. He was a lovely player."

We arrived at the apartment. Almost all of the Chicago neighborhoods at that time were the territory of one gang or another. The gang graffiti in our neighborhood was for the Latin Kings, the Cobras and the Insane Popes. We parked the van in front and walked around to the back entrance.

When Cuz realized that our apartment was up the wooden stairway on the third floor he said, "I'll never make it Cuz," and he started tearing up.

I said, "If you don't mind, I can carry you."

He was very light at that time. Barbara carried his bowling bag. Up the stairs we went and into the back door of Jack Reid's apartment. The fire radio was blaring as usual and Cuz asked what it was. I told him that Jack was a fire buff. Cuz couldn't sit comfortably after the operation without a lot of pillows. We got him situated and he pulled out his concertina. He placed an embroidered tea towel over his leg so that he wouldn't destroy his pants. He was high strung and very talkative and said, "My hands are ringing wet with nerves, Cuz. Would you believe, I haven't played in years?" He made sure I had the tape recorder ready to go.

"Is it on, Cuz?"

"Yes, it's on," I told him

He tore into a reel, "The Old Torn Petticoat That I Bought in Mullingar". Towards the end of the tune, he let out an ungodly scream and it was like him, pure wild. I still have that tape, and many others that we made over the years. Cuz put tunes on the tapes for me, jigs, old rare songs that he learned from his grandmother, reels, slides, polkas, marches, airs and about a hundred tunes that he composed himself. Tunes dedicated to people he knew back home in Kerry, like "Tadhg and Biddy on the Cock of Hay" and "Scollards" as well as tunes about people he met in Chicago like "Johnny Harling's Delight" and "Mickey Chewing Bubblegum". Cuz told me he had actually made the last tune when he was about fifteen but didn't have a title for it. The title came about when he saw his nephew in Chicago chewing bubblegum when it was first invented.

He was full of stories from the past forty-five or fifty years in Chicago. He met nearly every Irish musician who came through town. Among the Irish in Chicago, each county had its own club, where they met for ceilis, wedding dances and funeral functions. Cuz went to all of them, not just the functions for Kerry. He played all the Irish dance halls and hundreds of weddings. He still remembered who got married and who was related to whom. Although he called them all "Cuz" he knew everyone's name. He could play all the sets and dance them as well. Set Dances require different tunes for each figure and there could be four or five figures in each set. There were Kerry Sets, Clare Sets, Galway Sets, the Lancers' Set and the Caledonian Set to name a few.

When Cuz found out that we were looking for another musician to replace Kevin, he said, "Come down to the South Side Saturday night. I think I might have someone for you."

We went down to the South Side. I think it was a Kerry Club. We were asked up to play and when we left the stage Cuz brought over a tall, curly-haired, very thin fellow who was about our age, early twenties, and said, "Cuz, this is Chuck Heymann, and he's a good musician."

Chuck, or Charlie, Heymann was from Chicago. He played the guitar and concertina and he could also sing. He had a head full of Irish music and was very easy going. He didn't talk or drink much which struck us as unusual. He was very tolerant of everyone and everything, and cared only about music.

When Barbara's brother married and bought a house on Dakin and Lockwood, he offered to let us use the upstairs. It was walking distance from Shamrock Imports, on the Northwest side near Six Corners. Paige and Donna never complained about all the practicing we did with Chuck upstairs. Flanagan had taught us the importance of a good honest foot, so they had to contend with three big, honest feet banging away in the little house day and night. Later we put in a dance floor and started doing step dancing and tap dancing as well. On top of that, Cuz was a frequent visitor and his motto was, "You're going to have to scream if you're gonna play with me, Cuz."

*****

We returned to Boston shortly after Chuck joined us and played a few Irish bars in Dorchester at Field's Corner. Field's Corner was in decline at the time, but there was still a lot of good Irish music and dancing there. We showed up at The Irish Rover, a big dance hall with a music pub in the cellar one Sunday about noon. As we were heading down the stairs, a man coming up challenged me, "Oh, big fella, huh. Think you can fight? I'll fight cha."

I said, "Oh no. We're just here to play music."

"What kind of music?" he asked.

"Irish music" I replied.

"Well, why didn't you say so? I'm the owner. Come on in."

He turned around and we followed him down into the pub. He bought us a round and introduced us to everyone there including Richie Dwyer, Finbar's brother, who was a great singer and button box player. We ended up working at the Irish Rover as the opening act for some of the Irish show bands that played upstairs like the Dermot Henry Band. It was quite a place, full of immigrants from the West of Ireland. One night a fight broke out on the dance floor. A couple of patrolmen came in to break it up and needed to radio for reinforcements a few minutes later. Afterward, I heard that twenty-seven policemen had been sent to the hospital.

Because of the bad publicity, The Irish Rover was shut down for a while. We continued to play different pubs in the area, but when the place reopened as The Shanagolden Club we stopped by to check it out. As we were leaving, I noticed that the doorman/bouncer was a tall fellow with very white skin, freckles and black hair combed straight down over his forehead. I did a double take. It was Paddy "Keep It Traditional Lad's" Hirst from Pat's Pub in Chicago. I was surprised to see him there because he had disappeared from Chicago about six months before. It was rumored that he had been shot and there were a lot of theories about how and why the shooting took place. I could see through his shirt that there was a four by four inch bandage across his stomach, so it might have been true. I didn't ask him anything about it and was just glad to see him alive and smiling.

We noticed on the trip from Chicago to Boston that Chuck was a good driver. He could drive for hours without getting tired. One night after a gig in Holyoke Massachusetts, at about one a.m., we loaded up the car and with Chuck driving, set off for the next gig... in Denver. I remember asking Chuck somewhere in Indiana if he was tired of driving.

“Nope,” he said.

I asked, “Chuck, you haven’t said a word the whole way. Is there anything bothering you?”

“Nope.”

I was trying to help him stay awake, so I tried again, “Are you thinking about stuff?”

“Nope.”

“Do you have any tunes going through your head?”

“Nope.”

“Are you thinking about your family?”

“Nope.”

“How about politics or history? Can you think of anything that’s crossed your mind?”

“Ahhh....no.”

I didn’t ask any more. I realized that the reason he didn’t get tired or need to sleep was that he didn’t waste any energy. He was the ideal driver. For the next six or seven years Chuck took over as wheelman and there was plenty of driving to be done. I was glad about that because I figured I had used up all my luck as a driver.

*****

Though we were often on the road, we were based out of Chicago in those days. One Sunday afternoon we walked into Hanley’s House of Happiness down on the South Side. There were about twenty Irish musicians sitting on stools along the bar playing away. Many of them were playing button accordions with one leg crossed over the other and cigarettes dangling out of the sides of their mouths like Joe Cooley. Even though Joe had left Chicago many years before, his impact on Irish music there was obviously still being felt.

Nearly all the South Side musicians were in Hanley's that afternoon. Seamus Cooley, Joe's brother and a fine flute player, was assembling the wooden flute that he carried in a greased paper bag. Frank Burke, the fiddler from Mayo with hands so large that his fiddle looked like a toy, remembered us right away from the Bogan High School concert. Jimmy Considine and Joe Shea, both box players and both from Clare, were sitting on stools with their accordions at the ready. Albert Neary, a flute player and nephew of Eleanor Neary who had recorded tunes on the piano back in the thirties, was sitting nearby. Frank Thornton, another flute player and his box-playing son Jimmy, were there as well.

Johnny McGreevy, the Irish fiddle master from Chicago, also remembered us from the concert. He said "By Golly" so often that it had become his nickname. He had a student, Liz Carroll, who was rumored to be a fantastic player although we hadn't heard her yet.

Seamus and Joe Cooley with Martin McHugh on stage at Hanley's House of Happiness

Hanley's House of Happiness had an unofficial, oft repeated byline attached to it, "One Thousand Tunes, One Thousand Fights". I saw fights in many bars over the years, but never at Hanley's. They say that there are no fights when the music is right. One of the weekly Irish Radio Hours was broadcast live from Hanley's on Sundays.

Many in the crowd that came to there for the music were very knowledgeable about the tunes and the players even though they didn't play instruments themselves. They also had a lot to say about the dancing, the history and the politics of Ireland. Most were Irish born and had brought the Culture to Chicago with them.

Chicago was a kind of Mecca for Irish music, partly due to the great work of Chicago Police Chief, Captain Francis O'Neill back at the turn of the century. O'Neill collected Irish tunes from the multitudes of immigrants in the city and published them at a time when the music was disappearing in Ireland. It is said that to help in this task he lured musicians who could write music to Chicago with the promise of jobs on the force and that they were sometimes referred to as "Tune Detectives". The musicians continued to come long after O'Neill had passed on to that Great Session in the Sky. Even today, Irish musicians coming to America travel to Chicago to meet the inheritors of O'Neill's work. They had immigrated in the twenties, thirties, forties and fifties and are in their eighties or nineties today. Many of the visitors end up making Chicago their home and so the saga continues.

The 6511 Club on South Kedzie was a favorite spot for the Irish living on the South Side back in the seventies. Tom Flanagan, the owner, was a tall thin man with reddish hair who always wore sunglasses as his eyes were very sensitive to light. His ears were sensitive too, for Irish music, and he encouraged the people who played or just loved the music to make themselves at home.

There was a man serving behind the bar at The 6511 Club with the quick moves of a bantam weight boxer and an even quicker wit. This was "Sligo" Jack Finan. He had a distinctive white patch in his otherwise dark hair and sang and played guitar when the opportunity arose. Sligo Jack had a big following with the after-work construction crowd and pensioners. Both men and women loved him because he had the kind of charm that you seldom see anymore. Every woman in the place he addressed as "Princess" and every man, no matter what his age, as "Me son."

Many of the Irish musicians worked in the construction trades. Kevin Henry, from Sligo, made his living as a steel worker high up on the city's skyscrapers. He worked a tough job with long hours, but even before he retired, his first love was always music. He is a story teller, singer, piper and flute player of the first degree. I have been told that Kevin always marks the anniversary of Chief O'Neill's death by putting flowers on his grave and paying his respects. Irish musicians are always passing through Chicago giving concerts followed by after-hours parties and sessions until dawn.

Kevin Henry, Co. Sligo

Men like Kevin rarely missed these nights out but still showed up at work the next day with only an hour or two to lie down in between. Kevin Henry isn't the only one who kept these kinds of hours. This was the way of life for many of the best Irish musicians, men and women and it demonstrates the devotion of this generation of the stalwarts of Irish music in Chicago.

Kevin and Sligo Jack hosted the sessions at The 6511 Club. The sessions could start just about any time and last until any hour depending on who showed up. There was of course a juke box and a T.V. in the bar, but when there was live music they were shut off and it became a different place. When Kevin or anyone sang a song or did a recitation, there would be silence in the bar as everyone wanted to hear.

The bar was in a dodgy neighborhood. One night when we arrived with our instruments for a session, we noticed a guy holding a cinder block over his head just outside the door. He informed us that he would brain the next person who walked out. We ordered him to get the hell out of there and when we walked in we saw another guy, apparently the first man's pal, stretched out on the pool table getting his ankles readjusted. We heard he had caused a disturbance and broke a few things around the place. He had insulted everyone and was using a phony ID. When the ruse had been discovered, he began shouting that the bar was at fault for serving him when he was under age and threatening the staff with the police for accepting the phony ID. He had been asked to leave several times before ending up in his current predicament, but he had belligerently vowed not to leave until his mother came to get him.

When the mother arrived, she berated everyone in the place as a bunch of Irish drunks and promised retribution as soon as she collected her son. The phone had been pulled out of the wall during the fracas. She must have found a pay phone on the street to summon the gang of men who pulled up in two Cadillacs about fifteen minutes later. The door was quickly locked and barred. The men outside started to bang on it with baseball bats and heave the cinderblock at the windows. Fortunately, the windows were glass block and they could do no more than crack them. Then we heard sirens. The police precinct headquarters was only a few blocks away. We peeked out and saw the attackers piling into their cars. As they pulled away, Tom Flanagan, the owner with the bad eyes, pushed past us with an armload of full beer bottles and pelted the cars as they sped up the street. He had surprisingly good aim and made every bottle count. After four or five direct hits, he came back inside with a big smile and said, "I recognized a couple of them. They're off duty cops."

So, that night the cops chased the cops. The session did not take place that evening. With the exception of Chuck, we were too wound up after all the excitement. Chuck, the ascetic, was undisturbed.

Pete Furlong from Wexford owned the original Abbey Pub at Addison and Narraganset on the Northwest side of Chicago. It was a nice place with a long bar, a small front room and a larger room in back for Irish music, which was the only kind of music that Pete wanted. He had a big West of Ireland crowd as well as many Irish-American families and a live radio show on Sunday nights hosted by Bobby Ryan. Pete gave us plenty of work. One night we met a band that had just arrived in town, Mick Wallace and Jerry Goodwin. They called themselves The Irish Brigade. These two boys were so homesick for Limerick that they broke out crying when they heard the music that reminded them of home so far away.

Jimmy Cummins, from Swinford, County Mayo, was one of my favorite regulars at The Abbey. He was a humorous kind of a stubby fellow with a twinkle in his eye and he was full of stories. Jimmy would ask for "The Yellow Tinker", "The Dawn" and "Lucy Campbell's", reels that he heard when he was a kid. He didn't play music, but he knew the names of the tunes and songs he liked. He would walk up to the stage, squint up at me and ask, "Tomasheen, would you ever sing "Donaleen" for me?"

What he meant was "Donal Og", a rare song that had been translated from the Irish and sung by Rae Fisher. Jimmy was all ears when there was live Irish music. When the music wasn't playing, he was a wonderful story teller or "seanchaí". Once on a break I was sitting at the bar and Jimmy told me about waking up at home in Swinford when he was a child and walking out of the cottage door.

"I walked out the door and what did I see right in front of me but a big huge mountain. So high that I almost fell over backward looking at it. I turned around because I thought it might fall on me. And when I turned around, what did I see, but another mountain, almost as tall right behind me. Everywhere I turned, only mountains and more mountains."

We got back on stage and started the next set. About a year later, I drove through Swinford myself and looked for mountains but couldn't see any. It was one of the flattest places I had ever seen.

Some of the young fellas, and some of the not so young fellas who frequented the Abbey were inclined to fight. I knew most of them and knew that they loved the music and didn't want to cause a disturbance. It was important to greet them, letting them know that we knew their names and were glad they were there. This way they wouldn't feel out of place. When they felt unwelcome they were most likely to fight.

Friends of mine from another band played there one time. Although they knew these guys too, they made the mistake of ignoring them and the troublemakers had to find something to fill the time. I came in the next day to see the result of the ensuing row. It started when one fella, who didn't have much English, finding himself in need of the gents and not wanting to have to ask anyone, decided to relieve himself unobtrusively in the corner of the crowded bar. The owner saw him and grabbed him. A couple of the guy's friends, one very large and one very small, broke a bottle on the owner's head. The off duty cop at the door ran over to straighten things out and his arm was broken. People began moving towards the door as the bottles and ashtrays started flying. One fellow, asleep on the bar was picked up and thrown through the false ceiling where he was left hanging. The whole place went up for grabs with fists and glass flying everywhere. The band tried to ignore what was happening and continued playing.

The next day there was glass embedded in the cork paneling surrounding the stage, but the area just behind the musicians was generally glass free. With just a little imagination, I could see blank spaces in the shape of the musicians and their instruments. There were warrants out for the culprits, but they were never apprehended. They grew up, married and raised families and you would never think that they would do something like that if you met them today.

Some pubs had jukeboxes with Irish songs and tunes on them. I would load up my cassette player with fresh batteries and record off the jukebox the songs and tunes that struck me. I got "The

Homes of Donegal" from the jukebox in the Abbey. I first heard "The Copperplate" reels on the Abbey jukebox and recorded them as well. This is a method of tune collection that has gone by the wayside as technology changed.

I might as well tell a few stories about another pub, Ireland's 32 on Milwaukee Avenue just north of Montrose. The police called it "The Bucket of Blood", a name that was not wholly undeserved. Sonny Carmody and his lovely wife Eileen owned the bar. They and their three sons lived upstairs. Sonny's uncle, Terrence P. Teahan, otherwise known as Cuz, lived one short block away. Sonny and Eileen were from Castleisland and grew up with the music. They also had a crowd of regulars, almost exclusively immigrants, in their small bar. It was a drinking bar with no food but it did have a pool table that was the cause of its reputation as a fighting bar. Unless you were known when you walked in, there was dead silence. The patrons waited to hear your voice so that they could tell what county you came from. If you happened to know someone there to speak with, you were in luck. It wasn't a good place for a stranger unless you had very good people skills.

The pool table was used for gambling. The betting was private, but the arguments over the fairness of play often became very loud and public. They placed a piece of plywood over the pool table when there was going to be music. It was the only way to keep the peace.

Eileen had a beautiful voice and loved to sing. She was tired of all the fighting that erupted regularly and was worried about Sonny's habit of vaulting over the bar one handed to break up the fights. When a fight started, the usual way of dealing with it was to hustle the combatants outside. This saved some wear and tear on the bar and the bar was off the hook as far as the law went.

One night we walked in to Ireland's 32, and we couldn't believe the change in the place. There were only a few people there and

Sonny was moping at the end of the bar with his chin in his hands and a sad old look on his usually cheery face. "She talked me into getting rid of the pool table. She thinks I'm too old," he confided in us. Because he was really depressing everyone, we didn't stay long.

About a week later we stopped in again and the juke box was turned up blasting Irish music. Sonny was behind the bar, running up and down and wisecracking. Eileen was serving too, and everyone was happy. The pool table was back.

Tommy McEvoy was a singer and guitar player. His brother was Johnny McEvoy, a musician well known in Ireland. Tommy lived in St. Louis and was visiting Chicago. He came in to The 32 one night when we were playing and wanted to do a set. I was apprehensive and hoped that he wouldn't get hurt. It could be a tough crowd. Being the entertainer that he is, Tommy started off with jokes and patter. When he started playing, he jumped off the stage with his guitar and walked up and down the bar singing, dancing and mugging. I thought, "Oh my God! They're going to kill him," but he was so good natured and having so much fun that all of those rough boys ended up cheering him on and thoroughly enjoyed his show. He had no fear of them and it turned out to be a great night.

Cuz would walk over and play with us occasionally. One Tuesday night, he got up on stage by himself with his concertina and I happened to have my tape recorder with me. Cuz played all night. He told stories about Castleisland, Padraig O'Keefe his neighbor and teacher and all the music, dancing and songs from his place back home. Dennis, a fellow from West Meath who worked for Aer Lingus was there and was very curious about Cuz and his music. If he had been a professional interviewer, he couldn't have asked better questions. He wanted to know where Cuz learned each tune, who played the tunes and where they got their names. It was a good recording of Cuz Teahan at his best.

One Saturday afternoon we were playing Ireland's 32 after a funeral service. A fellow who had been causing trouble for Eileen when Sonny was home visiting Ireland had been told that he was barred. The young man threw a pint glass at Sonny, bouncing it off the bar. Sonny, who was dressed, as usual, in a white shirt and tie, sidestepped the glass which shattered harmlessly behind him. Soon Sonny was smiling as he dodged the flying glasses, bottles and ashtrays that the enraged would be customer was firing at him. In frustration, the fellow came over the bar after Sonny who made a beeline out the back door. Sonny was around fifty-two and the patron was maybe twenty-two. He chased Sonny up the back stairway to the apartment. Sonny got in first and locked the door. The kid beat his way through the back door window with his fists. By that time Sonny was out the front door talking to the cops, who arrived quickly as they often got calls from the bar. The kid came in the backdoor of the pub again, dripping blood all over the floor. He was told to leave because the cops were out front. In the mean time we had gotten on stage and started playing a waltz for dancers who were still dressed in their funeral finery. The cops entered, saw all the blood and broken glass on the floor and asked, "Where's the fight?"

Everyone on the dance floor smiled and said, "What fight?"

Cuz gave me a tape that he had made back in 1952 on an old reel to reel tape recorder that he had lugged back to Ireland when they first got electricity in Castleisland. Eileen Carmody and the children, who were still very young, wanted to make a tape for Sonny who had already come to Chicago. Eileen wanted to make sure that Sonny didn't forget Ireland and she thought the best way to prevent that was through music. Cuz set up the tape recorder in the cottage and invited all the neighbors, including Padraig O'Keefe. The tape starts off with Sonny's dad saying, "Hello Sonny! This is Daddy."

What follows is some of the best old time Kerry music and singing that you could ever hear. The neighbors each say, "Hello

Sonny" and introduce themselves before doing their piece. Cuz's mother plays tunes on the concertina with Padraig O'Keefe and O'Keefe accompanies most of the singers on the fiddle. Sonny's boys sing songs in Irish and his daughter sings "Noreen Bawn". Eileen then comes on the tape and says, "Hello, loveen. It's manys the time we sang this song together." Then she sings "The Isle of Innisfree". They wrap it all up at two o'clock in the morning with everyone singing "Doonaree."

Chapter 7
Two Tweed Suits

The aqua van was towed away during a Chicago snow storm. There wasn't much life left in it so we let it go. Chuck had an old Volvo and we put a cassette of "Hello Sonny" into the tape player and headed to the Twin Cities which, with all our trips back and forth, was starting to feel like a far Northwest suburb of Chicago.

Shortly after Chuck started playing with the band, Barbara, who had owned a horse, wrote to Ann, the horse trainer, describing him as a guy with big teeth and long legs. She thought Ann might be interested. It was at the Riverside Café, a coffee house on the West Bank in Minneapolis, that they finally met. The Dayhills were playing to a nice crowd. Everything went smoothly until the end of the night when Ann disappeared into the bathroom. Barbara went in to check on her friend and returned, reporting that Ann had locked herself in a bathroom stall with a bottle of whiskey and refused to come out until Chuck agreed to take her home. Chuck was quite surprised, but he went ahead and took her home. Not long after, on our next trip to Ireland, we had "buy suits for the wedding" on our list of things to do.

We went to Castleisland to see the people and places Cuz had told us about in so many stories. The first thing we saw when we stepped onto the main street in Castleisland was a man dressed like a baby in a baby buggy being pushed into a pub by a bunch of roaring men. We learned that it was a baby buggy drinking contest. Everywhere we looked there were fancy prams with men dressed as babies being pushed at high speeds in and out of the twenty or so pubs along the street. In each pub, the "baby" had to slosh down a pint of Guinness. Then out the door they rushed and into the next pub. There was quite a hullabaloo. As the bets were being placed, there was laughter everywhere. We could see that Castleisland was a lively town.

We had a night of music in Terry Teahan's Pub which was owned by one of Cuz's nephews, also named Terry Teahan, and there we met a local tailor with whom we arranged to meet the next day. He was an old style tailor who did not have a shop. His manners were very quaint and he was given to odd sayings. He took our measurements with pieces of string right there in the pub making quite a production out of it. It was an interesting experience but did not inspire confidence that we would be seeing the finished suits any time before Chuck's first anniversary. We decided to head up to Dublin to buy the suits as recommended by the younger Terry Teahan when he saw the state of affairs with the tailor.

Before we left Castleisland, we were asked to play a Station at Pat "the Hat" McMahon's house. A Station is a Mass said in a house and it is usually followed by a large party. It is a big honor to host such an event. The preparations often extend far beyond cleaning. The host family might buy new curtains or table linens. Rooms in the house might receive new paint or wallpaper. The family prepares for days and sometimes weeks. The best of food and drink is purchased, prepared and laid out. The family wears their finest clothes. If the clothes are not fine enough, the entire family might buy new outfits for the event.

The McMahon house was near The High Chaparral, a big night club just outside of Castleisland. The T.V. shows, "High Chaparral" and "Dallas" were in vogue at the time. It was just before everyone was asking "Who shot J. R.? " I always found it interesting to hear the Irish take on the American T.V. shows that were being broadcast in Ireland. One fellow, after seeing the beginning to the "Mary Tyler Moore Show" and hearing where we were from, asked us, "Do you really throw your hats in the air when you are happy?"

The afternoon before the Station, we were walking around an old graveyard. Chambered cairns were built over the burial vaults with door slabs that had, in some cases, sunk in or fallen over. There were moss covered Celtic Crosses and interesting, if spooky-looking trees, all leaning away from the prevailing winds. It was getting dark and starting to blow, and the rain was not far off in the west. We heard the hoarse, wheezy sound of heavy breathing coming from somewhere among the tombs. We were hastily leaving the graveyard when we turned around and saw something emerge from one of the cairns. It was an old matted, dirty wolfhound/ greyhound mix of a dog. We had noticed long bones and a few skulls in those cairns a little earlier.

The party after the Station lasted until dawn and as soon as we were able the next day, we headed for Dublin. We booked into a B & B in Howth near the area where Brian Boru had driven the Vikings from Ireland nearly a thousand years before. We located a tailor shop called Kevin and Howlin near Trinity College where we were measured up, this time with a real cloth tape and chalk. We would soon have very nice three piece tweed suits for the upcoming wedding.

We went to O'Donaghue's where we met John Kelly who was the heart of the Dublin traditional music scene. He was very kind to us. He asked us to play and then joined in on his fiddle. As Yanks, it meant a lot to us that he seemed to think we were on the right track. He sent us to a music club at The Four Seasons. Many well-known singers and musicians were there all taking their turns up on stage. We took a turn as well. It was wonderful to be there.

At the bar after we played, I met Tommy Peoples, the Donegal fiddler. He had been with the police force and I knew he had the reputation of being a hard man. I was a little wound up after playing on the same stage as so many much more able musicians, but was honored when Tommy Peoples offered to buy me a drink. When he handed me my pint, it slipped through my fingers and burst on the floor. "Not to worry," said Tommy and promptly called for another.

The lady that ran the B & B near Howth was always talking about "The Governor". She would look at a broken window blind and say, "I'll have The Governor take a look at that." We were getting curious about who The Governor might be but did not want to pry. She would sometimes cook meals for us in the evening, and as we were eating she would sing a few songs that The Governor liked. It wasn't until we were leaving that we finally met The Governor who, it turned out was her husband. We had sometimes suspected as much but were never quite sure. He had been working in England.

We had met Frank and Mary Griffin from Roundstone, a town in Connemara, at the Abbey Pub in Chicago. In the Griffin's Chicago basement at one of their Sunday afternoon get-togethers we were introduced to Sean and Eileen McDonagh. Sean gave us the key to a house he had bought on Inch Island near Buncrana in Donegal and we were planning to make use of it.

As we were leaving Dublin, we picked up the tweed suits. Then we stopped in the train station not far from the tailor shop to get a bite to eat in the cafeteria. Chuck left his concertina on the table when he went to get in line. After buying our food and returning to our table, Chuck stood for a while and stared. He eventually took his seat and said, "My concertina's gone." It was a very good concertina.

"You'll never see that again," I said.

We felt gutted and helpless. Chuck could play other instruments, so we made do, but that was the end of the concertina on that trip.

We had no idea what to expect when we walked over the little causeway, past the swans on Lough Swilly, to Inch Island. The key that Sean had given us was gigantic. It was five inches long and had a fancy handle about two inches in diameter that looked like a medallion with metal curlicues. It was as heavy as cast iron, but was probably tarnished brass and was about five times the size of any key I had ever seen before. It looked like it might be a joke key.

We trudged along a road to a little village that had a small shop which also served as the post office. The man there directed us to the house nearby perched up on a hill. It turned out to be a large manor house with stone barns and a small cottage next to it. At the bottom of the sloping lawn was an ancient tennis court. I was sure that the key wouldn't open the door to this house, but with some wiggling and pushing, we were able to step through the back door into a large mud room that led to a gigantic kitchen with big pantries and a long farm table capable of seating about a dozen people. We crept through the rest of the house in amazement through large sitting rooms and parlours with ornate fireplaces. Upstairs we found six bedrooms, each with very high ceilings and its own fireplace. The tall windows looked out over fields with sheep, cattle and horses and on to Lough Swilly shining in the sun. The electricity was not turned on, but we located some candles. The plumbing worked. We suddenly had a great place to stay until Sean and Eileen arrived with their three daughters the next month.

The good thing about being music crazy and having plenty of tunes and songs to work on is that we didn't need much in the way of other amenities. A radio with a tape player that worked on batteries was handy to have. We usually brought along cassettes of musicians we had recorded like Flanagan and Cuz Teahan, and when we heard a good song at a party, we often asked the singer to record his or her party piece. Also, in Ireland you could record traditional music right off the air from Radio Na Gaeltachta or RTE programs. There was no end of good music to learn and practice. There wasn't much money to be made as Yanks playing Irish music, but we enjoyed it and there were enough gigs to get by as long as we kept travelling.

One thing that we didn't have was laundry facilities. Barbara and I would wash our clothes by hand in a sink or tub, but Chuck reached the point where he couldn't stand the state his clothes were in and decided to do something about it. He stuffed an army surplus duffle with every piece of clothing he owned and hitchhiked to Derry City about eight miles away on the other side of the border. When he arrived back on Inch, he related his adventures.

Chuck is a tall lanky fellow. He was wearing an oversized army surplus trench coat that matched his duffle bag and when he reached the city center after crossing the border in somebody's car, he found military checkpoints around every corner. The check points were staffed by British soldiers with machine guns. They were surrounded by mesh and barbed wire and had gates through which people had to pass. At each check point, Chuck was stopped and searched. When he told the story he didn't seem to understand why he was stopped, not being given to looking at himself in the mirror. I suspect his height, bearing and clothing had something to do with it. He would be thoroughly patted down and questioned, and ordered take off his trench coat and empty out the contents of his duffle bag down to the last pair of skivvies and dirty socks. This happened over and over again, both on the way in and on the way out. At some point, Chuck got turned around which resulted in going through that many more checkpoints. Chuck was amazed at the security in Derry, but being the most harmless person on God's green earth, he just laughed it off.

We enjoyed exploring the Island. Because we didn't have a car, we walked around and around. We really didn't know much about Inch except that it was beautiful. When Sean and Eileen arrived, we were very glad to see them and they were happy that we hadn't destroyed the house. Their four young daughters were with them and the family was back to stay. They had many plans for restoring the old house. Sean's father Martin had been a groundskeeper for the old landlord of the estate. Sean remembered as a young boy riding bicycles up to the house with his father carrying panes of glass to replace broken ones in the big house. Now Sean had been able to purchase the house by rehabbing old brownstones near downtown Chicago. We had a good couple of nights with Sean and Eileen and then boarded a bus and headed for Connemara.

About fifty miles west of Galway is the town of Carna. We stopped there because we had met Johnny Mulkerrin and his sister Mary in Chicago. They had encouraged us to go to Teach Na Tra, the beach house in Ardmore just outside of Carna. Carna is a Gaeltacht, or Irish speaking area, and their mother Margaret, who was known far and wide as Momo, and father, Patrick, or Dado, ran a guest house for students who came from all over Ireland to be immersed in the Irish language. Irish was the language spoken in the house unless they were talking to us Yanks. Momo ran the house while Dado ran the farm. The house looked out over Galway Bay near Feenish, an island that could be reached on foot at low tide. The fields around the house that made up the farm, each surrounded by a stone wall, were small and rocky like most of Connemara. Once, in the Griffin's basement in Chicago, I overheard two girls, one American and one who had just arrived from Connemara, talking about the place. The American girl said, "I've seen where you come from. You got nothing but rocks there."

The Connemara girl replied, "Oh no. We have shtones too."

Dado grew potatoes, carrots, cabbage and "suedes", which we later discovered were "swedes" or Swedish turnips, which in America are usually referred to as rutabagas. We sometimes had to work as hard to understand the meaning of the English words as we did the Irish ones. He also raised Connemara ponies and white Charlois cattle and battled rabbits which were everywhere.

Momo was about seventy when we first met her, but was still a big, powerful looking woman and a fabulous cook. She had lived in America and worked in the "Big Houses" in Boston and New Orleans. She told us stories about her time there and one thing she mentioned was that many thousands of Connemara men were buried in New Orleans because they had died of malaria and yellow fever while digging the canals there. Since she kept track of all the locals who had gone to Boston, Chicago and St. Paul, she had many questions for us whenever we stayed there.

Dado, by contrast was a small, wiry fellow with glasses and didn't speak much English. His favorite English phrase was "Oh ho" which he used as a general purpose response to most of what we said. He understood more English than he spoke, and when I helped him in the fields a few times he used enough English to let me know what he needed.

Big Johnny Mulkerrin happened to be home on a visit from Chicago when we were there and he took us to Mac Mellit's in Carna, a pub with music and a big dance floor. We met Seamus Mellit, who ran the pub with his brother and his father. We were the only non-Irish speakers in the place and being surrounded by people speaking another language was a new experience for me, although I was trying to pick up as much Irish as I could.

One day at Mellit's, a big busload of Americans descended on the place. They seemed very loud and when they came through the door, one of them shouted, "Are there any Americans in here?"

Barbara, Chuck and I looked at each other and then stared down at the bar until they left. We were grateful that the locals had not given us away. One night, after hours we met Finbar and Eddie Furey who came to hang out at the late night singing session there. They were popular in Ireland and all over Europe at the time. Eddie Furey said, "We love coming out here. It's the only place where people still tease us about the length of our hair."

The flute player Marcus Hernon was around in those days and would come in to Mellit's. He was about sixteen at the time and wore a big old black trench coat wherein he kept his wooden flute handy. Coleman Folan, Coleen for short, was the last man living on Feenish Island. He was a good friend of Marcus, although there was about a fifty-year difference in age between them. Coleen would wade into Carna from Feenish at low tide and sometimes had to wait days for the tide to be low enough to reach his home again. The island once had families living on it, but the rabbits had ruined the land by eating the vegetation and burrowing, causing the top soil to be washed away by ferocious storms and high tides. Coleen was alone out there, but even with no neighbors and no electricity, he managed to be a happy man. He had written many poems and songs, all in Irish and had mastered the art of sleeping in hedges without getting wet.

There were many singers around Carna. They were sean nós, or old style singers who sang mostly in Irish. Josie Sean Jack McDonagh, Johnny "Volkswagen" McDonagh and the Canavan sisters all lived in the area. Joe Heaney was also from Carna but was not living there at the time. Radio Na Gaeltachta often came to Connemara to record them and the Carna singers entered and frequently won Oireachtas competitions.

One day Momo looked down the road toward the beach through her "binockles" as she called her binoculars, "Quick, all of ye, out the back door now. Its Seamus Devane and he's on the drink."

We were pushed out the back door. Then she stepped out the front, chatted with Seamus and sent him gently on his way. "He's a terrible man on the drink," she said when she came back in into the kitchen, "He's barred out of all the pubs for fifty miles around."

"Still," she said, "If a cow is having a calf and having a hard time of it, Seamus is the man to call. He'll go in with his two hands, turn it and pull it out safely. Oh, and such a dancer. He knocks sparks out of the floor. And, did you know, he made a flute out of a leg of a chair. The man is pure genius, but he's a divil on the drink."

A few years ago I saw Seamus Devane in Kinvara at Cruinniu Na mBad or the Galway Hooker Festival. He was dancing with a few of his grown grandchildren and they were all knocking out sparks.

Momo could see the good in anybody, but she always spoke what she thought. She once told me that I was a man that nothing happened fast enough for. I scratched my head about that one for years. Then I remembered Cuz saying that I was, "dying for excitement like Rourke's dog". I was in my mid-twenties and life was moving fast. We travelled constantly. A month was the most we spent in any town at one time. Bedtime was dawn and we seldom rose before noon, although we were sometimes still up.

We travelled up to Clifden and had a look around. Clifden is out on the end of Connemara past the Twelve Pins, a series of mountains in the West. It is a rocky and wild part of Ireland. Chuck had been unsuccessfully trying to reach Ann by phone for quite a few days and it was bothering him. As we were driving a borrowed car around the Sky Road above Clifden, Chuck started going faster and faster along the winding mountain road. I had never seen Chuck upset about anything before. I could see that he was fed up with making phone calls and not hearing back, communications not being then what they are today. I thought it was good for him to show some frustration, so I kept saying to him, "Faster Chuck, faster. It's ok. It's good to see you mad!"

It was good. I think Chuck had his first pint that night and reached Ann on the phone. It was time for us to get back to St. Paul for Chuck and Ann's wedding.

*****

The Oddfellows Hall on Raymond and Hampton in St. Paul was the site Ann found for the wedding party. It was up a long, steep stairway in a building about a hundred years old. The Oddfellows are a benevolent society that we didn't, and still don't, know much about. They had never rented the place out for an Irish party before. The hall eventually became a home to four different Irish dance schools and a rehearsal space for several Irish dance groups, as well as being the place for ceili dances and parties. It all started with Chuck and Ann's wedding.

Martin McHugh and his sister Kathleen at Chuck and Ann's wedding.

The wedding itself was in Edina, a prosperous suburb of Minneapolis. When the formalities were over, everyone made their way back to St. Paul and packed the hall. The lovers of Irish music were used to mobilizing. There were at least twenty-five musicians and scores of guests all ready for a big time. Ceilis were all the rage and everyone knew the dances. Irish immigrants made up about a third of the crowd. Chuck's family and his musical friends came up from Chicago. There were half a dozen kegs of beer, cases of Irish whiskey, cases of Irish Mist and plenty of sandwiches. Peggy Flanagan, a young waitress and sometime fiddler we knew from O'Gara's helped with the food. Everyone took their turns singing, playing music and dancing.

By four in the morning, the guys wearing suit coats invented a new dance as the cleanup started. One man would sit on the floor and the other would swing him around in circles by his coat tails. The tweed suits made in Ireland were tough enough to stand the abuse and the floor got cleaned up a bit. By six a.m. we had finally finished all the food, but there was still a keg and a half of beer, a half case of whiskey and several bottles of Irish Mist to finish. By eight in the morning, those who had stayed to the bitter end had polished it all off. The only thing left to dispose of was the ice in the troughs that held the beer. The chunks of ice were thrown off the roof and into the street, hitting a few of our cars. We called it a night.

Chapter 8
The Jig Is Up

In the spring of '74, I finally got a chance to hear some of the All-Ireland champions that Barbara, Kevin and I had missed the previous summer in Listowel because of packed venues. Every year Comhaltas Ceoltoiri Eireann organizes a U.S. concert tour that includes some of the winners of the All-Ireland competitions. The Comhaltas Tour came through town and gave a concert. The Dayhills were playing at O'Connell's on Grand Avenue in St. Paul and after the concert the musicians were brought to the bar. The back door opened and in walked Joe Burke with his accordion. Paddy Ban, Mary Bergin, Patsy Hanley, Paddy Berry, Gabe McKeown and others followed. It wasn't long before several of them joined us on stage. We had a great night of music and were honored to meet all these very fine musicians.

The bars in St. Paul closed at one a.m. in those days and we were packing up. At about one thirty, the great Joe Burke was sitting on the edge of the stage playing a tune on his box when Bill O'Connell, who was running the bar along with his brother Steve following the death of their father Fran, walked up to him and said, "Okay Bub, time to go."

Bill didn't like Irish music. He was more of a disco man. We were shocked at his rudeness at the time, but Bill got his about a year later. He liked to have late night disco parties in the Art Deco bar. The cops knew he was having these parties with his disco buddies and they were out to get him. At about five in morning, when one of his debauches was in full swing, someone went out the back door and left it ajar. The cops moved in quietly down the back hallway and when they reached the main room, Bill was up on the bar disco dancing for his cronies. One of the officers roared, "That's enough O'Connell, the jig is up!"

The bar was shut down, the O'Connell boys lost their liquor license and the bar was later sold. It was purchased by Tommy

Scanlon from County Kerry who eventually turned it into a proper Irish pub. Fortunately for us Ray MacCafferty from Derry was opening a big bar and restaurant right up the street and we didn't have to play again at O'Connell's after the unfortunate end of that Comhaltas evening.

During the 1970s many American cities had a special place where the Irish revival created a sort of magical haven for people craving an Irish atmosphere and the craic. There had been a fresh influx of immigrants from Ireland in the 50s and 60s. With the onslaught of disco and leisure suits, and the generally commercial culture that was being imposed on America, the time was ripe for an earthier, casual approach to music and behavior. The charm of Guinness, lively banter and the new found appreciation of Irish heritage encouraged large crowds to come out for Irish entertainment. The political situation in Northern Ireland and the nightly news also made Irish Americans and others acutely aware of some of the injustices and historically difficult problems that the Irish faced. Rebel songs from hundreds of years ago and those that were more recent told compelling stories with immediate relevance. The humorous songs with bawdy words and choruses that invited the audience to chime in, along with the laments and lively dance music attracted all sorts. You would find grand dames elbow to elbow with hippy chicks, judges drinking with janitors and white collars, blue collars and even clerical collars all mixing together. They packed the pubs where the music was found. MacCafferty's on Grand Avenue was the spot in St. Paul that became that special place.

Ray MacCafferty was born and raised in Derry City although his family had come from Donegal across the border. His older brother, Charlie, was born on Inch Island before the family transplanted to Northern Ireland and he came over to St. Paul first. Ray followed when he was in his middle thirties and bought several farms in Western Minnesota which he rented out while living in St. Paul. He had a dream of opening an Irish place in town. He had owned the Rocking Horse in Derry City before immigrating, so he had experience in the trade. With his wide range of acquaintances, Ray knew all the right people and that made him the perfect man for the job.

He sold the farms and put the money down on a building which had been Pedro's before it was fire bombed by some Las Vegas gamblers. It had reopened as The Noble Roman, a gay bar that featured telephones on each table for flirting. Ray took it over and MacCafferty's became the mightiest Irish bar that St. Paul had ever seen.

He hired Chef John Logan from Dublin, who already had his own following and Andy Vaughan from Lahinch, County Clare, who had been president DeValera's chauffeur and became MacCafferty's resident quirky bartender. Two lovely ladies, Frances Keating from Tipperary and Bridget Coleman, widow of State Senator Nick Coleman and mother of the current Mayor of St. Paul, opened an Irish import store in the basement. Pat Igo, who had worked for many years at O'Gara's, was installed as manager. Ray hired a great group of waiters and waitresses and even hired his attorney Terence O'Toole's son, Mike, to park cars although he was only fifteen and didn't have a driver's license. Soon Mike acquired the nickname "Slam Bang" O'Toole among those car owners who used his services. He hated the nickname, but it stuck with him the rest of his life.

A huge, L-shaped dining room had photographs hanging on the walls taken without permission directly from Leon Uris's book "Ireland, A Terrible Beauty", blown up to measure six feet by eight feet. The pictures surrounded the whole room and were gorgeous to behold. The bar, which was in the middle of the building, was partially separated from the main room where the stage was located. It quickly became a favorite hangout, day, night and early morning for attorneys, mechanics, clergy, cops, hippies, yuppies, politicians, immigrants, shopkeepers, actors, musicians, former nuns and scroungers of all descriptions, each in ruthless pursuit of fun.

Ray loved Irish music. After our first month at MacCafferty's, he asked us to stay and be the house band. We told him no, but that we would like to come back three or four months of the year. We suggested that he book the groups from Ireland that were playing Boston and Chicago and were willing to travel. So, Ray had a long string of some of the finest pub bands around playing his bar and the place rocked. St. Paul became a favorite city for Irish musicians on the road. Many of the musicians that were just passing through ended up married to locals and are still here.

Ray kept an apartment upstairs in a building next to his establishment for musicians and he had Irish music six nights a week. The staff would bring cases of beer and liquor up to the apartment for the almost nightly parties and never charged the musicians. There was a lot of singing, tune playing and general hilarity in the little apartment, but no complaints from the others tenants in the building and I don't know why.

A friend of mine named John Concannon, originally from Galway, told me a story about being in that apartment one night. When a reefer being passed around came to him, he took a big toke. As he blew out the smoke he was shocked to see through the purplish haze a uniformed St. Paul patrolman looking at him from across the room. The policeman came towards him and John didn't know what to do. The policeman smiled and John started to panic. Then the patrolman said, "Don't worry, son. I brought the bag."

Andy Vaughan, the dapper man from Clare, was behind the bar when three elderly ladies came in and ordered Andy's specialty, Irish Coffee. Andy was fastidious about the proper construction of a true Irish Coffee, and he would put on an elaborate display of adding the whiskey poured over the back of a spoon, the hand-whipped cream and the brown sugar. With a splash of Crème di Menthe he finished making the three beautiful Irish Coffees and placed them, with a flourish, in front of the much impressed ladies ... who took spoons and stirred them up. Andy instantly grabbed the three now defiled Irish Coffees off the bar and dumped them down the drain, saying, "You can't do that to my Irish Coffees." The ladies stared in astonishment as Andy stalked to the other end of the bar to fume. When he eventually cooled down he made them fresh Irish Coffees and added three large pieces of cake for which he didn't charge them.

Ray MacCafferty used to say that Andy ought to be weighed in and weighed out when he came to do his shift as bartender. His cash register never seemed to have much action on it, no matter how busy the place was. Andy was fun to have around. He and his wife, Josie, used to dance a lovely two-hand jig which they taught to quite a few young couples around town.

One night Ray said to me, "There's a queue around the block to get in tonight, Tom."

I said' "What's a queue?"

"You don't know?"

I didn't.

The room where the music was played held about two hundred comfortably. The bar held about a hundred and the dining room a hundred more. The place was a roaring gold mine, but it was full of leaks. It was starting to run itself almost like a living thing and was nearly impossible to control. It was a lot of fun and it lasted about five years, until Ray died at the age of forty-one. Without Ray, MacCafferty's went out with a whimper.

MacCafferty's was still going strong when Chuck came in one day and mentioned that he had received a call from Chicago. His concertina had arrived from Ireland and was at his parents' house. Barbara and I were totally flabbergasted. Barbara said, "Someone had a guilty conscience."

The idea that someone would steal a valuable concertina and then have second thoughts about it was unlikely. The odds of that person going to the bother of looking through the receipts and scraps of paper in the case to find the owner's address, packing it up and sending it across the ocean were astronomical. I said, "Only an Irishman would do something like that!"

Chuck, as was typical of him, didn't seem unduly surprised.

*****

We had met John Curtin, a retired St. Paul mailman from Kinvara, County Galway and his wife, Leah, who was American, at one of the Irish Northern Aid ceilis. It was about this time that he brought the three of us over to meet his friend Paddy Hill.

Paddy rented the upper floor of a duplex on Geranium Avenue just off of Rice Street in St. Paul's North End. He lived there with his second wife, Sinda, who was from Germany. Paddy answered the door wearing a plaid flannel shirt. He was huge, with a big bald head and very thick glasses. He had a high and very musical voice and old fashioned manners from the mountains of Tipperary where he had been born in 1900 in Silvermines near the town of Nenagh.

Paddy was complimented by John on how well he looked and Paddy said, "You know, John, when I was a kid, about seventeen, I went to a lady to have my fortune told. She looked at my hand and said that I would live to be seventy-nine years old. I laughed and thought that she was crazy. No men lived to be seventy-nine back then. And now, here I am, almost seventy-five. You just never know."

John Curtin said, "Oh no, you just never know."

Paddy looked at me and saw that I had a fiddle. He said, "Do you play the fiddle, Tom?"

I said that I tried, but that I wasn't much good. He said, "Tell me this, Tom, can you play 'The Blackbird'?"

I said that I would try and I when I finished, Paddy said, "Oh thanks be to God, you're an Irish fiddler. If you can't play 'The Blackbird' you might be some kind of fiddler, but you're not an Irish fiddler."

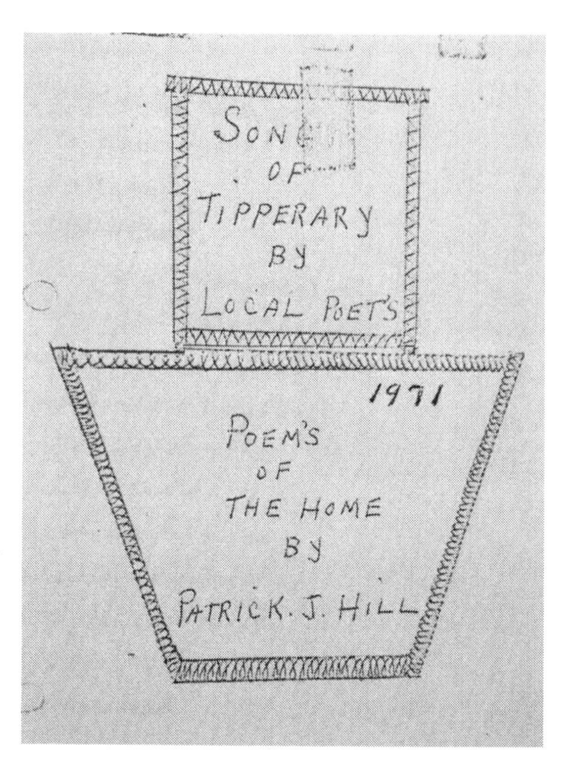

Paddy sat back in an overstuffed chair after he made sure that we had something to drink. He pulled out one of his notebooks, of which, I found out later, there were seven, opened the book and said, "John tells me you would like to hear some of my old songs."

"We would if you feel like singing."

"Oh, I might, let's see.... . What kind of Irish songs do you like?"

I asked if he had local songs from his place in Tipperary.

"How about 'My Fight for Irish Freedom'?"

Pat had joined the British Army when he was fifteen to fight in WWI. The Irish were not liked in England, and many Irish people felt disdain for the recruits from Ireland who volunteered to join the British Army. Paddy came home on leave in 1917. He was stopped near his home by some fellows on bicycles who asked, "Who are you?"

"Why, I'm Paddy Hill."

"What are you doing here?"

"I'm home on leave."

"Home on leave from what?"

"Home on leave from the Army."

"What Army?"

"Why, the British Army."

"Well, Pat, how would you like to join a real army?"

That is how Paddy Hill joined the IRA. Within a week, he told us, he was passing on the skills he had learned in the British Army to his comrades. Pat became a Captain and fought first through the War of Independence and then on the Republican side of the Civil War that followed. The Republicans were the side that wanted a United Ireland and were against the Treaty that signed away the six counties in the North, as opposed to the Free Staters who wanted the Republic even if it involved giving up those six counties for the time being. Paddy's song "My Fight for Irish Freedom" was, as he explained, wishful thinking. The last line of the song states, "We stand before the world, as a nation once again."

When he finished he noted, "But we don't, do we?"

John Curtin replied, "No, we don't."

Paddy turned a few pages in his notebook and said, "Here's a little music hall song that I always liked. It's called "I Can't Change It."

It was a cute song and after he sang it he commented, "Yeah, I always kind of liked that one. But, back then in Ireland, when we were kids fighting those wars, you daren't sing a music hall song, or they would chase you and the song out of there."

Paddy's wife, Sinda, was out in the kitchen. She seemed happy to have people over who were interested in Paddy's songs and stories. She kept bringing in tea and coffee, beer and whiskey, cookies and sandwiches.

Paddy told me that he had known my great uncle, Tom Dahill, the former Chief of Police. He said that he had been invited over to the Dahill house before I was born to play music and told me that Tom was a good Irishman.

They say that Paddy Hill never wore an overcoat. He did, however, wear hats and usually a plaid flannel shirt, as he did that first visit. I noticed that the wrists, visible under the cuffs of the shirt, were very wide. Paddy had put in over forty years at the Union Depot working in the railyard in all the extremes of weather that Minnesota has to offer. He said that after Bridget, his first wife, died he thought he was a goner too. He developed gangrene in both of his heels.

Patrick Hill, County Tipperary

Sinda was his nurse. After they married, she treated and cured the gangrene with some home remedies from her place in Germany. Sinda didn't seem to have a particular interest in Irish music, but she took great care of Paddy and you could see that she loved him deeply.

Pat was glad that we had a tape recorder because he wanted to put down as much of his music for us as possible. We were over with that tape recorder every couple of weeks when we were in town. He had written hundreds of songs about his home in Ireland. There were songs about wakes, cattle markets, courting, saving hay, fights, leaving home and politics. He had poems and songs that he had written starting when he was fourteen and he was still writing and rhyming about life in St. Paul and his trips back home. He wrote letters to his friends in rhyme and he worked so much on his writing, that when he spoke, the words at times came out in rhymes.

He always wanted to know where we were headed next. Chicago? Denver? Boston? And when would we be back? He made sure to let us know that we were always welcome. After a few hours, Sinda would come into the room and say, "Pat, it's time for your pills." And we would say good-bye for now.

When I went home after our first visit and listened to all the songs he had given us, I remember tearing up because I knew he wouldn't last forever.

Paddy had one son also named Patrick. There was some kind of rift between father and son and I never met the young Patrick Hill. Patrick married the daughter of another transplanted Irishman, originally from Mayo, named Dominick Caulfield. My family knew the Caulfields. Dominick was also a poet, storyteller, step dancer and singer and over the years he gave me songs and poems. He lived into his nineties and never lost his love of telling stories. In his later years my mother would run into him at Mass. After Mass he would walk over to the Lunds grocery store where he held court near the spot where the customers could get a free cup of coffee, sit for a moment, and be entertained.

I met one of Paddy's granddaughters a few years ago and she told me that, in spite of the strained relationship between her father and his father, she grew up knowing Paddy Hill. They lived nearby and she and her siblings were encouraged by their father to visit Paddy frequently.

I think it was the next time we stopped by that Pat gave me his fiddle. Pat had Parkinson's and couldn't play it anymore. He told me that the fiddle had been given to him by an old man, Tom Martin, another Irish fiddler, when Pat came to St. Paul in 1923. Inside the fiddle the label says, "Reconstructed, St. Paul Minn, 1880." This is the fiddle that I play to this day. I gave my other fiddle, the one given to me by the girl in Massachusetts, to John Flanagan, Pat Flanagan's son in Denver. He played it well until his untimely death back in the eighties at the age of twenty-seven.

Chapter 9
The Hand of the Fool Killer

Throughout the seventies, the folk music scene in Denver was booming with many fine songwriters, musicians and dozens of Folk clubs that were happy to have Irish music. The Dayhills, both when Kevin McElroy was still with us and later with Chuck, played Denver frequently because we could always find work, but the main reason we went there was to visit the Flanagans.

The Irish Fellowship Club of Denver had a Saturday night ceili every month for twenty years or so right through the eighties. Pat Flanagan on his button accordion and his son John on the fiddle formed the core of the music along with about ten other musicians, among them another fiddler named John Nielson, Maggie McBride, Eileen Niehouse and a man named Hayes. Many of the dancers were from Ireland. There was a master of ceremonies, usually Pat Murray, who would call the dances and between the dances would introduce the singers among whom I can name Sean Sheehan and Mary Casey off hand, but there were many others. Any Irish musicians travelling through town were invited to play or sing. The Denver Pipes and Drums would play a few tunes. It made for a very enjoyable night out. The way these evening entertainments were set up was a tradition that didn't begin in Denver. This was the way it was done in Irish communities all over the world.

We ourselves always invited singers up to perform their party pieces or to play a tune or two when we had gigs. It added to the fun and sometimes these impromptu performances started people off on their own careers. Mostly, it created a community feel to the evening. People enjoyed seeing those that they knew up on stage doing a little something.

Yet, sometimes people ended up on stage that had no business being there. I remember one New Year's Eve, back when Kevin was still with us when we were playing Shannon's in Boulder. Kevin had just bought a new, hand-made Mossman guitar. The

Irish crowd was up from Denver dressed to the nines. Locals from Boulder were there, as well as people who had come down from the mountains. They all converged on Shannon's.

Not long before midnight, an argument started at the back of the long room between a woman decked out in a fur coat and a woman who was part of the then newish animal rights movement. A scuffle ensued and when a few guys tried to break it up, new ructions erupted in several spots. Soon the whole back of the room turned into a sort of a scrum that was rolling slowly towards the stage. We kept on playing, keeping our eye on the crowd and hoping that the melee would dissipate before reaching us. Instead, it grew larger and larger until it finally crashed over the stage. Our mics went flying and one of our tall speakers fell, crushing Kevin's new guitar. Kevin and I used our boots to encourage people to leave the stage. Barbara had long well-kept fingernails, perhaps inspired by Maeve Mulvaney and used them to pluck up a few of the fallen heroes by the backs of their necks and kind of toss them out of harm's way. They settled down just in time for the singing of "Auld Lang Syne", after which the owner served free lasagna to all as magnanimous gesture to bring in the New Year. The lasagna was laced with hashish.

When the people on the stage had actually been invited up, rather than being part of an invading horde, it was a good thing for us. The songs they sang were often local songs from back home which hadn't been recorded or written down. It wasn't only from those that performed that we learned wonderful but little known material. Requests for songs or tunes from listeners, vaguely remembered, often started a hunt that could take many years to complete. Some I eventually found and some I'm still looking for. Has anyone ever heard "The Bum from Omaha"? Paddy Hill once told me it was one of the best songs he ever heard and he knew a good one when he heard it. I have been looking for it for nearly forty years now.

The Dayhills had one self-titled album out when we first started playing Denver regularly. Fast Mary Hedlund, who was the first TCRG, or board certified Irish dance teacher in the Twin Cities and had been given her nickname not because of her social tendencies, but because she liked her reels played fast when she danced, thought we should record. We booked time in a sound studio in the basement of a North Minneapolis house and Fast Mary paid for it. When Laura Benson and Jim Ransom of Biscuit City Records in Denver heard that album, they asked if we would re-record it in their state-of-the-art studio and put it out on their label. The Biscuit City label was named for the lump of vinyl used when pressing records called a biscuit. That record sold fairly well and we recorded two more albums with them, *Mom's Favorite* and *The Dear Little Isle.*

*****

Marty McHugh was squeezing a lot of music out of his accordion around St. Paul. He had come over in 1951 from Castlerea in County Roscommon and his wild box playing and charming personality, not to mention his outrageous sense of humor, made him a big hit in Irish circles from the time he arrived, on through the sixties, seventies, eighties and nineties and right up to the present. Martin was always in demand. He and his box were wanted for every Irish event that took place and Marty sometimes had to dodge people. Paddy Hill and John Curtin told me that they would have to send out a posse to search the local bars when young Martin would "forget" about one of the many dances or get togethers for which he was supposed to provide entertainment.

When we met Marty in the early seventies, he hadn't been playing out as much, not because he and his music were any less popular, but because there had been a reduction in the number of Irish events due to the demise, more than ten years before, of the Irish-American Club of St. Paul. The Irish-American Club held a ceili every Saturday night from the time of its founding until the early sixties. Prior to Marty's arrival, the entertainment had been provided by Mike McGivney, Mike Hughes, Mike Nash and Mike Sullivan, known as the four Michaels, as well as Tom and Kitty Donahue, Paddy Hill and Dominic Caulfield. The Club had been disbanded in 1962 when the entire McDonagh family left over some disagreement that is lost in the mists of time. About half of the Club was made up of McDonaghs.

By the mid-seventies, St. Paul's temporary lull had ended and Marty was back in demand. He had been one of the younger musicians in St. Paul in the fifties. Now he was a bit older and the aspiring young local musicians were flocking to him. He was starting to enjoy their company, but was meeting so many new people that he had trouble keeping track of their names. He developed the habit of calling any girl whose name he had forgotten "Killarney". Along with some of the musicians he fell in with, he formed The Plough and Stars Ceili Band and later The Northern Star Ceili Band. Marty used to say, "We may not be stars, but no one can say that we are not plowed."

I remember seeing Martin one New Year's Eve at MacCafferty's. He had been at the bar the early part of the evening, but as the night went on he seemed to have disappeared and people kept on asking, "Where's Marty?"

The night progressed and the crowd grew. The Mooncoin Ceili Dancers, a St. Paul dance troup founded by Fast Mary and a few others, showed up dressed as Straw Boys. They had used two entire bales of straw to make hats, skirts and masks. There were copious amounts of straw sticking out of every part of their clothing. At the end of the night the straw was everywhere, in the bar and in the restaurant, because the Ceili dancers had danced everywhere. MacCafferty was still finding bits of straw in the place six months later.

At about four in the morning, people were finally leaving and picking up their coats from a big pile in a corner booth of the bar. Suddenly, someone shouted, "Hey! Here's Marty!"

Marty had laid down for a quick snooze in the booth sometime early in the evening and someone had probably put a coat over him to keep him warm. As the night went on and the crowd grew, people just started throwing their coats onto the pile, burying Marty in the process. We were relieved to have found him, glad that he hadn't suffocated and together we all celebrated the New Year, nineteen seventy...whatever.

*****

Paddy Hill liked to take Barbara, Chuck and me out to lunch when we were in St. Paul. He would take us to Gannon's or The Coachman and he always insisted on paying although he was living on a pension. One day we were sitting with Paddy and John Curtin at Gannon's eating lunch when Paddy asked me, "Tom, would you ever want a set of Uilleann pipes?"

I was still thrilled at having been given the fiddle and it took me a moment to register his question. He went on to say, "We know the widow of a man called P. J. Linehan. He's been dead quite a few years, but she has his old set and I could talk to her and see if she would let you have them."

I said that of course I'd be interested, but then more or less forgot about it because it seemed so unlikely. A few days later I got a call from John Curtin.

He said, "I wanted to let you know. Paddy called Mrs. Linehan and told her all about you. She said that yes, she would like Tom Dahill to have the set, so Paddy and I drove over there to pick them up. Now, this is what happened. When she opened the door she said, 'I'm so sorry. My daughter got talking to a man on the bus today. He was a highland piper and she brought him over and gave the set away.' I'm really sorry Tom, we tried our best."

Even though I hadn't really thought, when I first heard about it, that I was going to be handed the only set of Uilleann pipes in town, I suddenly felt very bad, and then even worse, having discovered how close I had come to actually holding them in my hands.

The next night I was out at Ann Heymann's chicken coop when I got a call from Teddy Tonkinson. Teddy was a merry red-headed highland piper with the Brian Boru Irish Pipe Band whom I had met many times around St. Paul. He always wore his saffron Band kilt when he was out on the town and played the spoons. All the girls were crazy about him because he danced. He liked to waltz and when he danced jigs and reels, he made up his own outlandish steps.

Teddy said, "Get over to my house right now Tommy. Your pipes are in my basement. Andy brought 'em over along with a couple of his buddies and they have it in pieces all over my workbench. They're talking about taking a reamer to 'em to make 'em louder. I know they're supposed to be yours, but don't say a word or you'll never get them."

Chuck and I rushed over to Teddy's place and down to the basement to discover that all the pieces of the old set were indeed spread out over the workbench. There was an unspoken hostility in the air, but I still managed to get close enough to take a good look at them. I had never had an opportunity to see a set up close before but I knew the kind of music they made. This set was made of African Blackwood with brass keys and ivory fittings. There were two chanters, one of which was stamped, "Rousome". The old leather case had a hand printed label that read, "P. J. Linehan, Reed Maker" and there were fifty or sixty hand-made reeds of Spanish cane in small boxes tucked inside. Teddy kept looking at me and I could see that he was willing me not to do anything stupid. He glanced towards the stairs. The three others were giggling and I was afraid for the set, but Chuck and I headed upstairs and out the door. I know that on the way back to the chicken coup, I had a conniption, but Chuck was his usual even-tempered self.

I talked to Teddy later that night and he said, “Just stay calm Tom and see what happens over time.” Teddy was a bit older and wiser than me, so I heeded his advice.

Through the years the thought of the pipes would come bubbling up and I would start getting upset. The only way to tamp down the feelings was to tell myself that if I were meant to play the Uilleann pipes, the local set would have come to me and the only thing for me to do was to keep working on the instruments that had already come to me - the fiddle, guitar, mandolin, and tenor banjo. It was also around that time that I picked up a Paolo Soprani B/C two-row button accordion in a seedy pawn shop on Diversey Avenue in Chicago.

*****

In the spring of 1976, we picked up the Bicentennial issue of the *Irish People Newspaper* from Maureen at Shamrock Imports. The entire back page was covered with celebratory patriotic messages sponsored by Irish-American businesses in Kansas City, Missouri. That piqued our curiosity and the next time we passed through K. C. on our way from Chicago to Denver, we stopped to have a look around. We found a place called Egan’s in the phone book and dropped in. We booked a gig and the owner, Mike Egan, got the word out. The next night the place was packed with some of the big Irish families of Kansas City, the Quinns, the Glynns, the Carneys, Barrys, Cahills and Kellys, the O’Connells, O’Connors and the Cullinanes.

A couple of squad cars had parked out back. We thought that they were expecting trouble, but later learned that the name of the cop driving the first car was Terry Kelly and in the other was Officer Bill Cahill from County Limerick. They had their windows down to hear the music coming out the doors and windows of the pub. When the music started, some of the young fellows inside said, “This is great, but we don’t know how to dance to it.”

“What should we do?”

"Let's fight!" and they did. During one of the little scuffles, a young guy landed on the stage, but Barbara quickly removed him with her talons. The fights were all in good fun and the cops didn't seem to mind.

After the gig at Egan's, we were asked by one of the Quinns to play an Irish Northern Aid ceili at Redemptorist Parish, so on the way back from Denver, we stopped in K. C. again. About three hundred people showed up at the school. The floor in the gymnasium where the ceili took place was buckled into waves, some of them two feet high. The Carneys and the Cullinanes, both families from Ennis and the Glynns from Labasheeda taught the dances and soon all the fighters from Egan's were transformed into dancers as well. Whenever we played Kansas City after that, we could always count on a good crowd. We really liked the people and the developing Irish scene there and it became one of our regular stops.

A group of playwrights, actors and eccentric musicians called the Foolkillers were based in Kansas City. They had a theater called the Foolkiller Theater and the troup had written some entertaining plays. We enjoyed seeing their productions and playing a bit for them afterwards. We got to know some of them very well and often stayed with Foolkillers Bob and Diane Suckiel. Bob was an ex-seminarian, a Polish-American from Chicago, who had become a railroad engineer. He was also one of the foremost collectors of ribald cowboy songs, like "Charlotte the Harlot" and "The Castration of the Strawberry Roan." Diane was a nice singer. They were both very good comic actors.

I was told that the Fool Killer was a character from a Missouri folk tale that was a spirit-like ogre, who watched people do foolish things letting them get away with it for a while, and then one day, perhaps when a kid was walking along a bridge railing, would give a little shove, and the fool would die.

The Foolkillers were definitely an underground theater and had to move a few times because funds were always short. For a while, the theater was housed in a building on Main Street that the troup was renting from a banker who worked right next door. He usually parked his car in the shared parking lot out back. One of the Foolkillers, Dale, had a severe drinking problem and the courts had ordered him to take Antabuse, a chemical that made him very ill when he drank, which was nearly always. Our friend was up on the roof of the three-story building, getting sick, when he toppled over the parapet, landed on the hood of the banker's car, a Cadillac or Mercedes or something like that and died. The banker had been trying evict the Foolkillers for quite a while. He must have thought, "Well that's one down."

We played a Foolkiller festival in Mountain View, Arkansas, in very primitive surroundings and met many well-known folk singers there including Utah Phillips, Rosalie Sorrells and Glen Orlin. It was a great ragtag festival with a chili cooking contest where, it seems, the hottest chili won. They nearly set the woods on fire with the winning recipe.

I went for a hike with a few others to the Red River and happened to be in the lead when we ventured onto a giant cottonwood tree that had fallen into the water. We had gone a ways when I took a step and my left leg went right through a rotten patch in the trunk. I fell out over the river with my left leg caught in the tree. Someone grabbed my hand and pulled me up. As I scrambled out of the hole, I caught a glimpse of a bunch of cottonmouth snakes in a tangle around my sandaled foot. It was a Foolkiller's hand that had saved me. There were a lot of cottonmouths around the camp and they were known to crawl into open tents at night looking for something warm to curl up next to, but the Foolkillers didn't seem to mind.

Chapter 10

Come To the Glenshesk

The Glenshesk Pub in Chicago at 4102 N. Kedzie, named after one of the nine glens of Antrim, was a particularly good pub for hearing rare songs and tunes. It was also a place that had a lot of set dancing long before it became a fad in the nineties. The owners were from the North, but the regulars were mostly from the "Wild West" counties of Ireland. The conversations overheard were mostly in Irish and very few Americans ventured in on a regular basis.

We played standing up on a stage elevated about three feet off the floor. At the time nearly everyone smoked including ourselves, even when we were on stage. An exhaust fan built into the wall behind us would draw smoke, and long strands of hair covered in dust through the stage lights, past us and through the vent. The restrooms were behind the stage, so we would see everyone in the place eventually, as they walked by and gave us a nod and a wink or maybe shouted a request. Sometimes they would slip us a piece of paper with an announcement or the name of someone that they wanted us to invite up onto the stage for a song. The songs that were sung were often in Irish and unaccompanied.

One of the many fine singers there was Nora Grealish McDonagh. She sometimes asked us to her house and made tapes for us of some of her songs. Another singer, Paudeen Flaherty, gave me his version of "The Setting of the Sun". Pauraceen Beag McDonagh, Nora's brother-in-law, was someone who was usually ready to sing when asked unless some scuffle or another took precedence. There was also Eileen Heneghan who, like many of the regulars, was from Tourmackeady in County Mayo where Pat Flanagan was born. I remember her best for "Boating on Lough Ree". It was a sad song, but when she sang it she always had a lovely smile on her pleasant round face.

Nora had a friend named Mary Con Staff Joyce Flaherty. She was a tough, forty-something, red- haired woman from Carna in Connemara. Because Mary's full name was so long, her nickname was "The Gadhar", pronounced "Gyre" which means "the dog" in Irish. She didn't drink but was mad for dancing and, like many set dancers, she chewed gum incessantly.

Mary left home for London in the '50s when she was fourteen and lived in Camden Town and Cricklewood. She was there when the Irish music scene in the East End of London was in its heyday. Like Mary Flanagan and Jimmy Cummins, the Gyre knew all the tunes by name and the players who played them. She was a ringleader. When she left London for Boston several of her friends and their families followed. She left Boston and came to Chicago and again many families followed her lead. Later she moved to San Francisco and the same thing happened. It was not always the same families who followed, but people knew that where Gyre was, that's where the craic would be.

She took a shine to us and our music, and used her power as one of the Queens of Connemara, to boost our band at every opportunity. She was full of fun and had high standards for liveliness. If she dropped in, which she usually did when we were playing, and didn't think it was lively enough, she would make a beeline for the payphone and place a few calls. The people she rang would make a few more phone calls and within an hour the place would be packed with people who loved music and wanted to dance.

After a night at the Glenshesk, we liked to eat at the Harris Restaurant on Irving Park Road. It was open all night and there was a late night disco next door. We would come in with a crowd of ten to twenty and get our tables. Everyone would settle and put in their orders. A few of us might slip out to go next door and suffer through the loud disco music and flashing lights for the sake of one more round. Then we would hurry back into the Harris where the food would have arrived. The table would be covered with steak and eggs, slabs of ham, pork chops and other forms of “Hungry Man” breakfasts, and for Chuck, Cheese Blintzes, a North Shore favorite.

*****

We were staying with Barbara’s brother. About once a week Cuz Teahan would walk over in the afternoon to tell us stories about Chicago, County Kerry and Padraig O’Keefe and once he gave me a big lump of rosin that O’Keefe had made himself. Padraig had been Cuz’s school teacher, lived across the road from the house that Cuz grew up in and would stop by to play music with his mother. He taught as many children in the Sliabh Luachra area to play as were interested.

Padraig had a method of writing out fiddle tunes, using the lines of the staff to represent the strings and using numbers to indicate which fingers to use. This helped kids who didn’t read standard notation. He also wrote out the tunes for concertina and melodeon using numbers for the buttons and a plus or minus sign for the push and pull. Eventually, O’Keefe lost interest in teaching school subjects. He quit his job and hit the road as an itinerant fiddler. He travelled far and wide around Ireland and was even rumored to have been in America.

O’Keefe often didn’t have a fiddle of his own, but back then in Ireland, many homes and pubs kept a fiddle or a concertina for wandering musicians. He was fond of the drink and the distances to be travelled were hard on the feet in those days of leather brogues. Once, O’Keefe borrowed a bicycle from a lady that Cuz knew. She didn’t see Padraig or her bicycle again for a long time. When she finally did spy Mr. O’Keefe, she marched up and demanded, “See hear Padraig, what happened to my bicycle?”

“Ma’am,” answered Padraig, opening his mouth wide, “If you look way down deep in here, you might just see the handlebars.”

O’Keefe was a musical genius, as anyone who has heard his music knows. Unfortunately, he had a hard life and towards the end, Cuz told me that many people who had been encouraging, turned their backs on him. Cuz spoke fondly of the man and had a lot of O'Keefe's North Kerry style in his music.

Terry Teahan was particularly friendly to strangers. He couldn't care less what sex, color, race or religion anyone was. He never drove a car and walked all over Chicago, talking with everyone he met and calling them "Cuz". He seldom had any trouble.

One afternoon though, after visiting an Irish lady, the last in an old Irish neighborhood, Cuz started walking home. He strolled through a black neighborhood, a Mexican neighborhood and a Puerto Rican neighborhood, and then was mugged in a Polish neighborhood. He continued on through the one remaining gang infested neighborhood and finally arrived at his home near Montrose and Milwaukee, a little surprised, but amused at the irony.

When you have Irish friends, and you are a young working musician, you never go hungry. Barbara and I almost never cooked at home. Cuz liked to take us out and treat us to a meal at a place near his house and "The Gadhar" would take us to fancy restaurants. She was the one who told me to always order the end cut of a prime rib because that is where the best flavor is. Sometimes when Barbara and I finished our breakfast in restaurants, usually around noon or one o'clock, and it came time to pay, the waitress would say, "Somebody already got it for you."

Irish friends would pay for our meals and leave without our knowing it. It was a sort of a game for Mike O'Leary from Offaly and a few others. We would try to figure out who had treated us so we could thank them the next time we met, but they would never admit to doing it.

I learned "The Lambs on the Green Hills" from Mike in the middle of the Atlantic, at 30,000 feet on the way to his sister Sheila's wedding in Scotland. The way he sang it, he would put on a big smile at the end, while repeating the last line. If you know the song, you can see that a grin at that spot, changes the whole feel of the song and makes it , rather than tragic or pathetic, almost light-hearted. At the wedding we met Mike's father, Paddy. He was one of the people who did a great rendition of "The Cremation of Sam McGee" by Robert Service.

When Cuz Teahan would stop in at the Glenshesk, there was always a commotion at the door and you would hear him before you would see him. He was about seventy at the time and he had a loud, high-pitched voice. He would be shouting something like, "Hello Cuz! How's your bladder!"

Cuz was fearless and he was old enough not to care what he said or to whom he said it. Most people loved him for it. He wore checks and stripes in all colors, bedroom slippers tied on with ribbons and hats, sometimes with a feather. He had beaten cancer and was full of music. He was in constant motion and he was as at home on the dance floor as he was on the stage with us. When Cuz was playing with us, he would always watch the dancers closely saying, "You want to get the music under their feet."

In his style of playing, rhythm was more important than hitting every note perfectly. The musical keys he played in depended on which of his instruments, the concertina or the melodeon, that he happened to have with him. If he tired of playing, he would be on the dance floor like a shot and he had the good old moves of a natural dancer.

Cuz sometimes played with his "women", "The Screaming Banshees" who were Una McGlwe, Maida Sugrue and Mary McDonagh. They didn't call them the "screaming" banshees for nothing. They were very proper, nicely-dressed, fiddle playing women in their fifties and sixties, but they matched Cuz scream for scream. Whether he was with the Banshees or without them, Cuz would go wherever there was music and fun to be had. He once jumped on a plane and came to St. Paul for "Paddy Hill Day", held at the VFW in Mendota and sponsored by Irish Northern Aid. Cuz got along great with Paddy Hill and I remember that one of the songs he sang was "Nancy Hogan's Goose", a particularly ribald song that he claimed came from his grandmother. He danced, played and sang all day, then jumped back on the plane and flew home to Chicago.

One night at the Glenshesk Cuz played a tune called "The Chieftains Are Coming" that he had composed because he was excited that the band was coming for a concert at the Shubert Theater in Downtown Chicago. A few nights later Cuz attended the concert. He showed up late and walked right through the crowd and up onto the stage. He approached each Chieftain and shook hands, calling them all "Cuz". They chatted away agreeably for at least fifteen minutes. Cuz had stopped the show and most of the hometown crowd loved it. They knew he belonged on that stage.

*****

Johnny Mulkerrin and his sister Mary, who had told us about Carna and Teach Na Tra before our last trip to Ireland, were both regulars at the Glenshesk. Johnny was the biggest and strongest man in Irish circles at the time. He was a great footballer for the Connemara Gaels in Chicago and as far as I know, he never got into fights. He was just too big and a nice fellow besides. When he was around, there was never trouble because everyone knew that Mulkerrin was there. Johnny wanted to hear the music and didn't want interruptions. Mary was the same. She was there for the set dancing.

When Johnny and his wife, Barbara moved back to Connemara permanently he was missed. Without his calming presence, guys who never even thought about fighting were free to let their pugnacious tendencies come to the fore.

When we played the Glenshesk, if we got started late, a break was too long or the music had ended for the evening, there was often a bit of a brawl. I remember clearly standing at the end of the bar talking with Barbara one night when a row broke out at the other end. While we stood there conversing, a bottle flew between our heads and we took that as a sign that it was time to get back up on stage.

One Sunday night, not long after Johnny's departure, Maureen O'Looney was broadcasting live from the Glenshesk and we were playing. A guy from Ireland was having a hard time making himself understood when talking to his loutish "narrowback" cousin. "Narrowback" is a slightly derogatory term used by some Irish immigrants to describe their American-born children, who never had to work hard enough to get properly muscular shoulders.

We were between tunes, deciding which set of reels we would play next. The shorter Irish cousin was growing more and more annoyed and when the American cousin, gigantic in comparison, grabbed his shoulder, I saw trouble coming. The Irish guy's knees bent as he loaded up for the upper cut. Maureen was still chattering away into the microphone at her table in front of the stage when the American got clobbered by his stocky Irish cousin. The narrowback flew up in the air, staggered across the dance floor and fell on Maureen's table with a crash. Without missing a beat, Maureen continued, "So you come on down to the Glenshesk Pub where we are having a wonderful time tonight here with The Dayhills!" and we started into our next tune, the gentle waltz "Give Me Your Hand."

Chapter 11
The Priest's Curse

Liscannor the seaport where the fishermen dwell.
I went with my mother to St. Bridget's Well.
The day it was bright and the sun it did shine,
O'er the graves of our dead and Cornelius O'Brien.

*****.

On the west coast of Clare, just north of Lahinch, is the old fishing village of Liscannor, where the band spent a lot of time in the late seventies. It was only a few miles from the Cliffs of Moher. We played the Anchor Bar when we were there. The owners, P. J. and Margaret O'Donnell, saw us at the Glenshesk when they were visiting Chicago and invited us to stay with them and play the pub whenever we were in Ireland. They put us up in a house next door.

An old fellow who lived across the road from the Anchor would drop in daily for a hot whiskey. I don't remember his name, but each morning at about eleven he could be seen walking very slowly, being near ninety, toward the pub. Margaret would see him coming and start preparing his hot whiskey. By the time he arrived, it would be ready and waiting for him. He would sit by the turf fire and enjoy his drink and his time in the pub. He was a quiet sort, but pleasant, and after an hour or so, he would get up and say, "Good-bye now. Good luck. See you tomorrow."

Everyone in the pub would say, "Good-bye now. Good luck. God bless," and he would slowly walk home to his little cottage by the sea.

Later in the afternoon, Margaret would start making another hot whiskey and say, "Here he comes again." Looking out the window you would see this man making his way back to the pub.

He would greet everyone, take his hot whiskey to his fireside seat and after a nice sit and a little chat, he would say, "Good-bye now and see you tomorrow."

He often came back for a third time. The man squeezed in a lot of extra tomorrows this way toward the end of his life. He later fell into his fire at home. This was something that happened back then. When tending the fire, old people would have heart attacks or strokes and occasionally fall in. Sometimes, like in the cottage I later owned in Kinvara, an iron contraption was built to prevent such accidents.

Chuck was a natural musician. He cheerfully went along with all of our wild capers, but the whole time I'm pretty sure he was really thinking about music and, as far as I know, nothing else. He could often be found lying on a bed or sofa in the house in Liscannor, sometimes still wearing the long nightgown that he slept in, with his accordion on his chest practicing. He would learn tunes off of tapes he made of the musicians that we met along the way. He was always ready with the tape recorder to catch a party piece or a nice set of tunes from the Irish radio.

One day Chuck came down from his room with two reels that he had off the radio, "The Dawn" and "Rattigan's Reel". I picked up "The Dawn" from him that day because I remembered that Jimmy Cummins, the seanchai from the Abbey, had been asking for it. I learned "Rattigan's" as well, but can't think of it now. Nobody had ever asked me for that one and I never ran into anyone who played it, so it went out of my head. You had to be a hunter to build a repertoire and Chuck was and still is a great collector of Irish music. If I need to find an old recording that one of us made, all I've ever had to do is call him and he makes me a new copy.

Andy Vaughan, the bartender from MacCafferty's, had a brother named Joe that worked for the Irish Tourist Board. He was stationed in O'Brien's Tower on top of the Cliffs of Moher. The tower was built by Cornelius O'Brien as were many of the bridges in the area. At the time, the tower at the Cliffs was a bit off the beaten track. They have since built an interpretive center and two large parking lots there.

Joe was from a family that had lived in the area a long time. He had been a school teacher and knew all the local history. He was a very good man to have explaining and telling stories to the occasional travelers who showed up to view the Cliffs. Besides manning the tower, Joe ran a small gift shop where you could purchase postcards, keychains or cassette tapes. He was paid by the Tourist Board, so he didn't have to make money off the gift shop. He enjoyed meeting the people who came from all over the world and he was a genial man who loved his job.

The fly in the ointment for Joe was Micho Russell. There was a pathway along the Cliffs built of Liscannor flagstones with odd naturally occurring Celtic-looking patterns in them, leading up to the tower. Micho set himself at the bottom of the footpath a quarter mile away and had first crack at anyone coming to visit the tower. He loved to tell stories about the area as well. He sang a bit and played the tin whistle. By the time Micho was done charming the guests and regaling them with local tales, there wasn't as much attention paid to Joe as he deserved. It galled him to have a freebooter hosting the tourists. Both of them made up stories for the fun of it and to annoy each other. The tourists who managed to meet both men didn't know which stories to believe.

Cornelius O'Brien, who was born in the late eighteenth century, was a legend in the area and I heard many tales about him. I'm not saying that these are true stories, but here are a few of them. The tower that he built is said to be situated on the Cliffs in such a way that Cornelius could watch the ram that he had placed among the sheep on the tiny island below for inspiration in the boudoir.

O'Brien had a huge estate between Liscannor and the Cliffs. The local priest, scandalized by O'Brien's philandering, supposedly put “The Priest’s Curse” on him and his estate. The priest said that within a year the crows would be flying through his castle. Within the year, as the story goes, the manor house was hit by lightning and burned. The colonnade of oak trees that lined both sides of the long drive leading up to the estate were all hit by lightning or blown over in the course of the next twenty years. The ruins of the old estate to this day look haunted.

St. Bridget’s Well, which is also near the Cliffs, was moved slightly by O’Brien from its original pre-Christian location. The well is at the end of a narrow stone grotto and the walls and ceiling are covered with prayer cards from funerals, hand written notes, eyeglasses, canes and crutches, obituaries from newspapers, photographs, and all manner of tributes. The specific items are changed, but somehow the same each time I have visited. As you walk down into the grotto you hear the sounds of birds and dripping water. There is supposed to be an eel that appears in the well, which means, when seen, that a pilgrim’s wishes and prayers will be granted. Fast Mary Hedlund told me that she had nightmares about that eel.

A lovely old cemetery surrounds the Well and just outside the cemetery, to the front, towards the road and a bit off to the side stands the giant obelisk marking the final resting place of Cornelius O’Brien himself.

We were having great nights at the Anchor Bar. Set dancers from as far away as Ennis, like the Taltys, would drive out when we played. Flan Garvey from Inagh would come along with his friends. They would all show up with their favorite set dancing shoes and make a night of it, joining the many good set dancers from the local areas around Liscannor and Doolin.

Stephen McNamara was an old-time bodhran player who had made his own drum out of goat skin with big old pennies in the rim like a tambourine. No one made bodhrans for you back then and he explained to me how to make them in his style. I made several and it was a messy business involving a trip to a rendering plant, the use of lime and the scraping of hair. Stephen played with a one-ended stick that had a leather loop for his thumb. He was an excellent player who listened closely to the other musicians and matched their every rhythm and phrase. He knew just how to lift the music.

P. J. and Margaret took us to Lisdoonvarna one night in September when the Matchmakers' Festival was in full swing. We were at a ceili in a hotel where a lively band was playing and the room was jammed with dancers. I, myself, was ceili dancing with a pillar off to one side doing a dance that I had made up on the spot, when an older fellow in a tweed suit and cap came up to Barbara and asked, in all sincerity, "How would you like to live on a farm with six cows?"

It took a moment for Barbara to realize that she had just been proposed to. She was polite and said that she was already married. I gave up my Irish pole dancing ways then and there in case in the momentary pause as she was gathering her thoughts, she had considered the proposal. The matchmaking was a serious business back then, and there weren't many ways for a farmer to find a wife.

One night we were sitting in Margaret's kitchen in their house next to the pub having tea and sandwiches at three or four in the morning when we were all startled by a loud, unearthly moan that turned into a drawn out wail. All conversation stopped. Margaret's mother was the first to speak.

"There'll be someone dead in the village tonight."

When we got up the next day the first thing we heard was that Joe McHugh, the well-known and well-loved publican who owned the place next door, had died.

We had been doing well in Liscannor as a band, until Stockton's Wing came along and created a musical sensation that blew us right out of the waters of the west coast of Clare. They were a spectacular group and played unbelievably exciting traditional music.

We fled to the far end of the Dingle peninsula, out beyond Dingle Town to Fionach in the Kingdom of Kerry. There we met up with Seamus Begley, a fine box player and singer with whom we had previously spent some rollicking nights in Chicago. Seamus was playing his regular gig at An Cuine, his local corner pub and we had more rollicking nights with him there playing slides and polkas for the Kerry set dancers.

Returning from the pub to the Begleys' farmhouse one night in pitch black darkness we were having a hard time negotiating the way. Seamus went up ahead of us and, with matches, lit the tops of the hedges on fire. Although the tops were dry and caught easily, with all the rain in Ireland there was no danger of the fire spreading. It was a fine way to light the road. The next morning, Seamus's father sang "The Lovely Irish Maid." He gave me the words and it is a song I still sing, although I've never been able to sing it as well as he did.

Seamus took us up to the Three Sisters, mountains on the northwest tip of the peninsula that had broken off on the seaward side leaving sheer cliffs rising out of the Atlantic. We lay down in the tall grass at the edge and looked out over the ocean. We could see ships, fishing trawlers, dolphins and even whales going by far below. All around us every kind of seabird whirled and dove. It was a windy yet peaceful place. Sometimes, when I am having a hard time falling asleep, I imagine that I am laying up there and it doesn't take long until I am in dreamland.

Aidan Kelly lived in St. Paul, but was originally a Wexford man and we had promised to meet up with him at his family's farm near Camross. He knew Paddy Berry, one of the champions who had come to St. Paul on the '73 Comhaltas tour whose singing of "Ballyshannon Lane", one of the best 1798 rebel songs, made it famous. Paddy was also rumored to have dreams about the 1798 Rising in which he is actually there.

A song is the story of a place. Aidan decided that since I had the song from Paddy Berry, he should take me down Ballyshannon Lane, a few miles from the family farm. He took me on a tour of the little road and showed me the place where Evoy had his blacksmith shop and forged the pikes, where Doyle's house stands, Keating's Bawn and where the Kehoes had probably lived. The places that I saw that day along Ballyshannon Lane always come back to me in memory when I sing the song, making the events seen in my mind's eye more real.

Barbara, Chuck and I played bingo one night in Camross Cross and had to walk a couple of miles down a very dark road to get back to the Kelly farm. About half a mile away from the farm, we all suddenly stopped and could not move on. The hair on the back of my neck was up and we were sure that there was something just ahead of us on the road. We couldn't go forward, so we had a smoke while we tried to figure out what to do. Then we heard a car speeding towards us from the direction of the farm. The woman behind the wheel stopped and through the open window called out, "Get in! Did you see her?"

It was Aidan's mother.

We asked, "See who?"

She said, "Just get in. I'll tell ye later." She didn't say another word until she had us back in her kitchen with tea, sandwiches and whiskey. We asked what she meant out on the road. She said that it was a "Sidhe" that haunts that crossroad. The Sidhe sits on the big stone alongside the road just beyond where we had stopped and combs her long hair with a silver comb. Mrs. Kelly told us that over the years, people had been frightened to death there and when she heard that we were walking home, she set out right away to intercept us and bring us back safely.

One night Aidan Kelly took us down to Rosslare for a session. The Wexford Mummers, friends of his, were there as well as Paddy Berry. The session was full of singing. An old friend of mine, Nick Coleman, a newspaper man from St. Paul who has a passion for rebel songs happened to be there too sitting next to Paddy Berry who sang "Ballyshannon Lane". At Paddy's request, Nick sang a song. He was embarrassed about the sound of his own voice and afterward apologized. Paddy said to him, "That's alright, son. It's the story that counts."

The Wexford Mummers were the real center of the evening's entertainment with heroic recitations in the first person such as "I am Brian Boru, the Brave and True" and "Father Murphy". They acted out scenes from ancient Irish history, sang and danced, and cracked their wooden swords as they told the epic story of Ireland in a way I had never seen or heard before.

After our stay in Wexford, we decided to go back to Inch Island and Buncrana. I wanted to call ahead to let the McDonaghs know that we were coming, but I couldn't think of the number at the time so I asked the operator if he could help me. I could hear the Dublin in the operator's accent. He said, "Just stay on the line. I'll get back to you."

I had been standing there in the phone booth about ten minutes when I heard his voice again. "Do you still want to make that call, sir?"

"Yes."

"I'll be right with you."

In another ten minutes he was back on the line. He said, "Looking for a number for the McDonaghs on Inch Island, sir. I can't give you a Inch McDonagh. Would you take a Moyle McDonagh?"

I thought about that for a moment. After a few seconds, I started laughing and gave up on the call.

In the derelict train station in Fahan not far from the causeway leading to Inch Island, Sean and Eileen McDonagh had opened

The Railway Tavern and were flying it. They started out with a pub and restaurant and added a disco out back later. They had remodeled the big house on Inch and were living in it with their daughters. Sean's mother Molly was living in the little cottage next to the big house. We came, stayed, played and had a ball, as we did every time we journeyed that way.

The McDonaghs had also started a pirate radio station and each member of the family, adults and children alike, were involved. They had made up monikers for themselves and each developed their own programs and played the music they liked best. They came close to being shut down several times, but moved their transmitter as necessary and never got caught.

Sean was setting up concerts at various venues around Buncrana. Christy Moore stayed at the house on Inch after playing a solo concert for Sean. Late that night we were all sitting around the big table down in the kitchen having a singsong. An off-duty Provo was playing guitar and singing the Donovan song "Catch the Wind". We were all very quiet, as usual when someone is singing, and trying to be polite, but with that song we were having trouble keeping straight faces. Each verse ended with the phrase, "Ah, but I may as well try and catch the wind." Chuck was sitting quietly, seemingly lost in his own world but towards the end of the song, he joined in on that phrase and sang, fairly loudly, "I may as well try and pass the Wind".

Everyone at the table finally cracked up except the singer, who was outraged. Chuck smiled benignly and looked so innocent that no one was really sure he had actually said it.

In the morning, one of the young McDonagh girls came downstairs and saw a body laid out on the couch, a blanket covering its face and torso with only the feet poking out of the end. She started to worry when she saw how still the body was. There was no sound or movement at all. She was even more frightened when she noticed that the boots were still on. She later found out that the "body" was actually a sleeping Christy Moore, who was a fierce man for the craic in those days.

*****

After Inch, we returned to Chicago. We were playing the Glenshesk when I got a call from my sister Patty who was working as a nurse in St. Paul. She had been taking care of Paddy Hill. His gangrene had come back which put him in the hospital. They had removed one leg and he did pretty well for about a week. Then they had to remove the other leg. When he woke up from that surgery and found that both legs were gone, he faded fast. He died at the age of seventy-nine, just like the fortune teller had predicted all those years ago.

Patty had called to let us know that the funeral was the next day. We cancelled our gig at the Glenshesk and drove the four hundred miles to St Paul, arriving in the morning in time for the burial. It was winter, and freezing cold at Calvary Cemetery. Paddy had told Sinda that he wanted me to sing. At the graveside, I sang the song that he requested, "Sean O'Dwyer a Glenna".

Although we part in sorrow,

Sure, Sean O'Dwyer a cara,

Our prayer is God Save Ireland

And pour blessings on her name.

May her sons be true when needed.

May they never fail as we did.

Oh, Sean O'Dwyer a Glenna,

You were worsted in the game.

*****

Chapter 12
Flying the Coop

Ann's old Chicken Coop in Long Lake, about half an hour out of town, was the place to be for late night parties and sessions when in St Paul. Martin McHugh and members of his several ceili bands and anyone who was mad for the music and the craic would make their way out there after gigs often over icy roads. As we played music and danced through the hours approaching dawn, we found that some of our friends could not drink and stay awake at the same time. In order to prevent injuries, we found it best to consign to the Mouse Room those who had fallen asleep on the floor, thus becoming hazards to the dancers and themselves.

The Mouse Room was a tiny room with a large bed and many small, furry full-time residents. We carried the sleepers to that room and lay them on the bed, which might already be occupied by three or four bodies tossed sideways across it. Some of these folks were planning to work the next morning, so it seemed like the right thing to do.

Ann Heymann was playing with us now and we were a four piece band for about six months. She was playing the harp and the whistle. She kept her beautiful harp in a huge, yellow-brown fiberglass case on wheels which she pulled by a strap through the streets of Ireland and America. The case was as noisy as it was ugly. The wheels squealed and scraped every time it moved. It was especially bad on sidewalks. You could tell that passersby wanted to say something, but after one look at Ann's determined face, they usually decided to keep their own counsel. That case protected Ann's harp from both the elements and theft by stealth.

The four of us played Kansas City at a place called The Irish Brigade, named after a popular band founded by Mick Wallace and Gerry Goodwin, the homesick boys of Limerick. We knew from experience that this pair was a tough act to follow. We had played a gig in Davenport, Iowa, the day after The Irish Brigade had played the final night of a long engagement. The stage was a shocking site. There were ladies undergarments strewn all over and topping it all was a gigantic bra made specially, we were told, to wrap up the boys. At least in K.C. the stage was reasonably clear.

After Kansas City we went up to Boulder to play at a restaurant that we hadn't been to before. Shannon's where we usually played when we were in Boulder was no more. The roof had caved in during a snowstorm and they never reopened. There would be no more high times on Pearl Street, at least not at Shannon's.

Before playing the gig at the new place, we decided to get a bite to eat in the restaurant. The special listed on the menu was Rocky Mountain Oysters. Chuck, Barbara and I ordered the special. We hadn't had oysters before and wanted to try them. The orders arrived and we started eating. When the waitress stopped at our table to check on us, I told her that the food was good and didn't taste fishy at all, she asked, "Don't you know what they are?"

I admitted that we didn't. When she told us what they actually were, we switched to hamburgers. Ann was a vegetarian at the time and I think for a while after that Chuck became one as well.

When we returned to Chicago we played a few more gigs with Chuck and Ann, but it was becoming obvious that they would make a great group on their own. Ann was getting better and better on her wire strung harp and Chuck had a huge repertoire of songs. They liked doing more concert style venues where they could feature the harp, an instrument which for obvious reasons works better in a concert hall than in a pub. They took off and never looked back. They are still playing all over the US and internationally.

Barbara and I had worked as a duo before and were sure we could do it again, but when we met up with Cuz Teahan shortly after we split with Chuck and Ann, he said, "Why don't you call Liz?"

We called Liz Carroll and asked if she wanted to tour with us and she said that she would. When we told Cuz that she was going to come with us, he said, "Ask her about The Windy City Ceili Band and Buncrana."

I bought an old Ford station wagon and made a few phone calls. We had one quick rehearsal with Liz and it was time to hit the road. We picked Liz up at her parents' house on the South Side. As we were leaving her parents blessed us with copious amounts of Holy Water at the door and her father, Kevin, told me pointedly to watch out for his daughter. Liz was an all-Ireland, under-eighteen fiddle champion and had won the Senior All-Ireland the next year. She could also really play on her father's button accordion. Her parents made sure that we knew that we were taking the Crown Jewel of the Chicago Irish on tour and we were very protective of her.

Liz had grown up with the music, so there was no pub song or tune that she hadn't either played before or could pick up in a few minutes. She had gotten a lot of her music from her father and Johnny McGreevy, as well as from all the other South Side musicians. Liz was doing what she could to carry on what she had learned while adding her own bold style to the music.

First up on the tour was Davenport in Iowa. Then it was on to St. Louis, Columbia and Kansas City in Missouri. In K.C. we were booked to play an Irish Northern Aid dance. Liz's mother was from a town near Shanagolden in Limerick and had relatives and connections in town. The McAliffes, the Shines and the Cahills were all going to show up to hear Liz play so she was a little wound up. I asked her what she did to calm her nerves. She said that she prayed. It was Corpus Christi Day, a fact that had escaped me, to Liz's surprise and since the dance was held in a parish hall, Liz was able to attend Mass before the gig while Barbara and I went to a bar.

After the ceili, we continued on to Omaha where we played an outdoor concert at Peony Park and then headed west towards Denver. On the way, I finally remembered to ask Liz about The Windy City Ceili Band and Buncrana. The story as I remember it was that Cuz wanted to show off the young musicians of Chicago. He decided to put together a band to play at the All-Ireland Fleadh Cheoil. He called the group "The Windy City Ceili Band." Besides Liz, there was Jimmy Keane, John Williams, Martin Fahey, Barry Foy and some others.

The competitions are a fairly formal affair. There are judges seated at a big table taking notes and the crowd is quiet and respectful. There are rules for the bands, and they rehearse extensively, often making multiple attempts to win the top honor, the title of All-Ireland Champion. Most of the kids had competed before and won so they were not intimidated by the situation. Cuz told them, as he told everyone who ever played with him, that they would "have to scream." When the Windy City Ceili Band was announced, the audience saw a dignified gentleman in his seventies walk out onto the stage followed by a well-behaved gaggle of neatly dressed young people.

Chicago had a good reputation for traditional Irish music from Captain O'Neill's day and everyone knew the story of Irish music in Chicago. The band started out with their set and Cuz was tapping one foot and then the other. He could look very serious when he wanted to. Soon he was heel and toeing it with both feet. Then he threw back his head, holding his concertina up high off his knee and let out a mighty scream. The youngsters took their cue and let out their own war screams. Cuz was shaking his head back and forth and soon the pins he had used to tame his hair started to fly out in every direction and his shock of grey hair, which had been pinned down flat was now free and flying around in a spiral above his head. The audience erupted in shouts and laughter with the occasional "Go Cuz" or

"Up the South Side" heard above it all. When they finished the set, Cuz pulled up his left pant leg as high as he could and shook his leg at the judges and said, "How do you like that, Cuz?" I was laughing so hard when Liz told the story that I nearly drove off the road to Denver.

In Denver, after visiting the Flanagan's, we played the Folklore Center. Then we headed back East to Chicago for a week before continuing on to Portland, Maine via Montreal.

Liz enjoyed being twenty-one. Her parents had ideas about the supervision that would be required on the tour, but Liz had her own ideas. She was a little bit wilder than we had bargained for. When we were playing in Portland, we stopped at a disco after a gig. Liz decided that we should give them a blast of Irish music and had the owner shut off the sound system. The disco crowd did not appreciate the interruption of their music to listen to jigs and reels played acoustically and it wasn't long before they became rude. As we were leaving, I noticed that a couple of empty beer bottles had been placed under the tires of our old station wagon. Liz wanted me to take on the crowd right there on the sidewalk, but I decided it would be better to just leave and that is what we did. Irish music isn't for everyone.

We had a little time between gigs after Portland. Barbara and I left for Washington D. C. where we were playing next at a place called The Four Provinces. Liz said she would meet us there in a week.

When we arrived in D. C., Barbara and I decided to check out Matt Kane's place called Bit O'Ireland. Sean Tyrrell had told us about it when we were in Boston and had been playing it for years. Butch and Maeve played there as well. It was once the biggest venue for Irish music in D.C. and one of the best on the East Coast. From the time it opened in 1960 it was a favorite haunt of politicians, police and military personnel. Tip O'Neill and the Kennedys were regulars.

We thought that maybe we could arrange an impromptu gig. In the late seventies, you could still just show up, do an audition and be hired that way. It wasn't necessary, but it helped to have the recommendation of other musicians. The world of Irish music was much smaller then and most musicians and pub owners knew each other.

Our timing was off. We showed up just as they were shutting the doors for good. Matt Kane and his wife invited Barbara and me out to their beach house in Ocean City for a few days because they felt bad that they couldn't hire us. They were hospitable and treated musicians very well.

We met up with Liz after a week and played at The Four Provinces and another pub owned by a Kerry man called John Barry. When the gigs in D. C. were finished, the tour was over. We were tired and at loose ends. It was time to try something new.

Part Two

Chapter 13
Mystified By the Oddness of Hank

At MacCafferty's one night back in 1978 I met a fellow from Slidell, Louisiana, named Bob Lacey. He liked Irish music and commented that it must be a fun way to make a living. I told him that it wasn't as easy as it looked. He said that if I ever needed a change, I should try working in the oilfield and he gave me his phone number in Louisiana. I stuck it in my wallet. A year later the band had broken up and I became convinced that music was ruining my life. It was time to find a real job so I headed for New Orleans while Barbara stayed in Chicago waiting to see what happened. Within a few weeks, I drank up most of the musical equipment that I had carried south and it was time to call Bob Lacey about a job.

He gave me the number of the outfit he had worked for, Otis Engineering, a wire lining company, in Belle Chasse, Louisiana. When I filled out the application in the office, they told me they didn't have any openings. That didn't worry me because Bob had warned me that they would say that. I repeated to them what he had told me to say, "I've checked out the competition and decided that you're the best outfit. I'll be here every day waiting in the office until someone doesn't show. If you don't hire me, I'll go down the road to Camco." Camco was a rival company.

So there I was every morning meeting people and chatting with the receptionist while listening to The Commodores who always seemed to be on the office radio until one day Derwood Jones, the manager came out and bellowed, "Dayheel, get your ass in here. You're hired."

Although Dayheel struck me as funny, I didn't correct him. Some of my friends had started calling me "Downhill" and I was hopeful that Derwood's version was a step in the right direction. The next morning at 5 a.m., I reported to the job and was sent out with Terry Jones, a "Stump-Jumper" or native Mississippian, on a 40-foot work barge heading down the broad Lower

Mississippi in a fog through a place called Tiger Pass on the way to a somewhere referred to as "The End of the World. " Terry steered us out into the channel, which was filled with gigantic tankers and shipping traffic of every kind, put me behind the wheel, lay down on his bunk and cautioned, "Keep the green buoys on your right."

Then he went to sleep and I, who had never handled anything larger than a row boat, was on my own. I always told myself in these types of situation, "Don't worry. Either you will die or you won't." It hadn't occurred to me that I could really hurt someone else or cripple myself if I made a mistake.

I was twenty-nine, wearing a white hard hat and red coveralls with "Clarence" stitched on the left pocket, working with people who described themselves as 'Coon Asses' and had bumper stickers that said "Oilfield Trash and Proud of It." I was a Minnesotan living with people who didn't like Yankees, but they didn't connect me with the North. They called me Irish Tom because all I talked about was Ireland. I liked them and they liked me and they didn't want me to be a Yankee.

We would go out to fix wells on the bayous and estuaries and couldn't come home until the job was done. The work was hard, dirty and dangerous and I loved it. We made a base pay of $5.65 per hour, but often by Wednesday morning we had 40 hours in and were on overtime. We received hazardous pay on wells that had pressures over 2,000 pounds per square inch and more for wells with the poisonous gas, H2S. Most of the money we made wasn't spent because we were too busy. Barbara came down from Chicago and found a job at a restaurant across the road from the apartment we had rented in Belle Chasse.

After working for a while as a trainee, or to use the local vernacular, a worm, for various operators, I was sent out with Joe Rosson, the meanest, most demanding and hard to get along with old Texan in South Louisiana. For some reason, we got along fine. Joe had been working oil wells all his life in Texas,

Louisiana and Venezuela and just wanted everything done right. He ran off most of the worms that had the misfortune to be assigned to him because he had rules that they couldn't understand or live up to. For instance, on Joe's barge "Old Nellie", the oldest in the fleet, the worm was allowed two paper towels per day to keep the aged oilfield barge spotless. When working on high pressure wells with hundreds of working parts all covered in oil, miles of stainless steel wire, along with the tools and engines that needed constant maintenance, not to mention windows, it seemed like a lot to keep clean with two paper towels per day. I asked Joe if he could do it himself and he answered, "Hell yes!"

When I asked him how, he pointed to a pile of rags, a bucket of diesel, a bucket of detergent and a bucket of water and said, "Figure it out."

I found that by using the diesel soaked rag on the oily tools, then a detergent soaked rag to wipe them down, rinsing the whole works with bayou water and finally giving everything a coat of fine oil I could save the paper towels for the windows and get it done.

Joe was a great teacher in what I came to think of as the "Texas Tradition." He would tell me or even show me how to do something, but after that I was on my own. He answered any question I had about the special tools we used or the mechanics of the wells, but he would only answer once. If you asked the same question the next day or the next week, he would say, "Look it up. I already answered that one." I didn't mind and enjoyed the challenge. The more I learned about oil wells, the more I loved them.

On the barge there was a 30-foot crane that we used to lift the lubricator, which was a 6-inch-wide pipe that came in 3 ten-foot long telescopic sections that were coupled together. There was a pulley and a stuffing box on the top end of the lubricator. A tool string, really a long steel rod that weighed a hundred pounds or more, ran down the inside of the lubricator pipe, attached to a giant valve that we connected to the well head. The tool string was tied by a special wire knot to a 2-mile-long stainless steel wire. The two miles of wire were wrapped on a big metal spool with a motor and a gauge that told us exactly how far down the "hole" we were. When we opened the big wireline valve, the lubricator would pressure up to match the pressure of the well and we could lower the tool string down the hole through the pulley and stuffing box to work deep below the surface of the earth. Sometimes we worked a mile or more down the well, under pressures of up to 20,000 pounds per square inch. It was like working on a bomb.

The technology was invented in Texas back in the twenties by Otis and Halliburton, who used the back axel of a truck to operate the spool and wire when working on land wells. Now and even back in the seventies, electronic versions were being developed, but the old system is still used on many wells. The precise work we could do was something that still amazes me. I was fascinated by all the various jars, knuckle joints, kick-over tools, perforators, blow out preventers, dogs, mandrels and all the rest of the oil well paraphernalia.

One of the most common tool combinations we used as wireliners was a pair of twenty-four inch pipe wrenches, sometimes used with four foot cheater pipes to increase leverage. We used this combination to make up or break connections on the lubricator or tool string. These particular tools were sometimes used in other ways as well.

Company pick-up trucks were assigned to each crew of two. I remember hearing about one operator who, as a joke, threw a rattlesnake into the passenger side of the truck as his worm was about to climb in. The worm, seeing the snake on the seat just in time, grabbed his twenty-fours and went after his partner cursing and throwing the big wrenches at him as he ran away. Both of them eventually burst into laughter, realizing that they would have a good story to tell when they returned to civilization.

One rainy night on a rig in the Gulf about a month into the job, at three in the morning, I found myself hanging upside down by my knees from a board fifty feet above the drilling platform. I had a pair of twenty-fours and two cheater bars and was trying to break a connection on the lubricator to free a stuck tool string. There was another fool up there on the slippery boards with me, holding onto my legs in case my ankles suddenly gave out. I never saw a safety harness in the entire time I was in the oilfields and had been working for days with very little sleep, but I was caught up in the excitement of the drilling platform and didn't feel any fear. I was doing things I had never before imagined.

It wasn't uncommon to rack up a hundred to a hundred and ten hours a week. Most of the time, it was just Joe and me on the barge in the estuaries, but we would get called out for a few days at a time to the rigs in the Gulf as well. When we were up on the drilling rigs, they fed us well. They would ask whether we wanted one 16 oz. steak or two when we came in for breakfast. Sometimes there were long delays as we waited for others to finish their work so we could do ours. During the lulls we would climb down ladders to the water and fish for red snapper on one hundred foot lines.

The oilfields stretch over one hundred miles south of New Orleans, down the Mississippi all the way through Tiger Pass and out into the Gulf of Mexico. At night in the Gulf, the lights from the drilling platforms and refineries made it look like the barge was surrounded by distant cities. With the frequent flares that appeared and disappeared among the lights, the whole place took on an air of the demonically surreal. I now knew what they meant when they called it "The End of the World."

On weekends I liked to go to a laundromat near New Orleans' Garden District. It was a good place to wash your clothes because it had not only washers and driers, but live Cajun music and blues, delicious po' boy sandwiches and a bar. It was nice to order a drink, eat a meal, have a dance and do your laundry all at once.

The Happy Cajun was another place we liked to frequent. It was a dance hall on Airline Rd. in Metairie that was owned by Alan Fontaineau, an accordion playing, singing radio personality who hosted a live radio program from the bar that was very popular with the Cajun crowd. He had plenty of guest musicians and singers on the show with him. The place and his show reminded me of the pubs and live Irish radio hours in Chicago. The hall's atmosphere was similar to an Irish pub where most of the people were Irish speakers from rural Ireland who were transplanted to Chicago. In this case, it was French speaking Cajuns from the country replanted in New Orleans.

One night I was driving back from New Orleans to Belle Chase, about twelve miles south of the city, with a friend from work who happened to be from Connecticut. As we drove through a tunnel under the Mississippi, my buddy threw a string of firecrackers out the window. I glanced in the rearview mirror and saw the firecrackers blasting away on the windshield of a cop car. When we got pulled over, they let me go without much ado, but I could see that they relished taking my friend away to be booked. At least I thought that was the plan. Don showed up back at work a few days later with no formal charges, but he had been beaten to a pulp and it took a week or so until he was back to his old smart-alecky ways.

There was plenty of exotic wildlife in and around the bayous. I knew a wireline operator down there who ran traplines on the side. His nickname was Gator and he was one of the old time Cajuns. He told a story one day about how he took a shot at a nutria which is a kind of thirty to forty pound fur bearing rat with horrible-looking yellow teeth that is native to South America. A few had gotten loose in the Louisiana bayous from a fur farm and having no predators, spread all over the Gulf. Gator said that they were highly intelligent and could tell who was out to get them and who left them alone. Gator had taken his shot, but only wounded the nutria. The outraged nutria jumped into the water and started swimming straight at Gator and his friends. Everyone scattered in all directions, but it was Gator that the big rat wanted and it continued to pursue him with murder in its eye. Gator escaped with his life and never said what happened to the nutria.

There were plenty of alligators as well. They were very curious and could be called if you just yelled, "Hey gator, hey gator. " We sometimes fed them bread or scraps left over from meals, which probably wasn't too good an idea because they would gather around the wells where we were often standing on platforms that were only a foot or two above the water and that was when the water was low. When the water was high, the gators could get even closer. When it was so high that we were actually standing in the water, we could only hope the water moccasins might keep the gators at bay.

When we pulled the barge up to a well, dropped the "spuds" or weighted metal pilings that held us in place and jumped off, the first thing we had to look for was copperheads. They liked to lie sunning themselves on the circular cement platforms that surrounded the wells and it was a serious matter to get a poisonous snake bite at the End of the World. There were no roads for fifty miles around and if you got hurt or died, no one but oilfield personnel would hear about it. The companies did their best to keep accidents from outsiders.

The oil companies ruled, and they were all about the bottom line. We did pressure tests and flow tests when a new well was drilled and provided estimates of volume for the companies. No matter how good the estimate for the well, the policy was to write it off as a dry hole, cap it and wait, as the saying went, until gas was five dollars per gallon. It was a way to recoup the expenses of drilling.

The companies didn't like to pay much for drilling rights either. Often families that owned the land where wells were located were cheated out of revenues. Occasionally a family would win a law suit and get money out of a company that had kept it for years. However, winning in court against the oil companies was the exception, not the rule.

The company men had all the say about how things were done. Sometimes new managers liked to up production by overproducing the old wells. It was a way to make a name for themselves but they often ruined the wells in the process. The old Cajuns who knew each well, its history, and what it could do had a saying among themselves, "Keep a Small Mind." The managers were going to do what they wanted to and were not interested in the advice of underlings. In the end, the company men came and went, but the old Cajun oilfield people stayed.

There was one newly minted oilfield engineer that was hired right out of college by one of the oil companies that contracted with Otis Engineering. He used to pick me up in his brand new black 1980 Pontiac Trans Am. His favorite song was "Midnight Confessions". He admitted to me that he didn't know a damn thing about oil wells because he really went to college for the parties. Now he wanted to establish some credibility with the oilfield workers and asked me if he should pick a fight to earn some respect. I told him, "No! These people really know how to fight."

I was sorry that he felt like a sham, but he did make lots of money and with time, if he stayed in the oilfields, he would most probably age into credibility and respect. I don't know if he stayed.

The huge flocks of waterfowl that winter in the Louisiana bayous are legendary. In northern Minnesota we sometimes see one or maybe two loons at a time swimming across the lake wearing their summer plumage and we think it's lovely. In south Louisiana you see thousands of loons at one time. In their winter plumage, they lose some of their stateliness, but the sheer numbers make them impressive ..... Until they try to move. The loons land with an ungraceful plop and then take off running on their big feet, flapping maniacally until they gain enough speed to fly again. The oilfield workers amused themselves by steering toward huge flocks to make the loons go through their ridiculous looking efforts to take flight.

As a wireline operator trainee I would have to eventually know everything about the maintenance of the wells. I was very motivated to learn and studied all the written manuals and memorized all of the parts, tools and nomenclature used in the business. I was making up for lost time. I hadn't done anything but play music since the age of fourteen and now I was pushing thirty. My mother had suggested once just after high school that it might be a good idea to learn a trade, but I was writing three or four songs a day back then and ignored the advice. Later, in Rowley I thought about getting a job when money was tight, but it wasn't too hard to resist the temptation.

Bob Lacey had told me two things about working in the oilfield. "Never sit down on the job and never ask when you're getting off." This advice served me well because Joe Rosson didn't put up with any slacking from his worm. Once Joe had me trained to do what needed to be done, he would lie back in his bunk and begin musing, often about Hank Williams, his favorite subject when musing. He would say, "I just can't understand it."

"Understand what?"

"How a guy would get the idea to write a song about a wooden cigar store Indian."

"You mean Kaw-Lija?"

"I just don't get it. What would make somebody think of that?" He was totally mystified by the oddness of Hank whom he had heard once in the forties in a Tyler, Texas honky-tonk.

Joe listened to and loved all kinds of music, including Led Zeppelin, but he didn't play himself. He was oilfield all the way and musicians were another species to him. Joe wore a severe crew cut and he used expressions like," hot diggity-dingdong", and "well Sani-flush." One day I asked Joe when he was going to teach me how to drive the barge. He said, "Right now. Get behind the wheel. Take us to P.P. 131," and he lay down on the bunk.

I hadn't been paying particular attention to the maze of waterways in that bayou, but after being there for about six months, I had an idea of how to get to Plaquemines Parish Well No. 131. As we approached, I woke Joe and said, "We're here."

He said, "Put her in reverse when we get close," so I put it in reverse but because I was still throttled up, I killed the engine. Old Nellie plowed into the well and instantly we were engulfed by a sound like a jet taking off. It was so loud I couldn't think and I ran into the cabin to stuff pieces of my precious paper towels into my ears. I thought I would go deaf. The roar of that well could be heard for miles around and in five minutes, a half dozen company boats showed up to see what had happened.

Joe got up calmly, walked over and closed the flowline that had been broken in the collision. He closed it very slowly as all valves under high pressure must be closed or opened. I was mortified. I know that with all the crashing and scraping of metal, and all the natural gas that was coming out of the broken flowline, we could have been blown sky high, but Joe was nice and easy about it. After some joking and laughing and Joe changing the subject quickly, the company men left in their boats. Then Joe said to me, "Always rev her down and put her in neutral before you put her in reverse." After that I was allowed to drive and I was a careful pilot.

Occasionally I would be sent out with other crews because the company wanted me to gain experience in a variety of situations. When you were out on jobs with people you didn't know there would usually be a few pranks and challenges. There was always someone who would try to get your goat. I remember one big guy who called himself "Uncle Pervy". He goosed me when I was climbing up onto a well and without thinking I jumped off and put the steel toe of my boot to his backside. He said, "You wanna fight me?"

I said, "No I don't, but if you mess with me I will kill you." We got along fine after that.

Our apartment off the highway in Belle Chase was a fifties era, two-story building with open walkways on the second floor to reach the upstairs units. It faced an identical building across a shabby courtyard. We were on the ground floor and were friendly with the guy who lived above us. Bobby liked to come down and play old time music like "Red River Valley" and "Sweet Betsy from Pike". He played the harmonica and I would back him up on the guitar.

I came home from work one evening and saw a police car and a firetruck in the parking lot. The firemen were hosing down the balcony just outside our neighbor's front door. The water that spilled over the balcony and onto the sidewalk in front of our door had a reddish tinge to it. I asked the cop what happened. It turned out that our upstairs neighbor was entertaining a woman who worked just down the road as a bartender. The bartender's boyfriend had knocked on our neighbor's door looking for her. Bobby opened the door and gave the man both barrels of a shotgun right in the chest. The police searched the murdered man's pockets and found a California driver's license and a small unopened pocket knife. They arrested Bobby, who was a local, but let him out the next day once they determined that the shotgun blasts were “self-defense.”

Bobby seemed very proud of himself telling the story and laughing about it. Others in the building were not impressed. He put on a crawfish boil for the neighbors with plenty of Dixie beer to smooth things over, but those who showed up didn’t stay long. Bobby moved out a few weeks later.

I had been raised Catholic but was way out of practice. Barbara grew up in a Methodist house and had been warned by her late mother never to marry a Catholic. When we decided to marry at nineteen, we talked to my parish priest Father McDonagh in St. Paul. Once he had finished listening to one or two of our opinions, he said that he wouldn’t marry us and we decided to elope. When my mother heard about our plans, she talked to Father McDonagh again and he told her to let us get married in Barbara’s family’s church because that way I would still be a bachelor in the eyes of God. That is how Barbara and I ended up being married in a Methodist ceremony.

Most of the people Barbara and I had been meeting in Boston, Chicago, Ireland and now in Louisiana were Catholics and that must be why, around this time Barbara decided she wanted to convert. I wasn’t too keen on the idea, but somehow we ended up at the local parish rectory. We were invited in by the parish priest and Barbara started to explain why we were there. The priest interrupted her saying, “That’s nice sugar, but this is Mardi Gras. Come back and see me when Mardi Gras is over.” We never went back, but we did enjoy Mardi Gras in New Orleans.

Chapter 14
Farewell to Clarence

Bob Lacey, the man who referred me to Otis Engineering, invited us to Slidell on the other side of Lake Pontchartrain where his mother lived. He had an excursion planned for us on the Pearl River. When we got there we met Bob's mom who was a petite, genteel southern lady wearing a plain blue dress. On Bob's advice, we had brought a big burlap sack full of oysters as a hostess gift which we presented to his mother. We left Bob's Mom with the oysters and he took us out back to where he kept his canoe. We put the canoe on top of his car and being in a hurry to get to the river did not bother searching for rope to secure it. Instead, we just reached out the car windows and held onto the canoe as we drove. At the river we put the canoe in the water and climbed in.

We headed upriver through cypress groves hung with Spanish moss and thick, green vegetation along both banks. The sound of birds filled the humid Louisiana air. A few miles upriver, after poking around a bit, we turned around to go with the current which was fairly strong. We were paddling down the river enjoying the day when suddenly there was a resounding thump and the canoe sort of skidded off toward the right bank. I thought we must have hit a log or a rock. Bob shouted, "Big gator!"

Barbara and I hadn't seen alligator, but we believed Bob. According to him, it had given us a whack with its tail and to knock us off course the way it did, it had to be at least twelve feet long. The canoe was about fourteen feet long. When we reached the landing we were more than happy to climb out and head back to the house for the meal that Bob's mom was concocting from the burlap sack.

Once in the kitchen, we saw oysters everywhere cooked in every way imaginable. There were Oysters Rockefeller, Raw oysters, Oysters Casino and Oysters Bienville and more that I can't remember the names of. It seemed like the only kind of oyster dish that wasn't there was Rocky Mountain Oysters. We ate them all and washed them down with Dixie beer. I've eaten plenty of oysters since, but none of those experiences have ever come close to matching that afternoon's feast.

*****

I showed up for work one morning at 5 a. m. and was informed that we were being sent out on a job on a high pressure H2S well owned by a company called Aramco. H2S can be fatal if inhaled even in small quantities. Before we left, I was told to test a wireline valve for 25,000 pounds per square inch pressure. In the yard behind the maintenance building I ran into a friend who was going out on the same type of job, so we decided to test our valves together. We capped both ends of the wireline valves and used a compressor to pressure them up. Both of our valves tested okay, so off we went, he with his trainer, and I with Joe.

It was a lovely spring morning and after driving to Port Sulfur we boarded the crew boat for the thirty mile trip to Old Nellie. Once aboard, we motored out into the Gulf to a jack-up boat next to the well about three miles off shore. A jack-up boat has three legs and can be lifted thirty feet off the ocean floor to provide a stable work platform. We rigged up our wireline valve, lubricator and tool string and started doing bottom-hole pressure tests at a depth of about a mile and a half. The well registered about 20,000 psi. Then we started flow line tests, running the well at different volumes to see if there was any drop in bottom-hole pressure. We were estimating the potential of the well and it was looking like a winner. Then the four-inch O-ring on the bottom of the wireline valve sitting atop the wellhead started cutting out. When an O-ring cuts out, the sand and debris in the well rush to the new opening at, in this case, 20,000 psi. The opening might start out the size of a pin hole, but with all that force, the wireline valve can be eaten away rapidly. For that matter so can the entire wellhead. This is one of the reasons why blow out preventers were invented. Unfortunately they don't always work.

At the moment the O-ring cut out, our tool string happened to be stuck at the bottom of the well with a $200,000 measuring device attached to the end. Otis Engineering didn't want to cut the wire and lose the device and the Aramco didn't want to risk losing the jack-up boat, so they pulled the boat away, leaving me alone on the well with my legs wrapped around the wireline valve and two twenty four inch wrenches in my hands. It was suddenly very hot and humid and the beautiful day was looking ominous. All other personnel were on company boats about a hundred yards away using bull horns to give me directions on what to do next. Everyone had advice, but I was listening to Joe. After what seemed like a few hours the jack-up boat returned and Joe and I cut the wire and let the expensive measuring device fall into the "rat hole" at the bottom of the well. We then shut down the well, replaced the O-ring and re-rigged to go "fishing" for our lost tool string with a spare tool string.

It took that night, all of the next day and then another night and day to accomplish our mission. We did not stop to sleep and didn't take that many breaks. I'm not sure how we did it, but Joe could probably tell you. I think we took the lost tool string out in pieces which meant that we had to pull up the spare tool string and re-rig it to go back down twenty times or more. While we were working, Joe heard on the company radio that the friend I had been testing valves with behind the maintenance building had trouble similar to ours with the O-ring. The sand and debris in his well ate away his wireline valve until the whole mess exploded. The explosion crushed the right side of his body and ended his days in the oilfield.

There were huge heater tanks on the jack-up boat that were used to test the oil's viscosity and they, along with the Gulf sun that beat down on the steel deck combined to raise the temperature during the day to around 120 degrees Fahrenheit. Being from the north, it was a bit hard for me to cope, but we finished the job. In the end, we pulled the hundred and fifty pound tool string, a mile and a half of wire and the measuring device out of the two inch hole at 20,000 psi and the well was ready to produce. We thought we could call it a day.... a very, very long day.

Then the company man said, "Let's shut her in and we'll write it off as a dry hole."

After all that, they were going to plug it with cement. I suppose someday when it costs five dollars per gallon, I might drive using gas from that well.

When Joe and I arrived back at the Venice docks it was Wednesday evening. We had been out since Monday morning. We were on overtime and also were earning hazard pay for the high pressure and more hazard pay for the H2S gas that was in the well. We had made some good money and had plenty of excitement, but no sleep. We jumped off of Old Nellie at the fuel dock but forgot to put her in neutral. She started moving off and I couldn't get the dock lines tied on fast enough. I tried to hold her, but she kept moving away from the dock and I was pulled off by the line that was still in my hand into water filled with copperheads and water moccasins, alligators and chemicals, oil and rubbish and all of the things that make the oilfield fascinating.

I was thinking about swimming back to the dock, but then I heard Joe shout, "Stay with the boat!" so I kept ahold of the line which was hanging off the back of the old barge as she decided to head towards a jungle of flowlines. Some of them were visible above the surface and some were under the water. One spark could have blown up the whole shebang. Fortunately, Old Nellie got hung up on the flowlines at the edge of the forest stopping her forward motion and Joe, who had enlisted the help of a crew boat, was able to pull her off without a conflagration. This time we managed to tie her up properly. We cleaned up the barge, jumped into the truck and drove like hell back to Belle Chasse.

When we arrived at headquarters, I was still wet from my little swim at the Venice Docks. I heard Derwood Jones yell, "Dayheel, get your ass in here. We're breaking you out as an operator."

I had gained field experience in conducting bottom-hole pressure tests, installing gas lift valves in low pressure wells and subsurface safety valves that shut off the flow of oil or gas in an emergency. I even knew how to do the less than glamorous job of cleaning paraffin out of clogged wells, but to move from worm to full-fledged operator in the company, you also had to pass a difficult written test that covered things like specific weights for various fluids, pressure gradients and details about the care and maintenance of the well at all stages in its life.

Derwood Jones was telling me that I had to be back at five the next morning to take the day-long test, which I did. I passed.

Passing the test meant that I was now a wireline operator. I would be making more money. I would be a licensed professional. I would be assigned a work barge and my own worm whose training, life and well-being would be my responsibility. I had a lot to think about, but I was too tired to think.

Walking out of the building, a huge metal structure, I heard the strangest sound coming from the other end. It was the song "Cars" by Gary Numan, turned up loud and echoing off the metal walls of the cavernous building. The eerie New-Wave synthesizer scared the hell out of me and I suddenly knew that it was time to go.

The next morning, I came into the office and told Derwood Jones that I had received a call from Ireland. There was a family emergency and I was the only one who could take care of it. I had to leave for Ireland immediately.

A few days later Barbara and I were walking the streets of Galway.

Chapter 15
Plenty of Fish in the Sea

On the plane on the way to Ireland I had time to think about why I acted as I had. I must have known that I was a hazard on the job. My concentration was impaired by the hundreds of jigs, reels and songs going through my head at top volume and I couldn't count the number of times that Joe had saved my hide when I had done something stupid. I was trying to suppress the music, but after spending most of my life filling my head with it I found that it was harder to stop the process than I had hoped.

When I was a worm, I was only responsible for myself, but the idea of being responsible for someone else changed everything. Accidents were all too common in the oilfield and I don't know that I would have had my mind on the work enough to keep from blowing myself and my unfortunate worm to kingdom come.

Barbara was just as happy not to be playing on stage and I was still wary of making a living in music, so when we landed in Galway, I was again looking for "real" work.

In spite of my ruminations on the way over about my reasons for leaving the oilfields, the first place I tried to find work in Ireland was in the oil industry. I had read in the trade magazines that were left around the office at Otis Engineering, that one hundred and eighty miles west of Galway there was a new offshore natural gas field called the Porcupine Banks. I was hoping to get hired on there, but when I went in, they told me there weren't any openings. I think I was relieved. Since I didn't have a Bob Lacey around to tell me who to talk to, I figured that there was no danger of being hired in the oil business and decided to try commercial fishing.

I started talking to the fishermen at the Galway docks but had no luck there. We headed west to Connemara. It was either out at Teach Na Tra or at Mellit's that we ran into Paddy Connelly who was home visiting his people in Carna.

When we first met Paddy he had been working as a Guard on the Aran Islands and we had stayed a week with him on Inishmore. The pubs on the island were supposed to close at eleven thirty, but if a Guard brought the band, the pub could have a late night. All the pubs wanted a turn for the late night so in that one week we played every pub on the island. He was stationed in Donegal now and when I told him I was thinking about fishing, Paddy said, "Come with me and I'll bet you can get a berth on one of the Killebegs trawlers."

When Paddy drove us to Killybegs, we could smell the town before we could see it. As the town came into view around a bend, there was a huge fleet of over a hundred trawlers and a fish meal plant which was producing the smells, as well as fishmeal. Killybegs was built in a beautiful setting up the side of a mountain overlooking Donegal Bay.

We stayed with a family Paddy knew named McGuinness. They were purse seiners fishing for salmon, but the season had just ended, so they didn't have a use for me. I made the rounds every day on the pier, asking at every trawler if they had an open berth. My prospects were looking gloomy for finding work until one Saturday night when the McGuinness's took us down to a pub in the town for music and a few drinks.

The pub was long and low and packed to the gills with fishermen and their families. No food was on offer, but there was a lovely haze of smoke to go with the drink. At least sixty people were in the pub sitting at long tables. There were no boxes, whistles, pipes or guitars. This was a singing pub where each singer would take a turn and everyone would join in on the choruses. Towards the end of the evening I met a fellow named Mickey McLoughlin from Derry. He had been singing up a storm all night and when he found out that I was American, he said, "Let's sing an American song."

We started singing "I Can't Stop Loving You", a Hank Williams song that was a big hit for Ray Charles. That song was a big hit for us that night as well. Mickey and I got up on our feet and were encouraging everyone to join in with us. We all had our hands up in the air, roaring the refrain, "I can't stop loving you!" until delirium took over. Mickey asked me what I was doing in Killybegs. I told him I was looking for a berth. He said, "I'm the engineer on the Gerona. You're hired. She's a singing boat and we go out tomorrow night at eleven. Just show up and I'll clear it with the captain."

The next day Barbara and I set out to find a place to live. We rented a caravan about a half mile out of town up a steep hill. After moving our things to the new place, we walked down to the Hotel Bar where I made preparations to start my new job. I met the men from some of the other trawlers. The crews tended to stick together, and when I met one of the fishermen from a trawler, he would introduce me to any others of his crew that were there in the bar. I learned as much as I could by asking questions and listening to advice on how things were done. The pints and shots kept coming throughout the day and into the evening until eleven o'clock rolled around and it was time to board Gerona.

The Donegal accent can be hard to understand. Me being a Yank and brand new to commercial fishing, it was difficult at first to pick up on what was being said to me. The jargon was all new and the accent made it all the harder. I had spent quite a bit of time around Inch and Buncrana, but the Donegal in the speech was stronger here.

At the pier the first of the Gerona's crew that I met was Paddy Quigley. He greeted me with, "Nice fraysh breeze. There'll be whytin' in it." The wind was blowing in hard from the sea and whiting is a fish often used for fish and chips.

Paddy told me that he was from Kilcar, five or six miles west of Killybegs and was the oldest man in the fleet. He was fifty-two, but he assured me that he could still run the rail. That meant running around the eighty foot trawler while at sea on the six-inch band of steel on top of the gunwale. Paddy had whiskers since he only shaved on Fridays and short gray hair. Looking at his wiry frame and seeing the look in his eye, I had no trouble believing he could still run the rail.

Later, when I got to know him better, he told me that when he was a young man he proposed to his sweetheart but she turned him down. He was hurt. His mother, trying to help with the words many a mother of a broken hearted boy has used before said, “Well Paddy, there’s plenty of fish in the sea.”

Paddy said, “Well then, by God, I’ll go catch them.”

He became a full-fledged fisherman and swore off women for the rest of his life. Paddy would spend all of his pay each week buying drinks for everyone and throwing his money around so that, having been paid on Saturday he was broke by Sunday evening. Everyone called him “The nicest kid in town” and Paddy called himself that as well. Our skipper, Noble Morrow, usually held back a little of Paddy’s cash to give him later in the week. Paddy showed us by example what it meant to be a hard worker. When he was at sea he knew how to stick to business and never shirked. He showed greenhorns how to splice lines, mend nets and do all the other jobs that needed to be done on board.

Mickey McLaughlin arrived and nodded to me as I was talking to Paddy. He boarded and a few minutes later I heard the two cats, five hundred horsepower Caterpillar engines, firing up. Mickey, being the engineer had the most important job on board. It was crucial to keep the engines working properly because if you lose power in the North Atlantic where the wind and rollers are always pushing the boats towards that rocky shore, you must have plenty of power or ship and crew are sure to perish. When we were steaming out, we would not see Mickey for the first few hours because his station was below in the engine room.

Captain Noble Morrow knew the sea and all the underwater features on the fishing grounds that the Killybegs fleet worked.

He was an expert diver and had explored the wreck of the original Gerona which was a warship of the Spanish Armada that had gone down in a storm off Antrim after leaving Killybegs in 1588. It was carrying the survivors of two other Armada ships that had sunk near the town. Noble came to Killybegs to fish when he was sixteen and had been at it ever since. He understood what the other ships were liable to try because he was familiar with all the captains, their crews and their histories.

I noticed a couple of fellows slip on board who were very quiet and nondescript. Eventually I found out the reason for that. Their situation could be described by pointing your first two fingers down and wiggling them like running legs. They were from Northern Ireland and I won't bother mentioning their names because they were made up anyway. Our captain came from an old family in Sligo or Mayo and oddly enough sometimes made statements that seemed loyalist in nature.

Ronan, the last of the crew to board and the one that the others had spent nearly an hour waiting for and cursing, was our cook. He was a sullen kid of about fourteen, half asleep and obviously not happy to be there.

As we moved out toward open water, I commented that it was a fairly rough sea. Someone said, "We're still in the harbor. Wait 'til you feel the bay."

The sea came up as we worked our way out and so did the contents of my stomach, but I wasn't the only one. My method of tolerating sea-sickness is to not fight it. Many sailors just chalk, or chuck, it up to being part of the job. Whiting boiled in milk was the local cure if anyone wants to try it. Mickey swore by it. But then, he swore about everything anyway.

After a while I found out that we had gone out with another trawler. She was our sister ship, Loretto, another eighty-footer named after a sunken Spanish Armada vessel. Our two captains were hard-working, banged up, and experienced trawler men. They both had herniated abdomens. To deal with the hernias, they would sometimes lie down on the deck and tie themselves up with whatever kind of cloth rags they could find.

A few more miles into Donegal Bay the rollers coming in from the open ocean started to get bigger. Paddy Quigley said, "There now, she's feeling the bottom."

As the rollers enter shallower water, they turn into what are called ground swells. Until we moved beyond the shelf into deep water, we were meeting twenty to thirty foot swells. I think that is why when you ask a seaman landing on a pier how it is going he might answer, "Up and down."

After steaming out for five hours or so it was time to shoot our net. The night was black, rainy and unbelievably windy. The big nets that are used in commercial fishing are more complicated than one might think, with different sections for different purposes. The buoy attached to the end went off the stern first. It was followed by the cod end, the bag, the weighted mouth and then the big net with wings. The whole thing is pulled along by the warps or long ropes and cables with which the net was attached to the trawlers.

There are two main hazards when shooting a net. One is having your foot in the coils of a warp. When the net is going out the coil can suddenly tighten around the foot and drag an inexperienced or distracted fisherman overboard feet-first. The second hazard involves the Claddagh rings that almost all of us wore. We shot the nets without gloves and the crown of the ring can easily catch on the net resulting in a lost finger or being dragged into the water finger-first. I never saw or actually heard of anyone getting maimed or killed by a Claddagh ring, but more than once I came close to being a victim of the warp. I was saved by a shout of, "Tom, your foot!"

The Loretto pulled up alongside and we threw a warp and shackle to them. Both ships slowly spread out until they were about a mile from each other. For the next four hours, we trawled at low speed. The day was beginning to dawn and it was time for breakfast and a snooze.

We generally stayed out for three days and nights and the first meals were pretty good. Breakfast was sausage, rashers of bacon, black pudding, fried tomatoes and eggs. With the boat rolling around the only way to cook the eggs successfully was in "popeyes", eggs fried in a hole in bread. Ronan made the hole by taking a big bite out of the center of each slice and was again cursed by the crew for it. For lunch and dinner we had ham and cheese and occasionally a chicken. All the pots and pans had to be held onto the top of the stove by metal bars called fiddles.

The cookies, crisps and candy all rapidly disappeared and the disappearance was always blamed on Ronan. Mickey often said, "The wee cook is a jackass. The only thing missing is the big ears." Being a cook was a thankless job. By the last day we were often out of nearly everything so a few saltines found in the back corner of the pantry was considered a bonanza.

Down below the galley was the crew's cabin which had six bunks, three upper and three lower. They had high sides to keep you from rolling out in rough seas. After a while I could tell, when lying in my bunk, the size and direction of the seas by the movement of the boat and the sounds and speed of the engines. I always slept well on board. For me the twenty minute sleep grabbed in a bunk at sea was better than three or four hours in a bed. When it was time to get up, we had to be ready at a moment's notice so we slept in our clothes and had our sea boots ready to jump into. Our oilskins were hanging handily behind the galley door.

I will never forget the first morning that we pulled the net. Both boats were side by side, about fifty yards apart and the warp drums were rolling and pulling the net closer and closer. Then Loretto came up very close and one of her crew threw their warp over to us.

Both ships were in the swells. The Gerona was sometimes thirty feet above Loretto and sometimes we were that far below her.

The two trawlers often crashed into each other as they prepared to pull the net. Everyone was swearing and there were faces made between the two crews with much loud criticism of the captains. This was part of the routine and part of the fun. Once both ends of the net were onto the pulling gallows, we all hauled it in by hand from the stern with the help of the big hydraulic spool up on the gallows.

Next we turned to folding the hundreds of feet of net. My face and neck started burning and my eyes started watering and soon I couldn't see. Thinking it was the salt in the water, I yelled across to Paddy Quigley, "Man, this seawater really stings."

Paddy shouted in reply, "It's the jellies." The jellyfish had broken up in the wings of the net but even dead and in pieces they still had the ability to sting.

When we had the bag up alongside, we were surrounded by scores of screaming seagulls and cormorants diving deep into the water to pull fish from the bag which was nearly a hundred feet long. It was full of every kind of fish. The water was sparkling gold and silver from the herring scales that were floating up to the surface. Some of the crew started jumping up and down when they saw the evidence of the herring and yelled, "Big money in the bag".

Looking over the side I could see the net clearly twenty feet below the surface. The ship and the bag were doing a kind of dance in the sea.

While the skipper was trying to get a line around the cod end it was chaos, but we were finally able to pick it up with a crane. It looked like a gigantic ball, ten by ten and it was filled with fish. We hauled it up over the rail and above one of the ponds which were like corrals used to hold the fish until they could be sorted. Noble broke open the clasp with a mallet and down spilled herring, haddock, mackerel, hake, whiting, cod, ling and small sharks, dog fish, sole, plaice, squid, octopus and wee fish of other species that had been caught up in our bottom trawl.

The cod end was closed again with the clasp, and more fish were maneuvered into it from the bag by lifting it up with the crane. The refilled cod end was again positioned over a pond and dumped. The process was repeated until the bag of the net was empty and our deck was full of fish.

We wore heavy rubber gloves to sort the piles of flopping fish by kind. All of a single species were then gathered together and boxed. Four boxes made up a cran and after four to five hours, we had filled hundreds of boxes. Mackerel, because they were tough, could be boxed up and covered with ice in the hold after being unceremoniously shoveled through a pipe. Other species were delicate and required more care. These were lowered down into the hold in their boxes to be iced. The boxes were then stacked. The cod and the flat fish had to be gutted before being placed in the boxes and that attracted more bold screaming seagulls.

In the midst of the sorting we shot the net again following the same procedure, but this time it was the Loretto's turn. Generally, we alternated shooting the net, but often times we on Gerona had to shoot our net again because Loretto was a "Jonah" boat. She was unlucky. Her net often fouled on underwater rocks or stays and seemed to constantly be in need of repair. We would often curse her, her crew and her captain. Later I wished we hadn't because this Loretto would soon join her Armada namesake on the bottom. The captain and crew drowned the following spring when the Loretto sank while attempting to shelter behind a small island in a storm. Years before, near that same place, the captain's father had once tried to shelter and lost his ship, his crew and his life.

By the time we had the deck cleared of fish and hosed down it was time to haul again. This process continued day and night as long as we were at sea. The excitement of being on the wild ocean with the wind and waves and the prospect of taking a bumper haul kept us awake and fairly alert.

As Mickey had mentioned that night in the pub, we were a singing boat. We sang every kind of song from Elvis to Christy Moore. We did Irish songs, Motown and lots of country while we were sorting and stacking fish. There were endless jokes and stories as well. Sometimes when the weather was good and the Gerona was on the way back to Killybegs, riding on top of the deck house, I would light my pipe and think that it was nice to be a fisherman.

The Killybegs fleet sold their catch at the pier where the prices were governed by the law of supply and demand, and the fishing co-op. There was a lot of complaining that the co-op was in with the buyers and about corruption in the Wednesday and Friday evening fish auctions. The auctions were not loud affairs with shouting and loud bargaining. A tourist on the pier might not even notice that they were happening. Buyers would walk around inspecting and bidding, but the prices agreed on would not be known to the crew until Saturday when they were paid.

Most of the fish went to the big buyers, but, by custom boats would give away fish to locals who asked for them.

There was often a big letdown for the crew of Gerona after we arrived at the pier. The law of supply and demand dictated that if every boat had a hold full of fresh fish the prices went way down. On the other hand, if a boat was in early before the docks were teeming with the freshly caught fish, the price would go up. Because Noble never wanted to go in until the hold was full, while other trawlers would go in early with lighter loads trying to catch the best price, Gerona was often the last in and by that time the price was usually down. Noble would sometimes dig into his own pocket to give us enough to stay with him.

After Wednesday evening in the pub, we were ready to steam out at five a.m. on Thursday morning. We usually got in late on Fridays. Saturdays we worked a half day cleaning, painting and repairing nets and doing any other maintenance required on a trawler. Then we were paid and our time was our own.

Chapter 16
Tom Gawddommit

Sunday was the day off and Killybegs was beautiful. Not going to Mass was unusual in Ireland in those days, so Barbara and I would sort-of hide out in the caravan all morning. The town was always quiet until after Mass. Then everyone would be out swanning around the piers or strolling along the foot paths in the town and down by the sea. Barbara and I would join them. It was a cheerful scene, and everyone was in good humor in spite of the rumors that were always in the air of tragedy and death or impending new taxes and rules. All the pubs and restaurants did a brisk business, but our favorite place to go was Melley's Fish and Chips. It was a great gathering place and it seemed that everyone in town wandered in at some point during the day.

One of the Melley's regulars was a big older fellow with red hair turning white. He was from New York and his name was Danny. He came over to Ireland as a tourist after a stint in Korea on the advice of an aunt and liked it, so he just stayed and lived a quiet life in Killybegs. He had over stayed his visa by twenty-five years or more. Kids had been born, grown up and moved away in that time but Danny stayed put. Although he was a Yank and had no connections when he arrived, he came to play a big role in the town.

Danny was a fixer and knew who needed jobs and who wanted a job done. He would make the arrangements. Because he was over sixty-five and could use the bus for free he would run errands for fishermen that were too busy, and if a lady in town was too frail to get down to the pier, Danny would pick up fresh fish from off the trawlers and carry them up to her. Fishermen would come and talk to him when they were ready to marry. After their little talk, Danny would fix it with the jeweler in Donegal Town so that when the fellow brought his fiancé into the shop to buy the ring, the only rings on display would be the ones that the fisherman could afford.

He was not a citizen, but at the time the Irish government was not so strict about immigration. As long as foreigners didn't make nuisances of themselves, they could usually stay as long as they liked. But there was a catch. Danny never visited home because he was afraid they would not let him back into Ireland.

Another person who qualified as a regular at Melley's was Barbara. She spent long hours at the shop reading and visiting with Danny or whoever else came in. She seemed to get along with everybody. Danny and several others offered to help her find a job, but she seemed content with the way things were. I sometimes think that Barbara knew that Killybegs was just a stopping place in her life and did not want to create too many strong ties to the town.

Evenings on Donegal Bay were lovely, but at times the fog, clouds and wind made things confusing. One night two guys came out of a pub and one said, "Look at the moon."

The other said, "That's not the moon, it's the sun."

They were still arguing about it when a man passed by on a bicycle and they asked him which it was, the sun or the moon. He looked up and scratched his head and said, "I don't know, but then, I'm not from around here."

There was a Bulgarian factory ship that season anchored out in the bay. They were fishing within the twenty mile limit that Ireland was trying to win from the EEC. The official limit was three miles. The Bulgarian ship would come in sometimes and tie up at the pier. Although they bought fish from the Killybegs fleet, they were not appreciated by the locals. I was told that the Bulgarians had come in for a night at the Hotel Bar shortly before I arrived in town. It did not go well for the Bulgarian crew. Arguments erupted and fists flew and they barely made it back to their ship. As a large group they received no failte in Killybegs and from then on the poor old Bulgarians had to stay on board. I think that if one or two had disembarked they would have been welcomed as individuals, but leaving the ship alone or in small groups in the early eighties was probably not an option for them with the Iron Curtain and their government's fears of defection to the West. The poor old Bulgarians.

Because Killybegs was a busy harbor, stories of drownings were common. Often the fishermen drowned not at sea, but in the harbor. The trawlers were usually rafted up three or four deep along the pier. Jumping and climbing between the boats in bad weather when they were rafted up like that was dangerous, and fishermen returning late after a night in the pub would sometimes fall between them especially if they were under the weather themselves. Many didn't swim or they hit their heads or they became entangled in lines. The outcome usually wasn't pretty. I was told that dozens had died falling between boats in the last few years.

One Saturday night Sean McGuire, the mighty fiddler, who was one of my favorites, was playing at a hall up the side of the mountain. I was in the pub and assumed that I would go, because I never missed a chance to hear good Irish music. However, as the night worn on the time to hear him came and went. It eventually dawned on me that I had missed the concert and I took it as a sign that the spell that Irish music had me under was finally being broken. I have kicked myself ever since. I figured I would have another chance to hear him play, but I never did.

One morning at dawn we were pulling our net about three miles off the Stags, a rock formation off the coast of Mayo in a squall. We were standing in the stern of the boat fresh out of our bunks and barely awake. I was apparently looking out of sorts and Mickey said, "Aye shoorly, Tom, you know we are all here because we love this life and this is where we really want to be."

I was pondering these words when the boat took a dirty roll and a huge sea came down, soaking us and knocking us all into the scuppers in a heap. I jumped up and hollered, “Yes! This is the life. This is great!”

I was suddenly cured of my melancholy and for the next few hours I was all smiles while the rest of the crew looked gloomy and resigned as they went about their work.

On the summer Solstice, we steamed out of the harbor past St. John’s Point. The Baal fires were just being lit all up and down the coast of Donegal. We could see the huge bonfires along the coast of Sligo and Mayo far to the south as well. They were called Baal fires after the old god, but were also known as St. John’s Eve fires. They made a beautiful sight whatever you wanted to call them.

About this time I was asked to stand my watch at the wheel and was left alone in the pilot house while the captain and the rest of the crew slept the half sleep of trawlermen. After being shown the radar and the radio and being given a rudimentary introduction to the autopilot, I was told to keep her between two blips on the radar screen as we steamed out into the North Atlantic. A slight twist of the dial on the autopilot would keep us centered between the blips which represented trawlers on either side. As we moved farther west away from Ireland the seas rose and the rain, wind and spray blocked all vision from the pilot house windows. Time passed and I noticed that there were ten or twelve blips on the radar screen. We were all in a line abreast of each other and all headed out to the fishing grounds thirty or forty miles off shore. When the weather improved, I could see the running lights of the Killybegs fleet, the biggest in Ireland, spread out to the port and starboard of the Gerona.

I pretended to myself that taking my watch was no big deal and just hoped that nothing would go wrong. I had no idea what to do if a problem occurred. I didn’t even know how to recognize if there was a problem. After four hours of pretending that I knew what I was doing, the captain rose and told me to wake the crew. He said that we would be shooting the net in half an hour.

The days and nights were spent shooting and pulling the net and sorting tens of thousands of fish with stinking rubber gloves. I would sometimes have two, three, or even four fish between the fingers of each hand which I would throw into the boxes. The seagulls screamed and tried to snatch as many fish as they could. The trawler was always moving with the sea and keeping your balance was of prime importance. I was pretty banged up but I got better at not slipping and falling after a while. My two thumbnails that had turned black and fallen off when I was in Louisiana had started to grow back. I thought that I might lose them again, this time to commercial fishing, but I never did. The places where the nail hadn't grown back yet didn't sting, and I think maybe the salt water was good for them.

One day we were pulling our net and were having trouble getting a line on the cod end. The captain told me to get on the winch that was attached to the crane. I ran to the winch, but since I had never operated it before, I pulled the lever the wrong way. The captain who was leaning over the rail, called me something unrepeatable and suddenly I was running across the deck apparently with the intention of picking him up by the legs and tipping him over the side. Fortunately, Mickey knew what was going through my mind better than I did. He guessed my intentions and tripped me, saving me from what would have been a pretty big mistake. Sometimes when everyone is excited things are said and done that really don't mean much. Noble Morrow was a good captain and as an expert diver, he never hesitated to jump into the sea himself to cut away nets or lines that had fouled our propellers.

After we iced and stacked the boxes of fish in the hold, we would hose down the deck. In heavy seas, the boxes would sometimes work themselves free and we would have to climb down to repack and restack them, bracing them with boards. One day I was the last guy down in the hold after a cleanup. Suddenly, through the open hatch a flood of water, fish scales, fish blood and fish guts poured down on my bare head. I roared, "God damn it, turn off the hose!" The hose was shut off and there was silence from above.

A few days later, I was walking down in the town when a kid going by called out, "Tom Gawddommit, how are ye doin?"

In the Melley's shop the girl behind the counter said, "Tom Gawddommit, what will ye have?"

I realized that my kind of cursing wasn't the kind that they were used to. The Irish used a lot of words that in America would be way out of line, but what I said in that fish hold was a shock to them. So, once I figured out what was going on I told them, "It's not Gawddommit. It's Goddammit, damn it." The nickname stuck. Gawddommit!

One afternoon on Gerona, out in the bay, we were singing our usual assortment of Irish songs, rock and roll and country favorites when Mickey said, "There's a singing contest in a few weeks at the hall. Maybe we should enter, just for the craic."

The rest of the crew wasn't too thrilled about the idea of singing in public. Then Mickey sang a song that I hadn't heard before. It was a local song about a trawler sinking in Donegal Bay in 1937 called "Donegal Danny." We didn't harmonize when we sang that one. We just sang in unison. We sang as loud as we could because the engines were always running and the seagulls were always screeching and the wind and the waves were always sounding. Later I heard versions of that song with banjos, guitars, harmonies and a stomping beat, but I always like the song sung straight out.

On a Wednesday evening in midsummer as we were unloading the catch, a bus load of tourists visited the pier. They were taking pictures of the Gerona and us, the Donegal fishermen. I said, "Watch this, boys."

I jumped off, strode over to the tourists, and boomed, "How're ya'll doin? Are ya'll from America?"

They looked confused and a little shocked. I said, "Its sure good to see some of my fellow countrymen!"

One of them asked, "Where are you from?"

"Well...... I'm from Texas!" Thus was Texas Tom born. I don't know what got into me at that moment, but I was full of "hot diggity ding-dongs" and "well Sani-flushes" and all the funny talk I had heard in Louisiana from Joe and the Texans and all the oilfield gang.

The tourists looked like they wanted to tear their film out of their cameras, but we all had a good laugh. Texas Tom has returned from time to time to haunt me, but it only happens to me in Ireland, never in America. I have come to believe that there is a little Texan lurking in each of us just waiting for the right time to appear.

We never did sing "Donegal Danny" in the town hall, but we had a good season of fishing. None of us became rich, but we got the job done. "And that's good too," as old John Curtin in St. Paul used to say. When the take was divided, each crew member received half a share, the boat earned three shares, the engineer one share and the captain, I think, two. Mickey was thinking of moving to a bigger boat that would be able to fish out farther, stay out longer and, hopefully, make more money. He asked me if I wanted to be the new engineer for Gerona. He figured that because I was a Yank, I would know all about the Cats.

Caterpillar engines are indeed made in Indiana, USA, but I told him that doesn't mean that Americans know everything there is to know about them. I did not want to be in charge of keeping those engines running in the dangerous, rocky waters of the west of Ireland and to be the one to blame if we were all killed. I felt bad to say no, but was hoping to make it through life without causing any deaths.

The season wound down and winter was coming in early. Already, in September people were talking about Christmas.

Barbara and I hadn't been seeing much of each other the past year with all the crazy hours in the oilfield and on the trawler. We went for an evening walk along the lanes near the sea and started talking about St. Paul. Just as the topic of going home came up, a meteor lit up the sky over the bay and split into three parts. We decided to leave the next day.

On that Monday morning, we boarded a bus going to Sligo Town. From Sligo Town we went to Galway and then on to Shannon where we caught a flight to Chicago. On the first leg of the bus journey there wasn't an empty seat so I stood for the entire trip. I noticed that I didn't need to hold on to anything. My balance was better after my stint as a fisherman, at least for a while.

From the airport in Chicago we went straight to Barbara's brother house where I scanned the want ads in the morning's newspaper and found an old beater of a car for a hundred dollars. Paige drove us over to where the car was and we bought it on the spot. Paige went home and Barbara and I jumped in our "new" set of wheels and roared off towards St. Paul. There had been no stopover in Chicago. I was always in a hurry back then. We drove as far as Janesville, Wisconsin before we pulled over for a snooze.

Chapter 17

The Poor Old Dog Was Drowned

While we were driving to Minnesota, Barbara and I talked about not wanting to perform again. We wanted to live where we were sure no one would notice us. I always thought of St. Paul as a sort of rabbit warren. There were always people that I knew popping out of doorways and coming around corners. So when we arrived in the Cities, we crossed over the Mississippi to Minneapolis.

St. Paul actually borders Minneapolis, and the two cities are often called the Twin Cities, but they are many miles apart as far as the natives of St. Paul are concerned. Vice president Hubert Humphrey from Waverly, Minnesota, when asked about the difference between Minneapolis and St. Paul, is often misquoted by St. Paulites as having said that Minneapolis without St. Paul was just a cold Omaha. Minneapolis is the bigger of the two cities and is better known to the national press. It is more cosmopolitan and filled with people, often Lutherans, who were not born there. St. Paul is the state capital as a result of political shenanigans in the 1850s, and more parochial with large, often Catholic families that have lived there for generations.

We parked the car on Hennepin Avenue and found ourselves in front of the Green Mill restaurant. I was surprised to see a Green Mill in Minneapolis. The original had been a 3.2 beer joint on Hamline and Grand in St. Paul. Reminiscing, I told Barbara that when I was a sophomore in high school at Cretin, a Catholic military school, some of my cronies and I would occasionally go into the little joint. We would sit in a corner booth and order pitchers of beer and smoke in spite of our ages. The professors from the school would stop in there as well, to sit at the bar and drink. We saw them and they saw us, but no one said a thing. As long as we all stayed quiet and behaved, both teachers and students, everyone was happy. I thought that this arrangement was very civilized.

We felt out of place standing there and probably looked a little lost. A car honked at us and we ignored it because we were incognito and unrecognized. The honking continued and eventually the window rolled down and Peggy Flanagan, the sometimes fiddler who worked at O'Gara's stuck her head out and called, "What are you two doing here?"

Peggy Flanagan

We thought quickly and responded, "We're looking for an apartment."

"Where are you staying tonight?" she asked.

We admitted that we didn't know and she offered, "Jump in. You can stay with me."

Within minutes our stint in Minneapolis was over and we were back in St. Paul. We stayed with Peggy until we found a funky old duplex around the corner from O'Gara's. Barbara started working at a restaurant down the street. I went down to the Mississippi river front checking out the barge towing outfits.

I hired on with Capital Barge and worked as a deck hand. The Mississippi River separates St. Paul from Minneapolis and the water flows south through five more states, the last being Louisiana where it enters the Gulf of Mexico. From there the Gulf Stream current takes it around Florida, up to somewhere around North Carolina and then sends the warmed water across the Atlantic to brush the West Coast of Ireland. I thought about how my work outside of music seemed to be connected with the Gulf Stream. I'd worked off shore in Louisiana, on the fishing grounds off the coast of Ireland and now was back near the source of it all on the Upper Mississippi. I liked the work, but the season was ending. Soon the barge traffic would cease for the winter and the river would freeze over.

I stopped in around the corner at O'Gara's and started talking to Kenny Murray, the wiry veteran bartender who had been working there forever. I told him that I was looking for work.

Kenny said, "You should try the wonderful world of bartending. Talk to Timmy."

O'Gara's is an institution in St. Paul. Jim O'Gara had worked at Dahill's Bar and Restaurant, my great uncle's place, back in the thirties. In 1941 he opened his own little bar on the corner of Selby and Snelling. It became the main watering hole for the Irish in town and is still well-loved by the locals. Tim O'Gara was Jim's son and was now running the bar. I asked him if he would try me out as a bartender and was surprised when he hired me right away. The next evening I was togged out in a white shirt, black pants, a tie and a white apron. I was put under the tutelage of Mr. Kenny Murray and although he was a thin, little snappy fellow and I was six foot two, and a big lug, he referred to me as "You little puppy."

Kenny had a quick wit and moved like a dancer behind the bar. His regulars, who sat along the bar tended to order the same drinks like Windsor and Coke, Hennessey's and tap beer. When someone ordered a whiskey and water, Kenny would say, "A hoo-hoo and Oahu, yes sir."

When I poured my first measured shot for a customer, Kenny said, "No, no, you little puppy, this is how it's done."

He held the shot glass an inch above the highball glass and started pouring the whiskey and whistling, "Ring Around the Rosie", letting the whiskey overflow into the highball glass. He would whistle the phrase twice as his eyes looked first to one side of the room and then to the other. Then he would add a quick splash of water saying, "There you are miss" or "sir." Kenny was very popular.

The staff at O'Gara's had all been there for many years. When you were hired at O'Gara's, it was usually a lifetime position. I assumed that I had found my station in life too. My birthday was in September and I was now thirty years old.

Martin McHugh, the box driver, was a daily communicant at O'Gara's. We were old friends by this time and always had a good laugh when I was working behind the bar. We liked to use whatever Gaelic we knew and have conversations that only we could understand. Marty would say, if anyone inquired, "There are many dialects of Gaelic, the Connemara Gaelic, the Donegal Gaelic, the Kerry Gaelic and our own dialect, the Gibberish Gaelic."

Dowdling is a kind of Irish mouth music used to lilt tunes. Marty would dowdle tunes that he thought I should have, like "The Bird in the Bush" or "Christmas Eve" and I would dowdle along with him. I learned quite a few tunes from Marty that way while I was working.

Not long after I started bartending, Josh Dunson, a friend who was a folk music promoter and agent from Chicago, called and asked if we would go on a tour of Australia with Joe Heaney the sean nós singer from Carna. I agreed without thinking. I think I actually meant to say no because I had been trying to quit the music business. Josh set up the tour making all the arrangements, and then I changed my mind. Joe was a friend and a great hero of mine. He had recently stopped drinking and I was afraid that if we were on tour with him, he might drink again. I might also have been afraid that I wouldn't be able to drink the way I was used to. Living next door to and working at a bar had a cumulative effect and it was starting to take its toll. A funny thing about working at O'Gara's was that although you weren't supposed to drink on the job, you could take a pint glass, fill it with ice and keep it topped up with gin or vodka and drink it like water. It was okay as long as you didn't look or act like you were drinking.

Jack Fallon, another old friend of mine walked into O'Gara's one afternoon and was surprised and dismayed to see me working behind the bar. Jack, besides being a pilot, teacher and all around good guy, was the founder and president of our local branch of Comhaltas Ceoltoiri Eireann, the Irish music association. I found out that day that he had another talent that I didn't know about. He started drawing humorous but pointed cartoons that all harped on the idea that it was a disgrace for someone who could sing and play Irish music to be bartending. He wouldn't let up and at about ten that night, after four or five hours of his lampooning and badgering, I threw off the tie and apron in disgust and walked off the job heading for the West Bank, the old hippy district.

Over the past year Ray MacCafferty and the Curtins had been busy setting up the first Minnesota Irish Fest. It was to be held at the St. Paul Auditorium and Barbara and I had agreed to play it before I walked off the job. We didn't really want to because we hadn't played as a duo since the early seventies, but our picture was already on the poster. We managed to perform and it turned out to be a very good festival indeed. Cuz Teahan and his Screaming Banshees rocked the hall as did other local and out of town musicians.

Barbara and I knew our marriage was ending and as soon as the festival was over, I jumped into another hundred dollar car that I had bought a week before from a guy that I had worked with on the river. He said he would bring the paperwork for the sale later. He never did. He told me that he had lost the key but a screwdriver worked just fine. I started her up and drove to St. Louis. On the way down I remember being pulled out of the ditch a few times by farmers. I don't remember going in. I kept thinking, "I've got to go to where the music is."

I had met a bar owner, Nick Carter in Washington, D. C. a few years before and he had told me to stop in if I was ever in St. Louis. Since I was now in St. Louis, even if I was not in the best of shape, I headed for McGurk's at Twelfth and Russell in the Soulard District, an old Hoosier neighborhood just starting out on the path to gentrification. When I walked in the door, a Dayhills' recording was playing on the house speakers.

John D. McGurk's is named after the crewman who was scared stiff of work, made famous in the song "The Irish Rover". The pub was the brain child of Nick Carter and his business partner Jim Halloran. When it started out, it was a little corner bar at the bottom of a hill but it had expanded over the years taking over the small brick shops, one by one, on the way up the hill. Eventually the bar was half a block long and included a restaurant. From the top, you can look down through the telescoping rooms to the stage. The original stage, which hasn't moved, is located against the wall at the Twelfth Street end and sitting on the stage looking up through the rooms you can see everything. Up the street, separated from the last building of McGurk's by a little walkway, was a place called The Palace, rumored to be former slave quarters, where they now put up the travelling Irish musicians. When I arrived that fall night, it was still the early days of McGurk's and there were only two rooms open.

Micheal Cooney, Joe Burke, Richard Lavin, "the Old Master"

Nick Carter had great taste in traditional music. He loved to talk about and listen to Irish music more than anyone I ever knew and he put his money where his mouth and his ears were. Mick Wallace and the Irish Brigade were the first to play on the stage when McGurk's opened. Dan Devery, the box player from Offaly, Tommy McEvoy and the inimitable box driver, Larry McNally from Wexford already lived in St. Louis and played at McGurk's often.

Nick also brought more of his favorite musicians over from Ireland. A roster of musicians that played McGurk's and stayed at The Palace for a month at a time playing five or six night a week would look something like this: Joe Burke/Ann Conroy, Andy McGann, Michael Cooney, Paddy O'Brien of Offaly, Daithi Sproule, James Kelly, Andy O'Brien, Martin Hayes, Sean O'Driscoll, James Keane, Tony McMahon, Jimmy Crowley, Jerry O'Sullivan, Kevin Burke, Jackie Daley, and Micho Russell. Those are just some of the musicians that I heard there. Their pictures hung on the walls for decades. Most Irish musicians of the era would agree that John D. McGurk's pub was the greatest Irish music venue in America during those years.

It was Nick that introduced me to Danny Devery. He had a lovely wife, Ellen, and a family out in St. Ann's Parish on the west side of St. Louis. Dan played the button accordion, but told me that what he really loved to play was the concertina. Danny worked in construction and had massive arms. I would hate to be the concertina that landed in his hands. He loved to play and would practice every night in the little house in the Parish 'til all hours. His stomping foot would shake the whole house and he often growled and groaned when he played. His kids were teenagers at the time and they would turn up the T. V. full blast and sometimes the radio too, to drown him out. I know because I would stay there for weeks at a time.

We played gigs together for a year or more and put on some hard miles. Danny had a very active imagination and expressed his ideas and opinions to me with his elbow. I was black and blue on my arms and ribs because he was always jabbing me saying, "Ya know what I mean, Tommy?" Jab, jab. "Ya know what I mean?"

Danny was a dedicated musician and had played for many years with the man he called "The Old Master", Richard Lavin, who was a fiddler from the Sligo/Mayo border area. Many former residents of County Clare lived in St. Ann's Parish and Dan and The Old Master played all the Irish dances.

Richard Lavin's son, Kevin, owned a pub called The Shamrock where Danny and I liked to go. The cellar of the pub always had several feet of water in it and I don't know why. Kevin Lavin had been a boxer, so many of his clientele were boxers or former boxers. It was at The Shamrock on December 8th, 1980 when I heard on the television that John Lennon had been killed. I put my head down on the bar and cried. A lot of people took naps in that place, so it wasn't unusual to see someone with his head on his arms. When I stood up to leave a few hours later, there was a puddle of tears on the bar.

The Shamrock was about three miles from Danny's house. I used to walk over there most afternoons. Along the way there was another bar that was at more or less the halfway point where I would stop. One of the first times I was there, I heard a song playing on the jukebox that had been haunting me on the trawler in Donegal although I didn't know the title or the lyrics. It was just the melody that was going through my head. I walked over to the jukebox to see what it was. It turned out to be "The Rose Colored Glasses" by John Conlee. I played it again and from then on, every time I walked in I went straight to the jukebox and played that song. I had an idea that it would sound good on the button accordion. I dropped in on a regular basis for several weeks until one day as I entered I heard the bartender say to the waitress, "Here comes Rose Colored Glasses." I don't know if he meant me or the song, but I turned on my heel and left never to return. It does sound good on the button box and I still sing it once in a while.

Danny had a great way with words. When we played gigs together at McGurk's, The Glenshesk in Chicago, in St. Paul or in Kansas City, I would lean into the microphone and say, "Well, Dan. What do you think we should play next?"

Danny would turn toward me as if we were having a conversation and, keeping his mouth near his own mic, say something like, "Well, Tommy. We have a lovely little bird in Ireland that will stand on one leg in a field ..... and then hop over onto the other leg! And then she will fly straight up into the air. Up, up, up 'til you can't hardly see her. Then, if you listen close .... you will hear the most beautiful sound of sweet music coming from her as she flips and flops and soars and tumbles all the way down, singing all the way ..... until she lands. Then she might do it again. We call her the lark, Tommy."

"Should we play "The Lark in the Morning" for them, Danny?"

"I think we should."

"All right, Danny. Here she is, ladies and gentlemen, the Lark in the Morning."

Sometimes I would say to Danny, "I'm going to sing 'The Lambs on the Green Hills.' Don't play along 'til I get past the first verse. Okay?"

"Okay, Tommy. Okay."

I would start singing and after a couple of lines I would hear Danny starting to play. And, after the first few notes from his box, I would hear his low growl. The growling would get louder and louder until I gave him a kick in the shin and then Danny would say, "Oh, sorry, Tom, sorry." Danny was kind of rough and he understood the need to be kicked occasionally.

One night in his kitchen we were playing and drinking poteen when I received a phone call from Barbara, at about three in the morning. We were chatting away when Danny started playing and trying to talk to me. I said, "Fuck off, Dan, I'm on the phone" and continued speaking with Barbara.

The next thing I noticed was the barrel of a shotgun pointed into my belly. I was still on the phone and I commented, "That's a nice gun Danny. Is it a twelve gauge or a twenty?"

Danny said, "It's a twelve. Don't ever tell me to fuck off in my own house again."

"Okay, Dan. No problem," I answered.

Danny and I were good friends. He liked to call us "The Bog Men." Before a gig he used to say, "We'll start cutting the turf at the low bank, Tommy, working toward the high bank, just like in the bog."

Devery and other older players had an honest and direct style of playing that had a power that more refined styles of playing somehow lacked. Pat Cloonan in Chicago called it "Nature". Cloonan, himself a box player from Connemara, had plenty of "Nature" in his music. It was the kind of "Nature" that went beyond nature.

Danny Devery

Danny liked to say we were missionaries bringing the "Real Irish Music" to people who needed to hear it. There were usually a few in the crowd, who, though they had never heard the music before, would prick up their ears. We were just playing the good old meat and potatoes kind of tunes but we would see a look of amazement in their eyes.

We set up at a bar in Alton, Illinois, one night and were just starting a set when I noticed a pinball machine being played in the room. I asked the bartender to turn it off and he replied, "We make money off the pinball machine."

I had never played in a bar where a T. V. or a pinball machine was on. It just wasn't done back then, so I said, "Well, we're done here."

I started packing up and told Danny we were leaving. Later, as we drove along he said, "Tommy, I have car payments to make."

I apologized, but told him that I just wouldn't play when the machines were going. We did find plenty of places to play, but we had to travel quite a bit.

I had parked the beater that I had driven down from St. Paul on the street near Dan's house. I had noticed when I passed by that the parking tickets were piling up on the windshield. Then, one day, the car disappeared. I guess because it had Minnesota plates, a popped ignition, and a screwdriver for a key, the Missouri cops decided it had been stolen and abandoned. When I thought about it, I realized that they were probably right.

Nick Carter at McGurk's was very good to me. One day he decided that I looked down in the dumps so he gave me a wad of bills and said, "There's a Corvette parked outside, Tommy. Here are the keys. Why don't you run down to the Ozarks and have a good time?"

So, I took off to the Ozarks for a few days. I don't remember much about that trip except that I was very careful not to smash up that beautiful car and that I met Mark Dinning who was singing in a little roadside bar. He'd had a hit with the song "Teen Angel" years before and he still had a beautiful voice. He was friendly and we had an interesting talk about music and the music business.

Around St. Patrick's Day that year, Danny and I drove to Kansas City to play a couple of weekend gigs at the Grand Saloon. We had a good time playing for the big Irish-American crowds that showed up. As we were leaving the bar at the end of the second Saturday night, shaking hands and saying good bye to everyone, the owner's brother, a big guy who liked to pick fights, casually muttered to Danny, "Goodnight, asshole."

I was already outside the door on the sidewalk when Danny grabbed me and repeated the big guy's comment. He said, "I'm going back in to take care of him."

I wanted to stop Danny from going back in so I pulled a knife out of my pocket.

"I'll take care of him, Danny."

"No, no. Tommy. Don't do that."

So, I let him talk me out of it and we left in peace.

I felt bad that Dan had to work his job. He was a Union pipefitter and when he wasn't laid off he had to be up early even if we had been out playing most of the night. Danny told me not to worry. He said that at the building sites he was looked after. "They'll just throw a piece of plywood over me when I snooze and wake me if a foreman shows up."

Kansas City was and probably still is a rocking, fun-loving town. It was an early jumping off place for the Wild West as the Santa Fe and Oregon Trails both originated at Westport a few miles from downtown. It is on the Missouri River so it has been a center of trade and entertainment for nearly two hundred years.

I gravitated more and more to Kansas City because it reminded me of St. Paul. I liked the fine old commercial buildings, mansions, beautiful neighborhoods with stone fountains, parks and boulevards. There were big Irish parishes there and families that enjoyed each other and liked to meet for Irish music and dancing. In the summertime on Sundays there was a big gathering of Irish families at a certain park where the Carneys, Quinns, Glynns, Bells and Cullinanes used to congregate. Although my friend Larry McNally from Wexford often said, "You can't have Ireland over here," you can have a great time over here with Irish-Americans.

I would stay with the Foolkillers, Bob and Diane. I could always stay there for free and as long as I wanted. Their neighborhood was a little rough, but I kind of liked it.

The main traditional musicians in Kansas City had come from Shanagolden, County Limerick. They were Tom Shine who played the fiddle, his sister Kitty Shine with her concertina and the two McAuliffe brothers who were also fiddlers. They were older and not playing out anymore when I met them, but I was given a tape of their music that came from a few old recordings made at a train station in the forties at a coin operated recording booth. On the recordings they played polkas and waltzes with old-fashioned style and plenty of Nature.

There was an active Irish Northern Aid branch in Kansas City as well as the Ancient Order of Hibernians, and the Hibernians Ladies Auxiliary. Each group sponsored concerts and ceilis and there was always something happening throughout the seventies and eighties. Such events were going on all over America and "Freedom for Ireland" was the byword.

Most people who were interested in Irish culture believed that the answer to Ireland's problems was to somehow force the British Army out of the North. I even knew some English-born people who believed the same thing.

Rebel songs were popular and frequently requested, and Irish literature and books on Irish History were discussed and passed around. The Irish nationalism that was in the air in the pubs and concert halls was popular with some and bothered others.

In Westport, which over the years had been consumed by Kansas City and had become one of the city's entertainment districts, I played at a place called Harling's Upstairs. In a previous incarnation in had been the Falcon Club, a drinking and card playing establishment dating back to Prohibition days.

Jerry Wyatt was now the proprietor and he gave me a chance to play solo. I had never been up on stage alone before and wasn't sure I could perform by myself, but I had a lot of encouragement from Casey from K. C., who was a great friend of mine back then. When I tried it, what really surprised me is that when a single fiddle strikes up a tune, a crowd will respond in a completely different way than when there is backup. As long as the rhythm is there, a solo fiddle has a certain power that brings out a sympathetic response from a crowd even if the player is only just competent. Jerry Wyatt was happy with the large numbers that came out to the bar.

Tommy Wyrsh was the head bartender at Harling's. He had recently lost his own pub. It had been near the University and several small private colleges. When he bought the place, it was called The Pizza Pub and had a large sign with that name over the door. Tommy took the P and the B off the sign and called his place Pizza U and added the slogan underneath "An Educational Experience." It was definitely the craziest pizza pub I had ever been in. There was live music, activities and goings on too diverse and sometimes perverse to mention. I don't think that Tommy kept any books at all and that was why he was now managing Harling's and Pizza U was but a fond memory.

As in St. Paul, in Kansas City we all seemed to be connected in one way or another and sometimes in more than one way. Tommy Wyrsh was a case in point. I'd known him since The Dayhills played Kansas City for the first time. He was one of the boys who came up with fighting as a substitute for dancing and we'd become friends over the years. Tommy was an O'Connor on his mother's side and his uncle was the banker whose car had fallen victim to the falling Foolkiller.

Chapter 18
Just Call Me Cushy

I was tired of travelling and playing music so many nights a week and I got the idea in my head of moving to the North Woods. The previous year I had been up to Webb Lake, Wisconsin, with John Logan, the chef from MacCafferty's. That trip happened just after Christmas when John Logan had to bring some Irish stew up to The Lumberjack Saloon for "Shorty's" birthday party. John asked if I would like to ride along and I said, "Certainly." We hit the road with two big steaming cauldrons of stew in the back seat and stopped at every municipal bar along the way so the trip took a bit longer that it should have.

John, portly and confident, looked like an oversized version of one of those porcelain chef statues right down to the big black mustache and checked pants and he drove a big white Cadillac. He was in a great mood, but even so his conversation was littered with ef-f-f-bombs. We were telling stories and I reminded him of the time he filled in for Andy Vaughan behind the bar. One of the customers, who had been overserved, was trying to tell a joke. The guy kept stumbling over his words, repeating himself and starting over. John appeared to be an attentive listener. After about ten minutes with little forward momentum in the joke, the customer stopped and belatedly asked, "Have you heard this one?"

John responded, "Not so far."

We arrived safely, if not soundly, at around ten o'clock that evening. The Lumberjack Saloon sat on a hill facing Little Bear Lake and had been there since the thirties. The building had big windows overlooking the lake and was built of logs, as were several cabins and a big bunkhouse on the property. We entered the bar where the party was in full swing. Shorty was indeed having a birthday but did not seem like the type to arrange a big blowout for himself. The owner, Gary Jeffson, a man born to the trade although he hadn't entered it until his early retirement from 3M in St. Paul, wanted to honor the quiet regular and had arranged to have the stew delivered. Many of The Lumberjack's regulars were fellow 3M retirees. There were also plenty of locals who were sometimes called "Jack Pine Savages." It seemed like everyone in the place was fairly stewed already with all of the singing and dancing. Some were throwing dice which was also a popular pastime. They had a game called "Shake a Day" that earned the winner a free drink.

We were told that we could stay in the bunkhouse along with the Rae brothers who were from Newry, County Down. The brothers had been playing MacCafferty's and were at the Lumberjack, along with their entourage, for a little R and R. I ended up staying for a couple of days and had been thinking about returning ever since.

It was at Harling's Upstairs in Kansas City one night that I figured out, on a bar napkin which was indecipherable the next day, how to make my dream become a reality. Carefully following the plan, I found a hundred dollar Ford pickup truck, added a camper for another fifty dollars and headed north until I arrived in the parking lot of The Lumberjack Saloon. That was pretty much the extent of my plan.

That parking lot became my home for the next four months. Casey from K. C. came along for the ride and more or less ended up staying and sharing in the adventures for the next couple of years. I would busk in the bar and played a few gigs in some of the other backwoods places like Eddie Perry's Booze and Canoes, The Cabaret, a big dance hall built of logs, The McKenzie Castle and a place called What The Heck, owned by the Hecks.

I made friends with a couple named Clint and Kathy Muller who owned ten acres in the woods nearby. They encouraged me to get some land because, even though it was summertime, winter would inevitably arrive making parking lot living impractical.

Land was cheap and could be gotten on a Wisconsin State Land Contract, which allowed a first time buyer with a down payment to secure a guaranteed five year loan to buy an undeveloped wooded lot. I still had the Paolo Soprani B/C button accordion that I'd picked up in Chicago in the seventies. I called Chuck Heymann and asked if he wanted it. He sent me seven hundred dollars which became the down payment on ten wooded acres just down the road from the Mullers.

I had "found" an old chainsaw in the back room of Harling's which I liberated and used to cut down a few trees to get the truck off the road and then pitched a tent. There are bumper stickers put out by the State Tourist Board that read "Escape To Wisconsin" and that is what I had done. I held on to the land for the next fifteen years and it became my home base.

I also held on to the chainsaw for a while until I eventually found the rightful owner and returned it. Big John Carney from Ennis came out of the back room at Harling's one night when I was on stage playing. He pointed at me and bellowed, "You stole my chainsaw!"

I said, "Oh, was that your chainsaw?"

"No. But I was going to steal it."

A year or two later I sent it out to Colorado where Wyatt's original partner, Billy Harling, had moved. He had left the saw in the backroom of Harling's Upstairs for safe keeping.

My land was eighteen miles northwest of Spooner. Where the hell is Spooner? That's the question that was emblazoned on the t-shirts that were sold in town. The lot was bordered by McKenzie Lake Road and Section 1 Road, both unpaved. The land in this part of Wisconsin was rolling and the soil was sand with only a few inches of topsoil. It was dotted with lakes and crisscrossed with little streams. The Namekagon River which flows into the St. Croix was just a few miles away.

I was over the moon. The land was covered with jack pine, red pine, white pine, birch, popple, oak and maple. There were ferns, blueberry bushes, wintergreen and lady slippers spread underneath the trees. There was no artificial light or facilities because there was no electricity or running water. There was no electricity or running water because there was no house. Casey and I cut an access road in from the McKenzie Road side of the property and made a clearing, saving the logs and burning the brush. Then we took the camper off the back of the pick-up and propped it up on camper jacks that I had borrowed from Clint.

Clint suggested that it might be a good idea to build a cabin and told me what I would need in the way of lumber and other materials. I ordered the lumber from a place in town and it was delivered and piled in the clearing. After the lumber arrived, I set about getting the rest of the materials. I headed to the dump.

I eventually became well versed in dump etiquette and procedures. To be granted the right to scavenge you would first find some junk to take to the dump and buy two six-packs of beer. You then went to the dump, got rid of the junk and handed one six-pack over to the man in charge keeping the other for yourself. Next you asked him if it was okay to pull over and park for a while. The man at the dump always had a pile off to the side of some of the better things that had been tossed out and there was usually some good stuff. Occasionally when one of the people who had retired up there passed away the heirs would take the entire contents of cabin to the dump. In consideration of the six-pack you were allowed to scavenge through this pile or, if you wanted to, go into the landfill and pull out anything that caught your fancy. I found many useful things at the dump over the years including two boats and a canoe which I hid on a couple of nearby lakes.

That first time at the dump, I managed to find some windows and a door which I brought home and added to the pile in the clearing. That was as much as I accomplished until the arrival of winter was imminent.

Just before the snowballs started to fly, Clint came over and the three of us, with a little help from any neighbor who stopped by, built a small cabin in a couple of days. Casey and I used candles and kerosene lanterns for light and a Coleman camp stove for cooking but the days were getting colder and we had no heat. Although a twelve by twelve cabin doesn't need much to heat it, we needed something to keep from freezing. A friend of mine from high school, Kevin Ashe, was staying at his sister's place nearby and he visited us a few times. One day he stopped over with an old milk can and an idea.

We made a "hearth" out of bricks spread out in one corner of the cabin. Kevin lay the milk can on its side on top of the bricks and cut a hole to which he attached a stove pipe and damper. He ran the stove pipe up through the roof with a flange that I had happened to find in the back room of Harling's. We removed the cap from the milk can, drilled some holes, and then attached a metal plate to it with a bolt so that it could swing to cover or uncover the holes. We replaced the cap, securing it with a chain that was looped through the handle of the milk can and used it to control the amount of air entering the stove. Then we poured sand into the can to keep the fire from burning through the bottom. The milk can stove was complete and the only problem with it was that it had a tendency to turn bright red in the middle of the night and start huffing like a living creature. I mostly burned wood in the stove but later I sometimes burned peat that I had cut out of bogs nearby. It smelled the same as Irish turf and that was nice to have in Northern Wisconsin.

A good chain saw is an indispensable tool for a jack pine savage. I bought a new Stihl chain saw and used it nearly every day that winter to get firewood since I hadn't stockpiled much in the fall. The chain saw started to feel like a new appendage. In addition to cutting firewood I used it to increase the size of the cabin clearing, to widen the access road, to cut out stumps and to add the finishing touches on any building project I had going.

I was starting to meet a few more of my neighbors. Most of the other "settlers" along the road were hippies and non-conformists of one sort or another. There were also a few retired special ops fellows who tended to be reclusive and didn't even speak to each other, possibly due to government regulations. All of us were constantly clearing brush on our places and had huge piles of it to burn and we used to have wheelbarrow parties to deal with it.

For the gathering, each couple would load up a wheelbarrow with beer and head over to the parcel where the brush was to be burned. A boom box would be blasting away and the fire would be lit. It was best if the night was a little damp because then there was no danger of setting the forest on fire and thus no limit to the size of the fire. We liked big fires. We joked around and played a few games like "Run Through the Big Fire" or "Jump Over the Big Fire" as well as the betting game "Will He Fall Into the Big Fire." Clint's dad was at most of the wheelbarrow parties. He was known as Uncle Suck, a reference to the speed with which he could empty a can of beer. His real name was Duane. He had grown up in the area and never left, although his wife, who, comparatively speaking was a high roller, had. He was a big-hearted guy with a humorous visage who visited his son and daughter-in-law frequently and was one of the proudest grandfathers that I ever met.

As the night wore on the men would become exhausted as well as inebriated, and would collapse into the now empty wheelbarrows to enjoy the fire from a seated position. This was convenient because at the end of the festivities all that the women had to do was find their wheelbarrow and set off through the pitch dark woods or down the pitch black roads. Many times they would end up tipping their load somewhere along the way. We were never sure whether or not the spills were accidental.

There was plenty of "speed beef" to eat which is what we called venison that was obtained during "settler season" which occurred in any month with an "r" in it. Our neighbors had large gardens and eventually we did too. Canning and freezing was a big part of life. Casey did most of the canning when she was with me, using kettles that I had found in the back room at Harling's.

Most of us tried to live off the land as much as we could. I used to say that I moved to Northern Wisconsin because I had heard that there was no work up there and I was operating on the theory that if I kept my expenses down, I wouldn't have to work too hard. The truth was that the work required to keep your expenses down was unrelenting. Putting up a supply of firewood, clearing the land, building shelters and out-houses, hunting, fishing and gardening to keep the larder stocked and later taking care of animals, cut into the time I could spend at the multitude of nearby roadhouses.

I was scavenging at the dump one Sunday and found an old refrigerator that ran on propane. I managed to lug it into the tiny cabin. I used it for five years until I got electricity and, in retrospect I believe it might have been a good idea to have vented it to the outside at some point. Although it took a long time to install electricity, I did manage to obtain a telephone line after about a year and it was a huge improvement.

One morning just a few days after getting the phone line I stepped outside barefoot, and probably wearing nothing else, to use nature's facilities. Out of the corner of my bleary eye, I glimpsed a big fat porcupine nestled under the threshold of the door that, but for luck, I would have trod on with my bare foot. I picked up an iron pipe to give him a whack but missed and hit the newly installed service box attached to the cabin wall. The box was smashed to smithereens while the porcupine waddled away unscathed. I checked for a dial tone and the phone still worked. A little duct tape repaired the damaged box and I was still in business.

I drank in the local bars until I had run up tabs that were big enough that the owners knew the only way I could pay was to play a night of music. There were about twenty little backwoods bars within ten miles of my place and I played nearly all of them.

The people in northwest Wisconsin had only so much tolerance for Irish music. They would sometimes ask, "Tom, you're not gonna play that Irish shit tonight, are you?"

I would answer, "Don't worry. Tonight it's strictly country," and play Willy Nelson, Hank Williams, Johnny Horton and such, the same kind of music my friend Texas Tom played. For variety, I would play jigs and reels on the fiddle and sing "Cushy Butterfield", a song I learned from Sean Tyrrell back in the Boston days. Wisconsin people liked hearing about a big bonny lass who liked her beer. I was asked to sing it so often that the old timers and others who had forgotten my name would just call me Cushy. When I ran out of money, I would call Jerry Wyatt in Kansas City. Jerry would mail me a few hundred dollars cash so that I could drive down to Harling's, play for a few weeks, check the back room and then hightail it back to the woods where a little city money went a long way.

I played the fiddle and guitar nearly every day no matter what was going on and when Cuz heard that I had sold my accordion to Chuck to purchase the land, he asked me to drop in the next time I was in Chicago. When I stopped for a visit he told me that his big one-row Baldoni was getting to be too much for him to play and he wanted me to have her. I was delighted and found room for Big Liz in the little cabin too. A day never seemed complete unless there was time to play music.

All the same, I didn't like having the feeling that music was all I knew how to do. I wanted to learn about the things that I had missed. In the Wisconsin woods, if you needed to know how to do something all you had to do was ask and there was no shortage of help available as long as the beer was supplied. Very few locals followed sports and the conversations in the little bars were often about chain saws, trucks, log skidders, boats, lawn mowers and snow blowers, gardening, hunting, fishing and what the DNR was up to. Everyone would put in their two cents worth about the topic at hand and each topic was thoroughly discussed.

One of the many things I didn't know anything about was auto mechanics and to keep the wrecks that I drove on the road, that was one of the first things I had to learn. A Texan named Russ Baker lived about a mile from me. I had heard that he was good with vehicles and mine needed some transmission work, so I went over to talk to him. The man who answered the door was in his early seventies but people around there said that if Russ Baker had done everything that he said he did, he would have to be two hundred and fifty years old. I asked if he could rebuild my truck transmission. He said, "If you just park the truck in my yard, take out the tranny and set it onto my work bench I'll show you how."

I hauled the truck into his yard with the help of a neighbor and a logging chain, crawled under and went to work while Russ went about his business in the house and yard. After three days, I had the transmission on his work bench. The reason it took so long was because Russ was a Texan. I figured that I should do it the Texas way like I learned from Joe Rosson in the oilfield. I wasn't going to cheat so I didn't ask any questions and did it the ignorant way. The truck was parked over a hornet's nest which I dealt with by laying a tarp over the nest and lying on top of it getting stung over and over. I didn't have a jack or use blocks to shim up the tranny, which weighed about a hundred and fifty pounds. Instead, I used my legs and one arm to hold it up as I unbolted the rusty parts and wrestled the tranny out. I also had to make a few beer runs.

Once it was on Russ' work bench, he showed me how to rebuild the old Ford transmission and then he gave me some very helpful hints on how to get it back onto the truck. I listened carefully and had the tranny reinstalled in a couple of hours. We were great friends after that and whenever I drove by and saw that he was around, I would stop in and listen to some of his stories. I learned why people said what they did about his age.

Russ was an ex-Marine with huge upper arms and curly red hair and he was covered with freckles. He appeared to be hale and hearty although he told me he had cancer and that he drove down to Mexico once a year to stock up on the Laetrile that he was sure was saving him. His life had been an interesting one and parts of it seemed almost unbelievable. He had been a paratrooper somewhere in Indochina and had spent time in the electric chair. That struck me as unusual and I asked him about it. He told me that he was about twenty and on leave from the Marines, enjoying himself in a Texas honkytonk when a fellow bumped into him on the dance floor on purpose to start a fight.

"So I gave him all six with my peashooter."

He was convicted of murder and sentenced to death. The time came for the sentence to be carried out and Russ was strapped into the chair. He told me he was as solid as a rock and ready to die. Then, at the last moment there was a commotion and the warden informed him that the governor had granted a pardon. He said, "That was when I broke down and cried like a baby for the first time that I could remember."

Russ figured that the pardon might have had something to do with his military service. He never said exactly what he had done when he was in the Marines, but indicated that he wasn't thinking right at that time of the murder. The experience in the chair changed Russ completely. He married for the first of six times, and decided to become a Baptist preacher. He studied the Bible until he could quote it like a pro and set off on his career. Russ tended to roar at the congregation telling them that they were all sinners and going to hell. The longer the sermon went on, the louder he roared. Some of his flock seemed to like that. His preaching career was terminated suddenly a few years later when, after a sermon, a member of his congregation put his nose to the water glass that Russ kept beside him on the pulpit and found that it smelled of gin. Russ eventually quit drinking and had been sober for about thirty years when I met him.

He played guitar, fiddle and mandolin and liked to sing. He was father to about eighteen kids who were scattered around the country. He had built houses, been a long haul truck driver and owned a logging business and sawmill. He was a licensed electrician, plumber and mechanic. Russ once told me that he had studied all the religions of the world but confessed, “I still don’t know a God damned thing about God.”

But he kept his minister’s license so that he could still perform marriages as a side line. He himself was married to and living with Dee, the tallest, thinnest woman I had ever seen. She was a folk artist and painted beautiful woodsy scenes with wildlife and flowers on bird houses that Russ built and also on a kind of tree fungus that the two of them collected from the birches where it grew. They had a camper on a pickup truck that they would take to flea markets on the weekends where they sold their work.

*****

In the winter it was very quiet. Casey and I would see maybe two or three vehicles roll down the road in a day. When you managed to dig your way out of the snow, the only place to go was to a bar. If you met someone you knew driving along, you both stopped abreast of each other and chatted away for maybe an hour ‘til another vehicle came along and you both continued on your way at a careful ten miles per hour with your eye out for deer or grouse or anything else that might look good in a pot.

Ice fishing was not a sport for those who stayed through the winter. It was just a fun way of getting food. We only fished when and where we knew we would catch something. Word would be passed on about where the crappies, bluegills and walleyes were to be had. With hundreds of lakes of all sizes and in every direction, there was no problem catching fish. When the ice was just thick enough and before it snowed, you could walk carefully out onto the lake and looking through the ice, you could see through to the bottom. You were looking for spawning beds and other places where the big fish tended to hang out. That is where you would chop your hole in the ice and wait for dinner to swim by. We called this “window shopping.”

I started playing some gigs with Al Christner who played guitar and was a good country singer. We called ourselves The Jack Pine Savages and played all the old-school country hits. Although Al himself was a very nice fellow and a farmer in his other life, the gigs he booked for us were in rough bars, the kind of places where hard drinking didn't even begin to describe it. Then one night poor Al had a heart attack and died driving to one of our gigs. I got the call when I was already at the bar and ended up playing alone. Things were becoming kind of dark for me. I used to play country music as a lark and didn't want to take it seriously.

That night a man named Dick Brooks stepped out of the crowd and said that he had heard that I played some Irish music. He asked if I would come along with him up to the Lac Courte Oreilles Reservation near Hayward, Wisconsin, and do a radio interview. I was not interested until he said that he would be buying the drinks and that I could stop the interview whenever I wanted to. I consented and he said that he would pick me up at my cabin the next day.

Chapter 19

Presenting a Unitized Front

Dick Brooks was the station manager of WOJB, a Public Radio Station that broadcast out of the Lac Courte Oreilles Reservation. The station had only been in existence a short time. It was founded with the intention of bridging the gap between Native Americans and their non-Native neighbors.

Because Dick was the manager, we could go on air whenever we were ready, which was a good thing because when he picked me up at cabin, I tested his word by asking him to stop at the nearest bar. He stopped, and we stopped a few more times along the way. He bought the drinks just as he said he would. It was fifty miles to Haywire, as I called Hayward, the Sawyer County Seat. Back in my teenage rock and roll days, my band had been convicted of felony bear theft and barred from Sawyer County until we were twenty-one.

Dick put us on the air live within minutes of arriving at the studio. He had a great interviewing style and soon had me talking, then singing, then telling stories and then taking phone calls.

I was not used to being asked serious questions about Irish music in Wisconsin. The Native Americans who called in seemed to relate to the political history of the Irish. They said that it mirrored their own in many ways with some significant overlapping of the timelines. Over three centuries, their land was taken, treaties were made and then broken and the people were starved, slaughtered or driven to the west. Their religion was banned and their language forbidden. The people were ridiculed in the press and the subject of racist cartoons. Even the idea of promoting alcohol to weaken the culture and to make a further laughing stock of the people was similar.

The callers also related to the music. They commented on the laments and heroic tales told in song and got a kick out of the comic songs as well. They talked about their own Indian fiddlers and their love of the kind of wild fiddling that comes from sorrow and pain, transmuted into ferocious joy and the will to survive.

The days were getting colder with the arrival of November and deer hunting season was upon us, the real one as opposed to Settler's season. The Deer Season was a major event in Northwestern Wisconsin. Entire families hunted together and those who had moved out of state often returned to participate. Schools were closed. I tended to avoid the woods during deer season because of the crowds. Fortunately, we were pretty well set for food. Casey from K. C. was waitressing at a few places. She was popular and kept busy. She also was able to bring home large pans of leftovers from her places of employment and this was another way of living off the land.

Eddie of Eddie Perry's Booze and Canoes had a sister, Gail Castle, who owned The McKenzie Castle which was situated on Big Lake McKenzie about two miles from my place. Gail decided to hire strippers that year and she asked me if I would collect the one dollar cover charge at the door and act as bouncer. Gail told me that she knew I wouldn't start fights but she figured that I would be good at finishing them. I agreed to take the job for the ten days of the season.

The afternoon before opening day I spent at the Booze and Canoes. As I was leaving, Eddie asked me what I was doing that night and I told him that I was working for his sister as the doorman. Eddie looked concerned and opened up a drawer behind the bar. He pulled out a .357 Magnum and said, "Take this, Tommy. It's going to be nuts."

I said, "No, no, Eddie. I don't need that."

He put the pistol back in the drawer and pulled out some brass knuckles and said, "Then take these, Tommy. You'll need something."

I refused and was trying to get out the door when he grabbed a can of mace, put it in my hand, and said, "You've got to have something."

I put the little can of mace in my pocket and went back to the cabin for a snooze. Later that night The McKenzie Castle was packed with blaze orange clad hunters and scantily clad strippers. The hunters were already in their outdoorsy finery even though the season didn't start until the next morning. They all had buck knives and side arms. The trucks in the parking lot sported full gun racks. Some of the hunters even had their binoculars with them, but I don't think that was for the deer. Things were going along fairly smoothly when, from instinct, I felt an altercation was brewing. After all the years I'd spent playing bars I knew the vibe.

Sure enough, up at the bar a scuffle began. One guy popped another and then his friend stepped in and got popped as well. These two then started swinging at someone who wasn't involved and soon everybody was hitting somebody because everybody looked the same in blaze orange.

I waded in keeping my eyes on the back of the head of the guy who started the melee, ducking a few swings. The fighters had formed into a tangled pile that moved in one mass into the dining room that had been closed just before the strippers' performance had started. I reached the heap and with the help of a few trusty locals, started pulling the brawlers off one by one. I hustled them out the door yelling, "Fight all you want, but not in here!"

After a few minutes I found the guy who started it all at the bottom of the pile. It was Eddie Perry, Mr. Booze and Canoes himself. I ran him out the door and told him to go home. It was cold and snowing and as I was walking back into the bar, I put my hands in my pockets. There, I felt a little can. It took me a second to realize what it was. Then I cracked up, thinking, "I should have sprayed him with his own mace."

About a mile from McKenzie Castle, high on a hill across the lake stands West Point Lodge. It dates back to the 1930s and like many resorts of the era hosted the gangsters from St. Paul and Chicago who were on retreat from the hurly-burly of city life. West Point Lodge used to rent out small rooms in the lodge itself and had cabins and a campground. The main attraction at West Point was Pete Shiel, who was called Petey Pie by those who knew him well. He was a huge man from Stillwater, Minnesota, with a gigantic personality. Petey Pie had long black hair and a big black mustache but was bald on top. He had been in the bar and entertainment business all his life.

Petey Pie was the kind of fast talking, loud, witty person that you rarely find in the North Woods. He had never fished, hunted, made a fire or driven a pickup truck. The owner of West Point, Dale, who lived in the Twin Cities, met Petey, bought him a tiny pickup truck and sent him to the woods where he put him in charge of the Lodge. The truck was white and if you saw it coming down the road, you knew instantly that it was Petey Pie's truck because his weight made it list to port to an extravagant degree.

Petey loved the woods and everyone he met in the area. He made up nicknames for them and built them up way beyond reality, turning them all into legends. He even won over some of the older people who usually avoided his type. They couldn't help but be charmed by his enthusiasm for all of humanity.

There was a sanctimonious-looking older guy who came into the lodge a few times. He was a large man who held himself ramrod straight and always seemed to have a disapproving look. He wasn't religious, but Petey thought he looked like a high ranking man of the cloth and started calling him the Bishop. The man took to his new nickname and became a regular. This was how Petey assembled a loyal following, young and old, male and female.

West Point Lodge was a big place with a huge kitchen, ten small rooms upstairs, a large veranda overlooking the lake and a good-sized bar. They didn't rent out the rooms in the lodge anymore, but some of them were occupied casually by bar staff or locals who were temporarily in need of a place to hide out or to meditate on their predicaments. Petey always closed the place to the public at the time established by law and was deferential to the police that dropped in from time to time. The authorities never thought to look for the things that were going on behind the scenes, so he was able to run a very happy ship over the few years that he was in charge.

Petey had a jukebox full of his favorite music, but he himself always provided the loudest and funniest entertainment. Although beer was only $0.30 per glass and $0.50 per mug, it added up fast and nearly everyone ran a tab. When it was time to settle up, Petey would do some figuring. He'd calculate the entertainment value of each customer and then surprise them by how little they had to pay to hang out there. Petey didn't drink himself, but he knew how to create a lively bar filled with eccentric characters that would draw new customers. People would come from all over to see if the rumors they heard about West Point were true.

Dale, the owner of the property was a nice older fellow and he would come up from the Cities from time to time to see what was what. Fortunately for all concerned, he suffered from narcolepsy. In the middle of investigations he would .... fall asleep.

Petey served what he called "units" in the bar. A glass of beer was a "unit." He called a drink poured to go "a road unit". Eventually he started referring to people as "units". He described patrons who had more to drink than usual as being "unitized". I remember once a man ordered a cranberry juice at the bar. Petey said, "Excellent choice sir. That's very good for your lower unit."

Petey used to call me T-O-M, tom-tom, Tom. Once in a while he would ask me to play some music at the lodge, probably to cover my tab. His favorite song from my repertoire of the time was "Louisiana Man" by Doug Kershaw, the Ragin' Cajun. Petey called the song "Beeg Feesh." Everyone had stories about Petey and if Scott Township had a mayor, Petey would have been it.

There was a family of Kivels up in Wisconsin living not far from me, in a cabin on Dubois Lake. Ed and JoAnne Kivel and their two teenage daughters loved to go out and dance. In Wisconsin all ages were allowed in bars as long as they were with their parents and there was nothing that these dancing Kivels liked more than live music. The daughters were very jolly and danced with everyone, but if Mr. Kivel detected that someone was paying too much of the wrong kind of attention to one of them, a cross-shaped crease would appear on his forehead.

I saw the cross a few times and was amazed at how effective it was at cooling the ardor of the most persistent pursuer, especially when combined with the murderous look on his face. I first met Ed and JoAnne and his brother and sister-in-law, Tom and Gloria at What The Heck and have played many parties, some weddings, and a few funerals for them over the years. Tom and Ed have passed on, but they both loved Irish music and were true gentlemen as well as great family men.

*****

I needed to make some city money so I called down to the Glenshesk in Chicago and booked a week there. It was my first time playing there alone, and when I arrived, the place wasn't as busy as it had been a few years before. I played the Wednesday and Thursday night but on Friday night towards the end of the evening Mary, the owner, said, "Tom, what you need is a drum machine."

She went on to tell me that she had noticed that all the solo acts seemed to be getting drum machines. I took offense at this and told her, "I'm leaving. Keep your money," and walked out.

As steamed as I was about the drum machine comment, I still needed money to bring back to the woods and so I headed down to McNeill's on Milwaukee Avenue and managed to get a gig for Saturday night. It was a Connemara and Mayo bar. Things went well there and I was asked to play the following weekend. I didn't have a place to stay, but McNeill had a house that he was selling and he let me stay there. It had already been emptied of furniture so I was back to sleeping on the floor. I did play the next weekend and earned enough to buy a one way ticket to Washington D. C.

Since I'd played D. C. in the seventies I thought that there might be work, but times had changed. The places I had played had expanded well beyond solo acts or closed and it was harder to pick up a gig on the fly. I wasn't having much luck, and took to playing on the street across from The Four Provinces, a place that had hired us to play a few years before but had already booked a band for the month. I had been busking there on the sidewalk for three or four days when a car full of Irish musicians, all Americans, pulled up. One of the girls broke out of the crowd, ran up to me, and gave me a hug. Her friends ran up behind her and pulled her away from me saying, "Stay away from him! He's dangerous!"

She said, "Are you kidding me? That's Tom Dahill. I've known him forever." It was Mary MacEachron, part of the O'Gara's session in the seventies who would later marry my friend, Sean O'Driscoll from Blarney, County Cork, whom neither of us had yet met. Mary told me recently that she remembered noticing that I had a toothbrush in my shirt pocket that day.

I knew that I needed to escape D.C. but didn't have any money to leave. I met a man of about forty with green teeth who offered me a job. He needed help in collections. He told me that he was heir to a fortune amassed by his late father who had invented a radar system that was used by the U.S. Navy. This fellow had spent somewhere around eight million dollars on recording studios, fancy cars and two small airplanes. I could tell that a fair amount was also spent on drugs. The poor man was down to his last $50,000 and what was left of his assets were scattered around the country. He needed someone to help him recover what he could. He also needed a good dentist. I took him up on his offer.

He was living in his mother's basement in Chevy Chase and we arranged to meet the next day at the mansion to discuss specifics. The next afternoon I made my way to Chevy Chase, located the house, which was indeed a mansion, and knocked on the door. His mother, a society lady who was imposingly dressed, especially in comparison to my somewhat disheveled state, answered the door. I explained that I was there for a business conference with her son.

We went down to his digs in the basement, lit up and started discussing business. The substance of our discussion changed rapidly given the illegal substance that we were smoking. The man professed a love of music and seemed to have done some work as a promotor of concerts. He asked me to make a few phone calls which, at that point he was unable to make himself.

First he had me call the Buddha Hall in Charleston, S. C. and book a date. Next he made me call Juice Newton's agent to see if she was available for the date we had booked. He had me do the same with Ronnie Milsap's agent. Both were available and by the time I left, I thought I was well on my way to being a concert promotor as well as having a new career in collections. I remained unenlightened as to what he really had in mind as far as collections went, though I remember him asking if I had access to a handgun.

I left the house, catching a glimpse of the mother who was on the phone in another room and started down the street whistling a happy tune and contemplating my good fortune. I was planning to catch a bus back into D. C. but on the way to the bus stop a patrol car pulled up alongside me. It seems that I had been reported as a vagrant and the cops placed me, my fiddle and my duffle in the back of the patrol car and drove me to the District line. They told me never to return to Chevy Chase. I guess the man's mother had other plans for her boy and it was not in my karma to book anything in the Buddha Hall.

I still needed money to get out of town, so I went into a high end violin shop on Connecticut Avenue and pulled out my bow. It was a good bow and the shopkeeper asked me about it. I told him about Jack Kerrigan, a regular at MacCafferty's and a nice old man. He was a little guy about seventy years old who dressed well and had the manners of a gentleman. There was a flower shop next to his house, and every day on the way to the pub, he would stop in and buy a bunch of roses, which he would parcel out to all the girls that worked at the bar and to anyone else who looked in need of one.

His father had been a fiddler in Ireland. Jack himself played the mandolin and fiddle, and favored Carolan compositions. I had just started playing Paddy Hill's fiddle and one night Jack took a look at the bow I was using. He returned the next night with a new bow and gave it to me.

The man behind the counter, when he heard my story, refused to buy the bow and encouraged me to find another way. He told me the bow was high quality and ordinarily he would buy it, but under the circumstances he would pass. I am glad to this day that he didn't buy it. I am still playing with that bow thirty-five years later.

I continued down the street and walked into The Four Provinces. I started talking to Frank Hughes the owner and told him about my situation. Frank picked up the phone and arranged an airline ticket to St. Paul for that very night saying, "Pay me for the ticket whenever you can."

My old friend, Kevin Foley, picked me up at the airport and it was good to be back in St. Paul. Kevin was friends with some of the Diffleys, descendants of an old Minnesota pioneer family and he drove us out to the original homestead in Eagan where some of them still lived. We had a night of it. Kevin loves to sing and so do I, and that's what we did. Afterwards we went on to Kevin's place where I spent the night and the next morning I made my way back to Wisconsin.

A few weeks later, I called Jerry Wyatt in Kansas City and asked when he had time open at Harling's. He had a couple of weeks at the end of the month and I agreed to take them if he was willing to send some cash for the gas. Jerry said, "Dahill, you old tinker, give me your address again."

Back in Kansas City, I was asked by Megan Tallman and a couple of her friends if I would be willing to play for some kids to whom they had taught some Irish dances. The performance was for the parents of the kids and was being held in a convent which housed a lot of retired nuns. Megan asked me how much I would need to play for them. I said I would do it for a bottle of Jameson's.

"It's a deal," said Megan.

The performance wasn't until noon, so I stopped in at Harling's at about ten o'clock to meet with Tommy Wyrsh, the manager, for what we called our daily devotional, a couple shots of Jose Cuervo. Megan picked me up and drove me over to the convent. The room they were performing in on the fourth floor was full of kids, parents and nuns. It was already hot with eight radiators blasting away and the windows were fogged up from all the warm breathing bodies. I played the fiddle for a few of the dances. While I was waiting for the next dance to begin, a very elderly nun sat down next to me and introduced herself. She told me that she had been born in Ireland and that she had taught music, including the violin, for many years before retiring.

When the nun first sat down I noticed a smell of lye soap which immediately sent my mind back to childhood and Sister Magnus. Sister Magnus was a nun from Limerick who had attempted to teach me and some of my brothers and sisters to play the piano. She had some success with my siblings.

When the next dance began, I could feel the retired music teacher's eyes on me. She was listening closely and I felt a tremor in my bow hand. The heat in the room was becoming unbearable. Sweat was pouring down my face and back and the shaking in my bow was becoming uncontrollable. The dancers were about halfway through a sixteen-hand reel when I had to put the fiddle down and dowdle for the rest of the dance.

I had never had trouble with my bow hand before. I chalked it up to the heat and the feeling of being scrutinized by the old Irish nun. As the kids were leaving the room, one of them asked, "Hey mister, why did you stop playing in the middle of our dance?"

I mumbled, "I took the wrong medicine this morning."

In the car on the way back to Harling's, Megan said, "Tom, I'm not giving you that bottle of whiskey."

I said, "Fair enough."

The Harling's gig was a success. The place was packed every night. Casey would always come with me when I was playing in Kansas City so that she could visit her Mom. She would work the door on Fridays and Saturdays collecting the cover charge which was ours to keep in addition to the guaranteed price for the music. I was also flogging records and tapes from the stage. I had the three albums out on the Biscuit City label that I had recorded with the old band and they were selling.

At the end of the week, just for fun, Jerry would sometimes give Casey my pay envelope. She would always have to count the money very carefully because he would try to short change her.

Casey would always catch him and then he would have a good laugh. He never tried that particular game with me.

I finally managed to earn the city money I had been seeking. I sent the plane fare back to Frank Hughes in D. C. and still had a good chunk of change left that would see us through a couple of months in the woods. We took off for the "Great White North."

It was great when I had a little money from travelling gigs, but in between those high times, living rough in the woods was starting to seem a bit grim. Subsisting on speed beef and leftovers from Casey's job and trying to scratch out a living from playing music in little taverns where the money just about covered my bar tabs was losing its allure. I was beginning to feel old.

Chapter 20
Dog-Tracking

One day the phone in the cabin rang, an unusual occurrence. A voice said, "Tom, this is Paddy O'Brien. I'm starting a new band and I would like you to play guitar, sing and back me up along with Sean O'Driscoll."

For a moment I couldn't believe it. Paddy O'Brien from Offaly, not to be confused with Paddy O'Brien from Tipperary, was a well-known box player. I could feel a big change coming and I was nearly crying. I felt so honored to be asked by one of the Greats. After our short conversation, I agreed and then jumped and danced all over the clearing in the woods shouting, "Yes! Yes! Yes!"

I bought a big old Ford station wagon, this time splurging and paying a hundred and fifty dollars. I was ready to hit the road with Paddy O'Brien from Offaly who was living in Minneapolis at the time. He had just started seeing a woman named Erin Hart. Sean O'Driscoll had arrived from Cork, met Mary MacEachron and they were fast becoming an item. We all met at MacCafferty's, which was sinking fast since Ray's death a short time before.

Paddy was in command. We listened to his plans for the new band, which he wanted to call "Hill 16" after the Section of Croke Park Stadium in Dublin that was said to have been built over rubble of O'Connell Street after the Rising of 1916.

Hill 16. Photo by Erin Hart.

Erin would take photos and put together some promo. Paddy and Sean were working on the repertoire. They knew most of the songs that I sang and would have no trouble knowing how to back me up.

On the first leg of our tour, Sean couldn't be with us, so Paddy and I set out for Iowa City to play a folk club there called The Sanctuary. On the way down Paddy was full of stories from his time in the heart of the Dublin music scene. I learned that he personally knew some of the real giants of Irish music. He told stories about Sean O'Riada, Tommy Potts, John Kelly and Seamus Ennis. He also liked to shoot pool as did I. We played the gig and the next stop was St. Louis.

On our way to St. Louis, as we drove along the freeway, we noticed first one, and then another hitchhiker jumping off the shoulder of the road and into the ditch as we rolled by. Paddy was looking out the windows of the station wagon first to the back and then off to the sides of the road. He said, "Tom, pull over at the next exit."

Paddy and I stopped in the next town and he peered under the car. After a few moments of silence he said, "It's broke."

"What's broke?"

"The bar that's holding the back axel in place. It's rusted through."

The hitchhikers were jumping into the ditch with looks of terror on their faces because they thought we were trying to hit them. We were dog-tracking down the road. The body of the car was skewed on the axel giving the illusion that the car was heading towards the side of the road and the poor hitchhikers, seeing that sideways slanted rabid dog movement, had nowhere to go but into the ditch.

Paddy said, "I think I can fix it."

I was disbelieving for a moment, looking at Paddy in his tweed jacket and glasses, but then, I remembered that he had grown up on a farm in Offaly. I realized that he might know something that I didn't. He said, "Tom, find a hardware store."

I started driving around the town, trying not to scare anyone while Paddy made a list of the things we would need. By the time we located the hardware store Paddy had the shopping list done. We purchased two turnbuckles, eight U-bolts, two six-foot lengths of wire cable, one roll of string and a piece of chalk and returned to the dog-tracking station wagon.

Right there in the parking lot, Paddy set to work. He used the string first. He tied knots to measure the distance between the wheels on each side and used the chalk to mark the pavement. Then he had me climb in and move the car forward a little.

"Stop!" he yelled, "Back her up."

He measured again and we repeated the process over and over until Paddy shouted, "Stop!" for the final time.

There was now equal distance between the two sets of wheels and everything was more or less in line. Paddy had a plan to keep it that way. Unfortunately all we had to lift the whole side of the car was the little wind-up jack that we found in the back of the station wagon. Paddy went under the car, now precariously perched on two wheels by the fragile jack, while I held it as steady as I could in the big Iowa wind. He wrapped the cables around some solid parts that he found under the car and ran the other end through the turnbuckles. Then he doubled the cables back to make loops and used the U-bolts to clamp the cables. We used one length of cable to hold the axel so that it couldn't move forward and the other to hold it so that it couldn't move backward. Paddy then tightened up the turnbuckles and screwed the whole thing up tight and we were ready to continue on our tour.

Paddy told me afterwards that he was "afraid of me life" that the station wagon would fall on him. Sometimes to make it to a gig on time when your options are minimal, you just have to take a chance and work with what you have.

I asked Paddy where he learned how to do that and he said that he moved to Dublin not only for the music but to apprentice as a mechanic. There was a lot more to Paddy than met the eye.

We arrived at McGurk's where Sean was waiting for us and adjourned to The Palace next door after having a sup in the pub. We were to play that evening and it was important to rest up. We knew we would be up all night and most probably until well into the dawn. That was the way it was done at John D. McGurk's.

At closing time the musicians who were performing, all the musicians that came to listen, the bar staff, and friends of the band would reassemble at The Palace. The building was long and low, with six or seven rooms, depending on how you count, and beds and mattresses everywhere. The outer door entered into a large kitchen where there was a couch or two that came and went, plenty of chairs and a table. It wasn't a fancy place, but the staff came and cleaned it fairly regularly and did the laundry too.

Almost every night the refrigerator was crammed full of beer from next door that appeared magically at no charge, when the staff arrived for the goings on. Instruments that were stashed in cars around the block would be retrieved and most nights there would be a session. By "a session" I don't mean a formal Irish music session, but the kind of session where stories and jokes and gossip and yarns are the mainstay. Tunes, a few songs, arguments and plenty of politics, both foreign and domestic, together with takeout food and tons of drink were the norm. There was always a fair amount courting going on, while, scattered throughout the Palace, the big personalities would each hold their own court.

Sean was about ten years younger than me and Paddy was nearly ten years older. We called Paddy "the Chief" because he was the man in charge. Sean and Paddy worked on the tunes intensively while I often just read a book and listened. Paddy had a gigantic repertoire of tunes to choose from and considered each note when working out a version of a particular tune. Sean played guitar as well as banjo and had some great songs.

My part in the band was fairly easy, playing backup guitar and singing the occasional song. I had hundreds of Irish songs to choose from that I had picked up over the years. Once we found the right key, Paddy and Sean had no trouble with my material. I played the fiddle a bit with them, but since they were so tight together, my fiddling on stage was minimal. Paddy gave me fiddle tunes to work on and I did practice on my own.

Backing Paddy and Sean on the guitar was a pleasure. I listened very carefully so as not to step on what they were doing and played the guitar like a bodhran, rhythmically, and not using too many weird chords. I've always played guitar in standard tuning and, having a piano background thanks to Sister Magnus, tend to keep a bass line running under the chords.

I learned a little about Sean's past on that tour. He told me that he had played Irish Football and Rugby when he was a kid in Blarney. After playing schools Rugby he played with a top level club team and toured in Canada and England. By the time he was twenty, his knees were damaged to the point that he knew he needed to find something else to do. He still has the look of a Rugby player.

Sean had played electric guitar as a teenager due partly to his love of Rory Gallagher and after he quit Rugby his focus shifted entirely to music. Sean stayed in Blarney practicing the banjo and in time started playing out with friends in duos and trios. He was still in Blarney when he got the call about Hill 16. Sean was delighted and honored that Paddy had heard of him.

One day, at an afternoon session in The Palace, Paddy was playing a pet tune for another great player. It might have been Martin Hayes. Paddy finished the tune and it was a beauty. A fellow from Tyrone named McArdle who played the mandolin and bodhran, commented, “That was nice Paddy, but I think I heard one bum note.”

There was dead silence in the place while Paddy pushed his glasses up on his nose with one index finger.

“Or it could be me,” said McArdle. We all laughed, except, perhaps, Paddy. McArdle had just earned his new nickname which stuck with him for years, “Bum-note McArdle.”

I was out in St. Ann’s Parish, visiting old acquaintances at the Shamrock when I got an urgent phone call from Nick Carter at McGurk’s. He said, “Tommy, get down to The Palace right now. Dan Devery is on his way over. I think he’s gonna beat up Paddy.”

I jumped into the station wagon and floored it breaking all the traffic laws to reach The Palace before Danny. I thought of Danny’s huge pipefitter arms and knew, from experience, that he was a rough customer when he was mad. And he was mad. Music mad, like the rest of us. It was all he really cared about.

When I arrived on the scene, The Palace door had been kicked in and wood splinters from the doorjamb were all over the kitchen floor. I shouted, “Paddy! Are ya in here?” fearing that he could be unconscious or perhaps dead.

I didn’t hear a sound. It was a hot day in St. Louis and I was sweating like a pig. The air conditioner was going full blast, but over the noise I thought I heard a couple of notes on the accordion. I thought, “Thank God, he’s alive.”

I cautiously moved to the bedroom door and opened it. There were the two of them, Dan Devery and Paddy O’Brien, in the bed leaning up against the head board, each with an accordion in his lap, a bottle of whiskey next to Dan and a couple of Budweiser's on Paddy's bed stand. They saw the look on my face and Paddy asked, "What's the matter, Tom?"

I answered, "Oh....I just didn't know if anyone was home."

I slipped out and went next door to McGurk's. Carter showed me, in the St. Louis Post-Dispatch, what had caused all the trouble. It was an article with a nice picture of Paddy O'Brien and a caption that said "Irish music finally comes to St. Louis" or something like that.

The caption had really upset Danny. He had been playing Irish music in St. Louis for the past twenty-five years.

*****

Paddy, Sean and I travelled together over the next few years as Hill 16, playing venues in all the Midwestern states. Sean O'Driscoll married Mary MacEachron. Paddy and Erin Hart married soon afterwards. When we weren't on the road, Paddy and Sean were both living in Minnesota and I was still up in Northern Wisconsin.

Progress on my lifestyle in Wisconsin was very slow. I extended the cabin by ten feet so it now measured twelve by twenty-two and finally built an outhouse, but the cabin was still without electricity and running water after all this time and I was still using the milk can stove for heat. I was not working at anything in particular and I think it was making me a bit peculiar.

Eddie Perry was having a big Halloween party at the Booze and Canoes and he asked if I would play. I said sure and after spending the afternoon at the Lumberjack Saloon, which was on the way, it was time to play. The place was packed. There were Indians from the Reservation at Danbury, retirees from 3M and the town constable whose wife was driving the patrol car, as usual, because he liked to drink and play the harmonica while on duty. Casey from K. C. came after she finished work at the restaurant. Eddie and Wendy Perry and their daughter Stormy, named after the song, were there, along with various neighbors of mine from Tobaccy Road, Petey Pie's name for McKenzie Lake Road.

There was plenty of fresh venison although hunting season was still a few weeks away, and all kinds of dancing and shenanigans.

On a break, I met a woman who introduced herself as, "Debbie-Forty-Four-Double-D-so-as-not-to-be-asked." I wasn't going to ask, but I could see the need for the moniker. Debbie-Forty-Four-Double-D-so-as-not-to-be-asked did her famous donkey kicks. She had a great way of putting her hands on the floor and kicking her back legs up as she brayed. I think she was a school teacher.

At about four a.m. it was time to head back to Tobaccy. Casey decided to ride with Clint and Cathy and I'm glad she did because about a half mile out of Eddie Perry's there was a sharp turn in the road and the curve was covered with loose sand. The big old Ford slipped on the turn and I was thrown to the passenger's side floor boards. The car went into the woods at about sixty miles per hour with no one behind the wheel. I didn't have to wait long for the big Ford to hit a tree. My head broke the windshield, the engine came off the mounts and the front end bent into a V. The tree didn't move but the car went up it about eight feet. I was a bit stunned, but happy to see that Clint, Cathy and Casey from K. C. were stopped nearby and I wouldn't have to walk home.

I made it home all right, but not all right. When I woke up the next morning, I couldn't lift my head so I had to pick it up with my hands and sort of carry it around that way. I stiffened up more over the next few days and actually had to crawl backwards with my head on the ground to get anywhere. I vaguely remember crawling into McKenzie Castle that way and having to use a straw to drink. I couldn't go to a doctor because any money I had needed to be spent on whiskey to counteract the pain.

After a month or so I was feeling a bit better except when I played the fiddle. My neck couldn't bend to the left unless I used my right hand to push my head down onto the fiddle. Once my chin was down, it wasn't too bad unless I lifted it off again, so I tended to keep playing once I started. I played that way for months.

Hill 16 had several gigs around St. Patrick's Day 1983. My mother and a couple of my sisters came to see us play in downtown St. Paul. After the show, my mother remarked, "You really grin a lot when you play the fiddle, Tom."

"That's not a grin, Mom. It's a grimace," and I told her some of what happened.

Paddy was sympathetic and had a solution. He said in all seriousness, "Tom, let's get some dynamite and we'll blow up that tree."

I said, "Paddy, it wasn't the tree's fault and besides, I never want to see that tree again."

Chapter 21
Paddy and the Tugs

As the summer wore on, Hill 16 played some gigs around Northern Wisconsin. We played The Beach Club on Madeleine Island in Lake Superior, an area I would later become very familiar with. Life in the woods was growing monotonous and I was wondering if, now that I was an old man of nearly thirty-four, the best of times were past.

One day Paddy called, "I've set up a tour out East and we have a recording contract in New York City."

We were to start in Boston, then move on to Philadelphia. From there we would head to New York where we would record the album. The tour would then finish in Portland, Maine, a town that I really loved. It sounded like just what I needed to break out of the doldrums.

Paddy and Sean were flying out. I bought a Mazda for a hundred dollars and talked Stormin' Norman, a quiet fellow who worked at West Point Lodge, into coming along. Norm was originally from New Hampshire. I offered to drive him up to his home town and drop him off before I continued on to Boston. We loaded up and hit the road heading east and taking it slow and easy. We had to because the clutch slipped, the tires were dubious, and the brakes were not good. We nursed the car along. I always carried tools and we stopped at a junk yard and picked up a few spare parts like an alternator, a fuel pump and whatever else we thought we might need.

Norm was good company. We had a lot to talk about. At least I did. I don't remember what he said so I probably just chattered away. After a few days and nights and getting lost in the New Hampshire woods, I dropped Norm off, got myself to Boston and met up with Paddy and Sean on the night we were to play.

We played The Purple Shamrock, a new place in Boston at that time down near the Fish Market. We had a good crowd and everything went fine until it was time to be paid. There was a big discrepancy between what we thought we were getting paid and what they thought the arrangement was. I tried not to get involved. There was a kid that had just came over from Ireland who got up on stage and sang a song that I had never heard, "Wonderful Tonight" by Eric Clapton. I thought it was beautiful, but I was distracted.

I could hear that there was no progress in negotiations with the bar manager. I found myself taking the Bose speakers and PA Head off the stage. I had them locked in my car before Paddy and Sean or anyone else noticed.

"Now we can negotiate," said I.

Paddy and Sean were mortified and they both told me, "You can't do that!"

So, I had to bring the equipment back inside and set it all up again. Paddy told the manager that we would be back in a few days to work it out. We had to be on Cape Cod to play in West Falmouth. Sean and I had no arrangements for sleeping so we just stayed out late and slept on the beach.

We played our gigs and returned to The Purple Shamrock a few days later. Sean acted as our spokesman. He told the manageress, "I'm not the same as I was a while back. I'm just after getting married and can't afford to not be getting paid."

She buckled and we were paid, which was good because we needed the money to get to Philadelphia. I left my car behind a building. None of the cars I drove had ever been stolen or even broken into no matter where I left them, even though there were often vintage instruments buried in the debris of the back seat. Sometimes it pays to drive junk. Off we flew to Philadelphia, I think by plane, but I don't remember for sure.

We made our grand entry into Brittingham's Pub, a fancy place on the Germantown Pike. Sean and I made our presence known by doing some impromptu step dancing on top of the bar, which was packed with the after work crowd.

After a while, Paddy and I went up to "our cells" as we came to call the eight by ten eighteenth century rooms on the second floor. Sean stayed below in the pub where he met the Brittinghams. They were an older distinguished looking couple always dressed to the nines. She wore a lot of classy jewelry and had a beautiful white fur coat that I saw myself later that night. They decided to take Sean out to eat and got caught in heavy traffic on their way to the restaurant. Sean said that the Brittinghams were surprised when he jumped out of the car and did a little more step dancing along the bridge railing.

We played Brittingham's for five weeks and had the run of the place after bar closing. We would stay up drinking the kegs dry and the lobster in the big industrial freezers wasn't safe either. We discovered that it could be eaten frozen and raw. The swamper would come in at eight a.m. and ask us how we were doing. When we said, "Good", he would say, "No you're not. Go to bed."

The jukebox would fire up at eleven on the dot when the bar opened and become progressively louder as the noon rush moved into full swing. We could drink for free from eight p.m. to eight a.m. When we were not drinking at Brittingham's, we often would walk up the Pike or take a bus into Philly to carouse.

One Sunday we were sitting in the bar listening to a band that had the crowd clapping, singing and shouting in all the appropriate places. Then between songs the lead man, whom I am almost sure was Seamus Kennedy, said, "Ladies and Gentlemen, this next song is the one where everyone takes their clothes off and shakes their jewelry." I liked that line so well that I stole it and still use it myself occasionally.

When the engagement ended the barman at Brittingham's added up our tabs. We could hardly believe it. Frank Brittingham later said that we were the only band he'd ever hired that ended up owing him money.

We left Philadelphia and caught a plane, thinking that we were going to New York, but between Paddy's accent and the accent of the person who sold Paddy the tickets over the phone, we landed in Newark, New Jersey. We had to take a cab to Manhattan and after that cab fare, we were truly stone broke.

Paddy knew a lady who took us all in for a couple of days and we slept on the floor of her living room about six stories up. The excitement of Manhattan coming through the windows from down in the street made it impossible to sleep for more than an hour or two at a time.

We played a gig at the Eagle Tavern and Julia Clifford, the great fiddler from Kerry, came by and sat in with us. We then went up to near 230th Street and Bainbridge in the Bronx where we played for the next few weeks.

We sometimes ended up sleeping on floors that already had eight or ten others sleeping there. Housing was expensive and I remember a few times when the landlord would bang on the door in the morning and chase the surplus sleepers out of the apartment. The area was crowded with Northern Irish who had overstayed their visas and were working in pubs, construction and music. Paddy always seemed to have a place to stay, but sometimes Sean and I had to find a park with benches to lie down on or a viaduct to sleep under. Sean asked once, "Tom, did you ever notice that the driest places to sleep are the places that people like to piss?"

It wasn't a glamorous time for us, but when we stepped on to the stage at eleven, everything would change. The music was always great. The squabbling and arguing would cease and Paddy and

Sean would crank out some of the finest versions of tunes around. Whatever else was going on was forgotten.

Erin Hart came out to meet Paddy and I would see her at the pub when I came in for the gig. Erin wouldn't be drinking, but she often put her head down on the bar and slept. It could be a rough place with tough guys and drunks and fights. Everyone knew Erin was with Paddy, but Paddy was often away with the music, so, just in case, Sean and I kept a sharp watch over her from the stage.

Sometimes the crowd would grow sullen and dreary and then, at around three a.m., the smiles would return and everyone was suddenly in a good mood. Sean would look at me and whisper, "The Candyman is here."

Later, when we would go into the tiny toilet on a break, the floor would be sparkling with little scraps of tin foil, the sign that the Candyman had come and gone.

Sean and I liked to shoot pool. The going bet on a game was five dollars and sometimes we didn't have the funds, but we would play anyway. We always won, although we shouldn't have. We only found out later, because no one would say it to our faces, that our band was also known as "Paddy and the Thugs." Sean was even taller than me, and given the way we looked and with all the rough sleeping, the way we smelled, the other players threw the games that we should have lost rather than trying to collect from us.

One Sunday afternoon I remember strolling along a street in the Bronx with Sean when we came to a corner and spotted a little pub across the way. We heard a boom box and out front we saw a bunch of kids in Irish dance costumes. There must have been a Feis somewhere and the kids were apparently waiting for their parents who were getting refreshments inside. The song that was blasting out of the boom box, so loud that we had no trouble hearing it from across the street was Cyndi Lauper's "Girls Just

Want to Have Fun." The teenagers, mostly girls but a few boys as well, were break dancing to the music. It was the first time I had heard that song, and every time I've heard it since, that scene comes to mind.

We visited Martin Mulvahill, father of Brendan, while we were in the Bronx. The Mulvahills were one of the truly fine fiddling and teaching families in New York at the time. They were from Limerick and, when they played, you would never hear better.

It was time to record, but we had one more gig to play in the Bronx. The night was a rough one. Afterwards Sean broke the neck of his banjo and had to superglue it together and I misplaced my guitar. When we went down to Manhattan the next morning, I had to borrow a guitar, as well as a pair of jeans. My pants had been destroyed somehow the previous evening. Paddy arrived in a distracted state.

Daniel Michael Collins, owner and founder of Shanachie Records along with his business partner Richard Nevins was producing the recording to launch his new label Meadowlark Records. The first attempt that afternoon wasn't too successful. In fact, we couldn't complete a single tune and we were miserable. Daniel Michael said, "Not to worry, lads, we'll get this yet."

He left and returned a bit later with a surprise. He brought with him a case of Budweiser and a bottle of whiskey. The recording was done in less than four hours, mostly first takes, and it still sounds good thirty years later.

For the last leg of the tour we were to meet up in Portland, Maine, for a one week stint. I reached Boston, picked up the Mazda and then made my way up to Maine, stopping along the way to visit a few places I knew from the old days when I lived in the Boston area.

I visited Ed Jesby, a science fiction writer and scientist for GE who was the brother-in-law of Patrick Quirke of the Baldpate Hospital. Patrick had passed on by this time and I was sorry that I didn't get to meet with him and ask him all the questions that I had since learned to ask of Irish men and women from that generation. I would have loved to have known where in Kerry he was from, when he immigrated and to hear his reminiscences about his early life in Ireland at the beginning to the twentieth century.

Patrick Quirke's brother-in-law was an interesting character in a different way. He had no formal college degrees in science or anything else, and, in fact was a convicted criminal who had done twenty years in a New York prison although I never asked what his crime was. Patrick had told me that back in the seventies Jesby, strictly on the basis of his natural electronic genius, was the only one not required to wear a suit in the research department at GE.

Jesby had long, long stringy gray hair and thick wire rimmed glasses. Sitting across the table from him the first time I was at his house when I was twenty-one, he told me that he could throw a knife and stick it between my eyes. I responded, "That's nice, but what good would that do?"

He laughed and started calling me "Four Eyes with No Glasses."

*****

We had a good time on stage in Portland but had trouble figuring out what to do with our time off stage after the excitement of New York and the Bronx. The only two memorable things for me on that trip to Portland were seeing Kevin McElroy after a gap of ten years and meeting two elderly Connemara sisters. The sisters invited me to the apartment they shared, poured some tea and taught me a song called "The Bogs of Shanaheever."

We finished our last night in Portland. Paddy and Sean flew out and I headed off into the New Hampshire Woods in the Mazda to find Stormin' Norman. I picked him up and we took off for Wisconsin, taking the northern route through Canada, then down through the U. P. of Michigan. The Mazda was on its last legs. We could barely make it up the hills and the car was falling apart around us. It got me back to the cabin and didn't move again for years.

There were other wrecks accumulating on my property as well. Near the dead Mazda was a forty foot mobile home carcass that someone had sold to me for fifty dollars. I had no real use for it until a farmer bought the frame, axel and wheels planning to use it as a hay wagon. He cut the top off the trailer and left it in the yard. I was bartering this and that in the fashion of the locals. If I could scrounge something of value to trade, I did. We bartered trucks, vegetables, venison, furs, musical instruments, guns, anything and everything. It was part of the fun of living in the backwoods.

One day Marilyn Heck, of What The Heck, took a look at my bar tab and decided that she needed to hire me for a night of music. On closer examination of the tab, she said, "And I'll need you to swamp out the bar in the morning. Then we'll be square."

I played the gig, and showed up the next morning at seven for swamping duties. When Marilyn came in at around nine she said, "About last night, Tom, when you're good, you're really good. But when you're bad, you are really bad."

Although I often didn't remember what I had done after about ten in the evening, I rarely received bad reports the next day. I decided to stay away from the Hecks for a while.

Casey from K. C. was making herself scarce. I picked her up a few times from a new job she had at a place called The Pines. It was a three-quarters house for alcoholics who had become wards of the state. Once when I picked her up she said, "You should come in and have a look around. See the place where you're going to be living someday."

I was soon on my way to St. Louis to play McGurk's with Hill 16. I was always a hearty eater but lately I had noticed that my appetite for food was finally under control. A half a hamburger a day was all I wanted to eat.

It was Halloween in St. Louis. A former bartender asked Paddy if he could sing a song just as a break was ending. Paddy gave him permission and the guy started singing "Alice's Restaurant. " Sean and I, knowing that the song takes a half hour to sing, stepped out the back door of McGurk's outraged. We were complaining loudly when a big bucket with a mop got in my way. I gave it a good kick and it flew into wall thoroughly dousing us both with the nasty water that had been used to mop the floors of the bar and kitchen throughout the day. As the last strains of "Alice's Restaurant" trailed off into the night, Sean and I arrived back on stage. We were still soaked with the stinking mixture, but at least we had quieted down.

When I returned to Wisconsin, Casey from K. C. was gone for good. And that was good. She soon married a friend of ours and had two great kids.

Donny Lovdahl, a neighbor who lived near West Point Lodge, was building a pole barn on his land. He asked me if I could dig some holes in the sandy soil for footings. I didn't have a running vehicle so he picked me up. I tried to dig, but my hands were shaking so much, that I couldn't hold the shovel. A trip to McKenzie Castle to quiet the shakes didn't help.

Gail Castle was planning the entertainment for the deer hunting season. She wasn't going to have strippers again and she decided to hire me to play music. The first night in the middle of the performance, I told her that I had to go and hitched a ride to my older sister's house in St. Paul. She'd moved back to Minnesota from Denver years before. She tried to put me to work by having me assemble a newly purchased record cabinet. I couldn't concentrate, so I went to the Half-Time Rec on Front Street, where The Irish Brigade was playing. I was sitting at the bar when a girl came up and asked, "Didn't you used to be Tom Dahill?"

She said her name was Kathie Luby and we started talking. I finished telling some wild story and she said, "You must have been drinking. You couldn't have been in your right mind."

I said, "I'm always drinking, so this is my right mind."

She gave me a look that I have never forgotten and I considered for the first time, "Maybe I've never been in my right mind."

I had fifty bucks in my pocket and I was suddenly afraid to drink it. I didn't know what I might do. I wandered off and the next morning, November 21, 1984, my youngest sister Judy saw me walking along Grand Avenue and asked me if I wanted a lift. I wasn't headed anywhere in particular, so she dropped me off at my parents' house. We visited for a while. Then my father said, "Tom, there's this jerk down at the Hospital who claims he can tell if someone is an alcoholic by asking him twenty questions. I think he's full of it. Should we go down there and make fun of him?"

I agreed, "Sure, let's go."

Jim Jensen, who had been the head counsellor at Hazelden, asked me the twenty questions and I answered every one of them "right". He asked me about music and said that he used to fiddle. Then he showed me his left index finger which wasn't there. I asked, "What happened to your finger?"

He told me that he lost it when he was shingling a roof and missed, hitting the finger with his hammer.

"You idiot," I blurted, "You could have been fiddling all these years instead of sitting in an office! Don't you know to hold roofing nails between your first and second finger soft side up?"

He gave me a shocked look, picked up the phone, dialed a number and said, "We have a man here with a very serious problem. We have to check him into the hospital, now!"

Now I was shocked. He called around several places but all the beds were full. I was pretty quiet by this time. He said, "I think we can get you in in a few weeks. Try not to die between now and then."

"Okay," I replied, and left.

My dad was driving me along West Seventh Street and he stopped at Kessler-McGuire Mortuary. He told me that he had promised that he would stop in for a wake. Someone he knew had quit drinking, started again and then had committed suicide. He asked if I wanted to come in with him. I declined, "No, thanks. I'll just get out here."

I trudged up to Slam Bang O'Toole's Spot Bar and told Slammer that the posse was after me and wanted to put me into treatment. Slammer said, "Don't let them catch you, Tommy. They'll brainwash you."

It was snowing hard when I left the Spot Bar and slipping and sliding I walked a couple more miles to O'Gara's with tears frozen in my beard and mustache. A short while later I spotted the posse, consisting of my dad and sister, Judy, coming through the front door. I was about to slip through the kitchen and out the back door when my dad shouted, "Shot and a beer, Tom. Come on, let's have a drink."

I never turned down a free drink in those days. It's a humble boast. And they had me. They went next door and bought a twelve-pack of beer. We went back to the house and had dinner. I drank mine. My dad said that he had found a bed for me but I had to take it that night. It was a one-time only offer.

I was driven down to St. Joseph's Hospital, escorted into the Detox Ward and when the door locked behind me, I felt relief when I heard the click.

Part Three

Chapter 22
Spin Dryer

"Did the room seem familiar to you?" my mother asked. It was visiting day at the treatment center. "What room?"

"The one down the hall where you were staying."

She pointed toward the Detox Ward, where I had spent a weird three nights strapped down to a bed with nurses coming in at all hours giving injections that they said would keep me from going into convulsions. There were windows all along the hallway for patient observation. "Not really." I said.

"Well, it should. You were there a long time ago. It used to be the nursery for the maternity ward."

When I was born right there in that ward, I'd been told that things did not go smoothly. I was a breach birth and my mother had nearly died having me. My head was lying on my shoulder and my legs were twisted up. When I was brought home Dr. Galligan, who was the old-fashioned kind of doctor that made house calls, showed my mother what to do with me. My mother would push my head and move it from side to side to get my neck working. She also had to exercise my legs which involved a lot of pulling. My older brother and sister thought she was being mean, but it was just what I needed. My legs became so strong that I learned to walk before I crawled. My first words, according to the family Bible were, "I want to go!" And go I did.

After my visitors left, I took a walk to the end of the hall and looked out a window towards the Mississippi. This would have been my first glimpse of the wide world if an infant's eyes could see. When I was daydreaming in school I would look out the classroom window at the trees and birds and imagine what kind of place St. Paul had been before St. Paul got here. There were dozens of creeks, streams, caves and waterfalls all along the river and we had all heard the story of "Pig's Eye" Parrant, the

French bootlegger who sold moonshine out of one of the caves and provided refuge to soldiers who had deserted from nearby Fort Snelling. The settlement that came into being was called Pig's Eye and would have retained that name if not for a missionary, Father Galtier, who changed the name to St. Paul. After school I would try to trace where the streams and caves had been before the city landed on top of them.

The river was freezing over. It was November and there was snow on the ground. Seeing the early season snow, I started to think about setting snares to catch rabbits like I did back when I was a kid. When I caught them, I would tan their skins and hang them on my mother's clothes line in the basement which I'm sure wasn't what she wanted to see when she went down for the laundry. But my mother was always a good sport. I would use the pelts to make hats, scarves and mittens as Christmas presents for my sisters, except for Mary, who wanted a live baby rabbit rather than a fur hat. Even though I was a city boy, I always thought I would be happier in the country.

My thoughts were all over the place as I stood there watching the blowing snow. Things had not gone so well. There was a spot on my land in Wisconsin where, out of the corner of my eye, I used to glimpse my body lying in the snow. I would think, "Oh, that's where they'll find me. That's where I'll die someday." That thought hadn't bothered me because I figured I had seen enough and lived a full life. Now, here I was, safe and sound in the former maternity ward of St. Joe's, out of the cold and in a place where many a header had gone before.

The counsellor assigned to me was Pat Moore. My very first request, on meeting him, was to have my fiddle brought in. He wasn't having it. He said, "Your fiddle didn't keep you out of here." And we both laughed.

The first night on the ward I had met a big fellow from White Bear Lake named Tom. He had been in the place before and knew the score. He showed me how to hold my finger over the hot water supply on the coffee machine to get a really strong cup of coffee. Tom got a call from his lawyer the next day relaying an offer from a judge. The judge said that if Tom stayed in treatment, he wouldn't have to do a two year jail sentence. I thought that sounded good, but Tom took the jail term and left the next day. I started to wonder if treatment was going to be worse than I thought.

I missed my first breakfast, but I was able to get up for lunch. They marched us down to the cafeteria and through the back door single file. Turkey, mashed potatoes, stuffing and pumpkin pie were being served. I flew into a rage. "What kind of joint is this? Pretending it's Thanksgiving! I ain't buying it!"

A fellow inmate said, "Hey man, it IS Thanksgiving!"

I filled up my plate, and ate the meal.

After I had a couple of days under my belt without a drink, I remember being surprised that I could still understand what people were saying to me and even respond to them coherently. I didn't know what I was like sober. I had been a firm believer in better living through chemistry, always kept myself topped up so the only "me" that I knew with was full of drink and other substances. Now, I had what some called a "broken drinker." The only way out was to get out of the drinking business.

I had entered the business early. All the people that I loved as a child were good drinkers, some better than others. I always managed to get a taste of beer at family parties when I was a kid. It accompanied the singing and dancing and storytelling.

I learned young how to acquire drink. There were ladies in my neighborhood who left their liquor bottles in the trash barrels out back, often with a half shot or more left in the bottle. Along with Timmy Tigue who lived next door, I would go through the alley, collect a dozen or so and we would mix ourselves a pretty stiff drink. I had learned that trick by the time I was six. Timmy and I would practice our staggers and swaggers and talking big, just like our cowboy heroes. Even if we didn't have any beer or whiskey, we pretended that we did. When we met on the sidewalk we would say to each other, "Do you want to come over to my beer joint, or should we go over to yours?"

And this is where I ended up.

After the first week I was starting to realize a few things. I thought that maybe I wouldn't have to die from drink. Life would be boring from now on and possibly long, but that was okay with me. I was too old to die young and leave a good looking corpse anyway. I was beginning to think that it might even be worth sticking around to see what might happen.

Pat Moore called me into his office, and when I stuck my head through the door, he asked, "How are you doing, Tom?"

"Oh, pretty good. How are you doing, Pat?" I said as I sat down.

"Oh, I'm fine. Do you know that you're an alcoholic?"

"How do you know?" I challenged him.

"Because you look like one!"

I broke out laughing. "Do I?"

"Yes you do."

"Thank you very much."

"No problem," said Pat.

While in rehab, I learned something about group behavior that stayed with me. There was a day for each of us to tell our own story to the group with counsellors present. A tradition developed that we thought was part of the treatment process. On the night before one of these sessions all the patients would attend a practice meeting. The men would set up the chairs and the women would make the coffee, and the "hot seat" would be prepared. The person whose turn it was to talk would sit in the hot seat. No one was allowed to say anything until they were finished telling their story. Then the group would tear into the speaker. The comments without a referee present could be brutal and the person would often be shattered after the experience.

The staff caught wind of this activity and put a stop to it. Pat Moore said that this kind of thing had happened many times before. It seems to be part of human nature that when people are thrown together into a group, they make up their own rules and traditions spontaneously. It reminded me of some Irish music sessions where the players, intending no harm, start to make up "rules" about how many times a tune must be played, what order they must be played in, or where people should sit. The rigid attitudes that develop around these rules that are not rules make it difficult for newcomers to learn and can drive them away.

*****

When I was a kid, I wanted to learn, but I didn't want to attend school. In fact, I refused on my first day of kindergarten. My mother said, and I think she had been through something similar with my older sister, "No problem. I have some work for you to do."

"Okay," I said.

And soon I was beating throw rugs against the side of the house, watching the other kids walking to school. I thought I had it made and shouted, "So long, suckers! " By the end of that day, between all the jobs she found for me to do and having no other kids to talk to, I was ready to try kindergarten.

It was a public school and I didn't know what to expect in a school that included everybody. Our family and friends were steeped in the old style Catholicism, no meat on Fridays, saying the Rosary on our knees, Holy Days of Obligation, and Latin Masses. We had the impression that the non-Catholic kids thought we were bad, and we thought that they were all, unfortunately, going to hell, no matter how much we liked them.

My first day of kindergarten, a kid smarted off to me, so I smacked him. My punishment was to sit in a small area off to the side where the classroom library was located. I wasn't allowed to participate. I was supposed to observe. The teacher sat down at the piano, played an arpeggio and sang with the notes, "Come and sit down if you please."

The kids sang back in the same key, "Come and sit down if you please." They sat down in a circle near the piano and the teacher raised the key one half step and sang the words again and again the kids echoed her. Over and over, higher and higher each time, they sang. Then they went back down again, one half step at a time until they were back into the original key. I wanted to sing. It was just about the only thing that I knew I was good at. I decided that I would have to find a way to behave or they wouldn't let me sing.

I was what my dad called "rambunctious". When I couldn't be controlled, my parents would send me to the Dahill Mansion which is what we called my Great Aunt Kak's house at 1230 James. It was a tiny mansion, only 821 square feet. Aunt Kak Dahill was a no-nonsense Irish-American business woman and she liked everything "posh".

Her brother, my Uncle Tom Dahill and his wife Aunt Helen lived nearby. Uncle Tom had been the Chief of Police in St. Paul during the gangster days of the 1930s. That was a time when gangsters and police were able to come to "understandings" to make life easier for both, so dealing with a wild young nephew presented no great difficulty. At either of the Dahill houses, they expected me to behave like a little gentleman and would tell me that I was the Irish one in the family. With those expectations, I did behave.

*****

I tried to behave while I was in the treatment center too. I wasn't resistant to the process and attempted to keep my mind open to suggestions. After all, I knew I hadn't gotten there by eating too many Cocoa Puffs.

I had to take a lot of tests and there were two that I remember. The results of one of them showed that I wasn't mentally ill which was a surprise and a big relief. The second test indicated that I had an anger problem. That sounded serious and Pat Moore gave me a bunch of pamphlets to read. They were written by my old friend Jim Jensen, who instead of writing pamphlets could have been playing the fiddle all those years.

A few days later, Pat asked me if I had learned anything about anger.

"Yes," I said sadly, "I turns out that anger is really fear in disguise."

Fear was a word I had never used until then. I knew all about paranoia, but fear? Hell. I was afraid of fear. Now that the booze and drugs were gone, I became well aware of fear for the first time. I was told that the only way to counteract the fear was to find a faith that worked. I couldn't find any theology that worked, but I had faith that if I just did what I was told, I might survive. Then it was family day in treatment. Pat Moore and I were sitting in his office when my parents and a few of my brothers and sisters came in.

My father was a former Golden Gloves champ and a WWII vet. He had been in the U. S. Army in the European Theater. He played harmonica and piano and would take my mother out dancing most Saturday nights when we were kids.

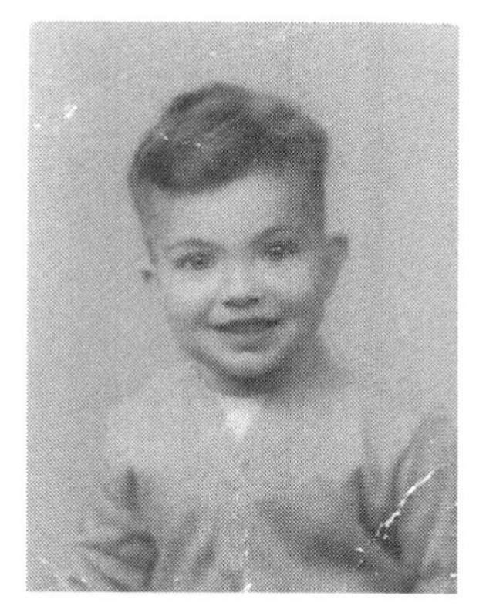

My dad loved being a father. When we went to bed at night, he would come up to each of us and sing a song like "Me and My Teddy Bear" or tell a story that he made up off the top of his head. He would tell stories about "Goofy", a not so bright soldier in the army, for the boys and "Susie Q" for the girls. My favorite bedtime stories were the legends of "The Pig That Was Always Smartin' Off". There was usually a moral to the story and more often than not it had to do with the consequences of pilfering cookies and sweets.

He had a big 1952 reel to reel tape recorder. He used it to record family get togethers where my mother and her four sisters, all tall women with long black hair, would sing songs in harmony and uncles would tell stories or sing their party pieces. It had a large green light that lit up when it was recording. Once, when I was about six, he asked me if I had anything to say into the microphone. I said that I had some jokes. He said, "Sing a song, Tom. Jokes get old, songs never do."

I don't remember much of what was said at family day, but I do remember that my dad, who I always thought I was very close to, went first. Pat had asked, "Tell me, what do you think about Tom?"

My dad answered, "Well, I really don't know the guy too well. We don't see him very often. Just once in a while around holidays."

After family day was over, I mulled over my father's comment about not knowing me. I started thinking about the people I'd met over the years and wondered how well I actually knew any of them.

*****

When I was seven, I had a piano teacher from County Limerick named Sister Magnus. She was tough and as a kid I thought that she didn't like me. My fingers were never quite clean enough for her and I was made to wash them several times each lesson. I copied what I heard her playing and pretended to read music for a few years. Then one day she asked my mother to stop bringing me to lessons because she explained, "He'd rather be chasin' rabbits! I see him before lessons with his bows and his arrows shooting at anything that moves."

Years later I visited her at Bethany, a home for retired nuns, and I played the fiddle for her. She was delighted to see me and she knew most of the tunes I played. She had been a concertina player back in Limerick when she was young.

I was put out of the classroom in the sixth grade for a minor infraction by Miss Gallagher. Miss Gallagher was feuding with my father and so my desk was out in the hall for about six weeks. I was supposed to sit there in the hall doing nothing, but I soon found something to do. I wandered down to the boiler room and met Pat Devaney from Connemara, County Galway.

He was the custodian and he had just arrived from Ireland. We got along great, even though he didn't have many words in English. We could communicate just fine by making faces and using our own sign language. He would laugh and say "What the Dickens" when I would light up a cigarette, and I would laugh when he would reach behind the boiler and pull out a half pint of whiskey. I would try to make sure he boarded the right bus for home at night, but Pat would climb onto any bus saying, "A bus is a bus is a bus."

Now I realize that he liked to ride around the city. He hadn't yet been able to bring his family over from Ireland and was alone although his wife and children all eventually arrived in St. Paul. Years later Pat Devaney and his sons Jerry and Mike were out playing cards and the boys decided to bring him to O'Connell's where The Dayhills were playing. They didn't let on that there was going to be live music. When Pat got out of the car in the parking lot, he said "Jerry, Jerry! Mike, Mike! Listen... Irish music!"

"No Dad," they said, "You're imagining it."

When they came in the back door, Pat cracked his hands together and said "What the Dickens!"

He hurried up to the stage where we were playing and started doing an old style Connemara step. Then he looked up in surprise and pointed at me.

"Jerry, Jerry! Mike, Mike! I went to school with that man."

"No Dad. That couldn't be."

I had blamed a lot of things on being a musician and wondered why I hadn't found something more useful to do with my life. I was given my first guitar for eighth grade graduation from St. Leo's. The eighth graders were released three days earlier than the rest of the school. On the last day for the graduating class, someone took a bicycle from the rack, ran it out onto the playground and jumped off. We all became involved and soon all the bikes were in a pile. Sister Paul Mary, the principal, appeared on the scene and we all ran. I zipped around the corner of the building right into the arms of Wally the Cop who just happened to be there.

I had been a thorn in Wally's side for years and he was happy to turn me over to Sister Paul Mary to be punished. She decided that, while the other graduates enjoyed three days of freedom, I would guard the bike rack until the rest of the school finished the year. I asked Sister if I could bring the new guitar. She said yes and so I sat outside for those three days practicing and learning a few songs. I had no idea that crashing bicycles would be the first step on the way to a musical career.

*****

I was starting to realize that the problems I'd run into along the way weren't caused by the music. They were the result of my particular type of drinking. In fact, the music had kept me out of more trouble than it got me into.

One day in Pat Moore's office, I announced that I was heading in the right direction and that I had given up alcohol. Then he gave me something to think about.

"When you say you're giving something up, you're implying that there was something good that you don't get to do anymore. What are you giving up?"

I considered that and tried to come up with anything that was good about drinking for me but couldn't do it. I never could control my drinking. I had just tried to control my behavior while drinking, but that had become harder and harder to do. I experienced blackouts and mistakenly thought that everyone else did too. I wasn't going to miss any of those things.

*****

In the past, alcohol and music had been tangled together. In my first week of high school in 1965 just after turning fifteen, I was asked by Jim Reid, a sophomore, Dan Hartnett, a junior, and Tom Enright, a senior, if I wanted to join a rock and roll band. We formed The Chaotics and had our first gig at a Rosemount High School dance about a month later making thirty-five dollars. Soon we were playing high school mixers, proms, dance halls and bars all over the five state area. We learned new songs as they came out on the radio, often several a week and figured out how to put them across to a crowd. We had a good agent and plenty of gigs. I never performed without drinking. For most of us, drugs and alcohol was a natural part of the rock and roll lifestyle.

Dan Hartnett and I turned out to be the core of the band. We went through fifty musicians over the course of four years. Dan and I were the only ones who were there from the beginning to the end.

On one of our Wisconsin gigs in Sawyer County, we picked up a felony bear theft conviction. We kidnapped Baby Bear, from a Three Bears display in town, put him on skis and sent him down a hill at Telemark, a resort near Cable, Wisconsin. After we were caught in a road block in Spooner, the taxidermist estimated the damage to the stuffed bear - missing toe and wrecked ear- at over two hundred dollars which made it a felony. It didn't help the situation that we had been hanging out in the sheriff's house with his daughter and drinking his booze while he was on duty.

We spent the night in jail. The next morning after our court appearance, we were run out of town and barred from Sawyer County until we were twenty-one. We changed the name of the band from The Chaotics to The Inmates and our parents had a meeting. They talked about breaking us up and then realized that if we weren't playing in a band, we would be loose on the streets of St. Paul. We kept on playing and even had the new name painted on the van.

The Minnesota State Fair had an area fenced off for rock and roll and called it "The Teenage Fair". The Inmates were booked to play one afternoon. We were running late when we showed up at the main gate which was manned by State Fair employees who were taking tickets and police who were keeping order.

Our bass player, Greg LeClaire, a huge wild-looking kid with long curly brown hair, was at the wheel. He slowed slightly as we passed through the gate and shouted out the open window, "Inmates here, we'll see ya!" and then sped off in the direction of the Teenage Fair.

The motorcycle cops mounted up and started after us with sirens blaring. Several cop cars joined in the pursuit. It wasn't any more trouble than we were used to.

Generally we were considered a little too wild for playing in town, but the agents in the Twin Cities often booked us for the out of town gigs. It wasn't uncommon for bands playing small towns to get jumped by the local boys while loading up the equipment after a gig. The agents knew we could play tough places and still come back in one piece. We always loaded the mic stands last as they were handy weapons for fighting our way out of town.

Once we stopped in Red Wing at an all-night café at about 2 a. m. on the way home from an out of town gig. We were in a borrowed Studebaker that belonged to the father of one of our band boys. As we were leaving the restaurant, we were attacked. We fought our way to the car and jumped in. They had a couple of baseball bats and smashed all of the car's windows and lights. The kid whose father owned the car was mortified because the Studebaker was his dad's pride and joy. We drove the fifty miles home with no lights.

In the morning, the kid came downstairs and found his father sitting at the breakfast table, his face hidden behind the newspaper. The son burst out crying, "Dad, I am so sorry!"

His father answered, "It's alright son, I understand. I used to play in the Big Bands."

The end of the band came when our new agent, in a wild fit of fancy tried to change the name to, "The Order of the Elephants." I said, "No way, man," and, at the age of eighteen I took a long walk away from rock and roll. I pulled out the acoustical guitar and started playing folk clubs and coffee houses. Soon after I met Barbara and we started playing together.

*****

Pat Moore said to me one day during a counselling session, "We are going to let you out of here in a few days because it seems like you're ready."

"Okay."

"We're going to let you out early, but you're going to have to go to a halfway house."

"Okay."

"Well, since you said okay, maybe you don't need to go to a halfway house."

I said, "Okay."

He asked me about my plans. I answered that I didn't have any. Then I explained that I was supposed to go to McGurk's in St. Louis to play music with a couple of guys from Ireland. I described the parties until eight a.m. and all the free booze and the carry-on at The Palace. I told Pat that I would have to cancel that.

"Yes, I suppose you do," he said. Then he thought for a moment and added, "Maybe you don't have to cancel."

"What? Go down there for five weeks? I'll never make it."

"But if you do make it through sober, you'll be stronger for it. If I set you up with an outpatient program down there, will you go?"

"Okay," I answered, "I'll try it."

Chapter 23
A Hungry Feeling

When I left St. Joe's, having been thoroughly dried out, my feet took me straight to MacCafferty's. It was just before Christmas and I had a few phone calls to make. I was on edge when I got there. I thought, "Well, I'll just get a drink at the.... Wait! I can't do that. That's okay. I'll just.... The cook usually has some...... No! No! No! What do I do?"

I called Martin McHugh. Marty had been quite a drinker and I'd visited him a few times in the hospital when he had bleeding ulcers. I knew he was off the drink now. On the phone he told me he was so dry he was a fire hazard. We arranged to have lunch at O'Gara's where the posse had caught up with me. We were sitting in a booth having a laugh, Marty being the master of humor both dry and droll, when an old pal of mine walked in. It was Smiling Pat all dressed up with a girl on each arm.

Pat used to beg me to quit drinking when he saw me at the bars. I thought he was crazy. He had been sober for six years, but that day I saw him order a drink for each girl and one for himself. Pat and his charming companions entered into animated conversation, and Marty and I continued our own conversation. Then I heard the sound of a slap. One of the girls with Smiling Pat walked out of the bar in a huff. Marty and I were dowdling tunes to each other when the other girl stormed off. Smiling Pat ordered another drink and started talking to a guy sitting next to him. That man soon left. Pat ordered another and struck up a new conversation farther down the bar.

Marty and I finished our lunch and left. Later I heard that Smiling Pat had cleared the bar one customer at a time and, after being shown the door at O'Gara's, was thrown through the window of the music store across the street. What happened to Smiling Pat was an educational experience for me.

Hill 16 had a gig to do in Collegeville the weekend after Christmas. I had never been on a stage sober in my life except for one night in Denver in 1976. On that occasion the others were so happy that I didn't drink that they took me to The Wazee Lounge on Larimer Street where there was a twofer special and we celebrated.

When Hill 16 took the stage in that Collegeville bar, I was scared stiff. Then I heard Sean and Paddy tearing into the jigs and reels and I was caught up in the tunes. Oddly enough, when it came time for me to sing a song I found it to be a lot of fun. I was excited after we finished the gig. It was only one night, but the thought crossed my mind that I could get to like being sober.

Then it was time for McGurk's. I can't remember how I got down there but I know that I had no vehicle of my own. I was fairly jumpy and didn't have much confidence that things wouldn't go south in a hurry. An older lady came up to me as I was standing at the bar and, just by looking at me, she knew I had been dried out. She told me that she had been sober herself for many years and said that she would stop into McGurk's often to see how I was doing.

Another time during that engagement a girl came up to the bar where I was sitting and commented, "Oh, recovering alcoholic, huh."

"How do you know?" I asked.

Pointing at the coffee cup that was sitting in front of me she said, "Shot." Then, pointing at the Coke in the glass she said, "Beer."

I had to laugh.

Most people didn't notice that I wasn't drinking and I noticed that other people didn't drink nearly as much as I thought they did. I did see some differences in how others approached me. A couple of friends brought in their new baby and it didn't start bawling when it saw me like most babies did. This baby even seemed to like me. A few people said that they had been praying for me but had been afraid to say anything before. They were right because I would have been insulted and annoyed. Now I was glad that they had been concerned.

Singing serious songs and playing difficult tunes is a demanding profession and being drunk was never part of the show. Some people who had known me for years assured me that my previous behavior on stage and in the bars wasn't that bad. I attributed that to the lessons I learned back in Boston when working for the Ox McCarthy. You could drink and drug all you wanted as long as you didn't show it. Out of habit I did fall off my chair on stage a few times in those first five weeks at McGurk's. Sean would just reach down, help me back up and we would keep playing.

One night while we were on break, a fellow jumped up onto the stage, which was a good three feet off the ground, and sat down in my chair. Sean, with his rugby face and physic, six-four, huge head, cauliflowers ears, and massive arms approached the stage and looked up at the oblivious would be entertainer. Then he picked up the chair, occupant and all, set it gently on the floor and ordered, "Don't do that."

When a night at McGurk's was over, we would adjourn to The Palace as usual and the party would begin. I would hang around in the kitchen for a bit and then slink off to the farthest bedroom, which had originally been a closet to read. The music would start up, great music, and the laughing and the shouting and all the usual carry-on. I would stay in my cell and that was fine. I was still too shaky to walk through to the kitchen to use the bathroom while the party was going on.

When I would finally emerge, after things had quieted down, it was usually light outside. The kitchen would be in a shambles and people would be sleeping wherever sleep had found them. I would chalk up another day off the drink.

The band was sounding better than ever. The new album was out and things were looking up. My old friend, Josh Dunson of Real Peoples Music, called and asked if we would like him to represent us. Josh's agency worked mostly with folk festivals and the college circuit. It sounded good, so we gave him the okay.

Josh went to work printing up brochures and other promo materials. Then we had a meeting with him in a downtown Chicago hotel. After dinner, Josh showed us the materials that he had printed up. They looked good, but there was one sticking point. In his description of the music, he had used the word "ballads". Sean and Paddy didn't want that word used in the publicity because it was out of fashion in Ireland at the time. Josh explained that everything had already been printed and it was really too late to change it. Sean and Paddy fell out with Josh over the issue and he never booked Hill 16.

I felt bad that we couldn't go with Josh as a band, but being a true friend, he worked out a way for me to have him as my agent when working solo. He told me that I wouldn't have to pay his percentage for the first year if I reimbursed him for the advertising and promotion that had been done for the cancelled Australian tour with Joe Heaney and that those payments could be spaced out until I got on my feet. This arrangement allowed me to become a primarily solo performer for the next twenty years.

*****

When I first returned to the cabin in the woods, I was shaken by what I saw. The old cars and pickups were covered with debris from the forest. The remains of the big mobile home, minus the frame, wheels and axels that went to the farmer's hay hauler looked exceedingly ugly. Most of the snow had melted revealing hundreds of beer cans lying all over the clearing. For a moment I wondered who had put them there.

The whole mess presented a good opportunity to start cleaning up the wreckage of the past.

I had been nervous on the way up knowing that I was just going to be dropped off. When we arrived, my heart was racing and when I spoke my voice was nearly an octave higher than usual. The friend who drove me up to the place, I believe it was Pat O'Neill, had mercy on me and stayed for a few hours until I was calmer.

Alone, I lit the milk can wood stove, turned on the transistor radio, lit the kerosene lanterns and climbed into bed with a book. I laid back and crossed my arms behind my head under the pillow and felt something strange. I lifted it up and saw a pile of pellets, D-Con Rodent Poison. I looked around the small room. From every shelf and all over the top of the gas operated refrigerator I could see pairs of tiny eyes looking at me, dozens and dozens of them. These were not only tough mice, they were insane mice. They were living on D-Con and apparently flourishing. I had left little boxes of the poison scattered all around the cabin. They had eaten the boxes and stashed the leftovers in my bed.

The mice were staring at me and seemed to be making plans. I threw a boot, hoping to frighten them. They disappeared and I tried again to read. After about five minutes, I noticed that they were back with a hungry look in their eyes so I threw the other boot and nearly knocked over a kerosene lantern. I got up and picked up all the D-Con and put it in a bowl by the door and that's when I saw my shotgun and thought about trying to blast them. Fortunately I was too tired to try this method of extermination, so I returned to bed, covered my head with the blankets and wrapped up tight. I slept for a while.

Early in the morning my dreams were disturbed. I felt a flutter, and then another across my face. The third time it happened I was awake enough to figure out what it was. Mice. They were chasing each other across my face.

I jumped up, dressed and walked over to Jo Mama's restaurant at the corner of County Roads A and H, about three miles away where I engaged in a little barter. I got a small, used wood stove and a hundred dollar pickup truck in trade for what was left of an illicit crop that I had grown in my garden the summer before.

When I returned to the cabin I picked up my shotgun and deer rifle and brought them to my neighbor's house for safe keeping. I'd known several people who had blown themselves away up there in the woods and I was not too steady yet.

*****

A few weeks after I returned to Wisconsin, I saw Rick Day's wife Terry down on the Hertle Reservation. Rick and I went back a long ways. He used to sleep in the afternoons at What The Heck where I also had taken naps. Rick would wake up and lift his head off the bar, see me sleeping across the way and then doze off again. Then I would wake up and see him sleeping. We seldom spoke but were friendly. Then he had disappeared. I asked Terry where he was, saying that I hadn't seen him in over a year and she answered, "Oh, he's around." When I finally ran into Rick himself that spring he told me that he didn't drink anymore so now I knew why he had disappeared.

Rick and a few other friends would stop by to check up on me and they helped me get things straightened up around the place. Stormin' Norman and I devised a plan to build a log cabin that would incorporate the original shack and over the next year making that plan a reality kept me busy.

West Point Lodge had added a campground the previous year and hired me to log off an acre or so of tamarack from a swamp. Tamarack doesn't rot so I wanted some for the outside walls of the new cabin. I had stacked the logs on site but the pile was shrinking rapidly so I drove in there with my pickup and hauled out about fifty big logs before they all disappeared. I took them to Clark Weaver's sawmill just across from What The Heck where he cut them in half lengthwise, giving me a hundred half logs that were ten feet long.

The original twelve by twelve shack already had a ten by twelve cement slab in front of it that I had poured when I attached an old mobile home kitchen to the cabin a couple of years before. I removed that kitchen and then used a car jack to lift the cabin off the old sinking cinder blocks on each corner which were all that held it off the ground. I removed the blocks and replaced them with railroad ties. Then I built walls around the kitchen slab and extended the original roof. The cabin now measured twelve by twenty-two.

When that was done, I dug an eighteen inch wide, three foot deep trench for a ribbon footing for the sixteen by twenty-two foot addition we had planned. I scavenged a couple of fifty-five gallon drums from the dump to haul water for the concrete. Then I went around picking up rocks and stones from lake shores and stream beds and piled them up nearby. I dug a little sand mine on the side of a hill near the cabin. Back at the dump I picked up all the bed frames, steel pipe and actual rebar that I could find. I was now ready to pour the foundation ribbon.

I built the forms for the foundation ribbon and picked up some bags of Portland cement on credit from Clark Weaver at the sawmill. Clark had a little bit of everything there, and we had an arrangement. If I didn't have cash I could pick up whatever I needed and pay him when I could. I would visit him every week whether I had a payment or not to let him know that I hadn't forgotten my debt.

I didn't have a cement mixer so I mixed the cement by hand on a mixing board I had made with two sheets of plywood. I threw all the rock and metal I had collected into the forms as I poured the cement leaving pieces of rebar sticking out at regular intervals. When the cement dried I could drill holes in the bottom plates, made from four inch tamarack slabs cut from the middle of the thickest logs I had, run the rebar through the holes and then bend it to secure the bottom plates to the footing.

Stormin' Norman had some eight by eight inch oak beams that he had scrounged for barter. We drove out to where he stored them and hauled back a huge load. These would be used for corner posts and for holding up the loft. We put up the oak corner posts and added the upper plates, again using tamarack slabs. We were constructing what was called a "Stockade" or "French-style" building. Many of the bars in the area were built this way and I'd spent plenty of time studying the technique.

I snapped chalk lines on the middle of the upper and lower plates and set the tamarack half logs up vertically, erecting the outside wall first. I secured them with eight inch pole barn spikes. When the outside wall was up, I stapled a layer of tarpaper to the inside. Then I attached three-quarter inch Bildrite fiberboard sheets over the tarpaper. Another layer of tar paper was stapled to the Bildrite on the inside. I then used jack pine half logs for the inside wall, setting them vertically but staggered so that the thin part of the inside wall would not come at the same point as the thin part of the outside wall. I fastened it all together with more pole barn spikes giving the new cabin sixteen inch thick walls to keep the Wisconsin winters at bay.

Then came the fun part. After carefully measuring and marking the openings I would need for the doors and big windows that I had scavenged from the dump, I pulled out the chainsaw. I cut the openings and without much trouble was able to install the doors and windows. Norm and I built the loft next and then used it as the scaffold to add the roof. We built the roof and a dormer using regular frame construction and rolled roofing.

I installed a floor in the addition, which was now the main part of the house. Rick Day came over from his farm and built the chimney. The wood stove I had bartered for after the "Night of the Mice" was too small to heat the new place and I replaced it with a barrel stove that someone gave to me. Life was improving.

The whole cabin was built for around two thousand dollars at the most.

Old Russ Baker, the Texan, agreed to come over and tell me how to wire the place as long as I kept him supplied with coffee. Suddenly, I had electricity. Now I needed water.

A few years before I had witched a well with a forked dowsing stick that had indicated that water would be found at a spot in what was now the middle of my living room. In sand country, the usual way to get water is to drive a pipe into the ground but that didn't work for my neighbor Clint. Driving could only be done if the water was reached at fifty feet or less. Clint ended up having to drill and finally found water a hundred and fifty feet down. I borrowed a well driving rig from Clark Weaver and started driving a sand point into the middle of the living room. A sand point is a pointed piece of two-inch pipe with holes in it to let water in and screens to keep the sand out. I was lucky. At twenty-seven feet, I hit good water and plenty of it.

I asked around and, with a little help, plumbed the place. A few more gigs from Josh, who was booking me in colleges now, and I soon had a flush toilet and septic tank. I was given an old claw foot bathtub by Dick Brooks and Sandy Lyons of WOJB. What had been the original cabin was now a good sized bathroom.

After being on the land for five years, I finally had all the comforts of a modern home with the exception of a furnace. Heating with wood was fine if you didn't mind a mess and a lot of work. I tried a couple of propane furnaces, but they were second or third hand and more trouble than they were worth, so I stuck to burning firewood.

My friend Kevin Foley was moving out of the house he and his wife, Shula had been living in since the MacCafferty days. I helped them with the move. Kevin was a big reader but wasn't planning to take all his books with him. He told me to look through them and take any that I wanted. We ended up loading four or five boxes of his books into my car. At home, I unpacked the boxes and was pleased with the variety. There was everything from *Moll Flanders* to *Johnny We Hardly Knew Ye.* I built a bookshelf in the loft that also served as a railing.

I had a big garden, a freezer outside that only had to be turned on in the summertime, a stove, an electric fridge, a sink, a toilet and a library. I was pretty comfortable up there.

Chapter 24
Burning Down the House

I was driving one day and saw Petey Pie come around the bend down by Mystery Lake about a half mile from my place. We both pulled over near the public landing. I jumped out of my pickup to have a chat. It was easier for me because he had a hard time extracting himself from his own little white pickup. The list to port was increasing as Petey continued to grow wider.

"Pie, what are you up to?" I asked

"I'm going to be a jack pine savage like you guys on Tobaccy! " When Petey Pie first started using that name for McKenzie Lake Road, most of us weren't sure whether he meant we were hillbillies like the book and song implied or whether it was a reference to the hidden crops some of us grew. Either way, we all started using the term. He told me that he was moving out of West Point Lodge. "It's too much for my head," he said. "I've got an A-frame a couple of miles up the road."

Thinking that Petey might be imagining things, I mentioned that there were no houses up that way. McKenzie Lake Road was all sand beyond my place and otherwise there were just logging roads. Petey said, "It's brand new. A guy had it built and I'm gonna live there and be just like Uncle Suck!"

Petey was all excited. "Come on, Tommy. You've got to see it."

I followed his pickup down the road through the woods laughing inside thinking of Petey, the greatest people person I had ever known, trying to live alone in the woods.

When I pulled up to the A-frame, Petey was as proud as could be showing me around his new home. It had obviously just been built and it was definitely in the woods as there was no clearing beyond what was needed for the house.

Petey couldn't wait to build a fire even though it wasn't cold. He said he wanted the fire for atmosphere. There was a Swedish-style stove in the living room that looked like a big upside down funnel with a stove pipe going up and out of the roof. Petey asked me to help him get it going. We put a fire down, then sat in the living room and chatted for a bit. When I was ready to leave I congratulated him on his new lifestyle and commented on the new bib overalls that he had donned for the occasion. I headed out the door, hopped into the truck and moseyed on home.

I had just sat down to eat my dinner when I heard the volunteer firetruck speeding down the road with the siren blaring. It was coming from the direction of the firehouse at the intersection of County Roads A and H. I heard the siren but probably had some tune going through my head and didn't really think about it. I usually sat and played the fiddle or Big Liz, Cuz's one row box, in the evenings, and I had completely forgotten about Petey Pie, the newly minted jack pine savage.

The next day I stopped in at the A and H Outpost, a bar and shop at the crossroads next to the firehouse. Tommy Farrell, the owner, who didn't like Petey much, said, "Your buddy burned down a house last night."

I found Petey back at the Lodge and he related the sad tale. "I was sitting there alone, smoking some wacky and watching the fire. All it needed was a little music so I put on some Molly Hatchet. Everything was so beautiful. The fire burned down, so I put on some more wood. It didn't burn right away so I threw on some more. Then it all took off at once and burned down the house. I got out just in time."

A man named Loren Bowen and I had become good friends after meeting at What The Heck. He was another colorful though drab-looking character and everyone referred to him as the One-Eyed Jack, but never to his face. He got the nickname because he had lost an eye more than thirty years before and never had it seen to. It was constantly weeping and looked pretty frightening until you got used to it. He worked as a hunting-and-fishing guide and had painted the letters, "DNR" and a big round face with a tongue sticking out on the door of his truck. He was also a handyman, and professional scrounger. He came out fishing with me on my boat a few times and we did odd jobs together over the years.

Loren lived on an old homestead that dated back a hundred years or so which is a long time in that part of the woods. The place may have been wired for electricity at one time, but Loren never bothered with it. His land was covered with old farm and logging machinery. He had every kind of vintage truck, tractor, thresher and cultivator. You name it, he had it. Where anything was, though, was a mystery to Loren. Everything was grown over. There were metal chairs overhead that had been lifted into the air by the trees that grew through the rusted seats. The bits of machinery that peeped through the undergrowth were blanketed with rust. The combination was enough to disguise the identity of most of the things in his outdoor museum and late fall or early spring was the only time you had a chance of finding what you were looking for.

Loren had arthritis. He went to a doctor who took an x-ray and told Loren that his spine showed up entirely black from the disease. The doctor told him that the only reason he could still move was because he had never stopped working.

Every couple of days Loren made the rounds. He picked up people's trash and, after picking out what he wanted, hauled the rest to the dump. I shoveled snow off of roofs with Loren one winter, which can be really hard work. I couldn't keep up with him and asked him why he cleared to much more than I did. He answered, "You work hard and fast. Then you stop and take a rest. I take small shovelfuls, work easy and slow, and I don't need no rest."

I was just starting with Josh on the college and festival circuit and the Hill 16 gigs came up now and then, but to fill in the gaps, I would head to my hometown of St. Paul, just a two hour drive from the cabin. When the gig was over I would high-tail it back up to my place. I had become accustomed to the quiet, slow pace of the back country and I dreaded the traffic and the noise of the city at the time. When I played in town I usually played at a new place on Grand Avenue that had opened just down the street from what had been MacCafferty's.

I had first met the owner of the new pub back in the winter of 1975. It was snowing and I was walking down Grand Avenue in front of Knowlan's Supermarket across from MacCafferty's. A man in a fur hat was shoveling the sidewalk with a big old-fashioned iron snow shovel. He looked up as I passed and called, in a distinctive voice, "Are you Tom Dahill?"

I admitted that I was and he exclaimed, "I can't believe that a great musician like yourself would be walking down the street just like anyone else!"

I looked hard at him to see if he was kidding, but he didn't give anything away. I don't know to this day whether Tommy Scanlon is pulling my leg when he makes unusual comments. You tend to remember people whose first words to you are something like that.

Now it was ten years later and Tommy had bought Fran O'Connell's and changed the name to Scanlon's. It picked up some of the slack left by the demise of MacCafferty's and was quite a place while it lasted. Tommy put the likes of Gus Gustavson and Lar Burke behind the bar. Lar was a genuine and genial fellow, a Vietnam vet who was involved in local Irish theater. Gus was a native son of St. Paul and a master of making connections and passing along the news since he knew everybody in town. It was a jovial place and featured traditional music. Marty and I played there as did every other Irish band in town, of which there were now many. Tommy, three or four of his brothers and one sister had all come to St. Paul in the early sixties. Once that generation had established itself in America, the next generation of Irish Scanlons started making the crossing and frequenting their uncle's bar.

Towards the end of Scanlon's reign on Grand Avenue, Tommy told me in that high voice that people love to imitate, "I'm thinking of closing the kitchen. There are more steaks going out the back door than to the tables out front." Tommy ran a very leaky vessel. He ran a slightly tighter ship when he opened The Dubliner on University Avenue a few years later.

I stopped in to a Sunday night session at Scanlon's with either the fiddle or the accordion, I don't remember which. The other flutes, fiddles and accordions were hard at it and I chimed in. In the middle of a tune, a guy crept up behind me and put his arms around my shoulders. The other musicians looked apprehensive and waited to see what I would do. They didn't know that I had already read all the pamphlets on anger. The man yelled, "I LOVE this guy!"

Now the others in the session were somewhere between embarrassed and appalled. The session players had become more and more straight-laced since the seventies had ended. I recognized right away that it was Danny Doyle. We had grown up together, and there was no way I could be mad at him.

Danny loved any kind of music. In his younger days he had been the best looking kid in town. With his black, curly hair, his blue eyes and his pale skin with a hint of freckles, the girls were crazy about him until they found out that he never worked. Not for long, anyway. He sometimes worked for a few days here or there. At those times he resolved to change his ways, but Danny never changed. I remember when we were kids in the neighborhood, if you didn't want to finish your cigarette, you would put it out carefully and stand it on the filter tip out of the rain because, "Danny will be coming by."

Danny slept on everyone's couch and was always welcome because he thought the world of everybody, and he let them know it. He was like Petey Pie in that way. People who really like other people tend to get along somehow, even if they live their lives outside of the accepted norm.

On that night poor old Danny looked awful rough. He died about a year later with Gus, the bartender, at his bedside. Gus told me that Danny had been in hospice and when they were turning off the machines that were keeping him alive he was listening to music on headphones. As he lay there, Danny had them play The Moody Blues. I imagine that the particular song he wanted to hear was "Go Now". Gus stayed with him to the very end and said that Danny's last words were, "It's my own damn fault. I should have quit drinking when I was twelve."

*****

To avoid having to travel down to the city too often, I started an odd jobs business in Wisconsin. I hand wrote a couple of posters saying,

Handyman Available.
Painting, Raking, Mowing.
You name it, I can do it.

The phone in the cabin didn't ring for a week or so. Then a lady whose husband had died saw one of the posters and called saying that she needed her lawn mowed. After I mowed her lawn, she sent me over to her sister's next door who was also a widow and needed some work done. It turned out that there were many widows of retired 3M employees in the area.

At The Lumberjack Saloon the so called Sunset Club made up of the elderly set met every afternoon to gaze out the windows over Little Bear Lake. The ambulance was called, often on a weekly basis, to pick up the men who had heart attacks at the bar. The carnage was something that people joked about. It left quite a few widows who sometimes lived another twenty years and they needed someone to help keep their lake places going.

I found no end of odd jobs to do. I raked seaweed out of lakes, put in and hauled out docks, shoveled snow, raked, mowed and painted. I couldn't keep up with the demand. I tried getting help from halfway houses in the area, but after paying my helpers, I usually didn't see them again.

Josh was finding more and more gigs for me. I played some college and folk club tours that he had booked including one that sent me all over the mid-West in the dead of winter. For that tour I started out in a blue Pinto hatchback, a vehicle favored by local poachers, and before I was even halfway to my first stop in Omaha, I was in trouble. The car developed a fuel leak near the carburetor and the engine caught fire....in the middle of Iowa farm country....at about two a.m. ....in a snowstorm. I pulled over and got the instruments away from the car, popped the hood and started throwing handfuls of snow onto the burning engine. The snow put the fire out, but the wires were melted. I walked back to my instruments and stuck out my thumb. The first vehicle that came by was a pickup truck pulling a horse trailer. The couple saw the smoke and pulled over.

"Where are you going?"

"Omaha."

"Oh ma God," the woman said, "so are we. Hop in."

The couple took me right to the door of Creighton University and dropped me off at about six in the morning. I played the noon gig, received my pay and started looking for a car. I found a Mercury Grand Marquis.

The car ran well at first, but over the next twenty-four hours, one by one each tire went flat and had to be replaced. The final tire blew out somewhere near Columbia, Missouri, as I drove to the next gig. It was about four in the morning and everything was closed. I couldn't continue so I pulled over and slept on the side of the freeway. I woke up a few hours later with the rising sun. I looked out the window and saw a tire store about a hundred yards away.

I decided to head for The Palace where I knew I could get rested up and maybe even sort out the car a bit. When I arrived, I took a look under the hood and saw that the main water hose was blown up like a football and was on the verge of exploding. I changed it along with the thermostat and all the belts and hoses I could see.

With its wide windshield the Mercury was a great car for taking in the scenery, especially since I didn't have any distractions close up. The rear shocks were shot and the back end of the car was so low that the long hood of the Grand Marquis pointed heavenward making it impossible to see anything directly in front me. I decided to deal with that later.

I continued on the tour, finishing up at The Ark in Ann Arbor, Michigan. Before leaving Ann Arbor, I had to replace the radiator and water pump in the parking lot of an auto parts store. By the time I finally arrived back at the cabin, I had a pretty good runner.

The following September, Josh called and told me that he had booked me on another tour. I set out in the Grand Marquis and played a couple of colleges out East before heading for the final engagement, a folk festival at Lincoln Center in New York.

In New York City I parked the car as close as I could to Lincoln Center, opened up the trunk, pulled out the instruments and ran to make the venue on time. Some of the festival headliners were Doc Watson, Odetta, and Richie Havens. There were about 60,000 in the plaza in front of the outdoor stage. I made my way down to the lower level green room and was introduced to Doc Watson. He was a terrific blind guitar player and singer. He told me that this was going to be his last tour, but he continued playing concerts for another ten years.

I figured that I wouldn't be able to hold on to my bow, my nerves being the way they were after seeing the size of the crowd. Leaving my fiddle down below, I went to the backstage area and watched Richie Havens finishing up his set. I was up next.

Richie came off the stage totally drenched with sweat and said, "Good luck."

I wondered what Josh had gotten me into. The announcer introduced me and then walked back to where I was standing and said, "Fifty minutes."

I repeated what I hoped I'd heard, "Fifteen?"

"No. Fifty." I nearly fell over.

I walked out on stage and said into the microphone, "Hello. I just came down from Wisconsin. I don't think there are this many people in the whole state."

From several spots in the crowd I heard shouts of, "Wisconsin! Wisconsin!"

Looking at my guitar I said, "I lost my song list....about twenty years ago. So I'm just going to sing "Cushy Butterfield", and I hope you like it."

The crowd chimed in on the chorus, "She's a big lass and a bonny lass," and I could see that I was going to survive. I decided to play the festival like I would a pub, not explaining much and just trying to entertain. All the good energy from the crowd melted away my fears and after about twenty minutes I wanted to run down to the green room and grab my fiddle. But there was no time. The fifty minutes flew by and it was soon over.

Afterwards, I was off to the side of the stage selling some records when Odetta came up and asked for a cigarette. I gave her one and she growled, "Don't tell my friends that you gave me this," in her powerful, gravelly voice.

I said, "If they give you a hard time, just tell them it gives you voice muscle."

She laughed, "Heh, heh, heh. Voice muscle. I like that."

I picked up my things and returned to the car, relieved to see that it hadn't been towed. Unfortunately for me, the trunk had been popped and fortunately for someone else, seven hundred dollars in cash was missing from my suitcase. I tied the trunk shut and drove straight back to Wisconsin. The strange thing about it was that for the next two years, every time I did my finances, I was exactly seven hundred dollars short.

Chapter 25
Bite the Hand

I got a call from The Pines, the three-quarters house that Casey from K. C. had invited me to tour back when she worked there. They wanted a couple of rooms painted. While I was painting, I met some of the clients. They were wards of the State of Wisconsin, but most of them were good humored people nonetheless. One fellow told me that there was a horse outside that he wanted to show me. So, on a break from the painting, I went out to have a look.

She was a skittish brown mare with a wild look in her eye. Even though she had no spots I was told that she was pure Appaloosa. Her hooves had never been trimmed because no one could get close to her and they looked terrible, growing out in every direction and kind of curled. If she had been loose in the fields, the hooves would have worn down a bit naturally, but she was only able to move about in a small paddock and the situation had gotten out of hand. She was a pet horse for the facility and they called her "Old Bite-The-Hand."

I always liked horses, not that I knew a lot about them. When we were kids, my older brother, Larry, and his friends had permission to ride some horses out in Mendota just across the Mississippi from St. Paul. Mendota, which translates roughly to "Where the Waters Meet" started out as an early frontier settlement springing up where the Minnesota River meets the Mighty Mississippi. It is a tiny town which has now been surrounded by city.

I would tag along with Larry and his friends on my bicycle. We would bring sugar lumps to lure the horses over and when we caught one, we would jump on bare back and just hang on, riding wherever the horse wanted to take us. The horses would run around the fields until we fell or were tossed off.

When I finished the painting job, I asked the manager of The Pines about the mare. He told me that he wanted to sell her because some of the residents had been abusing her. One had hit her with a two-by-four. I hadn't planned on having a horse, but I did have ten acres of woods. I said, "Don't pay me for the work. I'll take the horse."

I went home and grabbed my chain saw. I made a little clearing in the woods behind the cabin and put up an electric fence attaching the wire to trees around the perimeter. I found a lady vet in Shell Lake who worked with horses and she met me at the Pines. We closed the doors of the small barn to the residents so they wouldn't spook the horse.

The vet looked over Old Bite-The-Hand, pronounced her fat but healthy and because she had had a good way with horses, was able to clip and trim the hooves. She brought a trailer with her and plenty of rope. It was a job and a half coaxing Old Bite-The-Hand into the trailer, but we loaded her up and hauled her out to my land.

Now I found myself with a circular corral made of electric fence containing one abused horse and no experience in caring for horses. Yet.

I worked constantly on my new project. I mucked out a cow barn for a friend and received plenty of hay in return. Then I started digging holes eight feet apart for a barn sixteen by sixteen, to shelter the horse. Once I had the holes dug, I used cabin left overs and salvaged wood to build. I still had some oak beams from Stormin' Norman. I painted the ends of the beams with drain oil from the pickup and set them upright in the holes. Then I used two by twelves salvaged from the dump for stringers and left over slab wood and half logs for the walls. More salvaged wood and rolled roofing topped it off and, in about a week, with the help of some friends, I had my little barn up. It is still standing as is the cabin thirty years later. When I look back at the work I did so quickly, it wears me out and I feel like taking a nap.

Old Bite-The-Hand had come with a halter and I spent a lot of time walking her, brushing her and trying to lead her. She didn't seem to appreciate all the work I had done to provide her with a better environment. Although she never actually bit me, she had been traumatized by her time as a resident at The Pines. In the end, I was able to put a blanket on and walk her, but that was as close as I got to gentling her.

I asked questions of anyone that owned horses. Eventually I met a fellow in Minong who owned quite a few of them. He offered me a trade. He would take Bite-The-Hand and a hundred dollars and in return I would receive a spotted Appaloosa. I took a look at the gelding, a big, tall thin fellow and we saddled him up for a test drive. As I was working with him, I kept calling him "fella" and that became his name. I took the deal and the Man from Minong threw in the saddle and a hackamore bridle at the last minute. He brought Fella over to my place in his trailer, picked up Bite-The-Hand and hauled her off to her new life.

I had good times with Fella riding through the woods on sand roads and logging trails that stretched for miles to the north, south and east of my place. I had been given a great introduction to riding fast and jumping with horses a few years before with Steve Allie.

I had met Steve at Harling's Upstairs where he and his friends, some dressed in grey uniforms and some in blue, would come after meetings. They were avid Civil War reenactors and loved to sing and dance so we hit it off right away. Steve owned horses which he used in the reenactments, training them for cavalry charges and other military maneuvers. We were sitting at Harling's one night when Steve invited me to join him on a reenactment of an 1866 Jesse James' bank raid in the town of Liberty, Missouri.

The next week, Steve and I rode up to the old bank building in Liberty. It was next door to a Seven-Eleven. We filled our saddle bags with beer from the convenience store, went out behind the bank, dismounted and skulked around a bit. We were near the main entrance when Steve shouted, “Now!”

We dashed around the corner of the building, jumped on the horses and took off at full gallop. In about two blocks we were out of town. We left the road and set off up and over the hills, then across the fields, jumping anything that got in our way. Steve assured me that this was the route that Jessie James had taken when he had robbed the bank. I followed him for miles at top speed and it was a great ride. Steve had trained the horse was so well that it didn’t matter who was on his back even when jumping fences or going over downed trees. It was like riding in a Cadillac convertible with the top down, steady as could be and smooth. The only problem with the whole event was that the beer was badly shaken up. The memory of that ride and other rides with Steve were a big part of why I ended up with a horse.

Fella was a good runner and he liked to chase deer through the woods. They always escaped, but we enjoyed the chase anyway. He had one baffling habit. He would suddenly lie down on his belly in the road with his legs splayed and his neck stretched out flat to the ground. The first few times it happened I thought he must be deathly ill. It was a mystery to me until someone told me that it was just a trick he had learned to get a break.

By the time the Man from Minong came by and taught me how to trim Fella’s hooves and keep his frogs clean, I had removed trees from a couple of acres and cut the stumps level to the ground. I nailed more electric fence wire to the trees around the cleared area to complete my pasture. Fella and I were getting along fine.

I went down to St. Paul to play a gig with Marty at Scanlon’s. As I was entering through the back door, I walked right into Dan Gleason who was on his way out. Dan is an architect originally from Brosna, County Kerry. He is a good singer and "The Valley of Knockanure" is one of his best. We did some catching up and I told him that I was busy with horses up north.

"I have one that you can take if you want her."

"Are you kidding?"

"It's a barrel racer, an Appaloosa. My daughter used to compete, but she's gone away to University. I've been taking care of that horse for years and I'm tired of it."

"Are you sure your daughter wouldn't mind?"

"She hasn't ridden it in years. The only people that ride her are the ones that come out to my house and that's only when they have a few drinks in them. She's become a party animal. One of these days somebody is going to get hurt and I'll get sued."

"I'll take her."

"Her name is Pearl. Come and get her," said Dan.

Back in Wisconsin I located a guy with a horse trailer and we drove down to pick her up. Pearl turned out to be a very nice horse. She was a steady trail rider, but a little feisty at first. She hadn't been ridden by anyone other than Dan's party guests in quite some time and I suppose she had grown used to having the upper hoof. Now that I had two horses friends would stop by and we could go riding.

My sister Judy and her boyfriend Joe used to come up every summer for my annual "Hotdog Festival". I supplied the place and the hotdogs, and she would supply a crowd of friends from St. Paul. The local Jackpiners would be there as well and we had plenty of singing, guitar playing, fire-jumping and horseback riding.

Fella's first move when someone climbed aboard was to back into a pine tree in an attempt to dislodge the rider. He had a few

Tom, Pearl and Fella

other tricks as well, but if they didn't work, he would settle down and allow himself to be ridden. Pearl wouldn't let just anyone ride her, but she never gave any trouble *when she had small children on her* back. She was very careful with them. About a year later, I saw Dan Gleason again. "My daughter isn't speaking to me," he said, but he didn't want Pearl back.

Quiet Al was a neighbor of mine who owned Moon, a horse named after The Who's drummer and we often rode together. He was working for a big paper pulp mill when the employees tried to start a union. Word spread that the company had compiled a list of those that were to be terminated for union activities. Al got wind of it and happened to know where the list was kept in the company offices. Somehow, the list disappeared. No one was fired and no one was caught. Al kept working and kept his mouth shut. He didn't talk an awful lot, but there was plenty going on under his hat.

Quiet Al came by one day and, laughing, told me a story. He was riding Moon near the Namekagon River close to the town park of Earl when he came upon some people at a picnic table. There was a lot of food on the table and, what caught Al's eye, plenty of beer. Al, being a friendly sort, rode up, dismounted and, with the best of Wisconsin etiquette said, "Give me a beer."

Somebody at the table, not following the accepted customs of the area replied, "No."

Al was walking dejectedly back to Moon when the horse did what horses do. Al, without saying a word, picked up a big pile of Moon's output, walked back to the group and deposited it on the table. He mounted his horse and trotted off. You never knew what Quiet Al would do, but he was a great friend to have in the woods. We went through a lot together over the years. He was even married to a cousin of mine....for a while.

*****

In the summer of 1987 I met a girl named Lisa who was living in a halfway house and wanted to run away. I knew her mother and some other friends of hers and they all said, "She's gonna run away with somebody, so she might as well run away with you."

A short time later there was Lisa, me and the two horses living at the cabin. Lisa decided that there wasn't enough going on and not long after she moved in, we went out and acquired a couple of Malamutes, a male named Chinook, and a female named Angie.

The two Malamutes had very different personalities. Angie tangled with a porcupine once and only once. She never got stuck again. Chinook got into one really bad mess with a porcupine and ended up with quills all over his face and down his throat. I took him to the vet and paid fifty dollars to have them pulled. Two days later, he chased after a porcupine again but I couldn't afford another trip to the vet. Instead, I bought some Everclear, the hundred and ninety proof alcohol with the "caution, extremely flammable" warnings on the label and poured it in some milk. Chinook drank it and I rolled him up in an old carpet, put a stick crosswise in his mouth, tied it around his head and went to work with a pair of pliers. I pulled out every quill.

A week or so later, the same thing happened and I followed the same procedure. Chinook just kept attacking porcupines and I kept pulling quills by the hundreds. After a few more porcupine encounters and the resulting hangovers, he wouldn't drink the Everclear and I would just use the carpet to hold him still and the stick. Later on, I didn't even need the carpet. After months of this kind of carry on and a very unpleasant bloody carry on it was, he would just come and lie down in back of the cabin with another big mouthful of quills and wait for me to put the stick in his mouth and pull them out.

That summer there was a drought and hay was becoming expensive. It had been about a dollar a bale, but suddenly it was scarce and the price spiked. Lisa's father owned cattle, and as winter approached he sold off his stock. He happened to have six big round bales of marsh hay on his property that he hadn't used. I could only haul one at a time on the truck, but suddenly we were in the hay. It was moldy, but it was free.

Lisa got used to my daily practicing fairly quickly. One evening I was playing the fiddle and feeling content. I looked around the cabin happily and said to Lisa, "This is the house that fiddling built."

Lisa looked around, smiled and replied, "No, Tom. This is the house that Cushy built."

Lisa had a daughter and a son, but had lost custody. We talked about getting married and possibly getting the kids back. When our discussions became serious, the old Texan, Russ Baker came to mind. I remembered that he had kept up his minister's license with the idea that marrying couples might be a good sideline so we talked to him. Although it had been a long time since he had officiated a wedding, he agreed to do the job.

We hired a band and the wedding was held at the Scott Town Hall. Scott Township was the official name of the settlement at the A and H crossroads. While conducting the service, Russ the tough old Marine, was so nervous that he started shaking all over and stuttering. I was a little worried that he might not make it through the ceremony, but somehow he managed. The reception was held immediately after in the hall and my family had come up from St. Paul for the festivities. I remember one of my aunts, a good Catholic, saying to me when I was dancing with her, "Tommy, I just love coming to your weddings."

I was Lisa's third husband in seven years. Lisa's daughter lived with her first ex-husband and was fairly settled. She would spend a day or stay overnight once in a while but never lived with us. Her son Arthur had been staying with his dad, ex-husband number two, and did come to live with us. He was about five and very bright. He accompanied me on all my odd jobs and we got along. He liked the dogs and the horses and the woods. He was with us for about a year.

Tom with Art and Hippy the dog

One day in the cabin I turned on the radio and Arthur asked, "Tom, can we listen to the long music?"

I asked, "What's that?"

He turned the knob on the radio to a classical station and said, "This is it. This music is good for you. Rock music is bad for you....and country music is REALLY bad for you."

Art seemed to know a lot of the things that are important in life. My parents came up once from St. Paul for a visit. Art went out with my Mom to show her the horses and she told me that he had been very solicitous of her. He told her, "Don't touch the electric fence. And, whatever you do, don't pee on it."

I'd had Fella and Pearl about two years when I saw an ad in a local grocery store circular for an Arab gelding with papers for a hundred dollars. The horse had been a raffle prize, but the winner couldn't afford to keep him.

Now I had three horses.

I talked to a neighbor about a quarter mile away who had a twenty acre pasture. He wasn't using it and agreed to let me keep the horses there in the summer time. In the winter, all three horses could be sheltered in the barn when the weather was bad and when it was nice, they could run around in my pasture. The Arab at just over a year old was too young to be ridden. He was grey and I named him Pretty Boy.

The horses were eating better than we were and had medical care, which we didn't. They needed shots, hoof trimming, and were generally high maintenance. The handyman work, as much of it as there was, was not enough to care for the horses without going into debt. And then there were the dogs. Things were getting tight.

*****

Around this time I received another phone call. Cuz had died. I wasn't able to attend the funeral in Chicago, but friends who had been there described it. At the wake, Cuz held in his hands a concertina that I had given him as he lay in the coffin. I was told that just before the coffin was closed, Mrs. Teahan took the concertina out of his hands. Someone asked her why. She answered, "It's a waste of a good concertina."

Cuz would have liked the story. I could almost hear his wild, joy-filled scream.

*****

Lisa had a job at a meat and cheese processing plant in Minong for a short while and one day she came home with a surprise for me. It was a twelve pack of beer. I pulled out my shotgun and blasted it. Not long after that Lisa wandered off with a biker gang, and I never saw her again. Arthur went to stay with Lisa's mom when she disappeared. The last time I saw him he asked me, "Won't I ever see you again?"

I told him that if he ever wanted to find me, he should look for Irish music. I hope he does.

The situation had gone bust. I gave Pretty Boy, the Arab, to Quiet Al, who kept him for another twenty years. I sold Fella and Pearl to a nice riding stable in Rice Lake. The dogs, Angie and Chinook, went to a breeder. I held on to the land and cabin which were paid off. It was late fall and a new decade was approaching. I decided that I was ready to try city life again.

Chapter 26
Strictly Heavy Duty

I felt like a hillbilly when I arrived back in the city. I rented an apartment in a house called Big Pink, originally a giant duplex that was now divided into seven apartments and painted a becoming shade of pink. There were some good sessions around town. Both Sean O'Driscoll and Paddy O'Brien were spending a lot of time in St Paul.

Big Pink

Daithi Sproule, a singer and guitar player from Derry, was on the scene as well. He first visited St. Paul with Paddy O'Brien and James Kelly when they were playing together in a group called Bow Hand. Daithi liked St. Paul, found a local girl to marry and has lived here off and on for many years. He has a vast repertoire of songs in Gaelic, is an excellent guitar player and a very good fiddler. He tours with the group Altan now as well as playing solo.

Daithi enjoys going to sessions and one night in a noisy bar one of the other musicians, Tom Sweeney, had pointed Daithi out to his new employer whom he had invited to an evening in the pub saying, "That's Daithi Sproule."

The man was new to Irish music and had been indulging in pints and shots while taking in the scene. In one of those inexplicable hushes that sometimes comes over a lively room, his boss replied loudly, "What's a 'da-he-sprule'?"

I was playing a solo gig in the back room at Scanlon's when my sister Judy came in with a friend who was a realtor. Terry Smith asked me to give her bids on some painting jobs for a few condos and houses that she was selling as an agent. She drove me around to eight properties and showed me how to write up bids in a little book, a bid book, that she had brought along. A few days after I had turned in my bids, she called and said, “This is fine, Tom. Just double your price and you can do them all.”

Suddenly I was a painting and rehab contractor. Being used to country wages, I had no idea how much more you could charge for your labor in the city. It was easy work compared to the work in the woods, mostly because the majority of it was indoors and you didn’t have to drive so many miles for materials. Soon I was knocking off two or three condo jobs a week. Mostly the work involved “burnettizing” the properties. The term meant cleaning the place and painting the walls off white in preparation for sale by Burnett Realty, the company that Terry worked with.

One of the first jobs I did for her was on the Eastside on Jenks Avenue. It was a HUD house and there was a garage out back that had to come down, work that was right up my alley. I pulled out the old chain saw to cut the corners of the structure and used a logging chain attached to the bumper of my station wagon to pull it down. Then I cut up the garage with the chain saw and threw it all into a roll-off dumpster.

Not long after that, I was repairing and burnettizing a house on Dayton’s Bluff, also on the Eastside. A lot of very foul smelling carpet had to be torn up from one of the rooms where someone had kept pit bulls. The dogs had not been taken out much, if at all, and the stench was unbelievable. The trim work in the room had been gnawed and needed to be removed and replaced. There were holes to be filled in walls throughout the house, apparently made with fists, feet, and a few stray bullets.

Working alone in the dim interior I started to notice a sound. It wasn’t constant, just a strange chirp, like a forlorn cricket trapped somewhere within the walls. The noise came from different directions at varying intervals up to ten minutes apart and would only sound once so I couldn’t track it down. As I worked, some part of my brain would be waiting for the sound and I would flinch when I heard it. Finally, I found the source. Someone in the house must have had a great fear of fire and found a good deal on battery operated smoke alarms. In the end, I found eight of the things scattered throughout the house emitting their lonely peeps of death. The whole house gave me the creeps.

When everything was finally pulled out of the house I was left with a gigantic pile of trash. I sometimes hired friends to help me and one of those friends was Danny Doyle. I needed a trailer and Danny said he had one. He assured me that it was new and "strictly heavy duty." He agreed to help me haul the rubbish including the foul carpets to the dump that was under the High Bridge on the Westside. We loaded up the trailer, a flatbed about twelve feet long and tied everything down. The trailer was made of metal and looked well built. We hitched it up to the station wagon and headed off towards the dump.

St. Paul is built on bluffs on either side of the Mississippi and a trip from the Eastside to the Westside is only about three miles but involves crossing several bridges. We were in the middle of the Third Street Bridge just above the old Connemara Patch where there used to be a shanty town full of Irish immigrants when there was a sickening sound from behind. The trailer had buckled. There was an even more sickening smell as the load shifted and the carpets unrolled. The contents of the crack house fell off the trailer and spread across the busy roadway that serves as the main route from the Eastside into downtown St. Paul.

We jumped out to see if there was anything we could do. After taking a quick look, we jumped right back in and drove like hell. The "strictly heavy duty" trailer, now empty and bent nearly in half, was banging along behind us as Danny and I looked for a place to hide.

The last job I did for Terry Smith was at a house she had bought for herself. It was a brownstone row house on Summit Avenue near Dale in a neighborhood known as Crocus Hill. It was next door to one that F. Scott Fitzgerald had lived in when he was rewriting the manuscript for *This Side of Paradise*. Sinclair Lewis, the author of *Main Street* had lived just down the Avenue where he worked on a novel, never finished, about James J. Hill, the Empire Builder. Hill, who built his mansion on Summit Avenue and Archbishop John Ireland, who erected his Cathedral at the very top, loomed large in the history of St. Paul in the early part of the twentieth century.

Terry hired me to do some demolition and painting at the big brownstone. I hired a few other fellows and we tore out some walls and ceilings and hauled out the debris. Behind some of the walls upstairs we found hundreds of issues of National Geographic from the twenties that were apparently used as insulation.

Terry had hired separate crews for the carpentry and sheetrock and they were working right behind us. There was a lot of work for all the crews and cooperation as well as coordination was necessary to finish the job efficiently. There was plaster dust everywhere from old walls and newly sanded sheetrock.

As in many big old houses, there was a front stairway for the owners and their guests to use and a back stairway built for the servants. The house was going to be Terry's main residence, and she had definite ideas about what she wanted. She told me that the back stairway, spindles and all, were to be painted mauve. I had never heard of mauve, but went ahead hired another friend named Tim Fitzgerald, a Highland Piper, handyman and painter known as Fitz. With all the ornate woodwork it looked like it might take a week to finish that stairway, but Fitz had recently purchased some equipment, including a sprayer that he wanted to try out. I thought he might be able to finish it in a couple of days.

When Fitzy showed up for the job, I introduced him to the guys in the other crews. There were probably ten or twelve of us on site at any one time. Fitz set up his work station near the bottom landing of the three-story staircase. He placed a large boom box on a work bench and started arranging his tapes of the Clancy Brothers, the Dubliners and the Highland Pipes. When that task was finished to his satisfaction, he left for lunch.

He returned three hours later and brought in his shop vac, toolboxes, sanders, plastic sheeting and the paint sprayer. He piled them in the lower landing making access through the back and into the kitchen very tight. That was it for the first day.

The next day at about noon he returned and used the plastic sheeting to block off access to the entire back stairway making the front stairway the only route for all the debris to be brought out of the house and all the sheetrock to get in. Finally...he turned on the music. Loud. The Irish songs were not appreciated by the other workmen.

Fitz would disappear into the blocked off stairway to do some sanding, scraping and patching for about half an hour until the tape finished and then emerge to change the tape and make a circuit through the house cheerfully visiting with everyone. Fitz was a jolly type, about five and a half feet tall and maybe two hundred and fifty pounds at the time. He was so friendly that none of the guys complained to Fitz about the music.

On the days that Fitz had the Irish music blaring, it wasn't too bad, but when he got onto a jag of listening to Highland war pipes, the atmosphere became strained. Soon shouting, snapping, arguments and complaints were the norm with the Highland pipes providing the soundtrack to our misery.

It wouldn't have been a problem if Fitz had finished in a couple days, and it wouldn't have been so bad if it had only been a week. But after a month's time, there had been little progress on the back stairway and the other contractors were cornering me and insisting that I light a fire under him. Terry was hearing about it too and she refused to pay me or anyone working with me until Fitzy was finished. Finally the day came when Fitz took down the plastic and cleared out. And the stairway looked good....from a distance.

With the back stairway finished, our work was done and we could be paid. Before I had a chance to collect, Larry a big wild looking guy who was also part of my crew found out that our pay had been withheld and became so outraged that he ran over to Terry's office to confront her. I chased after in the car and he was just inside the door when I caught him. I escorted him away from the building and sent him back to start the final clean up.

I went in to talk to Terry. She cut me a check so that I could pay everyone and then, with a hint of a smirk, handed me a tax form to fill out. I had never seen one before and wasn't sure what to do with it. Asking around, I found out that I was responsible for the taxes on all of the money including what I had paid out to the people I'd hired. Contracting was more complicated than I had realized. Fortunately, I never had to do it again.

Chapter 27
Just Part of the Fun

I was escaping to Wisconsin as often as I could. The cabin was a welcome refuge since it now had all the comforts of a home and with the wives, girlfriends, horses and dogs gone, I could relax there.

I had kept up with Dick Brooks of WOJB and a few years before, at his request, had done a thirteen part radio show called *The Irish Kitchen Racket.* The show was mostly based on cassette tape recordings I had of the men who had helped me, Cuz Teahan, Paddy Hill and Pat Flanagan. There were others as well. That show led to a Wisconsin Arts Board grant for a five part radio program called *Songs of the Wisconsin Lumber Camps.* For that project I interviewed local old timers who had worked in the logging camps of northern Wisconsin. The songs and stories that I collected were mostly too lewd for broadcast, even on Public Radio. I did gather enough material for the program which was a good thing since I had already spent the grant money on the horses.

One winter's night not long after I had finished the radio series, John McCormick, a piper from the Brian Boru Pipe Band, drove Marty McHugh up to the cabin. John was just getting started on the button accordion and had been spending time with Marty. The three of us continued on to Sandy Lyons and Dick Brooks' place in Springbrook and recorded an album called *St. Paul to Donegal* for Flying Fish Records out of Chicago. We were short one song so we used a tape that had been made earlier on the Reservation of "Cushy Butterfield" with a mostly Ojibwa audience singing on the chorus.

The following year, which was 1988, I made another record with Glenn Walker Johnson. I had met Glenn at WOJB and he had given me a cassette of his harp playing. I put it in the tape deck on the way home and cracked up. He was playing O'Carolan music and would launch into rhapsodic variations which sounded distinctly Caribbean. He would play along for a while with just enough notes from the original tune to keep you from forgetting what it was and then gradually bring it back to earth. I called him up and asked him if he wanted to record. He not only agreed, he said he would bring along all the recording equipment. We recorded the album, *The Ragged Hank of Yarn* right there in my cabin.

I sent the master down to Josh Dunson of Real Peoples' Music who was still my agent and he brought it to Bruce Kaplan of Flying Fish. Bruce liked it enough to produce it. Now I had two albums out with Flying Fish Records. I was still playing Chicago, Kansas City and St. Louis sporadically in those years and having new recordings to sell helped keep the wolves from my door.

One day when I was in Wisconsin, I spotted a sailboat at a yard sale in Spooner. I drove by, trying to ignore it. I went out for a cup of coffee. I had seen a sailboat in the dump a few months before. It had been too big to move and in a very sorry state, but that vision had planted the kernel of an idea in my head that was trying to sprout as I drank my coffee. I drove back to the yard sale half hoping that somebody had already snapped up the little sailboat. It was still there.

The boat was twelve feet long and made of fiberglass over a foam core. Somehow it ended up in the back of my pickup and I headed home. I called Pat O'Neill who had driven me up to the cabin when I first left St. Joe's and was now a frequent visitor. He had grown up on White Bear Lake and was the only person I could think of that knew anything about sailing.

Pat came up the next day and we put in at the public landing on Rooney Lake. He showed me how to rig it up and with the wind blowing us offshore, we sailed out to the middle of the lake. The wind died and the boat, which apparently had cracks in the fiberglass, started to sink. The shell filled with water, but the foam core didn't allow the boat sink all the way, leaving the top of the hull level with the water. From the shore, we looked like two men sitting on the water in the middle of the lake with a mast, a sail and grim expressions on our faces. Using a paddle and occasional puffs of wind, we made it back to shore in a couple of hours. From that point on, whenever I sailed in that boat, I would stay close to shore and every twenty minutes or so I would beach it, pull the plug, and drain the core. Then I would be able to take her out for another twenty minutes of happy sailing. In the end, I think I got my fifty dollars' worth of enjoyment and experience out my first sailboat.

Back in St. Paul, I was looking for a car. Someone put me on to "The Volvo Man", Dave McEachran, who, if you gave him a hundred dollars down would fix you up with one of the fifteen to twenty old Volvos that he had stashed around the neighborhood near Lexington and Selby. The Volvos were parked everywhere. He had a range of prices for the cars and the final cost could be anywhere between five hundred and two thousand dollars.

Once you had given him the down payment you could drive it away and pay it off over time. Any repairs needed in the first thirty days, he would take care of. Dave always had a mechanic or two working for him under the radar. When the car was paid off, he would give you the title. Although it probably wasn't entirely legal, Dave had been operating that way for many years and getting away with it. Over all the years he had been doing business, he told me, only one person had failed to pay up.

Dave was still a big guy at eighty. He was originally from Michigan and loved to dance. He was out most nights dancing because, "The ladies love a man who can still dance." He added, "They keep me busy."

I went to his storefront abode, another not entirely legal arrangement, to talk to him and noticed that he had sailing magazines stacked around his very cluttered office. He was on the phone so I started paging through one of the magazines while I waited. When he hung up, I commented on the beautiful sailboats depicted. He looked at me and said, "You! I will sell you my sailboat."

A half hour later we were out at Hooper's Yachts in Afton, where Dave had his twenty-five foot, 1973 Hunter stored on a trailer. She was full of mold and mildew, but she had good lines, with a galley and sleeping quarters and was fitted with running lights and a motor. I looked at her and thought of Lake Superior.

It was fall, so I had the whole winter to clean up the sailboat and ready her for the next sailing season. I just needed a place to work and Fitz came to mind. Fitz would do anything he could to help out a musician and he was renting a farmstead out in Rosemont. I hadn't been out there, but when I called him he said that there was a barn on his place. He suggested that I bring the boat there and we could work on it over the winter.

When we brought the boat down to Rosemont, Wee Barry Nelson from Belfast and his two teenage sons Donny and Chris were there. After hearing their band, Penny Whistle, at the Half-Time Rec, the bar on Front Street in St. Paul, Fitz told them they could stay at his place as long as they wanted. As Fitz became more and more involved in the Irish music scene, one of the things he always did was put up travelling musicians when they were in town.

Fitz knew about many of the practical aspects of refurbishing the boat and rebuilding the trailer. We tore out the mildewed insides of the cabin, bleached everything and then used blue, padded car upholstery for resurfacing. We repainted the outside and Timmy rebuilt the brakes on the trailer and replaced the wheel bearings.

Meanwhile, I read everything that I could find on sailing and navigation and was a regular visitor at Hooper's where I hung out in the shop and offices and asked questions. By the end of the winter, I had learned about nearly every piece of equipment in the shop and how to read navigation charts. Bill Hooper and his business partner Brian were very patient but eventually Brian told me, "To learn how to sail, you just have to take the plunge and do it."

In the spring of 1990 Fitz and I towed the boat up to Bayfield, Wisconsin, and dropped it into Lake Superior. She didn't sink or even leak. The hull was sound. We couldn't get the motor running, but I used a long paddle to move her away from the city dock. I soon had to buy a new motor.

I got a gig at The Beach Club on Madeleine Island, one of the Apostle Islands, just three miles off shore from Bayfield. I loaded my instruments and a small PA on board. A couple of friends, a wild woman named Katie from County Kerry and her boyfriend Kenny came along for the ride. Just as they came aboard, it started raining and I soon discovered why the interior of the sailboat had been so moldy. The hull may have been sound, but the deck was another story. We were settled into the cabin when the rain started coming down in earnest and were soaked as water poured in through bolt holes and from around the deck fittings.

An Island Hippy named Moe was working the door at The Beach Club that night and at the end of the gig he started talking to Katie. Kenny a recent graduate of Hellgate High School in Hellgate, Montana, became a bit peeved thinking that Moe was paying too much attention to his woman. The Hellgate Kid jumped into action. He grabbed a hold of the hippy's ponytail and started swinging him around and around in the bar. I would have intervened, but I was busy tearing down equipment and the ruckus was all over before I saw what was happening. I still know that particular Island Hippy. Fortunately, he doesn't remember a thing about what happened that night.

The owner of the Beach Club at that time was a disbarred attorney who had once been the Dean of the Law School at St. Thomas College in St. Paul. His island name was "Bottom Feeder". He loved Irish music, drink and fun, not necessarily in that order. One night I slept in a room above the bar just down the hall from him. Bottom Feeder kept me awake with the screaming and moaning coming from his room. In the morning I asked him if he was okay.

He said, "What do you mean, Tommy?"

"I heard you shouting and screaming in the night."

Bottom Feeder said, "Oh, it's just part of the fun, Tommy, just part of the fun."

I leased a spot for the Hunter on the city dock in Bayfield and for the next fifteen years I kept a sailboat there. I went sailing whenever I could and found places to play when I was up on Chequamegon Bay.

Back in St. Paul, there was a new Irish pub called The Irish Well. The proprietor was John Dingley, a wiry and wily Welshman and an old friend from the MacCafferty days.

John is a man who knows a great deal about a great many things from stonework to history to UFOs to sheep husbandry. He is also a writer and performer and will probably tell you all about it someday. The Well, an entertaining spot, was walking distance from Big Pink and a good place to play gigs. There was a traditional session on Sunday nights that was always well attended.

Fitz was hired at The Irish Well and that was how he started in the bar trade. He began as chef and also learned the ins and outs of working behind the bar from Dingley. Fitz went on to work for Kieran Folliard the man from Mayo who opened Kieran's Irish Pub in Minneapolis and thus started an empire.

*****

I was running down to Chicago once or twice a month to play at Shannon's Landing. The bar was actually at the Lansing Municipal Airport in Lansing, Illinois, near Gary, Indiana. Shannon's Landing had existed first on paper as a business school thesis that Danny Harkenrider created for his Master's Degree. After a few years slaving away in management at US Steel, he had earned enough to bring his paper project to life. Danny ran Shannon's Landing successfully for many years with the help of his uncle and aunt, Louie and Kay McDonnell from Monaghan.

One night I was playing Shannon's and when I finished a song and the crowd cheered and clapped enthusiastically. When silence descended again a woman's voice called out loudly, "I never heard as bad!"

I peered through the smoke and the stage lights into the crowd and spotted Kay with a big grin on her face. She caught me good that time.

I usually stayed at the Harkenrider house with Kay, Louie and Danny when I was playing Shannon's. One Sunday evening we were all watching Public Television. It was Pledge Week, a fund raising drive that is conducted several times a year. Throughout the week, the Public Television station shows musical specials, among other things, to attract viewers and monetary commitments. During the "Pledge Breaks", the officials from the station appear and drum up support. In the background you see a bank of phones manned by volunteers taking the calls and writing down the pledges.

Tommy Makem was doing a Christmas special that night. Kay decided to call in during the break. We watched a volunteer pick up a phone with a big artificial smile on her face. Kay said, "I grew up with Tommy Makem."

The volunteer replied, "That's so nice you called in."

"I'd just like to say one thing," Kay said.

We could see the volunteer still smiling at the receiver. "And what is that," she asked brightly.

"I never heard as bad!" and Kay hung up.

We watched the volunteer look at the phone as her smile faltered and then magically returned, looking more real than it had before. I still occasionally imagine I hear her voice when I finish a song.

About a year after I started sailing on Lake Superior, I was talking to Bill Hooper and he mentioned that he was the broker for a twenty-seven foot Coronado. It was a bit bigger than the Hunter and in much better shape. I looked it over and found that I could actually stand up in the cabin.

Within a week of seeing the Coronado, I met a guy in a coffee shop in St. Paul. We were talking about boats and he told me he had a half formed idea of sailing down the Mississippi to Florida with his daughter. She was only nine years old and dying of the same cancer that had taken his wife a year previously. He decided right there in the coffee shop that he was going to carry out his plan and that he wanted the Hunter if I was selling it. He said he was handy and could fix anything that was wrong with the boat. I decided to sell it to him and buy the Coronado.

Timmy Fitz and I drove up to Bayfield to pick up the Hunter. It was early spring. The trailer's running lights and brake lights didn't work. The mice had probably gnawed on them over the winter. The license plates on the trailer were expired and I can't blame that on the mice. We were in a hurry and decided to just hook up the trailer with the three ton boat and take off. Fitzy's pickup truck was complaining loudly about the load and between the straining front end noises, the expired plates and the lack of lights, we felt conspicuous, so we drove slowly as we embarked on the two hundred and fifty mile trip to St. Paul. To quell our nervousness about the situation, we sang Clancy Brothers and Dubliners songs as we crept along. It didn't help.

We made it to Turtle Lake before we were stopped by the Wisconsin State Patrol. We were told to unhitch the trailer in a big parking lot across the highway from State Patrol Headquarters. Fitz received a ticket for hauling a trailer with expired plates and no lights. The trooper warned us not to move the trailer again until everything was legal.

It was getting late, and both Fitz and I had to work at The Irish Well that night. We left the boat and continued on to St. Paul but were back early the next day to rescue her. We did what we should have done in the first place.

We stopped at a convenience store and bought two flashlights, the kind of red cellophane tape used for taillight repair and duct tape. We covered the top of the flashlights with the red tape and duct taped them to the trailer to mimic running lights. We figured that having “working” running lights would imply that our brake lights worked as well. We managed to sneak out of Turtle Lake with the three ton boat without being noticed and made it to Hooper’s without getting stopped again. I covered the money Fitz had to pay for the ticket, but Fitz didn’t tell me until the next year that the strain of hauling the boat had ruined the front end of his truck.

The man from the coffee shop came out to Hooper’s and paid me for the boat. He started working on it that very day. I gave Hooper the money for the Coronado. He told me that he was going up north the next week and would drop it off in Bayfield. I named my latest boat Concertina because it was an instrument that I was trying to learn at the time.

Bill told me that the man with the plan more or less camped out in his parking lot while he worked on the Hunter. About two months later Hooper drove the boat down to the river and father and daughter started their journey. None of us ever heard anything more from them. We hope they made it all the way to Florida.

Chapter 28
Fat on the Land

I hadn't been to Ireland since working on the trawlers in Donegal in 1980. A lot can change in ten years for both places and people. I couldn't imagine going to Ireland without drinking, but my sister Judy encouraged me to go anyway. I bought a round trip ticket to Shannon for less than four hundred dollars.

Knowing that I only had two weeks I headed straight to Galway, the town I knew best. I found a B & B on Forester Street near the train station and met the woman of the house, Philomena Hollywood. She was a small lady with a big voice, and, coincidently, a champion button accordion player who was off the drink. Philomena knew a lot of my old cronies from the days at the Cellar Bar, The Quays, The Harbor Bar and all the rest. It turned out that many of my friends were still alive, which, given our lifestyle in our youth, was a pleasant surprise. There was plenty of music being played in the town, more than ever really.

As I walked around the streets of Galway, and talked to the people I met in coffee shops, restaurants and in Philomena's kitchen, I saw changes that I might not have noticed without the ten year absence. There were many more cars and the cars looked newer. People would talk about trading them in after driving them for just a few years. Probably because of the scrounger's eye that I had developed in Wisconsin, I spotted more and better quality discards on the roadsides and in the junk shops. There seemed to be more work than there had been in the seventies. After years of economic struggle, life was easing a bit for the Irish, but The Celtic Tiger was still just a cub.

Philomena had told me that Eugene Lambe was making pipes and living out in Fanore near the Cliffs of Moher. We were old acquaintances so I stopped in for a visit. He had renovated the old National School building using the lower floor as a shop where he made Uilleann pipes and wooden flutes and living on the top floor which had a panoramic view of the Atlantic with the Aran Islands visible in the distance.

Eugene was also a sailor and had a twenty-foot sailboat. He took me out fishing off the west coast of Clare where we caught pollack for dinner. We would sail out a distance and then drop our lines while the boat drifted back towards the rocky shore. Then we would sail out and do it again. Being on the ocean in waters that were familiar after Donegal, started me thinking about how great it would be to have a boat over here. I wondered if The Concertina would be strong enough to get me to Ireland.

I visited Eugene several times on that trip and we fished on Galway Bay more than once. He told me that Michael Casey in Kinvara, an old market town on the bay, was a man that I ought to know. He had several sailboats in his yard and Eugene said that Michael knew Galway Bay better that anyone after sailing it for more than forty years.

I was told to just drop in and introduce myself, so on the last day of my trip I knocked on Michael's door. He invited me in, made tea and sandwiches and then showed me his garden which kept him supplied with vegetables. We looked at the boats in the yard and went back into the house where Michael showed me some of his musical instruments. He played several and had them hanging on the walls.

He had just started showing me how to read ocean charts, which were different than those I used on Lake Superior, when the phone rang. Michael answered it. I kept inspecting the charts and tide tables while I waited and after a few minutes he hung up, swearing.

I didn't ask, but he told me anyway. His sister had requested that he find a cottage for her near Kinvara. Michael had looked and looked and finally found one that he could fix up.

"And now the bitch tells me she's moving to Florida."

"Is the cottage still there?"

Michael gave me the withering look that the question deserved and answered, "Of course it is."

"Can we go have a look?"

So, off we went to check it out. It was a traditional whitewashed stone cottage about three hundred years old just off the side of the road to Gort, a long mile out of Kinvara. The walls were three feet thick and the roof was galvanized steel. I could see that it needed a lot of work. There was a sign with a number to call for information. We took down the number and, since this was before cell phones, headed back to Kinvara to make the call.

Una Bermingham answered the phone. She was acting as the agent for Michael Deeley, the farmer who owned the cottage and, in fact, had been born in it. Michael Casey and I returned to the cottage while Una rang Michael Deeley, telling him that there was a Yank interested in the place and arranging for him to come out and meet us there.

When Michael Deeley arrived he at first thought Michael Casey was the Yank. Michael Casey is a tall man, a native of Dublin who holds himself erect and always looks very official. Galway and the west at that time were laid back compared to Dublin and the people were a little more casual, kind of like those in northern Wisconsin. Michael Casey was insulted to be mistaken for the Yank, but I was pleased.

Once the confusion was cleared up, Michael Deeley opened the padlock on the half door. I stuck my head in and couldn't help saying, "God Bless all here."

I could feel the generations that had lived in the place. Three hundred years of old thatch was visible under the galvanized roof, falling down in some places. There were sheets of cobweb draping everything. The strong scent of the turf fires that had been burning nearly constantly over the centuries in the open fireplace lingered and that smell combined with the smell of damp coming from the floor and walls added to the eerie atmosphere. Looking more closely around the room I saw signs of the people who had lived there, yellowed lace curtains in the window, a walking stick, a cracked milk jug, a few plates and saucers and the hooks, pots and kettles still hanging on the crane in the fireplace. Michael told me that his aunt, Maggie Deeley, had lived there until she died five years before at the age of nearly ninety.

I saw possibilities and asked Michael what he would take for the place. He gave me a number and we bargained back and forth a few times. Finally we agreed on eight thousand, two hundred and fifty punt or about ten thousand dollars and I reached in my pocket and gave him my last fifty punt note, telling him I would be back soon with the rest of the money. Michael Deeley spit in his hand, so I spit in my hand too and we shook on it. Privately I had no idea where the money would come from. Michael Casey and I left, and the next day I flew back to St. Paul.

The day after I landed, I figured that I should at least go through the motions of trying to secure a bank loan. I had no savings or checking account and, with the exception of the raid on the bank in Liberty, Missouri, had never had much to do with them. I had no credit history and my income was variable and usually didn't leave much of a paper trail. I walked into a bank in Highland Park since I knew where it was having grown up nearby. I thought, "All they can say is no, and that will be that."

The brass name plate on the loan officer's desk said Mr. Murray. I sat down across from him. He looked friendly enough. I introduced myself and the first thing he said was, "Aren't you Larry's son? The one who played at MacCafferty's?"

"Yes, that's me," I said.

"I really like your music. What can I help you with?"

I told him that I had just gotten back from Ireland and gave him the whole story about the cottage in Galway. I said that I needed ten thousand dollars. After I gave him a few sketchy details about my financial situation, he said, “Well, Tommy, I’m retiring in a few days.”

I looked down and prepared myself to let go of the dream.

“This sounds like fun. Let’s do it.”

I walked out of the bank a few hours later with a cashier’s check in hand and within a few days was back in Galway. Una Bermingham recommended a solicitor who drew up the paperwork. After taking a look, the solicitor, Colman Sherry, told me that he was willing to classify the property as “agricultural land of less than a third of an acre with an old dwelling house.” With that classification I didn’t have to pay the taxes and fees required for a finished house and under Irish law at the time, I didn’t need permits to repair an existing dwelling. The paperwork would take months to be completed, but in the meantime he told me, “You’re free to work away on it.”

And work away is what I did. I still had several weeks in Ireland and I got right down to it. Una Bermingham had a B & B in Kinvara and I slept there the first few nights.

Michael Deeley came by the first day and hauled away a few bags of fertilizer and some other things that he had been storing in the cottage. After that he stopped by often to see how I was doing and he would usually tell me a little bit about the history of the area.

He told me that the cottage had been built by the people in "The Big House" which was the manor house of the old Northampton Estate. Around three hundred years ago my cottage had been where the blacksmith lived. There had been many more laborers' cottages on the estate that had been taken down over the years and mine was the only one left. The Big House itself had been burned in the early 1920s by the locals and the remains, with the exception of part of a wall and a spiral stone staircase, were finally demolished in the thirties due to safety concerns.

The estate had been owned by a family named Murray at the time it was burned. I told Michael that the man in the States who had approved my loan was named Murray. I hoped that my Mr. Murray hadn't gotten into any trouble and that he was enjoying his retirement.

I decided to start by removing the old thatch under the roof in the bedroom. I was lucky because it came down fairly easily. Taking down the thatch in the other rooms would prove to be more problematic. I used a pitchfork to rip it down and started moving it out into the yard. I had to take a lot of the thatch down before I could see the top part of the walls. Michael explained that when his Aunt Maggie had been living there the thatch had gotten so bad that it no longer kept the rain out. Maggie didn't want to move and the county council didn't want to force her so they repaired the roof. Instead of removing the thatch, they had cut off the eaves and built up the walls a couple feet higher. They then built a frame so that they could put a galvanized roof over the old thatch.

The big chimney in the middle of the cottage served both the open fireplace in the main room, which had been the kitchen and a second small fireplace on the other side of the wall in the bedroom. The fireplace in the main room was so large that it could accommodate a stone seat on either side. You could sit inside the chimney with a small fire going and look up to see the stars in the nighttime sky.

It took a few days to remove all the thatch from the old bedroom. Some Travelers came by on the road just as I finished and asked me if I needed anything. They had a big truck and I saw an old divan that could be folded down into a bed. For five punt, I now had a place to sit and to sleep. I moved out of Una Bermingham's B & B and started camping in the cottage.

There was a small box for electricity put in by the council, but Maggie Deeley had rarely used it and it had been disconnected. To create a homey atmosphere, I went into Kinvara and bought some turf to burn, two kerosene lanterns and a transistor radio. When I got returned, I set the radio to Clare FM and went back to work.

In a shed behind the cottage I found an old plow, harnesses, animal traps, bottles and many other odds and ends. The yard was surrounded by stone walls and within those walls were more stone walls. One made an enclosure around an apple tree near the road and another, extending from near the back of the cottage across to the outside wall, sectioned off the back yard where a cow could be kept. For miles around my small parcel, there was pasture land crisscrossed with more stone walls where farmers, including Michael Deeley, grazed cattle, sheep and horses. The crags of the Burren loomed in the distance and atop one of the hills was a prehistoric ring fort.

Off to the West toward the distant uplands of the Burren I could see the lights of a few houses. To the south, about half a mile up the winding road was the Northampton National School near where the Big House had been and between my place and the school stood only one fairly large house. Across the road from me and up a little bohereen lived an old man named Jim Hehir. He had lived in a cottage very similar to mine, but it had fallen in and the county council had moved in a small trailer house next to the ruins.

Jim was a tall gentleman in his late eighties. He rode an old Raleigh "High Nelly" bicycle, the kind that had been used to beat the Black and Tans in the War for Independence. Jim loved to play Forty-Five and I often saw him riding along to card games at various houses up and down the Gort Road.

The closest dwelling to mine was about a hundred yards north down the road towards Kinvara. It was a cottage similar to mine but newer, only about a hundred and fifty years old and blocked from view by trees and underbrush. In it there lived two brothers, Gerry and Donal.

Gerry and Donal patrolled the road. Nothing happened along that stretch that they didn't know about. They were both bachelors and usually didn't speak to strangers. They kept a donkey whose job it was to keep the nettles in the yard down and to bray loudly and repeatedly at dawn.

I came out of the cottage one morning and went around towards the back to answer nature's call. Against the wall of the house I spotted an old bicycle that hadn't been there the last time I had gone around that way. I never found out who had made the donation, but it came in handy. When walking to or from town someone would usually stop and give you a lift, but the bike was nice for a change of pace. I used it to ride into town to buy things but realized pretty quickly that I would need some other form of transport for larger loads.

I met a fellow in Galway named Bob Cantwell and mentioned that I needed a car. He told me that his brother-in-law had one for sale. It was a rusty little old banger and the price was right, one hundred punt. The brother-in-law was a Guard and when he gave me the paperwork, he advised me to keep it in the glovebox and show it anytime I was stopped by the police.

Cars in Ireland have a small plastic pocket on the inside of the windscreen, split into two sections meant to hold the tax disc and proof of insurance. Both needed to be kept up to date. The disc changed color with each renewal, so that a quick glance at the windscreen would tell the Guards whether the paperwork was current. I purchased a box of colored pencils and doctored the disc to match the color for that period. That took care of the tax disc.

Next I tackled the proof of insurance. My sources told me to try to buy car insurance, even though I would be turned down because I didn't have an Irish driver's license. My applications were returned to me along with refusal notices which I put in the glovebox, as instructed, to prove that I had made an honest attempt. Then I found a bank deposit slip that looked like a proof of insurance paper and wrote across the front "Applied For." I stuck it in the other half of the windscreen pocket and hoped for the best.

My ruse with the disc and proof of insurance must have worked because I was usually waved right through checkpoints after a glance at the windscreen. The few times I was stopped I would show the booklet of original paperwork as advised by Bob's brother-in-law. The Guards would look at it, and seeing the name of a fellow policeman, would allow me to proceed with no bother.

When driving in Ireland you run into checkpoints every once in a while, never knowing exactly what they are for. Sometimes the Guards are looking for someone, sometimes they are trying to catch drivers who are over the limit and sometimes they have their own reasons. Kinvara had been a quiet little place but was becoming popular with artists and musicians and one night when driving back to the cottage from Galway City, I was stopped at a checkpoint at the edge of town. I was cleared as usual but before I drove on I asked, "Why is there a checkpoint here tonight?"

The Guard smiled and said, "Oh, it's Frankie Gavin's birthday party above at Winkle's tonight. We're stopping everybody coming in or going out."

Frankie is a famous fiddler and popular in Ireland and all over the world, but at the time was obviously not popular with the local Guards.

I drove the little car for years until the doors rusted off and used it to haul tons of materials to the cottage where, whenever I was in Ireland, I was hard at work.

Chapter 29
Coming Up Threes

My idea of sailing to Ireland was taking hold and I realized The Concertina was not a strong enough boat for an Atlantic crossing. I had seen a 1966 thirty-five foot Pearson Alberg for sale in a local magazine. Its hull was three-quarter inch fiberglass because in the early days of using fiberglass hulls they made them as thick as wooden hulls, not yet understanding the strength of the new material. These early models were said to be bullet proof.

At the time I was providing music for a ceili dance performance group that had formed about twenty years before. I knew most of the dancers and had been dating one of them for a couple of years. I'd told her about my ambition of making an Atlantic crossing and about the pier in Kinvara, only a mile away, where I could keep a boat for free.

She encouraged me to buy the thirty-five foot sloop, so we looked it over at a boat yard in Superior, Wisconsin, near Duluth. It wasn't hard to obtain bank financing for a boat in Minnesota, the Land of 10,000 Lakes. The banker explained, "People almost never default on boat loans. They tend to lose everything else first."

After the banker okayed the loan, I sold The Concertina. The Pearson was the third boat I'd had on Lake Superior. We scraped and painted the bottom and put her in the water. A friend from Bayfield, Greg Lashum, met me at the boat yard and we jumped aboard and headed for my slip. We sailed all night and got in at around three in the morning. We crashed into the pier when we arrived, but I eventually learned how to stop her properly. My plan was to take the boat to Chicago. From Chicago there was an inland route to Florida and from there I could sail on to Ireland.

It was September and there was still time to take the Pearson south as far as Chicago before winter set in. I needed crew so I stopped by Madeline Island thinking that an island would be a good place to find people with sailing experience.

The early French explorers had assumed that there were twelve islands in Chequamegon Bay and so called them The Apostles. It turned out that there were twenty-two and the whole area is now known as The Apostle Islands National Lakeshore. With the sailing I'd done with the Hunter and the Coronado, I knew the waters fairly well and had sailed around most of the islands. Madeline Island is the only one that is permanently populated now.

One of the best known of the Islanders is a man named Tommy Nelson. He is about my age and grew up there. He bought an old beer joint with a full liquor license that was infamous during the Viet Nam War days and was located just a little ways outside of the town of La Pointe, originally a French fur trading settlement dating from the year 1693. Tommy moved the entire building to a site in middle of town and opened it in 1990 as Leona's Café. It had only been going for a couple of years when it mysteriously burned down....for the first time. All that was known for sure was that it was a case of arson.

The cafe was totally destroyed without the benefit of insurance because Tommy had not paid the insurance premium. As a result of this unfortunate situation, Tommy came up with the first of many slogans associated with the place, "You got to be tough if you're going to be stupid."

Tommy was tough enough. He cleaned up the mess with the help of friends, covered what was left with an old circus tent and ran it as a bar and music venue. He changed the name from Leona's to Tom's Burned Down Café because he is a man who believes in truth in advertising. Then it was burned down again, by popular demand, on St. Patrick's Day, 2005. Phoenix-like, the

Burned Down Café rose again from the ashes and Tommy has been running it now for twenty-five years and counting.

I had started playing for Tommy when the Bottom Feeder's business at the Beach Club went belly up. In 1994 it was still early days at Tommy's Burned Down. It was the logical place to look for crew and I was in luck. The first two guys that I spoke to at the bar that afternoon were Tyler and Troy, both teenagers who immediately responded, "Yes. But we have to ask our mothers first."

They headed off to do that while I waited. When they returned, they announced, "Our mothers said no. They want to come instead."

"Really?" I said.

"No. Just kidding. Let's go."

Tyler had worked as a cook, spaghetti being his specialty and Troy, whose mother was from County Sligo, was at least as experienced a sailor as I, which wasn't saying much. Troy went off to buy the extra supplies that he and Tyler thought they would need and Tyler and I sailed the first leg of the journey on our own going to Ontonagon, Michigan, about thirty miles to the southeast of the Apostle Islands.

When Tyler and I left La Pointe it was getting dark. We cleared the lighthouse on Michigan Island in a few hours and that told us we were leaving the familiar waters of the Apostles. I looked at the chart and figured the compass course to Ontonagon. There was an old Loran satellite navigation system down below and I tried to explain latitude and longitude to Tyler so he could use it, but I could see that he wasn't concentrating so I let it slide. We sailed on for a while and soon found ourselves in heavy fog.

We couldn't see a thing. I wasn't worried, but Tyler suddenly stood up and hurried below. I didn't know what had happened to him. He came up into the cockpit about an hour later, having figured out the navigation system and he showed me where we were on the chart. I was pleased to see that once the fog set in, he was a fast learner. After that, we marked our position on the chart every hour.

We arrived in Ontonagon at about three a.m. I used the marine radio for the first time and asked them to open the lift bridge that spanned the entrance to the harbor. Troy arrived not long after we did. He had picked up groceries and extra fuel jugs and arranged to have his brother, Brian, drive him to Ontonagon. Tyler cooked up a meal for the four of us. We spent the night in port and the next morning Brian left for home. The three of us sailed on to the Keweenaw Peninsula. We decided to use the Keweenaw waterway, an eight foot deep channel that passed through the middle of the Peninsula, thus saving us from having to go all the way around. We had a good sail.

I had picked up a B/C accordion in St. Paul and brought it along. I sat down below and practiced, letting the boys sail the boat. We made the Houghton/Hancock docks in the middle of the Peninsula around eight p.m. As we pulled up to the pier, the boys were on the bow and somehow Tyler wrapped his right arm around a piling to slow the boat and managed to dislocate his shoulder. He was in a lot of pain, so after we tied up, we found the harbor master who gave us a lift up to the hospital about a mile away. As we were riding along in the car, Tyler's dislocated shoulder popped back into the socket. He saw a doctor at the hospital who gave him a big bottle of pain pills.

We set off again the next morning and a few hours later we left the waterway and were back on the Big Lake east of the Keweenaw. We continued down the lake against a huge east wind that brought with it a rain system. The storm lasted about ten hours. Darkness had fallen and we couldn't see much. We were motoring into the waves and every time we hit one, spray would shoot up thirty feet in the air showing up red on the port side and green on the starboard from the bow lights. The motor was a Ford tractor engine which, when installed in a boat is known as an Atomic 4. We were full throttle against the sea, often making less than one knot per hour while the boat bucked like a rocking horse ridden by a demented child.

After the storm passed the next morning, we were able to sail for Grand Marais, Michigan. We had burned up the thirty gallons of fuel in the tank and used up almost twenty gallons from the gas cans that Troy had brought to Ontonagon. When we reached the pier in Grand Marais we knelt down and kissed the ground. And, we weren't kidding.

Grand Marais had many, many shops selling pasties. Welsh and Cornish immigrants who worked in the copper mines of Michigan's Upper Peninsula had brought the culinary tradition with them. I'd never tasted them before, but the folded over pies with pork, beef, potatoes, rutabagas and onions have been a favorite of mine ever since.

The next leg of our voyage would take us to Whitefish Bay, a port of refuge that ships on that part of the lake would head for when there was bad weather. The Edmund Fitzgerald hadn't made it and sank nearby. I had the accordion out again and the boys asked me if I could play the Gordon Lightfoot song. I refused because I had been told by some sailors in Bayfield never to sing or play it because it was considered bad luck for a sailor. I was not about to tempt the fates any more than I already had. Anyway, it was time to stow the accordion because it was already growing dark and we were approaching Whitefish Point.

We meant to follow the sea lanes south down Whitefish Bay, but somehow, maybe because it wasn't quite dark enough to see the lighted buoys, we overshot the lanes and were heading for Canada. When we realized our mistake, we turned around. As we approached the sea lanes again, we could now see the lights from the buoys clearly.

We could also see a big Salty, an ocean going ore boat off a mile or two in the distance. We started across the lanes towards our port of refuge. Suddenly the huge ore boat, maybe a thousand feet long, was looming over us, blaring its horns and dazzling us with spotlights. I think she may have sped up to teach us a lesson. And the lesson was learned. She chased us out of the sea lane and I never attempted to cross a sea lane in front of a big ship again.

When we reached the little harbor there were no lights, electricity or water, but it didn't matter. We were happy to be close to done with Lake Superior. Our next adventure would be going through the locks just above Sault Ste. Marie which would take us to Lake Huron. We ate and sat around until nearly midnight. Our encounter with the big Salty had shaken us up and our nerves were still too jangled to sleep.

I addressed the crew. "Well, we have a good boat here and a pretty good crew. The only thing we are lacking is experience. Should we go and get some?"

My crew answered, "Let's go."

We jumped to it and headed out toward the Soo Locks on the St Mary's River. When we appeared upriver of the Locks and Dam, it was three a. m. Out of nowhere, through the rain and wind a Big Voice bellowed, "What the hell are you doing here at this time of night?"

It was an enraged lock keeper on a big loud speaker. We called him on our little marine radio to answer. I apologized and told him that we had never gone through locks before.

The Disembodied Voice boomed again through the foul weather. "Stay put for a while until we can let you through."

We spent the next miserable hour backing against the strong current, going around in circles and hoping that the engine wouldn't stall and let the river push us over the dam. I found out later that small craft usually wait until a big ship goes through the locks, preferably in daylight, and then tag along. We were worried about running out of fuel so we headed toward a wall with the intention of tying off when the Big Voice came over the loudspeaker again saying, "Get away from that wall!"

It turned out that it was illegal to tie up there because of security concerns. I should have known that because for a while, during World War II, my father had been a guard on the Soo locks.

Finally, they opened the gate and we entered the gigantic lock alone. The immense gate closed behind us. The water dropped much more rapidly than we could have imagined and we bounced and scraped down the wall fending the boat off in an exhausted panic. Then the gate before us opened. We sailed out and took a left. At dawn we tied up at a fuel dock in Sault Ste. Marie, Canada, and fell asleep.

The end of September was the perfect time to enjoy the privilege of sailing down the St. Mary's River that flows south from Lake Superior to Lake Huron and through some of the most beautiful wooded country I have ever seen. You could feel the history of the waterway and we finally were having ideal fall weather.

The boys did most of the navigation and driving of the boat. I relaxed, brought out the box and blasted away. Tyler and Troy were having a good time too, although Tyler was having a hard time staying awake. He was still taking the pain pills for his shoulder. We reached De Tour on Lake Huron, landed and strolled around the town. We stocked up on food and fuel, enjoyed a good sleep and headed west in the morning for Mackinac Island.

It was again beautiful weather and easy sailing, so as on the previous day I left the sailing to the crew and played and played on the accordion. I was very happy with our progress when we made Mackinac Island at about five in the afternoon and pulled into a slip. I almost never reported in to harbor masters to pay. Many harbor masters appreciate not being bothered, especially very early or very late in the sailing season.

Mackinac Island was nothing like Madeline Island and we did not feel at home there. We smelled fairly ripe, had little money and after a couple of pieces of fudge, our sweet tooths were satisfied. We agreed that the profusion of fudge shops and the lack of pubs was annoying. There were no cars on the island and after walking around for a while I returned to the boat and soon fell asleep.

The boys stayed out. They "borrowed" a couple of bicycles and rode around the island, met some girls and partied all night. They showed up at the boat around dawn looking no worse than they had the previous evening and were ready to sail off again before the harbor master woke up.

We sailed under the Mackinac Bridge, an impressive sight when you are in a small boat. I went for the accordion but it wasn't there. Troy and Tyler watched me search desperately for about five minutes before they cracked up and admitted that they had planned to take the accordion while I was asleep, put it in a box and mail it home to me in St. Paul. They decided not to follow through with their scheme but had hidden it. After a few more minutes of laughter they relented and told me where it was. It dawned on me that I may have been abusing my captive audience so I put the box away and cranked up the radio.

It had taken a week just to reach Lake Michigan, sleeping in port every other night, sometimes for only a few hours and we still had hundreds of miles to go to make Chicago.

We were taking turns at the helm and on one occasion, when it was Tyler's turn, I woke up and looked into the cockpit. Troy was fast asleep on a bench and Tyler was indeed at the helm. He was leaning back against the lifelines with a single toe on the wheel and sleeping soundly. A half mile away a big tanker was bearing down on us. We maneuvered out of the way just in time and I decided from that point on that Tyler wasn't driving anymore. Or at least not until the pain pills were used up.

We sailed south for two more days passing Beaver Island which had been an Irish settlement and continued following the east shore of the lake. We stopped in Ludington for a night after which we were back in the sea lanes. That late in the season there were very few small craft and most of the shipping traffic was big tankers and ore ships.

We stopped in Pentwater because the battery charger wasn't working. We had run out of time to get the boat to Chicago on this trip. I had some gigs coming up and Troy and Tyler were losing their enthusiasm. I called Eagle, an American Indian who worked as the doorman and bouncer at Shannon's Landing, telling him that I was stuck in Pentwater. He said, "I'll be right up, Tommy. You can drop me off and use my rez-mobile. Just bring it back when you're done."

I made arrangements to keep the boat docked in Pentwater. Eagle arrived in the car, a big old Oldsmobile, and he drove us south to his home in Hammond, Indiana, where he turned the car over to us. The three of us continued on to Madeline Island. It was a wild ride up North. Those boys drove fast and the old rez-mobile had a hard time keeping up with them. I fell asleep in the big back seat and a couple of times I woke up thinking that the boat was bumping the bottom and that we were out of the channel. I yelled, "Find deeper water!" and then realized it was just the rear end of the car hitting the pavement as we bounced our way back to Bayfield.

I played a couple of gigs in St. Paul to replenish the wallet and then drove the rez-mobile back to Chicago where I picked up Steve Walsh. I had met Steve a few years before when he used to come with his dad to hear me play around Chicago. Steve was an adventurous type who later became a Chicago fireman. He had agreed to replace the previous crew who were happy to be back to their lives on Madeline Island

After picking up Steve, I drove on and found Eagle who drove us up to Pentwater and dropped us off. I was planning to winter the boat in Hammond, which was in Indiana but is part of the Chicago megalopolis. Steve didn't know what to expect when we arrived in Pentwater. I wasn't too sure what to expect either, since the whole trip was pretty much a "learn on the job" enterprise.

We climbed aboard and when Steve was stowing his gear, he showed me the Glock pistol that he had brought along.

"What's that for?" I asked.

"It's for if anyone messes with us."

"We won't be seeing anyone out there."

We spent a few hours readying the boat. I found some shorts in the wiring and repaired the battery charger as well as the lights that had been giving me trouble. We were now ready to set sail and headed off into Lake Michigan at dusk. I always preferred sailing at night. During the daytime it is easy to lose sight of objects in the waves or in the glare off the water. The red and green lights, port and starboard and the running lights that are used at night make it easier to determine the presence of other craft as well as the direction they are travelling.

The wind was blowing steady from the north at about twenty-five miles per hour and the waves were building behind us as we sailed into more open water. After a few hours we had six to eight foot following seas and I knew the waves would continue to build as the wind moved the water down from the top of the lake. It was a wild ride, but I knew the boat had been built for heavy seas and I had seen how she handled the storm on Superior.

Steve had not sailed much and hearing the creaking and groaning of the boat and feeling the rolling and tipping, he started to worry about whether the boat would remain in one piece. We were nearly in the middle of the lake beyond the sea lanes and heading south when we caught our first glimpse of the lights of Milwaukee around midnight. When he saw the lights, Steve shouted, "Let's go there."

I explained that even though Milwaukee was closer as the crow flies, if we tried to head in that direction across those waves, we would lose most of our speed, the ride would be even rougher and it would take about eight hours. We were flying with the wind and waves behind us and I told him that it was probably about six hours to Chicago. Once I had explained, he agreed that Chicago would be best.

Next, we ran into a big fog bank. We were still heaving along at a good clip and after a bit we could make out the lights of the skyline of Chicago about sixty miles away. We could see the shapes of the buildings through the fog off to our left. What was troubling was that Chicago should have appeared ahead of us and slightly to the right.

We couldn't figure it out. I checked and rechecked our position and we were on the right course so we just plowed on through the fog towards the invisible downtown trying to ignore the ghostly one to our left. Eventually the light dawned in the east. The fog mirage disappeared and we found ourselves about ten miles off of Hammond Harbor.

This close to shore the swells were huge. With what might have looked like skill but was really just luck, we managed to swing around the sea wall and into the harbor without incident. The ordeal was over and Steve didn't have to pull a gun once.

I had a gig through Josh that afternoon playing the International Day at the Elmhurst College Student Union. Steve took me to a car I kept stashed at Louie and Kay's house and headed for home to take a long, long nap. I climbed into my car and made my way to the venue. There was music and dance from many different countries and I was there to represent the Irish. I played a few tunes, sang a few songs, cashed the check and drove home to St. Paul.

My third boat made it through three of the Great Lakes and was now safely in dry dock at the harbor in Hammond. But there was another third looming on the horizon.

I had and maybe still have a quirk of character that doesn't allow me to back down from a challenge. If someone asks for a fight, I find it nearly impossible to say no. Instead, I say, "Sure. Let's go. Right now."

Most of the time they back down. If they don't, I suffer the consequences.

One night, the previous spring my girlfriend stated, "My mother says it's time we got married."

As I said I never turn away from a challenge and I always got along with her mother, a feisty redhead from the North of Ireland.

"I'm not afraid. Let's do it."

I found out later that I should have been afraid, but at the time I was hoping for the best.

The date for the wedding was fast approaching. It was to be a Catholic wedding and we had already completed the marriage counselling that was required before the ceremony could take place. We agreed during counselling that once we were married, we would live in the cabin in Wisconsin where she would look for a new job and I would continue to pursue my musical career. In the spring we would take the boat down the Illinois River to the Mississippi, take a left and sail on to the Ohio River. When we reached the Ohio we would hang another left to the Tennessee

River, then take a right on the Tennessee to go south to the Tombigbee Waterway. The Tombigbee would take us to the Gulf of Mexico at Mobile, Alabama. Once we had exited the inland waterways we could sail down the coast to Florida. If needed, we would stop and ask for directions. If we ran out of money, I would play a few gigs. Then, if possible, we would sail on to Ireland. At least that was what I remember about marriage counselling.

My mother said that even though I had been married twice before, I had never been married in the eyes of God. But, in the eyes of the law this would be wife number three.

The reception was held at Danny Flanagan's, a restaurant on West Seventh Street and Randolph in St. Paul. My family all came and had a great time as usual. The fun-loving aunt, who came to my last wedding, echoed her previous sentiment, "Tommy, you have the best weddings!"

I'm sure she said the same thing to my brothers. My older brother Larry had already had three weddings and my younger brother Danny had two. The males and females in my generation of the family seemed to have something in common with the Malamutes Angie and Chinook when it came to the sometimes prickly world of marriage. Two of my sisters were also divorced, but unlike the males, never tangled with marriage again.

The reception evolved into a hooley. Brian Smith from Scotland, the founder of a band called "The Tim Malloys" was on stage singing with a drink in one hand, a cigarette in the other and a huge carved pumpkin on his head. It was Halloween. Teddy Tonkinson, John McCormick and the entire Brian Boru Pipe Band marched through several times. Sean and Mary O'Driscoll and many local St. Paul musicians played. I chimed in with the band off and on. There were even a few scuffles. Between tunes, Marty McHugh turned to me and said, "Tom. You are the Zsa Zsa Gabor of Irish Music."

Chapter 30

The Thatch Comes Down

I should have taken Marty's words more seriously. In general, the marriage would probably receive the same rating on a scale of one to ten, as your typical Hollywood marriage. In spite of high hopes, the carefully constructed plans for the future made during the pre-marriage counselling never came to pass. Moving to Wisconsin didn't happen and the boat never made it to Florida. Instead we continued to live in Big Pink.

There was one really good thing that came out of the marriage. Number Three saw an opportunity to start an Irish dance school. She rented a time slot at the hall where Chuck and Ann's wedding had been. Her first students were nieces and cousins from both our families. They told their friends and the dance school grew. Within a year or so she had to hire more teachers. My main role was playing music when needed and occasionally acting as a driver. It was a lot of fun and it was a good opportunity to practice the fiddle and the box. Some of the young dancers played instruments and showed interest in learning Irish dance tunes. I helped them by having them play with me at the dance classes.

Something in me rebels when I look at written music, but many of the kids could read so I would find sheet music for them. The kids that were three and four and just starting out in Irish dance classes when I first met them grew up and scattered all over town. I run into them here and there. Some are still dancing, and some are still playing and some have even started their own dance schools. Every one of them tells me that they have fond memories of Irish dancing. Over the years I have played many weddings, graduation parties, wakes and funerals for the families of Irish dance students and it has been an honor to know them.

*****

I started making two or three trips to a year to Ireland where I would work on the cottage and play music. Michael Deeley would stop by when he saw that I was back and we would have a chat. Once, during those years of frequent trips, I was not seen for nearly a year. When I finally made it back, Michael said, "Oh, we all thought you were dead."

Michael had never been to America and he had lots of questions about the politics and goings on "across over". He knew more about American politics and who was who in Washington than many Americans. Even though he didn't have relatives in America, like many Irish he thinks of America as a sort of extension of Ireland because so many immigrated.

I had no running water at first so Michael fixed me up with a "hosepipe" which was a two hundred foot rubber hose that I bought at a hardware store. We ran it from his cow shed up to the cottage and put a spigot on the end so I had temporary running water. I was going to need the water for the dirty job I was about to tackle. I had taken the old thatch down in the bedroom, but I still needed to get it out of in the other two rooms.

As I was tearing it down, I tried to figure out how it had gone up in the first place. From what I could tell, the rafter poles were pegged to the ridge pole that ran across from the peak of the gable to the chimney and tied with sugan, a kind of rope made from twisted straw. Then, every three feet or so, more poles, lined up parallel with the ridge pole, were tied to the rafters all the way down to the eaves. After that, a "skirt" of woven straw that looked kind of like burlap, was laid over the whole framework. Sod was laid on top of the woven skirt and tied down with more sugan. Then the thatching started. The thatch was laid in small bundles starting at the bottom and then layered upward like long shingles. The bundles were held in place with U-shaped "scallops", which were thin flexible sticks that curved around the bundle and tucked in on each side. Once the thatch on each side had reached the top, they were secured with more ties and scallops and then, on top of it all, another type of woven mat, much thicker than the skirt, was laid all along the ridge hanging down two or three feet on each side and secured with even more ties and scallops. Over the centuries, new layers of thatch were laid over the original when the roof leaked. By the time the steel roof had been put over it, the thatch was three feet thick in most places.

I had been able to remove the thatch in the bedroom with a pitchfork and a hand saw, but I had more trouble in the rest of the cottage. The bedroom thatch might have been easier to remove because the span was less, and there was more dry rot. Even some of the rafter poles were rotted.

I set up a step ladder in the main room and started picking away at the thatch with the pitchfork. Soon the sod began falling down on my head. I tied a kerchief over my mouth and started poking at it again. The soot of years of smoky fires and the dust of the ages soon filled the air. I ran to the hardware store and picked up a huge roll of plastic sheeting which I hung to seal off the bedroom where I was living.

I also bought a wheelbarrow at the hardware store and used it to haul the old thatch into the yard where I piled it on top of the bedroom thatch. I put a match to an old newspaper and lit the pile on fire. The fire lasted three weeks, always smoking because the thatch was damp and moldy and it often rained. The smoke from the fire would sometimes drift out over the road, like a fog, making it difficult to see. The neighbors never complained. Now and then older women walking down the road would appear out of the smoke with shawls pulled across their faces and say things like, “God bless the work” or “You are very welcome here.”

Stories circulate about people finding artifacts from Ireland’s troubled past such as pikes, swords and guns hidden in old thatch. There are also stories about finding money. Several times friends or neighbors stopped by offering to help. I would hand them a kerchief and put them to work. Soon we were all covered in black soot. Sometimes you could loosen a whole section by poking it over and over with a long stick until it would suddenly fall down all at once. Bird nests, mummified mice, and spiders, living and dead, rained down, but never any money or weaponry.

Eventually I had everything down from the rafters and was left with the ridge, which was compacted and didn't give way to the pitchfork or the poles. I could see that removing this part was going to be tricky, so I drove into Galway to find some help. I ran into Bob Cantwell, the man whose brother-in-law had sold me the car. He agreed to come out and have a look. He had no idea what he was in for.

When we arrived back at the cottage, I showed him the rafter poles that were holding the three foot thick heavy, solid remains of thatch all along the ridge fifteen feet in the air. Then I handed him a kerchief and showed him the chainsaw. I had taken apart my old Wisconsin chain saw and brought it over in a duffle bag. I said, "I have an idea. Watch this."

I fired up the chainsaw. Bob's eyes got wide. The sound it made had never before been heard in the ancient cottage in the west of Ireland. I nipped off one of the rafter poles by the chimney at the bottom. The ridge above the rafter buckled but was still held up by the rafter on the other side. I moved to the opposite rafter pole and cut it. The entire section came crashing down. Bob let out an encouraging scream and we were delighted with the progress. It took ten trips with the wheelbarrow to haul the fallen section out of the cottage and throw it on the fire. When we came back in we noticed that Mag Deeley's ancient electric service box had been knocked off by a flying rafter pole. We decided that next time we would be more careful.

We thought that it would be a good idea to cut the next pair of rafters under the other end of the ridge and so headed into the room that Maggie Deeley had named "the black hole." It was the room on the west side of the cottage where Michael Deeley, and I'm sure many others, had been born. At some point after

Michael Deeley's birth, it had been turned into a byer and was filled with a couple feet of old, dry manure. The gable wall in that room had been pulled down by ivy and Michael had rebuilt it with cement block. There was only one tiny window situated high up on the wall. Even with flashlights it was difficult to see anything in there.

With the help of the chainsaw, that section of ridge thatch came down fairly easily and again we hauled it all out into the yard and threw it on the fire. It was raining and the fire was a sodden heap.

Only the longest middle section in the kitchen/main room was left, held up by two pairs of rafter poles. I cut first one, and then another. A long section of the heavy compacted ridge hung down threateningly. There was one pair of rafters left and with the next cut the whole mess was coming down. The cottage had a front and a back door opposite each other. I handed the car keys to Bob, who was standing at the front door and asked him to go for help in case of serious injury. He said, "I don't drive."

I approached the rafter by the back door. I revved up the chainsaw and started cutting but the rafter bit back. The weight from above trapped the blade and I had to fight to free it. I then shifted the saw, taking a step farther into the cottage to cut the rafter from above. I barely touched the wood and it was all over. The rafter pole came after me like a spear hurled by an angry Neanderthal. I dove out the back door and it chased me and ended up stuck in the dirt three feet beyond the door next to where I sat. The ridge thatch had made a muffled crashing sound as it fell and a cloud of black dust followed the rafter through the door.

As I was falling on my ass out back, Bob was fleeing out the front door being chased by the same billowing black cloud. He told me later that he felt like he was in an Indiana Jones movie. He hadn't been able to see what had happened to me and didn't know for sure whether I was alive until I came around the corner of the cottage. Bob said that when he got home, he had to take three showers before the water going down the drain ran clear again.

After we cleaned up the mess, we went in to see the results. The inside of the galvanized roof was a beautiful shade of metallic blue, almost like a bird's egg. It looked strange in the old cottage. The peak of the roof was a least three feet higher than it had been that morning.

*****

Whenever I was staying in the cottage, I would go into Galway City several times a week. Ireland is not a big country but I was still surprised at the number of old acquaintances that I would bump into just walking down the street or sitting in a pub. Some I had met in Ireland years ago and some I had met in Chicago or Boston. Many, like me, travelled back and forth from Ireland to America frequently, and some had just moved home for good. Even if I had not seen them in years we were usually able to strike up a conversation as if no time had passed.

Back in the seventies, when Sean Tyrrell travelled to California with us, he told stories about a man he called John Henry Higgins, a friend of his from Galway. I finally met John Henry in a coffee shop in town around the time I bought the cottage. Because I knew some things about him and he had heard of me, we soon became good friends.

He was living just outside of the city in Connemara and making little Galway hookers the traditional way, carving the ribs, thwarts, planking and rigging out of pine. The sails were made out of red canvas. These hookers were table top sized boats meant for display in pubs and homes. John planned to sell them. He had gone around taking orders which he intended to fill, but he ended up only completing a few. He had made the mistake of showing other people what he was doing and the others, being more ambitious, took his idea and ran with it. Soon fleets of miniature Galway hookers were flooding the market.

This kind of thing happened over and over again to John Henry. He would have an idea for theater or arts or merchandising and when others saw what he intended to do, they would beat him to it. Some say that John Henry's ideas made Galway rich, but he himself was living pretty much as a pauper. He's philosophical about it. He tells the story of his latest "almost was" with a depreciating smile, peering at his listener through the thick glasses that make his eyes look big and then shrugs his shoulders. He knows that he is more of a dreamer than a doer, and he has something even better than his half executed plans. He knows how to enjoy life.

When I first met him, John had a currach, another kind of traditional boat, full-sized this time and one day he asked if I'd like to go out on Galway Bay with him. His boat was in Galway City, tied up at the wall near the Claddagh. As we reached the foot of the bridge over the Corrib River on the Claddagh side, John saw someone that he knew. The man had long, wispy brown hair and his shirt was unbuttoned halfway down. John said, "Ah Declan."

I looked at the man more closely and realized that it was Declan Hunt, the famous Boston rake of days gone by. He recognized me as well. We greeted each other and caught up a little bit. I asked him how long he had been back and he reckoned ten or fifteen years.

Declan was curious when I told him about the cottage in Kinvara so I invited him to come out and visit anytime. He said that he would be out in a few days. Then he asked what John and I were up to.

I had heard about currachs and seen a few of them. A currach has a hull made out of tarred canvas which is stretched over a frame. There is a song in Irish that tells of a tragedy at sea involving one of these boats. Livestock was being moved in one and a hoof went through the canvas. Those in the boat drowned in sight of their loved ones on the shore.

Though I had seen them, I had never had the occasion to say the word out loud and being unfamiliar with the proper pronunciation I answered, “We’re going out in John’s curragh.”

With a wink, Declan teased, “As in “Curragh of Kildare?”

John Henry rescued me and said, “Currach, Tom. A curragh is a flat plain. The boat is a currach.”

We continued on our way and reached the sea wall. John Henry’s currach was eighteen feet long. Normally, they are rowed, but John Henry’s had a little engine. We motored out the Corrib River. It was a beautiful day, warm, sunny and calm which was unusual for Galway Bay. We headed to Mutton Island a few miles out and investigated the old ruins of the coast guard station. The island was a kind of hatchery as well and there were thousands of seabirds about.

We chatted as we walked around and eventually got talking about Sean Tyrrell. John reminisced, “I remember when Tyrrell and I did our very first gig. It must have been back in the early sixties. We were both nervous about playing in front of people, but Sean was more nervous than me. Once we got started though, I was the one dying inside. I could feel myself getting smaller and smaller. I looked over at Tyrrell and he was getting bigger and bigger. That’s the difference between Tyrrell and me.”

We decided to push on toward Salt Hill. Salt Hill is a part of Galway City that was once, and still is, a kind of seaside resort with hotels and amusement arcades. John motored right up to the public beach.

As we approached the shore, we were confronted by disapproving looks and outraged comments. Fingers were pointed at signs spelling out the beach rules, one of which was "No motorized watercraft", and then the same fingers were shaken officiously in our direction. John beached the currach, leaned back against the motor, and lit a cigarette. I leaned back in the bow and tried to ignore the people with the same nonchalance as John.

"Get that thing out of here!"

"You're not allowed!"

In between the barrage of criticism and demands, I asked John under my breath, "Do you think we should get out of here?"

John said quietly and peaceably, "Those rules are new. I'm from here. I've been coming here all my life. I don't know any of these people, so we'll just take our time."

After about a half an hour and three or four cigarettes, John Henry said, "Let's go." We fired up the motor and headed into the bay making our way back to the Claddagh, motoring deftly around the few swimmers.

Another old friend Nora Grealish McDonagh, the renowned sean-nos singer from Connemara whom I had first met in Chicago, was now back in Galway and owned The Pucan. The Pucan was near the train station in the building formerly occupied by Cullen's, where I had gone on my very first night in Ireland. Her pub is named after a third kind of traditional boat, this time a small sailboat used to haul freight.

Nora gave me a lot of work in the first five years after I bought the cottage. I would sit in with the house band, The Stack of Barley, and Nora would pay me on the side. Billy Carr was the front man, a singer, guitar player and box driver. Tony Deviney played banjo and kept the women entertained with his outrageous flirting and ogling. Harry Horan from Feakle, County

Clare was a fabulous old style flute and whistle player. He was a short heavyset curly-haired man who often looked as if he was away with the fairies when he played. His nickname was "The Porter Shark". Harry liked to play jigs and reels and would call Billy "Strauss" if he thought he was playing too many waltzes. His whistle playing had a bubbly kind of sound that was intricate but humorous at the same time. I have heard hundreds of whistle players but none that could play like the old Porter Shark.

The Stack of Barley played some other places as well as The Pucan. I was playing with them once at The Harbor Bar, owned at the time by the great Delores Keane. It was a warm summer night and the tiny pub was full making it much warmer inside than out. We had no sound equipment and so were playing as loud and hard as we could. The place lacked ventilation and everyone was smoking. There was not a breath of air to be had. The other three musicians were all wearing Aran sweaters and dripping while I had stripped down to my shirtsleeves. I asked Tony Deviney, "How can you play? Why don't you take off those sweaters?"

Tony answered, "It's a poor ass that won't wear his harness."

Nora's husband, Colman McDonagh, added on to the original pub as Galway started roaring with the Celtic Tiger. He did most of the work himself. Philomena Hollywood, whose B & B had a view of the back of The Pucan, told me that she would see him out there working alone for a full year, at all hours of the night, building a disco. Later he added a country western bar above the disco. There were lots of legal challenges and arguments with the authorities, but in the end it turned out well for all concerned.

The Pucan was right on the tourist track but its cliental was mostly locals or visitors from other parts of Ireland. One night just before the disco opened, I was playing fiddle with The Stack of Barley and the place was packed. A bus load of French tourists arrived and wanted to come into the little Pucan.

Coleman heard from the bouncers that they were out front. He pushed his way through the crowd and out the front door and yelled, "No. They can't come in! I built this place on the backs of the Irish not the backs of the feckin' French!"

Nora was trying to get me as much work as possible so I could fix up the cottage. I needed lumber, plaster, cement, paint and any number of other things. And I had to eat, sometimes even two or three times a day. She asked me if I wanted to play some country western music out in Connemara. I felt a nudge from an old friend that was hiding deep down in my psyche who whispered, "Well hot-diggity ding dong, that sounds like fun."

After Nora had booked the gigs I asked John Henry if he wanted to play with me and he said that he'd give it a go. He was acting as a caretaker on a farm outside of Moycullen in exchange for rent. I went out to the cottage that he shared with his little Jack Russell Terrier, Peppy, to get a repertoire going. As we were running through some old country western favorites I heard the sound of rats scurrying under the floorboards. Peppy was snoozing in the corner and was totally undisturbed by the sound. I had thought that Jack Russell's were bred for killing rats and asked John Henry about Peppy's apparent lack of concern.

John answered, "Oh, yes. They're great for the rats. Peppy will kill a rat in a minute. But these fellas live here. Now if a strange rat came over from the next farm, Peppy would be on him like a shot, but he knows these boys."

We loaded John's a little PA into his old van and headed out west to do the string of gigs in the Gaeltacht area. We were billed as Texas Tom and the Wicklow Mountaineers. John Henry played mandolin and guitar. Texas Tom sang Hank Williams, Patsy Cline and Johnny Horton songs and then pulled out the fiddle and played jigs and reels.

There weren't any fights which meant that the crowd was listening. They danced to the songs, but when they heard the jigs and reels being played between the country classics, they asked suspiciously if I was a genuine Yank.

I would answer, knowing that it would make some of my fellow countrymen of the Southern persuasion pale, "Hell yes! I'm a genuine Yank. I'm Texas Tom."

Chapter 31
Escape Wisconsin

Back in St. Paul we were still living in Big Pink. The dance school was off to a strong start and Number Three wasn't showing any interest in sailing to Florida, so I decided to take the Pearson back to Bayfield and postpone the dream of sailing to Ireland. The boat was still down in the Hammond Harbor Marina over four hundred miles from St. Paul. It was very early in the season when I hit the road and headed for Chicago to assess the situation. So early that crusted snowbanks lingered on the edges of parking lots and roadsides.

The original name of the boat was "Partnership". Number Three never liked the name which was another hint of things to come that had slipped right past me. The boat had been taken out of the water for the winter and was sitting high up on jack stands. I noticed a convenient snowbank behind the boat and decided to take the opportunity that presented to change the name. I stood on the snowbank and painted the new name across the stern, "Anna Rita", after my grandmother and mother.

I had the boat put back into the water and as I was puttering around doing this and that, I became aware of a strong smell of gasoline coming from the bilge. I searched for the source of smell and realized that the fuel was coming from the carburetor. It would have to be rebuilt.

It was a Saturday and I was playing that night at Shannon's Landing. A couple of Southside musicians, Jimmy Thornton and Joe Shea, came down to sit in with their accordions. On a break, I was talking to Joe and told him all about the latest problem with the boat. When I mentioned that I had never rebuilt a carburetor before Joe said, "If you take it off the motor, I'll show you how to rebuild it."

He promised that he would come down the next day after Mass and, true to his word, early Sunday morning Joe appeared dressed in the immaculate white suit and fancy tan shoes that he had worn to Church that morning. We went below and he sat on the bench at the table while I made some coffee.

Once we were both armed with coffee, I opened the engine hatch and, in about twenty minutes had the slimy, smelly carburetor on the table in front of us. We started to take the carburetor apart and clean it. It was the Texas method all over again, although Joe, a native of County Clare, didn't know it. He was a bit less blunt than Joe Rosson and a lot more generous. There was no limit placed on the number of paper towels I was allowed to complete the job. Soon, we had to open the windows to air out the fumes. By the time we were done my hands and shirt were filthy, but the carburetor parts spread out on old newspapers were gleaming and Joe's suit was still spotless.

Our next step was to locate a 1966 Atomic 4 carburetor rebuild kit on a Sunday morning. We headed to the payphone at the harbor office where we let our fingers do the walking through the yellow pages. Amazingly, we located the proper kit at a store near downtown Chicago and the place was actually open. A few hours later we were putting the rebuilt carburetor back on the engine. We fired it up and it ran like a top. Joe left late that afternoon in his immaculate white suit and spotless tan shoes.

A fellow sailboat owner, Jim Newman, agreed to help me get the newly christened Anna Rita back home to Lake Superior. He caught a bus from Duluth to Chicago. I picked him up at the station and brought him back to the marina. We jumped on board and in ten days we were tied up at the Bayfield city dock. We were so early in the season that we didn't see one other small vessel on the entire trip.

*****

A mostly unoccupied cabin can be a liability. It is almost a tradition for local kids, especially around graduation time, to break when no one is home and have parties far from parental eyes. The parties involve alcohol which is usually, but not always, provided for free by the absent owner of the property. Often a few of the owner's things disappear along with the kids. I was staying in the Wisconsin woods less often. The first time I was broken into, a T. V., a camp stove and a few other odds and ends were missing. I didn't worry too much about it.

One afternoon about a month later, I stopped at the cabin on my way to St. Paul and came in the back way. As I pulled up, the back door was open and I saw a figure was running around inside in a panic. He tried to get out the front door, but couldn't figure out how to work the bolt so he gave up and came flying out the back door as I was jumping out of the car. I ran into the cabin, grabbed the shotgun from beneath the couch and hurried around to the front where the young man was desperately trying to start an All-Terrain Vehicle loaded with things from inside. It was the fanciest ATV I had ever seen and when I saw it I shouted, "Rich kid, huh?"

The guy gave up trying to start the vehicle and tried to run but I dropped him....with a fist. I said, "I'm just going to bury you out here where nobody will find you." With the adrenalin going through me, just for a moment, I might have meant it.

The guy was crying and then I saw that he was just a kid of maybe sixteen. I put down the gun and grabbed him by the ear. The phone in the cabin wasn't hooked up, so I said, "Come on."

I marched him down the road to a neighboring cabin where there was a phone, telling him that I was going to call the cops. He started crying even harder and howled, "Don't do that! I'll get kicked off the hockey team."

I still had him by the ear and asked, "What's your name?"

"Pat," he bawled.

I thought, "Shit, now I can't call the cops."

"Who's your father?" I demanded.

It turned out that I knew his father, an attorney in Spooner.

Resigned, I asked, "Where's he right now?"

I let go of his ear, walked with him to my old Volvo and took him to his father who was at the family cabin on one of the lakes nearby.

His father listened to the story and by the end both were wailing, the father from shame and the son for fear of being kicked off the team. The three of us worked out a deal. The kid would lead us to the place where he had stashed the things he had stolen during the first break-in and fix the window he had broken in the back door. He would also be required to pay a hundred dollar fine to me (payable immediately because I was broke), and mow my lawn for the rest of the summer. The father, being a lawyer, put the agreement in writing.

We went off to retrieve my things. The kid had a nice little campsite set up near a stream, about a mile beyond my place. I recognized some of my pots and pans, my fishing tackle and a couple of lawn chairs. Off to the side there were a bunch of empty beer cans stacked neatly in pyramids. Seeing the camp, I couldn't help feeling that this kid was a lot like me when I was his age although I never built the pyramids.

The three of us returned to the cabin, unloaded the ATV and put the loot back inside. Then we drove to their lake home. The boy showed me some baby flying squirrels he had caught and was keeping in a box while the father wrote the hundred dollar check. The check was handed over, and we all shook hands.

The next morning father and son fixed the window together and that summer, the kid not only mowed the lawn, he "groomed" the lawn. It had never looked so good. There were no hard feelings, but I did tell the bare bones of the story to the owners of a couple of taverns nearby. They gave the kid a hard time when he came in just to keep him on the right track. His father told me later that it worked and I like to think that the arrangement was good for the kid in the end. He was able to show his dad that he was not heading down the wrong path. His dad died a few years later.

*****

Back in St. Paul, Tommy Scanlon had rented out his first place on Grand Avenue and bought a bar called The Ace Box on University and Vandalia. The Ace Box was rougher than Scanlon's and the regulars were a motley crew. There was a flop house next door and a big paper factory across the way full of shift workers who liked to cash and spend their paychecks immediately. Then there was the hobo jungle a quarter mile away near the railroad tracks. The bar was also popular with truckers and biker gangs.

Tommy kept The Ace Box as it was for a couple years but talked about changing it into an Irish Pub with music. I didn't take him seriously until he cleaned it up, painted and got rid of the pool table which was the cause of many fights. Tommy decided to call his new place The Dubliner Pub. People would ask why he didn't call it The Kerry Pub, or The Kerryman's, being that he was born in Kerry. Tommy would answer, "Everyone has heard of Dublin. Nobody knows anything about Kerry."

Tommy wanted to clear out most of the old regulars when the place changed into The Dubliner and his opportunity came immediately. On the day Tommy's place was officially renamed there was a memorial service planned for John Logan, the chef at MacCafferty's who'd introduced me to The Lumberjack Saloon. Over his lifetime John had worked in cities all over the country and memorial services had been celebrated in each of them with his ashes being the guest of honor. The new Dubliner Pub was where he made a final appearance on his grand U.S. tour. The next memorial service would be back home in Dublin.

The Irish arrived attired in suits, ties and nice dresses. The old regulars sitting along the bar looked pretty scruffy in comparison. Tommy was gentle in his method and kept on serving them... until their money ran out. Then, pointing out the mourners in their Sunday best, he told each of the old boys, one by one, "You've got to go. And don't come back. This is a fancy place now."

A few weeks later, a newspaper man from the *Minneapolis Star and Tribune* came in and asked to write an article about the place. Tommy said, "Oh, no sir. Please don't do that. This place is strictly word of mouth." Tommy didn't want people coming in there looking for something that wasn't happening yet and it took about a year for The Dubliner to catch on.

During the transition, troublemakers of every description as well as the occasional former regular who hadn't yet received his marching orders had to be encouraged to leave. One method Tommy used was "the temporary price hike." The price would be raised two dollars or so on whatever the unruly customer was drinking and he would usually storm out the door with a few choice words but under his own steam.

Some of the troublemakers had to be removed by the staff. Tommy's son Dinny had a knack for escorting nuisance customers, otherwise known as "meatballs" out the door. Sometimes the meatball would get belligerent out in the parking lot, in which case Dinny would give him what he called "a little extra hospitality." He enjoyed his work so much that he was often referred to as "Mr. Hospitality." Later he became a fireman.

Finally The Dubliner became a safe place for college students and gentle people to frequent. When young women started coming alone, leaving and actually coming back again another night we all knew that the place had turned a corner. Sometimes Tommy would get nostalgic for the way it used to be and say, "I know I'm getting too old to fight. But still, it would be nice to be asked once in a while."

Tom ran a small ad in the local Irish Music and Dance Association newsletter for a while. It featured a football inside a circle with a line through it. Sports bars were popping up everywhere at the time, but Tommy had something different in mind. From the beginning in 1992 Tommy Scanlon hired live Irish music six nights a week and the Dubliner Pub became a center of Irish activity in St. Paul and a little gold mine.

Sometimes Tommy would have me play twelve nights a month if I was in town. Although I played alone, I had plenty of help from people in the crowd. Sean T. Kelly would belt out in his tenor voice "When New York Was Irish" or "Clancy Lowered the Boom." Bill Conlon often got up to sing "Daisy a Day" or "The Fields of Athenry." I invited any fiddlers or flute players up on stage if I could find them. The smoke was so thick on a busy night that I had to duck down below the haze to see who was there.

I myself had been a heavy smoker since the age of seven and was spending a lot on cigarettes. Since I depended on my voice for my livelihood I decided that it was time to quit. I had a session with a hypnotist and that night I went to the movie "Dances with Wolves" which was just under four hours long. I was amazed that I didn't have a need to light up as I walked out of the theater. I never had the desire to start up again and seemed to be spared the effects of withdrawal. Even at coffee shops, where the combination of a coffee and a smoke was such a habit, I had no need to light up. I would hear in my head the mantra instilled by the hypnotist, "I've smoked my last cigarette. I don't need 'em and I don't want 'em. I can be in a room full of people all smoking like chimneys and my only thought will be 'I'm glad I'm not smoking'."

One day, about a week later, I was sitting at the tables outside Dunn Brothers on Grand, drinking my coffee and having a conversation with a newspaperman who worked for one of the major dailies. He was an editor and his job was to decide which of the international news stories coming off the wire should be printed. We were having a mildly political discussion and, as usual, we were friendly and joking. A girl, another casual regular of the place, rode up on a bicycle and asked, “What are you two talking about on this beautiful Sunday?”

My buddy said, “Oh, he just wants to talk about the IRA.”

I had never talked to him about the IRA and we weren’t talking about it then. I splashed a little of my cold coffee on him. Then he threw a little on me. Fisticuffs ensued and soon our little round table was rolling around in the middle of Grand Avenue traffic. I managed to pop him pretty good and opened up a split on the side of his head. We came to our senses and I apologized. My hand was sore and he was bleeding from the cut. My white shirt and light colored pants were spotted with red. Feeling very small, I said that I would drive to him to the emergency room for stitches.

I went inside and asked for a towel because my knuckles were bleeding. My coffee cup was empty so I asked for a refill as well. The girl behind the counter, taking in the bloodstained shirt said, “Sir. Would you like to switch to decaf?”

On the way to the hospital, I asked if he wanted to press charges. My friend answered, “No, Tommy. I was a Marine, I can take a hit.”

I thought that the hypnotism was working like a charm. I guess I wasn’t doing as well as I thought with the withdrawal symptoms.

The smoky little Dubliner was doing well, but as happens in pubs and restaurants, there were down times. Tommy told me that one day he was sitting at the bar all alone and looking out the window. He kept on seeing former Ace Box regulars whom he had barred walking along the sidewalk in front of the pub. Overcome with loneliness, he grabbed a piece of paper and a magic marker from behind the bar. He quickly made up a sign and stuck it in the window. It said, “AMNESTY! TODAY ONLY!”

Tommy leaned out the door and called to a few of "the boys" who were walking past and, pointing to the sign, invited them in. Now he had people to talk to.

Music and dance were not the only parts of Irish culture that were being actively pursued in St. Paul in the eighties and nineties. Besides having the Irish American Cultural Institute, a literary society founded by Dr. Eoin McKiernan, there were several Irish theater groups. Tommy Scanlon joined one of them, Na Fianna Irish Theater and they held rehearsals in the basement of The Dubliner. Also in the troup were Dan Gleason, the man who gave me the Appaloosa, Kathie Luby, a singer and the woman who questioned my continued existence that night at the Half-time Rec, and Lar Burke who was a writer as well as being the old Scanlon's bartender. Other members were Sean T. Kelly the singing reporter originally from New York, Maeve O'Mara and Liam O'Neill from Cork who owned the Irish import shop Irish on Grand and Tommy Goulding from Waterford who had been John Dingley's "not so silent" partner at The Irish Well. This bunch never bothered to memorize scripts. Some of them never even read them. After getting the gist of the story from others they would ad lib the rest. Na Fianna won Irish theater competitions in Milwaukee, Chicago and Canada.

Besides playing The Dubliner in St. Paul, I was going to McGurk's in St. Louis which booked musicians for four or five weeks at a time. I also had fairly regular bookings in Chicago, Denver, Kansas City and a place called O'Malley's in Weston, Missouri, which was built mostly underground in caves at the site of an old winery. Josh was still booking me in colleges. Between the gigs, the boat, the cabin in Wisconsin and the cottage in Ireland, I was very busy.

*****

I met a wiry Finlander named Larry Rantalla wandering around in the northwest Wisconsin woods. He was investigating the flora and fauna of the sand country north of Spooner. Larry had been raised in Bayfield but fled the town as it became more crowded with summer people and winter sports enthusiasts. He had long, stringy brown hair and a huge wolf's head tattooed on his chest and stomach. Although he never finished college and had no degree, he was the recognized expert on local sedges, sphagnum mosses, and bog flowers. The DNR occasionally employed him to do survey work because they didn't have anyone who knew as much about the bogs as Larry.

He and I had become friends. Not long after the cabin had been broken into I invited him to stay at my place. I needed someone to look after my property and he was at loose ends. We worked out a mutually beneficial arrangement. Even though I had told him that he could stay in the cabin, he brought an old camper and dropped it off in the yard. After a few weeks, we got to talking and I asked him if he wanted to buy half my property for two thousand dollars. He would pay me a hundred dollars a month and that after twenty months he would own some land.

Jim Brooks and his wife Mary Sue bought a place in Wisconsin not far from me and started asking around to find out where exactly my place was. Jim is a news hound who can always sniff out a story and in fact owns his own newspaper in St. Paul, *The Irish Gazette*. With his sleuthing ways, it wasn't long before he thought they had located the cabin. They drove up a long driveway into a clearing and were confronted by a growling German Shepard and a long-haired bearded being that had emerged from a dilapidated camper. The man glared at them from behind a pair in incongruous wire-rimmed spectacles and the snarling wolf on his bare chest seemed to glare as well.

Jim and Mary Sue tried their professional friendliness and cunning in an attempt to get an idea of whether they had indeed found the right place but got absolutely nothing from the creature. Jim later had to ask me, when he met up with me in St. Paul, if he had found the right cabin. I was pleased to hear that the security that Larry was providing was so effective.

Once during Larry's tenancy I visited the cabin and found him stumbling about in the driveway. I climbed out of the car and he tried to talk to me but all he could manage were mumbles and groans. I immediately suspected that Larry had fallen off the wagon and yelled, "You bastard. You're stoned out of your mind."

Larry shook his head vigorously in the negative and pointed to his mouth saying, "Waabeehawathmmmoud!"

I saw that his tongue was swollen to at least twice its normal size and grabbed some garden dirt, ran into the cabin and used water to make a big handful of mud which I pushed into his mouth. Larry sat down and relaxed a little. We gave it about ten minutes and then he rinsed it out. We decided that he should have a second serving. After about a half an hour, the swelling had gone down and Larry was able to speak again. He had no idea how the bee had gotten at his tongue. Maybe he had been sleeping with his mouth open.

By that time Larry had been there for over twenty months and had paid me nineteen hundred of the two thousand that would have purchased the property. I thought he would give me the hundred dollars remaining and it would be a done deal but Larry surprised me. He said that he didn't really believe in owning land and kept the last hundred dollars. He stayed on for a few more months and then packed out.

I was stretched too thin and that fall I sold the cabin to Quiet Al's sister. I paid off the cottage in Ireland with the money and started thinking again about sailing to Ireland.

*****

Martin McHugh and I had an album out on Flying Fish and that summer we were booked by Josh Dunson to play the Winnipeg Folk Festival. It is a big gathering that is still held every year and features folk music from all over the world. One of the programs that year was called "Songs of Struggle."

There were singers from Guatemala, Poland, Alabama, El Salvador, Tibet and South Africa. Martin and I were asked to represent Ireland. A master of ceremonies spoke before each group did their spot providing a little background on the issues of each country. There were translators and sign language interpreters on the stage and about thirty thousand people in front of it.

Marty and I were scheduled to go up and do our spot just after Sweet Honey in the Rock, a mighty assembly of powerful Black women out of Alabama. They had incredible voices, complex harmonies and rhythmical singing. Their grand finale was an anti-Apartheid tribute to the women of South Africa. At the end of the song, they started to wail louder and louder, like police sirens, and then stopped suddenly, to the amazement of the crowd. There was a stunned silence and then a gigantic cheer went up.

As the group marched off the stage they walked right past Marty and me where we stood shaking in our boots listening to the thunderous applause that followed them. I hadn't decided what to sing yet and we hadn't even started talking about which tunes to play. One of the women from Sweet Honey in the Rock called out to us over the din made by the cheering crowd, "Next struggle, please!"

We walked out onto the stage and I sang "The Dear Little Isle", a song that touches on many aspects of the Irish struggle. The last line is, "But the Irish are somehow like wild, creeping flowers. The faster you pluck them, the quicker they seem to grow."

Then we played "Joe Cooley's Reel" and "The Sally Gardens" and got the hell off the stage. Marty jokingly muttered to me, "Another very successful tour."

Chapter 32
The Pipes Are Calling

I had not abandoned the idea of crossing to Ireland with the Anna Rita. I drove up to Bayfield to sail around the Apostle Islands as often as I could, expanding my knowledge. I was also making improvements on the boat to ready it for an Atlantic crossing someday.

When in Bayfield I usually played a few gigs at the Burned Down on Madeline Island, the Mecca in Lake Superior for fun loving people. Madeline Island means different things to those who find themselves there. It is the center of the universe for the Native Americans in the area and the Cape Cod of the North Woods for others. The population swells from about a hundred over the winter to thousands in the summer. Old logging families and farmers, both old style and ultra-modern, live there year round. There are artists of all descriptions both pro and con, musicians, ragtag to classical, poets, runaways and lots and lots of lawyers. There are nearly as many types of watercraft as there are people.

The full time residents tend toward being either characters, strong personalities or both. One former mayor of La Pointe, who let slip that he was on the island as a result of being in the Federal Witness Protection Program, got busted on the Bayfield to La Pointe Ferry for smoking and refusing to extinguish it. The fact that it was marijuana didn't make his situation any better.

Tom's Burned Down Café stands to the dismay of some and to the delight of many in the heart of La Pointe. It's considered an eyesore by the straight laced types who have built mansions on the island. Perhaps they object to Tommy's claim, displayed for all to see on a handmade sign above the bar, "We cheat the other guy and pass the savings on to you!"

Tommy has fought hard with the elements, natural and legal, that seem to have arrayed themselves to attack him and his odd bar. The tents and old sails that cover it have come and gone, blown away by the big winds and weather of Gitche Gumee. The fires that burn nearly every night send sparks high up into the evening air when Tommy's bar is open, while the activities spark controversy across the island and beyond.

There are plots each year to shut him down. With every new assault, the opposition thinks they have him dead to rights, but they are wrong. Tommy owns the land on which the bar stands. He used to keep wrecks of cars, trucks, boats and farm machinery strewn around out back. The powerbrokers on the island, including some of Tom's close relatives, tried to sue him for running an illegal junk yard. Tommy put out a call for help to metal sculptors and welders. He received a grant from the Wisconsin Arts Board and turned the whole property into a "Metal Sculpture Garden". In no time, Tommy was appearing on lists of prominent Wisconsin artists. There was much gnashing of teeth in the opposing camp.

Among the lawyers on the island was a man named Bruce Hartigan, a successful defense attorney called by some "The Ringleader" usually pronounced with a trilled "r". The name was originally bestowed on him by an Irish nun in the orphanage he and his brother had been raised in. Tommy credits Bruce with keeping the more serious legal assaults on the Burned Down and himself at bay.

Although with Bruce's help he has avoided convictions in the court of law, Tommy has strong political convictions. Every year he and his friends create an extravagant entry for the Fourth of July parade in La Pointe. They spend months planning and building the spectacle. These parade entries, like the float dedicated to electing "Cheney and Satan in 2008" and the whole scene at Tommy's are so outrageous they have to be seen to be believed. No mere description would do them justice.

After having steered the boat manually from Superior to Chicago and back, I knew that a self-steering wind vane system would be best for crossing the Atlantic. I got word of an old Aries wind vane for sale for two hundred and fifty dollars and snapped it up. I found out after I bought it that the model was considered one of the best designs ever produced. A new wind vane of that type would have cost nearly eight thousand dollars which was out of the question.

It took quite a bit to install, but I had plenty of help from the other sailors on the city dock in Bayfield. After a lot of experimentation and a good chunk of time we figured it out. The heavy bronze apparatus is installed on the stern of the boat. A wind vane on a long steel tube is attached the top of this apparatus. When the wind tips the vane, it turns a paddle that hangs off the bottom of the contraption into the water. The moving water catches the turning paddle and kicks it far enough over to engage the gears on the apparatus, on one side or the other. Those gears control arms that protrude out of the top. Ropes are attached to the arms and run through a series of pulleys to the cockpit where they are crossed and then wrapped around a stainless steel drum attached to the steering wheel. The ropes convey information about slight changes in wind direction to the wheel. To engage the system a spring-loaded metal peg is pushed into the wheel drum. The boat then steers itself, keeping a steady course in relation to the wind, and the sailor is free to think about other things.

When the sailing season ended and I was back in the Twin Cities, I happened to stop in at Molly Quinn's, a bar on Lake Street in Minneapolis to talk to one of the owners. Bill Watkins is Welsh-Irish, was born in England and then lived in Scotland before moving to the Twin Cities. He is a writer and performer, singing songs of his own composition. He has also written a couple of good books, *A Celtic Childhood,* and *Scotland is Not for the Squeamish.* We were having a chat when Bill said, "Excuse me a minute. I have to throw this guy out."

He pushed a disheveled, wasted-looking man out onto the street. As the man went through the door, I caught a glimpse of his face and thought I recognized him.

Bill returned to where we were sitting and said, "Sorry, Tom. That guy has been bouncing checks."

"What's his name? I think I might know him."

It was indeed Andy, the Highland piper who had the set of Uilleann pipes that had been promised to me all those years ago. I asked Bill if he knew where Andy lived and he rummaged around behind the bar until he found a card with his address and phone number. I told Bill a bit of the story of the Uilleann pipes and how close I had come to getting them when Paddy Hill was still alive. I asked Bill if he thought they might still be in Andy's possession.

Bill said, "I don't know. Wait a wee bit. Give him time to walk home. Go find some cash and see what happens if you show up at his door."

I left, and as soon as I was on the street I found myself repeating a prayer that I had originally heard from Philomena Hollywood in Galway when I told her how I was hoping that the deal on the cottage would go through. "If it's for me, let me get it. If it's not for me, don't let me get it."

It was a cold wet afternoon in early winter. After about an hour of slogging around the slush covered streets of St. Paul I scraped together a thousand dollars and made my way to Andy's door.

For all those years I knew that if the set didn't come to me, it was a sign that I was not supposed to be a piper. Buying just any old set would be defying the gods of music. This was running through my mind as a stood outside Andy's door and I was afraid of spooking him and thus losing my chance to become a piper. I knocked and waited and then knocked and waited again.

After about ten minutes I was thinking about trying the door when it suddenly opened. Andy stepped out and said, "Tom

Dahill, is that you? I didn't recognize you without the long hair and beard."

I almost didn't recognize him with the long hair and beard. The Andy of old had been a Highland Pipe Major and clean cut. He had changed a great deal over the years and it looked like they had been hard years.

"It's been a long time, Andy. Do you still have the pipes?"

"I do. They're right inside on the living room floor. Do you want to see them?"

I followed him inside.

There they were, still in the old case with the label that said "P. J. Linehan, reed-maker." I saw again, after twenty-five years, the African blackwood with brass keys, the ivory endcaps, the beautiful bellows and green velvet bag cover with gold fringe. I was kneeling on the floor examining them and exclaiming on their beauty when Andy commanded, in an imperious tone, "Take them and leave!"

I thought that he meant to lend them to me and asked, "When do you want them back?"

"I'm not lending them. Take them and leave!"

I pulled out the thousand dollars and asked, "Do you want to sell them to me?"

"I don't want your money. I have twenty thousand in cash in the freezer." He pointed at the door. "Take them and leave!"

I took them and left.

I brought the box back to Big Pink, put it on the couch and carefully removed the contents. After years of patient waiting and doing what Teddy Tonkinson had told me to do ("Don't say a word or you'll never get them"), all I could do was stare in amazement.

Mostly I had been able to put the pipes out of my mind, but sometimes, when I met a piper, I would tell him the story. One of those pipers was Michael Cooney from Tipperary who was playing in St. Louis. Michael got angry, a reaction that I had seen before when I told the story.

"We've got to get them. They should be yours."

Michael was ready to jump in the car, drive to St. Paul, break in and steal the set, especially when he heard that the Highland piper had sworn that no Irishman would ever play them again. I never took any of my piper friends up on these kind offers, but it felt good to know they were outraged on my behalf.

Now I had them. I had been listening to Uilleann pipes for years but I didn't know much about them even though I had read about how they worked and seen them played. The bellows under the right arm pumped air into the bag under the left arm through a leather hose. A brass lever on the stock turned on the drones, of which there were three, tuned to three octaves of D. The regulators, three stopped pipes with one reed in each, have keys that are used to play harmony and rhythm. The chanter is attached to the neck of the bag.

I attempted to put the parts together and after a few hours I was able to manage a few wheezy squeals and low groans. I could hear air leaking out from the bellows, the regulator keys, every joint, and from a big crack in the stock.

Timmy Fitz was now the general manager of Kieran's where I had a gig that night. I decided to bring the pipes along and show them to Fitz who was nearly as fascinated as I was. To us, they said something about the history of the Irish in Minnesota that was intriguing and at the same time unknowable. All we knew for sure was that they had been made in Ireland around 1900 by a master pipemaker and sent across. This was the only old set that had ever been in Minnesota as far as we knew.

I wanted them to get to know me so I brought the pipes up on stage and placed them carefully behind my chair. I opened the box just a little, so they would be able to see me and hear what kind of music I played. Working with the set would be something like taming a wild animal. I would have to take it slow and easy and find all the help I could. I was forty-nine years old, pretty old to be starting on the pipes. But I knew it was good that I hadn't had them in my younger days. I was too unsettled. Now, what I lacked in youth, I could make up for in determination. As I fell asleep that night, I pondered on how well the fates had taken care of things.

The next day I called the one fellow in town who I knew played the pipes. When I told him the good news he said, "I hate you."

We met up anyway. I picked up a few pointers and the phone number of another piper, Chad Giblin who, when I called, was excited and came over right away. Chad had all the books, tools and enthusiasm that I needed to get started. I knew plenty of tunes on the fiddle and box, but could barely get through any of them on the pipes.

Chad and I put our heads together and started an Uilleann pipers club which, to give it a sense of place, we called The Great Northern Irish Pipers Club. Misery loves company and we soon found four or five others who were struggling, if not to master, not be mastered by the Uilleann pipes.

We organized our first tionól or gathering of pipers in 2000. Fitz gave us the run of Kieran's for the weekend and we had Paddy Keenan, one of the most respected players in the world, as our guest piper. We were extremely lucky that he agreed to attend and teach when we ourselves could barely play. I'd read books that described, in painful detail the expensive tools, materials and exact measurements required to make reeds, but at the tionól, Paddy, in about twenty minutes and using only a jack knife, a cork from a wine bottle, a scrap of sand paper and a piece of broken glass made a reed that played and played well.

The Great Northern Pipers Club held a tionól every year after that. It has invited Michael Cooney, Billy McCormick, Michael O'Sullivan, Kevin Henry, Dave Power, Tommy Martin, Patrick D'arcy and many others to share their expertise and stories.

David Daye of Seattle made bellows kits that were airtight, cheap and readily available. He also made chanters of PVC. They were good for pipers who were just starting out and worked pretty well if you needed something to practice on when your own chanter was in the shop.

A great pipe maker, Kirk Lynch, who lives in Kansas City had used a Willie Rowsome set much like mine as a pattern for the first sets that he made. Somehow, one of his sets made its way to Pakistan where it was copied. The copies worked most of the time, if you were able to make them work. We eventually had five of these sets floating around town. If you sent in your stock, regulators or drones to be reconditioned by a master, you could plug in the Pakistani parts to cover you until your set was ready. They were life savers for the early Great Northern.

After years of neglect, my set needed some major rehab. Besides the leaks and the cracks, there were loose keys and missing pins. I couldn't bear to part with the entire set while the work was being done, but I'd been given the phone number of Benedict Kohler, a Vermont piper and pipemaker extraordinaire. Benedict patiently answered hundreds of my semi-coherent questions and eventually consented to rebuild my set a few pieces at a time.

When I finally had my whole set back from Benedict that winter, I started to put in eight to ten hours a day working on the pipes. I continued to practice constantly for the next five years. With help I learned to make reeds and troubleshoot my set. After such a long wait, I wasn't going to miss my chance to become a piper. It was, I'm afraid, an unpleasant experience for others who had to hear me, but, as Oscar Wilde commented, "at least they don't make a smell." I drove a few people crazy, mostly residents of Big Pink.

I never would have thought that skills I had developed when I was a ten-year-old kid making bows and arrows, chugs and go carts would be used again forty years later. That early practice with levers and springs, with carving, wrapping and tying, with using bees' wax, gluing, cutting and sewing with leather and sinew were handy to have when dealing with a set of pipes. They require maintenance whether the set is new or old and if you can't do the work yourself, you will seldom see your pipes. The weather can play havoc with the reeds, especially in Minnesota where the humidity can go from tropical in the summertime to desert-like in the winter when it's twenty below and the furnace is blasting.

The next spring the Anna Rita was returned to the water and when I was tied up on the pier in Bayfield it was usually quiet. I could make all the piping noises I wanted to without fear. In the early stages it can be a pretty gruesome experience for anyone to hear a piper practicing. By summer the pier became more crowded and I realized that there were people hearing me and, I could tell from the tapping of the feet seen through the porthole even listening to me. That was the last thing that I wanted. Then I remembered the wind vane steering. I could sail out into Lake Superior and engage the wind vane. Once I set a course I wouldn't have to touch the wheel. I had found the perfect way to practice the pipes and the boat became mostly a workshop and practice studio on water.

The wind vane worked like a charm. Many times the thirty-five foot boat would be heeled over and flying along. It could sail for hours that way with the wind vane making minute adjustments faster and more accurately than any human hand, while I sat in the high end of the cockpit piping away, with the halyards clanging, the wind roaring in the sails and water rushing by.

I started hearing details about the Linehan set's life before it came to me. John Curtin told me that after Linehan, whom he knew personally, died in 1950, his widow wasn't sure what to do with his set. So, like many other sets of pipes around the country, they were put in a convent with the nuns for safekeeping. When Pat Hill had asked Mrs. Linehan about the pipes in the seventies, she had retrieved them from the convent to give them to me. That was when the miscommunication between mother and daughter occurred and the set moved out of reach.

I found out later that P.J. Linehan had been a grain elevator inspector by occupation and eventually became a foreman. That was railroad work in those days. Many Irish musicians had worked for the railroads and had free travel passes, riding the rails from city to city to meet up with other Irish musicians. The air hole cover for the bellows on P.J.'s set is fashioned out of an old railroad pocket watch cover that has a locomotive etched on the front. That hints at the idea that the railroad had a part in his music. Perhaps Linehan, whom I knew to be a reed maker from the label inside the case, had used the railroads to deliver his finished product to the pipers who had ordered them or perhaps pipers had come to him.

P.J. could have easily travelled to Chicago by rail. Chicago in the early 1900s when the set came over was full of Irish pipers. Chief O'Neill of the Chicago Police Department had seen to that when he had invited some of the best Irish musicians to Chicago as he researched tunes for his great collection.

I was most interested in hearing and thinking about the pipes when they had been in P. J. Linehan's possession, but I also heard a few things about the set's time with Andy. I was hired along with a Highland piper from Brian Boru to play an outdoor wedding in Northern Minnesota. As we waited for the ceremony to begin, we talked pipes.

He said, "Did you know that that set of yours was in a pawn shop on Lake Street for a couple of years?"

It turns out that once, when Andy was down on his luck, he pawned the set and then apparently forgot about them. Another piper finally heard about it, paid the ticket and returned them to their wayward keeper. Fortunately for my sake, nobody knew what they were during their time in the pawn shop.

*****

I knew that the wind vane worked well and since the cottage in Ireland was coming along so nicely it seemed like this might be the right time to take the boat through the Great Lakes, out through the St. Lawrence Seaway and once in the Atlantic, up to Newfoundland and across to Ireland.

A friend, Patrick O'Donnell, had heard about the intended voyage. Patrick had founded a theater group called "The Titanic Players" that practiced and performed in the back room of Kieran's. The back room was known as The Titanic Lounge and featured traditional Irish music and theater. Patrick and Timmy Fitzgerald had decked over a twenty-five foot wooden boat to serve as the bar. It was meant to resemble a lifeboat. Pat hadn't sailed before but he and his wife Ann came up to Bayfield to check out my boat with the idea that Pat could possibly come along as crew.

Patrick, the man of letters, saw some potential for filming the trip and was talking about getting a grant as we set out on the Anna Rita for a quick practice trip around Chequamegon Bay. He was expounding on all the opportunities there would be to conduct interviews with the characters that we would surely meet along the way while I was explaining how a sailboat worked. I was showing them things like how to tie off halyards, how to tack and jibe, and how to trim sails for upwind and downwind, while Patrick was holding forth about the historically significant places we would see on our voyage. It occurred to me towards the end of the test sail, that Ann could probably crew a boat and Patrick could probably produce a decent documentary.

I wasn't so sure that I should be alone in the middle of the North Atlantic with a man who was part of "The Titanic Players", so I continued to search for crew. I stopped in at the Burned Down to ask Tommy for a recommendation. Tommy, of course, had one. His candidate was a strong looking guy about twenty years old and bigger than me who with his sun-bleached beard looked like a Viking. He was working for Tommy at the Burned Down and also crewing for sailboat races. He had been born on the island and lived on the water his whole life. The Viking sounded perfect, but I wanted to see him in action. We went out on the boat and he was quick to pick up on all that was needed. We got along well and he was excited about the prospect of a long voyage. The Viking was the ideal man for the job.

When I had the boat hauled out that fall, we were both anticipating spring and our cruise to Ireland. That winter when I wasn't practicing the pipes I was reading all the technical sailing books and first-hand accounts of sailing voyages that I could find. I had read the sixteen book series by Patrick O'Brien twice over by that time.

Around Christmas the phone rang. It was the Viking. When I picked up the phone he said, "Tom, I wanted to let you know. I can't go with you to Ireland 'cause I'm in a mental hospital."

There was a history of schizophrenia in his family and it had struck him. I felt bad for him, but if it was going to happen, I think it was better that it happened while he was on dry land, where he could obtain the help he needed rather than in the middle of the Atlantic with no one around but me. He got through the episode and the last I heard he had become a wooden boat builder.

In the late summer of 2001 I got my first piping gig. A friend of mine, Dave Maroney often came in to hear me sing in the pubs when he was hale and hearty. He had been told the story of the pipes, and knew I had been working on them. Then his health began to fail. His brother, Terry, called me when Dave had passed and told me that he had left a request that I play the pipes at his wake. I wasn't sure if I was ready to play in public, but since a friend had asked, I knew that I would do it.

We were all doing our best to make it a good send off. The Maroneys had old ties in St. Paul and we were all telling stories about the past. Terry launched into a story about how back in the days when he was going regularly to The Half-Time Rec, his mother had asked him where he had been the night before. Terry answered, "I was hanging out with Tom Dahill."

His mother said, "Oh, Tom Dahill was a friend of your father's."

Then she stopped and gave him a look. "Tom Dahill is dead."

Terry said, "But I was just talking to him."

Eventually, they worked out that she was thinking of Chief Tom Dahill, my great uncle. His mom had more stories about her family and Chief Dahill. She said that when Terry and Dave's Uncle Bill got paid he'd go on a spree. He lived near the farmer's market and would spend most of his pay on the drink. When he drank he liked to fight and he would usually end up getting hauled to jail. Tom Dahill would be called down to give him a talking to. "See here, Bill, we can't have this. Go home and don't let this happen again."

Uncle Bill would promise that this was the very last time and Tom would have him turned loose. Then he would head home and be a model citizen for twenty seven days... until the next payday.

I played my best for Dave at his wake and he had no complaints. I was on my way to becoming a piper.

Chapter 33

Very Welcome Here

The next time I returned to Kinvara, the thatch was down and the galvanized roof was all I had between the sky and me. There was three hundred years of whitewash on the interior walls of the cottage and scraping it off would be a big job. I decided to start in the bedroom, but I had to rid the place of some unwanted guests first.

I had given a key for the cottage to Tim Fitz and Marty McHugh. They stopped by, walked in and left on the run. The bees had taken over. I had placed blocks on top of the chimney to keep rooks from nesting in it when I was gone and unintentionally provided the bees with a nice sheltered place to build a hive. Looking up from the fireplace in the bedroom you couldn't see anything, but you could hear the whole chimney humming.

Declan Hunt's old banger careened into the yard at just the right time. We put our heads together and came up with a plan for the bees. We built a roof ladder out of two by fours. Declan climbed up with a can of poison and a saucepan. He sprayed the poison down the chimney and then used the saucepan to scoop out the comb. After scooping as far down as he could he tipped himself in to reach even deeper. From below all I could see were his two legs protruding out the top of the chimney.

When he finished, I started a fire in the bedroom fireplace, thinking that the smoke would keep the remaining bees quiet. Instead the smoke immediately filled the cottage and we realized that the hive was bigger than we thought.

I filled the saucepan with water to douse the fire and Declan climbed back up on the roof with an old rafter pole. He started pushing the whole mess down while I fashioned a hook out of heavy gauge wire and started working on the hive from below. It was only then that we found out how big it really was. I ended up with seven five gallon buckets of poisonous peat-smoked honey comb. Charlie Piggott had a problem with bees a few years later. He called a bee keeper and was able to save the honey which in retrospect is what we should have done. At least neither of us was stung even if we deserved to be.

With the bees gone, I could start on the bedroom. I decided to put in a ceiling before removing the old whitewash. There was a saw mill about ten miles away next to Coole Park, Lady Gregory's estate where she had hosted some of the leading lights of the Dublin literary and political scene around the turn of the last century. I bought lumber for all my projects there. I'd tie a big load of wood on the roof of my old car and drive back to the cottage very, very slowly.

The bedroom was about sixteen by ten. To make the ceiling I pulled out my chain saw and cut two by eights to make a frame. Then I used tongue and groove pine to make a ceiling with a trap door. I insulated it with fiberglass batts. The ceiling was nine feet high and the remaining area from the ceiling to the galvanized roof was storage.

Next, I scraped all the whitewash off the walls and then had to re-plaster them. I hadn't worked with plaster before, but I knew a guy in Galway called "one-eyed Paddy" who picked up odd jobs to get by when he wasn't working with horses. He came out two or three times to help me plaster the bedroom.

Paddy really did have only one eye. He was an ex-con and had served time in a Portuguese prison for doing what he did to the guy who took that eye, but he had a great sense of humor. He had grown up on the Bohermore where small shops and small houses crowd up against one another. The area is one of the oldest parts of the town. He was caregiver for his mother who still lived there. While we worked, he entertained me with stories about the old Galway that was quickly vanishing. We finished plastering the bedroom and then Paddy got busy with the horses and I was back on my own.

The two brothers that lived up the road, Gerry and Donal, were frequent visitors. They were once described to me as Peeping Toms, but weren't really. They were just watchful. If there was a conversation that they wanted to hear, one or the other and sometimes both, would stand behind a nearby bush. They would stay very still and, although their presence was obvious, they would act as if you couldn't see them. When the conversation ended, they would disappear. Michael Deeley would sometimes tell them bluntly to go away if he spotted them lurking and they always complied. One-Eyed Paddy had all the time in the world for them. He said that it was the best of luck to have such characters around.

Both Gerry and Donal were very intelligent in their own way. They had terrific memories. Gerry could tell you the scores of every hurling and Irish football match he had heard or read about and the names of the players going back thirty years or more. Donal could recite the names of the All-Ireland Champion Ceili Bands and who played in them. Although neither of them would talk to strangers, whenever I returned to the cottage, they could give me a complete description of any car that stopped by and its occupants. The descriptions were always detailed enough for me to know who had been looking for me. There was a lot said against them, but I think they were just not of this age and had been passed by in the mad rush for progress.

St. Vincent DePaul's in Galway City had a fine selection of furniture and other household odds and ends. If you arrived early enough on a Tuesday morning before they opened, you had a chance of procuring a few choice items. There were usually about two dozen fellow scroungers waiting for the door to open at nine. When they unlocked the door the crowd would rush in to put their marks on the items they wanted. You had to be fast to get your mark placed before someone else did. I picked up a few tables and chairs and some pots and pans that way which was the beginnings of furnishing the cottage. I painted the freshly plastered bedroom walls white and returned to St.

Vincent DePaul's. This time I found an old carpet, a bunch of candles and a "new" Coleman lantern. Back at the cottage, I put down a turf fire. It was really starting to feel like home.

My cottage was one long mile from Galway Bay and if I walked down the road towards Kinvara, I could see water after about a hundred yards. I could also see the Burren from my cottage. It is a two hundred and fifty square kilometer area of limestone plateaus and mountains that is famous for ancient dolmens, ring forts, castles and interesting flora and fauna. The Burren is an area steeped in traditional music and folklore. They say that if you get lost up on the Burren, which is easy to do as it is often covered in cloud, the best thing you can do to find your way again is to turn your coat inside out. That is one way to break the fairy's spell.

Deckie was working as a postman and delivered the mail in his car to all the out of the way farms and pensioners' cottages sprinkled around that remote area. He knew his way around the Burren better than nearly anyone since he had been at the mail delivery business for years.

Declan had one complaint about the job. He, like rural and sometimes urban postmen the world over, was driven nearly demented by the dogs. To defend himself, he asked me to bring him a can of mace from America since you can't buy it in Ireland. I brought over two or three cans, but they didn't work very well for him. No matter how far away the dog was, as soon as it started towards him, Deckie started spraying. By the time the dog was on him, the can was empty. The other thing that he asked me to bring over for him was a brand of boots made in Red Wing, a Minnesota town on the Mississippi River. At least he had good footwear to hightail it back to the car when the mace can was empty.

I wasn't the only one with a project going in the area. Michael's daughter, Martha and her husband, young Aiden Fahey, were the first to build a house nearby. Aiden built houses for a living and knew the ins and outs of the building trade in Ireland. Michael had given the couple a piece of land to build their own house on. The house they built was beautiful and big, which was what they needed for their ever expanding family.

I hired Aiden to help me out on projects that required more specialized tools than a pitchfork and a chain saw. He put in new windows and a teakwood half door. He also sandblasted the wall around the main fireplace to expose the old granite blocks that had been covered with layers and layers of old whitewash.

Once, when I returned from America, Aiden came down and told me of an odd event. He said that one morning he noticed that some mysterious workmen had come in the night and put in a septic system. He wasn't sure how it had happened, but the good news was that since the septic was already in, I could put in plumbing whenever I was ready without first obtaining a permit.

Michael Deeley continued to stop by to see how the work was coming along. There was plenty to talk about now that the old thatch was down. I told him that I was thinking about re-thatching over the galvanized roof someday if I could figure out how to do it.

P. J. Linehan's pipes seemed to like being home in Ireland and they were played at all hours, day and night, in between bouts of working on the cottage. One day a man who had been building a new house just beyond the Fahey's house walked over along with his brother and knocked on the door. They had been hearing the pipes and at first thought that it was a recording. When they started hearing the mistakes and the same phrases played over and over, they realized that a piper was practicing. The man was Fintan Sheehan and his brother was called Bernard. They both played music. Fintan played the flute and Bernard the pipes.

Fintan was originally from Kerry but had married a local girl, a nurse named Allison, which was why he was building in Kinvara. He was building a frame house, a novelty in Ireland. Nearly all Irish houses are built of block or stone, but Fintan had read about frame construction and decided to build an "American-style" house out of wood. Given the weather in Ireland, everyone thought that the brothers must be crazy.

Finton Sheehan, Co. Kerry

Fintan helped out on many of the projects at the cottage. Once, as practice for his own house, he designed and built a new set of stairs to the loft in my place. When his house was finished he would stop over with his flute after his kids were in bed and we would play and play. Later on, Fintan and Allison's kids, along with Aidan and Martha's, would come over with their tin whistles and give me concerts. They played tunes like "Maggie in the Woods" that they had learned at school.

By the time I had removed all the old thatch, Jim Hehir was pushing ninety and had given up riding the High Nelly. He hadn't given up the Raleigh bicycle though. He pushed his old friend along wherever he went, using it as a kind of walker and a companion. He liked to stop by for a chat.

It was the old custom that if you visited someone who was working, it was the neighborly thing to do to pitch in a little bit. I remember one day I had been working with a jack hammer taking down the abutment that helped to support the front wall. There were two or three friends over helping with sledgehammers and crowbars as we tried to knock it down. Jim came by. In the tradition of a good neighbor, he used his walking stick to clear a few small stones away. He was a good old man.

Gerry and Donal were used to walking right into the cottage the way they had when they were boys and Maggie Deeley had lived there. They continued on in the same manner after I owned the place. If I left the door open when I was working they would walk in, sit down and not say much. Usually they would say nothing except, "Yes, yes, yes" when I asked them if they wanted some tea or "'tis, 'tis, 'tis" when I made comments about the weather.

Once in a great while, they would help out when I was mixing cement and they did incredibly neat work with the shovel. They didn't do this often. Most of the time they would just stand around watching me work. Once I got used to it, I didn't mind. I even thought that their presence might be useful. I did a lot of work high off the ground on ladders and homemade scaffolding and since the cottage didn't have a phone line I liked to think that if I fell, they might flag down a car on the road and ask for help. Fortunately, I never had an occasion to find out if my hopes were well founded.

One day, the boys were sitting at the table watching me work. I had a gig that night and I told them that I needed a nap in before I left. I sent them out the door and took my snooze. When I woke up an hour later, I happened to glance out the window. They were both sleeping in the tall grass right outside my door.

I built a loft over the black hole but hadn't yet cleaned the room out. Deckie came over and in between playing tunes and chatting we cleared out the old dry manure, poured a cement floor and turned that room into a small kitchen and bathroom. A cellphone, my first, made it possible to call a plumber. After I had the place plumbed, I installed the sink that I had been using with Michael Deeley's hosepipe in the new kitchen and used the Coleman stove for cooking. Using the cell phone again, I arranged to hook up to the town water system and the electric grid. The cottage and I had joined the modern world.

Declan had a regular Saturday night gig at Gus O'Connor's in Doolin and Billy McCormick played the pipes with him. They had been playing that gig for years. When Declan discovered that I was learning the pipes he kept after me to come out and meet Billy. After about a year of nagging, I did take a break from working on the cottage to drive out to Doolin and there I met the man who would become my main influence on the pipes.

Billy was very friendly and invited me out to his house on Sunday, the following evening. He lived in Kilnaboy just outside of Corofin with his wife, Marie, and their two young sons. His house was on the Burren, about a half an hour drive from my place on narrow back lanes that had grass growing down the middle of them.

As I neared Billy's, the giant shell of a ruined manor house suddenly appeared on my right perched on a hill above the road. It had no roof and the walls were crumbling in places. The early evening light showing through the empty window casements gave it an eerie look.

Maura Rua's

I found out later from Marie, who was born and raised in the area, that it was the house of the legendary Maura Rua a formidable woman of the seventeenth century who may or may not have thrown her third husband out of the top floor window.

When I arrived at Billy and Marie's house we all sat at a big farm table and had a meal of boiled bacon and cabbage. We talked about piping, music and musicians. He took out his pipes and we played into the night.

Billy told me that when he was about twenty, he had come down to Dublin from Carrickfergus in the North where he had grown up, with some of his Belfast musician friends. Their mission was to play the reel "The Bank of Ireland" on the steps of the Bank of Ireland. At the time Billy had a small practice set, bellows, bag and chanter. They were playing away on the steps when a group of tourists from America came by. One of them was an elderly nun. She was enjoying the music and the day. She told Billy that she liked his piping and asked his name.

"Billy McCormick."

"My grandfather was a Billy McCormick. He was a piper too."

They talked about the coincidence and then she said, "I have his set. Would you like them?"

Billy couldn't believe his ears and probably, like me when Paddy Hill and John Curtin had first mentioned the Linehan set, didn't really think it would come to pass. But a few weeks later, the pipes arrived and he suddenly had a famous set of Uilleann pipes.

His set had been made in Philadelphia in the 1880s by William Taylor for a star pupil, Kid Eddie Joyce. Unfortunately Joyce hadn't been able to play them for long. He had a brain hemorrhage on stage at the age of nineteen. He didn't die but was never able to play well again. When he did die years later, his bereaved widow had to sell the set to pay for his burial. A man who was a friend of Chief O'Neill bought them and carried them home to Chicago. This man was Billy McCormick. When he passed away, the set, like mine, went to a convent, this time because his heir, the nun was living there.

Fox, badgers, hares and the occasional car would appear suddenly in the headlights as I returned home that night and on the many, many nights that followed over the years. As I descended from the Burren near Kinvara, the view opened up and I saw the lights of Galway City sparkling across the bay. When I entered my quiet cottage after the eventful evening, I went to sleep with the sound of the pipes in my head.

Billy had invited me to visit again the following Wednesday. He worked full time in a stone quarry, but even after his long day at work, he was always ready to play music. After he cleaned up we sat down again at the big kitchen table and started to go over tunes, or, as Billy called them "chunes." For the next ten years Billy worked with me showing me his techniques, up hand and down hand triplets, ghost Ds, hard Ds, crans, pips and rolls. It took me a long time to make my fingers do them, and many I am still working on, but Billy did his best and was infinitely patient. He showed me how to take all the tunes I had on the fiddle and the accordion and using the techniques turn them back into the piping tunes that many of them had originally been.

Tom and Billy McCormick, in Billy's Kitchen

From then on, whenever I was back, I would play with McBilly and Declan, along with Michelle, a banjo player from France, Christie Barry the flute and whistle player and sometimes Terry Bingham on concertina. We played mostly at Gus O'Connor's but also at the Royal Spa and the ancient Roadside Tavern in the town of Lisdoonvarna. I played fiddle mostly, but also some guitar. I occasionally played the pipes but Billy was so good, I reluctant to muddy up what he was doing by playing the pipes with him in public. His playing is very clean and bright. It's full of details and the intricacies are what make Uilleann piping so intriguing. People would sit as close as possible to watch Billy's fingers perform their magic and hear a master at work.

The cottage was still a work in progress. I met a man from Chicago by the name of Cloonan who was living in Galway. He was in the mood to come out to the cottage to see what could be done.

Since I had knocked off the buttresses that helped hold up the walls of the old cottage, we decided to reinforce them with concreate and some rebar that we "found" by the docks in Galway.

Then Cloonan had a really brilliant idea. Although the bedroom had a ceiling, the metallic blue galvanized roof was still visible above us in the main room and over the loft. Cloonan decided that a vaulted ceiling would be just the ticket. We got a load of two by twelve boards which Cloonan measured and marked with curves. We took them to Eugene Lambe who was now living in Kinvara. He used a band saw to cut the patterns and we brought the boards back to the cottage. Standing on some makeshift scaffolding we spiked the two by twelves to the rafters. Then we nailed knotty pine tongue and groove to the rafter framework and soon had with the curved vaulted ceiling that Cloonan had envisioned.

On breaks, Cloonan and I explored the bohereens around the cottage and some of the fields nearby. We found two ring forts in the fields behind the cottage, prehistoric circular stone enclosures that had arched doorways with steps on either side leading up to the tops of the walls. The ones we found were about a hundred feet in diameter and had walls twelve feet high and about ten feet thick. We walked around on top of them. The cattle in the field kept staring at us and seemed to wonder what we found so interesting. These two forts were not on any of the maps of archeological finds around Kinvara and so don't have many (if any) visitors. I did find them marked on an old ordinance map later, but ring forts are so common in parts of Ireland that they are considered almost a nuisance.

Cloonan did spot something near one of the ring forts that he found as interesting as the cows found us. I followed him over to see what it was. He was gazing at a big patch of magic mushrooms. He picked a bunch and left them in my sunny doorway to dry. He had them with him when I dropped him off in Galway that evening. I was back to pick him up the next morning, but I couldn't find him. I never saw him again, but a few weeks later I heard that he had been spotted preaching the Gospel on a street corner in Dublin.

Eugene Lambe came by and told me that he had a big pile of stuff under tarps out back that he wanted to get rid of. He needed room in his back yard because he was planning to build a boat. I ended up with three large glass-fronted cabinets, a gas cook stove and a refrigerator with a bumper sticker on it that read "Sober, but still crazy."

Eugene had never built a boat before, but he liked a challenge. He said, "Anyone can make pipes but not everyone can build a boat."

It was to be a thirty-eight foot sailboat with a steel hull. It took him a few years, but he succeeded. He rigged it up himself and sailed it all over the Atlantic, the Mediterranean and the Caribbean.

Around this time Brian Miller and Django Amerson, a couple of young musicians whom I knew from St. Paul, were in Ireland and came to visit. They had stopped by Eugene's first and Django in particular was impressed. Being a builder himself, he talked about the beautiful work that Eugene had done on the old school in Fanore and on the decommissioned Guard station in Kinvara where he now lived. He thought that Eugene was the coolest person he had ever met. We were talking and playing tunes in front of the fire when Django blurted out, "I wish he was my father."

I said, "He might be."

Since Eugene is quite a storyteller, I decided to tell one I had heard about him back in the seventies. Eugene had quite a reputation as a rake and had acquired the nickname of Lambe the Ram. He was becoming known as a fine pipemaker as well. He had a backlog of orders from people all over the world who had sent him deposits and were waiting for their sets to be finished.

Those were wild times and Eugene had forgotten about one of his orders. The buyer came to Ireland from America looking for Eugene and his new set. He found him in The Cellar Bar and Eugene promised to have the set ready in a few days. He had a half-done set in his workshop and worked day and night to finish it. It was nearly complete and all that Eugene lacked was some leather to make the bag and bellows. The hour was late and Eugene knew that the man would be over in the morning to collect his pipes before he flew home. Lambe stopped in a pub to brood. As he sat at the bar a nice looking girl came in and Eugene struck up a conversation. She was well dressed in the fashion of the day and staying in a B & B nearby. She invited Mr. Lambe over for a late night session. In the morning Lambe was gone and so was the leather skirt she had been wearing at the pub the night before. Later that morning an American boarded the plane at Shannon proudly carrying a newly minted full set of Eugene Lambe Uilleann pipes complete with bag and bellows.

We played on in front of the cozy turf fire. I think we were in the middle of playing "Sean sa Ceo", or "John in the Fog" when I suddenly jumped up, grabbed Mag Deeley's old cane and started banging the ceiling with it until the handle broke, yelling, "Get out ya bastards!"

I was addressing the rats that I heard up above. Brian and Django smiled, nodded and started talking about the lateness of the hour. They left soon after.

I needed to do something about the rats. There had been a shed out back of the house that Aiden had knocked and after that I had rats in the cottage. At first, I didn't realize it. I told myself that the thumping and rustling that I heard in the storage area above my bedroom was perhaps birds nesting, flying in and out and enjoying the cottage in much the same way that I did. In fact, I was pleased that I had never seen any evidence of mice. Eventually I had to admit that the absence of mice was due to the presence of rats.

I couldn't fool myself about them any longer when, one day, I went out to mow the lawn and had left a pint carton of milk on the table inside. When I came in a half hour later, the carton was tipped over and some of the milk was dripping down onto the floor. I picked up the carton, cleaned up the spill and headed outside again. When I came in the next time, the carton had been tipped over again.

I hurried down to the hardware store and bought a dozen big tablets of poison. I put them all around in the storage space and anyplace else in the cottage that I thought might be popular with rats. It was like hiding square purple Easter eggs. The tablets disappeared fast and in a few days I was back at the hardware store to resupply. The lady behind the counter told me to string the tablets on a wire so that they wouldn't be dragged away. They were all chawed down within a week. It took about a year, but I was delighted when finally I saw my first mouse in the cottage. I couldn't help but say, as the neighbors had once said to me, "You are very welcome here."

Chapter 34
Larger Than Life

One night at about two a.m., I was asleep on the boat tied up safely to the city dock in Bayfield, when I heard a very loud engine driving up the pier where no vehicles are allowed. It stopped alongside my boat. I stuck my head out of the hatch and saw Big John, a buddy of mine. He shouted, "Permission to come aboard?"

I said, "Sure," and grabbed some clothes. Suddenly the boat took a lunge to port as Big John stepped aboard. He weighed nearly four hundred pounds. When I climbed up into the cockpit with him, he shouted, "There's six of them after my soul."

Asking him what he meant wasn't necessary. He needed no prompting to continue. "Two Catholic priests, a Lutheran minister, one Rabbi, a Methodist and even the Mormons think I'm going to Hell and they're trying to save me."

Lights in other boats along the pier were starting to come on. Neither John's jeep nor his voice had a muffler. That was handy for Bayfield residents because if Big John was driving through town, the noise of his jeep gave them a chance to slip into a shop or around a corner if they weren't up to tolerating his overwhelming presence.

John was a metal worker and retired gangster in his fifties from St. Paul's North End. He was about six feet tall and had permed brown hair on his gigantic head. He was always either very subdued or totally overwrought. There was very little in between. He knew nearly everything there was to know about stainless steel, brass and iron and had an extensive shop that was full of lathes, punch presses, grinders, pipe benders and welding equipment. Big John had it all and it was all hot.

John had been the self-educated engineer of a criminal enterprise that pitched water purification and sewage treatment systems to small communities in the South. Once the bids were accepted and the deposit checks received, John and his front men would buy the back hoes, diggers, tools and trucks needed for the job and then disappear. The equipment would reappear in Minnesota for later sale and the gang would reappear looking more professional in the next town. They had never actually completed a project, but John was anxious to let me know that he really could design a sewage treatment plant, or a dam, or anything else you wanted. To prove it he would draw plans, in fabulous detail, right there on a bar napkin.

His former gang had been up to Bayfield several times in Cadillacs looking for him with new business ideas, but everyone around there knew that John was retired and his former coworkers never found him. That was why John loved Bayfield.

One day I went with John to talk to the owner of a marina who needed some metal work done in the aftermath of a big storm. When the man introduced himself as Nixon, Big John burst out laughing right in his face, sputtering, "Nixon! Nixon!"

Big John saw the look in the man's eye and stopped. He said, "Nixon wasn't a crook....he just got caught."

Dave Nixon didn't look amused, but he hired John to do the work anyway.

All John's medications were prescribed by his doctors, just not in the doses that Big John consumed them in. He swallowed anti-depressants by the handful, sometimes twenty or more at a time and multiple pharmaceutical doses of ibuprofen on a daily basis. When he was sad he would go into a restaurant and order ice cream in "the biggest bowl you have."

He had a toy poodle named Abby that he doted on. She always had ribbons on her ears and tail and John painted her toenails regularly in all the colors of the rainbow. He used to invite me up to his hideaway to watch "The Red Green Show" and he would roar with laughter at every sketch. He wondered why people thought that the series "Twin Peaks" was spooky. He said, "The people on that show aren't any different than the people around here."

One Sunday at Grunke's, John's favorite restaurant, we were sitting with a friend of his who, just a few months before had received a heart and lung transplant. John was musing loudly on the question of whether his friend was the same guy he knew before or some other guy now that he had a new heart.

The place was not very busy, so the other diners in the room could hear nothing but Big John. You could feel the tension and disapproval in the air of the restaurant as he talked on and on without noticing. A neatly dressed man about four and a half feet tall, who had been sitting at a table with some other quiet people approached and asked, "Sir! Could you please keep your voice down? You are disturbing us."

John turned bright red and I was waiting for the explosion, but he didn't say a word. He kept his head down and we finished up our meal. Ten minutes later after we had paid our bills, stepped out of the door and moved away from the restaurant, Big John yelled at the top of his lungs, "That little bastard!" and went on to describe all the things he should have done to the guy until he was laughing as hard as we were.

He jumped into his mufflerless jeep and blasted his way out of town and back to his hideout in the woods. That winter Big John died. His friend with the new heart found him frozen in the snow the following January.

*****

My Mom and Dad came up to Bayfield to see the boat. They were in their late seventies and neither had ever sailed before. It was early in the season and very windy so there weren't many other boats out. We were sailing along the northern side of Madeline Island when my Dad asked if he could take the wheel. We traded places in the cockpit. The boat was heeled over and going as fast as she could go. My Dad was wearing a cap and, sitting there in the cockpit smoking his pipe he looked like an old hand. My mother was climbing up and down the cabin ladder with coffee and snacks as the boat plunged along, looking as relaxed and at home as my Dad.

After a while my dad said, "Somebody told me that he heard you sing "Danny Boy" at a funeral. I thought you didn't sing that one."

My Dad used to ask for "Danny Boy" and even beg me to sing it back in the MacCafferty's days. He sometimes teared up when I refused, as I always did back then. He would say, "You know, it was your grandmother's favorite song."

I didn't have anything against the song, but I knew from my Boston days that if you sing "Danny Boy", the next request is either "When Irish Eyes are Smiling" or "McNamara's Band". Before you know it, the evening starts to resemble a Bing Crosby tribute show. In the seventies, the last thing a young hippy folk singer type wanted was to be known for that kind of song. In the eighties, when I was living in Wisconsin, the Spooner newspaper published an article about me with the title, "Whatever you do, don't ask for 'Danny Boy'."

Then, when I was about forty, I was playing a funeral for a man from Connemara and the family asked for it. I realized that I not only didn't mind singing the song, I actually kind of enjoyed it. After that I started to sing "Danny Boy" if the request was sincere. I still prefer to hear someone else singing it. After all, I'm not a tenor....maybe a fiver.

It was the turn of the century and Timmy Fitz made a live recording of me and a flute player named Larry Nugent at Kieran's. I had first met Larry at a session in Chicago at the Abbey Pub. He was from Fermanagh and had come over to live in New York in the early nineties. He had just moved to Chicago when we met. Later he married a girl from Stillwater. They had a big wedding in St. Paul and a reception just across the St. Croix River in Hudson, Wisconsin.

Number Three, sure that the lack of an invitation was a mere oversight, suggested that we crash the reception. Many of the old Chicago musicians were there and when they saw me they asked me up to sing. Larry and I have been fast friends since that day. He was often in town because Timmy Fitz was booking him to play Kieran's and some other places and putting him up in a building that he had bought on Rice Street in St. Paul.

We wanted to make a CD to sell at the upcoming Minnesota Irish Fair. Larry was under contract with a record label at the time and we couldn't use his name so we called ourselves "The Mystery Band of the Millennium." On the first night we recorded, Scotty Sansby, the drummer from my old rock and roll band, The Inmates, was in the crowd. I hadn't seen him since the sixties but I invited him to play with us knowing that he was a born percussionist. Even though he had never played Irish music before, he fetched some spoons and a washboard from his car, sat on a chair in front of the stage and, by tuning into our feet and fingers, was able to get under the music and lift it. We recorded two nights and there was a boisterous crowd both times. Between songs on the second night someone shouted out a request. I thought I heard "Danny", but I know several songs about Dannys.

"Danny who?" I shouted.

"'Danny Boy'?" he repeated.

We tore into a kind of rocking version of the song to fit the mood of the crowd. Texas Tom made a few cameo appearances that weekend as well. Fitz recorded it all and took the liveliest tracks, including the "Danny Boy" with the preceding exchange and put the whole CD together within a week. We called the album "Fast Spon Joe Lucks", slang for quick cash, because our reason for recording it was entirely mercenary.

At the fair Larry and I were up playing, when I saw Caitlin and Meghan Sweeney, daughters of a friend, Tom Sweeney. Tom played the fiddle and I'd known the girls from their earliest step dancing days. They were about sixteen and eighteen now. I asked them to walk through the crowd and try to sell a few of the CDs.

It was a beautiful summer day, and the audience at that stage sits facing the Mississippi River taking in the panoramic view of downtown St. Paul on the far side. Everyone was in a happy mood and the girls looked gorgeous as they moved through the crowd flogging the CDs while we played. They sold dozens of them in the fifteen minutes we had before our enterprise came to an abrupt halt. Fitz came roaring onto the scene in a golf cart and said, "You can't do that. It's against the rules."

"Then why did you record us?" I asked.

"All CDs have to be sold from the merchandise tent."

"Well, that's no fun!"

But Fitz was already speeding off in the golf cart to put out another fire somewhere else. When I told Larry what had happened, he jumped off the stage in the middle of the show to look for Fitz. He was going to take matters, and Fitzy's neck, into his own hands. Fortunately, Larry never found him because Fitz was practically running the festival and was never in one place for long. Larry cooled down, returned to the stage and finished the show.

Larry can play no matter how he is feeling. Once he has a flute or whistle in his hands, the music takes over. One winter night, when it was twenty below, I gave Larry a lift from Kieran's in Minneapolis to Fitz's building in St. Paul. The heater in my car wasn't working and there was black ice on the road. Larry pulled out the whistle and said, "Have you heard this one, Tom."

He started playing a jig. As I approached a red light and started to slow, the music slowed down. As the car idled at the light, the jig became a slow air. When the light turned, Larry's tune sped up along with the car and if I would hit a patch of the black ice, Larry's whistle skidded or spun along with the tires. Without the benefit of gloves, heat or a defroster, he kept the music perfectly synchronized with the car all the way to Fitzy's place.

Fitz was the man people would call when they wanted Irish music. He booked nearly everybody when they came to town. He not only booked them, he picked them up at the airport, put them up in his building, provided them with food and drink, made sure they got paid and promoted their shows. At the Irish Fair he saw to it that musicians and dancers were treated right. The Fair's hospitality tent, when he was running it, was a lavish affair and truly a place that brought the artists together. The clincher was he never took a dime from any musician for all the work he did.

Fitz was a big man, short, but big in personality and big in girth. That was what did him in. One night not long before St. Patrick's Day, Wee Barry Nelson flew in from Belfast and Fitz wasn't there to pick him up. He knew something was wrong when he called and Fitz didn't answer his phone. Barry took a cab from the airport to Fitzy's building on Rice Street. He and some others knocked on Fitz's door but weren't able to rouse him. Finally, Milo, a friend who also lived in the building, climbed in through a window and found him. Tim Fitzgerald was only forty-seven.

I received the phone call after it happened and was stunned. Later it sunk in and as I drove alone down the freeway thinking about the huge role he played in the local Irish music scene, I called out loud, "Fitzy, what are we going to do now?"

I wasn't the only one. All the musicians who lived locally and played the Twin Cities pubs seemed to feel the same way. Musician friends from all over the country and even Ireland were calling me to ask if it was true. Larry Nugent dropped everything and came straight to St. Paul for the wake. With St. Patrick's Day just around the corner, many local festivities were in disarray because Fitz kept track of most of what he was doing in his head. Organizers and performers scrambled to figure out where they needed to be and when they needed to be there.

Fitz was given a huge send off in the Titanic Lounge at Kieran's, the place he managed for so long. It was the last big event held there. Kieran's pub was moving. Fitz had helped to design and build the new place and the doors were to open on St. Patrick's Day.

Chapter 35

The More Charm Is In It

When I next flew to Ireland, I finished sealing off the cottage to the outside to keep the warmth in and the wildlife out. Declan came over and we tore up the old floors. We put down some thick plastic sheeting and, with a borrowed cement mixer poured new concrete floors. We laid Pergo flooring over the concrete with extra padding underneath in the main room for dancing. That took care of the floor. The next step was doing something about the interior walls in the main room, kitchen and bathroom.

John McCormick and his father, Ed, from St. Paul came over and stopped to see me at the cottage. Ed had been the pipe major of the Brian Boru Irish Pipe Band for many, many years, and John had played the Highland pipes since he was about ten. The two of them came straight from the airport and were still jetlagged. I showed them around the cottage and Ed had some great ideas for the walls. They decided that they would spend the first full day of their holiday plastering and whitewashing. Ed's idea for whitewashing was to use lime, white cement and plasticizer mixed together with water. He thought that this would repel the damp and would not rub off on your clothes if you bumped against it. When they left for their B & B, I went out and rounded up the materials.

The next morning the McCormicks showed up ready to work. We plastered a section of wall to the right of the front door. John and Ed were the experts and did the plastering while I watched and assisted. Later that evening we tried the whitewash mixture on the new plaster and it worked.

The following day I took the McCormicks out to see Connemara and decided to drop in at Teach Na Tra. Johnny Mulkerrin and his wife Barbara were running the B & B now. Dado had passed away, but Momo was still there. She didn't remember me. I was a little disappointed because I had such vivid memories of the times there, but she was getting on and it had been nearly thirty years since Barbara, Chuck and I had been regular guests.

John McCormick was playing quite a bit of accordion by this time and I asked Johnny Mulkerrin if he still played the melodeon. He said that he hadn't been playing because one of the buttons on his box didn't work. He brought it down and neither John nor I could resist opening it up to see what the problem was. It was John who spotted the reed that had rusted right off.

Johnny said that he had been planning for years to take the instrument into Galway to have it fixed, but had never gotten around to it. Somehow the talk turned to whether a reed could be fashioned out of a saw blade.

The next five hours were spent expending every bit of Connemara and Yankee ingenuity that we could muster between the four of us. Johnny sacrificed several saw blades and we subjected them to tin snips, an electric grinder, files, a lump hammer, a sledge hammer, solder, and beeswax.

At some point we had moved from the kitchen table to the outdoors. Spectators in the form of Connemara ponies, Border collie puppies and neighboring children came and went. As Johnny Mulkerrin was getting ready to strike a rivet (fashioned from a nail) with a sledge hammer to attach the new, but exceedingly ugly reed to the reed plate, Momo ran out of the house and called, "I remember you now, Tom."

The reed sounded in tune but still had the tone of a hacksaw blade. Johnny had a working box, John and Ed had been able to make use of their mechanical abilities and knowledge of reeds and Momo had remembered me. It was a day well spent.

*****

I had been asking around about the roof and several people had suggested that I talk to Charlie Piggott because he had thatched his own stone farmhouse when carrying out extensive renovations. I had met Maggie, Charlie's wife, back in Galway in the seventies just before they married, but had never met Charlie. He was living in Kinvara and I stopped by. He agreed to come over to the cottage to have a look.

Charlie told me what it would take to thatch the place, and then we had a few tunes. He was busy playing music and touring and said that it would be a year or more before he could think about giving me some help.

Later that week I was working away on the cottage, plastering on my own for the first time and not having much success. Just as I was becoming thoroughly discouraged, Charlie's van pulled up. He jumped out and said, "Tom, I was just driving by and I have a tune for you that you might like."

I invited him in. I showed him what I was doing and explained the trouble I was having.

"Watch me and tell me what I'm doing wrong."

I went back to mudding the wall and Charlie spotted the problem right away.

"You're starting at the bottom. Try starting at the top and working your way down."

I loaded up the trowel and tried it from the top, but I was still having some trouble getting the mud to stick.

"Take handfuls and just keep throwing it on until it sticks."

I tried that and soon got the hang of it. I was able to finish the rest of the plastering and whitewashing over the next few months.

Once I knew that I had the method down, I took a break and made some coffee. I joined Charlie at the table and asked him what tune he had for me.

Charlie smiled, "It's called 'Scatter the Mud.'"

He pulled out the box and taught me the tune.

Charlie invited me along to a few upcoming gigs and I played with him occasionally in Clare and Galway over the next ten years. He sometimes played with a mountainy character from East Galway, a bodhran and box player, sean-nos dancer and storyteller named Tomas O'Niallain. He was the epitome of the old style farmer musician of which there used to be many but now are very few. He wore the old tweed suit and cap and could do more to entertain a room than ten perfectly proficient champion musicians. He had quips about everything under the moon as well as the sun. When he would play the wooden edge of his bodhran with his stick he would say, "That's the bit on the side," and wink.

Tomas had foot trouble and always wore big leather work boots. Once he had to go to the hospital for an operation on his foot. His old time humor was a big hit with the nurses. One of them inquired, "We've heard that you're quite a singer. Would you ever give us a song?"

Tomas gave them his startled look and said, "There's an old song that I got from me father, but I couldn't sing it."

The nurses pleaded with him.

"Oh, it's awful sad. I'm afraid you won't like it."

"Oh we will. Please. Let's hear it."

"But it's very sad. I don't think I can. It's called 'The Lamb's Farewell to the Mountain'."

"Please. Please sing."

Tomas sat up a little higher in the bed, took a deep breath, and with heart rending feeling, loud enough to be heard throughout the entire ward bleated, "Mmmma-a-a-a-a-a……. MMMMa-a-a-a-a-a."

Tomas styled himself a rake and used to say frequently and loudly, "Every man loves his wife, and I love every man's wife."

Number Three was over once staying with her mother's family in Northern Ireland and had come down to the cottage to visit me. I was playing with Charlie and Tomas at the Pier Head in Kinvara. She didn't believe for a minute that Tomas was the philanderer that he made himself out to be and decided to test him. She ran towards him with her lips puckered, ready for a kiss. Tomas, with a truly startled look this time, nearly fell backwards over a table trying to escape. He was, after all, a married man.

My favorite quote from Tomas O'Niallain is this, "The oftener you play a tune, the better the tune gets to know you. And the better the tune knows you, the more charm is in it."

Deckie lived in a tiny trailer in the corner of a site that he had purchased cheap years ago. The reason the land didn't cost him much was because it was really just a bog hole and no one else would take it. Declan put the word out to everyone in the area that if they had any rocks, stones, rubble, tree stumps or anything else bulky that they wanted to get rid of, that they were welcome to dump it at Deckie's.

He built a sort of island that over the years he figured had become solid enough to build his house on. I'm not sure how he dealt with the county planning board, but block by block, he started to build a house. He never took a bank loan but just bought materials a little at a time. Whenever he had a bit of cash to spare he would buy five or six blocks and haul them home in his car. The doors and windows he picked up here and there and then made openings to suit. No one had thought that he would ever finish, but after two decades, he was nearly done and the house looked as fine as any other conventionally built house.

I sometimes played with Deckie in the pubs around Kilfenora where he would raise the rafters with his rendition of "Eileen Og" and raise eyebrows with his song "The English Royal Family." He didn't drink much himself, but every year before Christmas he would drive out to Connemara and buy big bottles of poteen. Back home he would divide it into smaller clear glass bottles, add a little food coloring and give them to friends as gifts.

For about a year I had been pondering the difficulties involved in thatching the cottage and I was starting to think that it might be more trouble than I was prepared to take on. I was debating whether to use some other material one day when Michael Deeley stopped by. I told him that I was thinking of using slate or a fiberglass to roof it.

Michael said, wistfully, "Don't you remember, Tom, when you used to talk about thatching it?"

Now my decision was made. Thatch it.

Charlie was busy with music and couldn't help out. He advised me to talk to Mickey Martyn in Kinvara who had taught most of the local thatchers. Mickey came over and told me what I needed to do to prepare the cottage. The galvanized roof needed to be cut back by about a foot to allow for the overhang of the thatch and the chimney had to be built up about eighteen inches higher. The biggest job was to build "barges" on the gable ends of the cottage. The barges were upward extensions of the gable wall meant to keep wind from getting under thatch and blowing the roof away. The barges needed to be eighteen inches high, about twenty inches wide and overhang the walls they were built on by two inches or so to keep water away from the wall.

I tackled the big job first. Billy McCormick came over to help build the forms we needed to pour the barges. My neighbor Fintan Sheehan and Declan also came by to help. We built the forms out of scrap lumber collected from our various houses. We "found" more rebar (I didn't know where to go to buy it) and I had a load of sand dropped off. I rented a cement mixer. We managed to get it all up, poured and drying in about a week.

Tom Sweeney the fiddler from St. Paul was over for a holiday. He stayed with me in the cottage for a week or so. I took him around to visit friends and play a few tunes. We also went to hear music in the pubs.

Back at the cottage we would take walks and see magpies, rooks, seagulls, larks, pheasants and cuckoos. There were hares, badgers, foxes and otters. Weasels, stoats and pine martens were fairly common sights. With all the wildlife around, I was surprised when Tom seemed to be most fascinated with the cows. Cow sightings are not rare in Minnesota, it being a very agricultural state, but Tom pulled out his camera whenever a herd of them came into view. He seemed to have a kind of love-hate attitude towards cows, photographing them at every opportunity, but becoming nervous when they got too close.

Tom worked for a trade magazine for handymen and knew quite a bit about building. He pitched in along with the others and together we raised the chimney and built a chimney cap. Because we all liked to play music, we worked casually. We would play a few tunes together in the cottage then wander out into the yard to do a little work. Then we would have a bite to eat, a few more tunes and get back to it. My friends would come and go whenever they wanted or needed to. We got everything done that way and the cottage was ready for Mickey Martyn.

I had enough money left for Mickey to make a start on the roof. His preparatory steps involved steel bars, rods, wires and anchors. Mickey got to work and I packed up to fly back to America. Before I left, Mickey told me that to finish the job he was going to need two big truckloads of reeds that came from estuaries in Turkey. They were cheaper and lasted longer than the reeds that came from the Shannon.

Once back in the States I talked to Edmund Tunney. Eamon as we called him played the Uilleann pipes. He had just obtained a Willie Rowsome set but had no chanter. I had two Rowsome chanters and Eamon and I came to an agreement. I would give him one of the chanters if he would buy the thatch. We made the trade and the money was sent on to Mickey. A few months later when I was back to Kinvara, Mickey had the front half of the cottage thatched and was three-quarters done with the back.

It was beautiful, eighteen inches thick with a nice overhang. It looked better than I could ever have imagined. The fresh thatch had a bright golden color to it. As I unpacked and settled in, the neighbors dropped in one by one to comment on the work. I wanted to hear what Michael Deeley had to say. He was over the moon about it and I was very pleased myself.

*****

Somehow over time, I had lost touch with Pat and Mary Flanagan. I had been running back and forth to Ireland and in between playing Bayfield, St. Paul, Chicago and Kansas City. In the middle nineties I had been out to Denver a handful of times playing at the Radisson Hotel and doing a few college concerts. I was playing the button accordion and Pat came to one of the concerts. I was nervous because I knew he was in the crowd. I had learned the music from him on the fiddle and thought he might not like the way I played the box. After the concert I asked with some trepidation what he thought of it and was relieved when he told me that it sounded just right.

I saw him for the last time a year or so later. He was in a wheelchair following a stroke that paralyzed his body on one side. He couldn't play himself, but he would sit in the wheelchair and play versions of tunes on his cassette player for the many musicians who visited his home and were still learning from him. I was able to visit him for a few sessions and he still had a great ear for the music.

I didn't travel out that way again for years and time had slipped away. I assumed, given his poor health that Pat Flanagan had died, but he was tough. I found out from John Nielson the fiddler, when I saw him a few years ago, that Pat had lived nearly seven more years. Mary passed away in the early summer of 2001 and Pat followed her six days later.

I regret not keeping in touch with these two who had so much to do with helping me learn the music. I have regrets when I think of opportunities missed with Paddy Hill and Cuz Teahan as well. The only way I can make amends is to keep playing the music that I learned from them. When they played or passed on the music, profit and fame were never the reason. They always played for the honor and glory of Ireland.

Chapter 36
Every Tom, Pat and Larry

I played at Tom's Burned Down every summer for years and sometimes invited friends to play. I brought Tom Sweeney along for some sailing on Lake Superior and a couple nights of playing.

Tom Sweeney

He is a gentleman fiddler and upright family man originally from Connecticut. We sailed around a bit and soon landed on the island. Sweeney had never been to Madeline Island before and didn't know what to expect. The marina was a nice, clean normal-looking place with a shop, fuel dock, restaurant and golf course nearby. We walked over to the pool. I said, "Let's go for a swim."

Sweeney asked, "Don't we have to pay?"

"Ahhh, don't worry about it. They don't care."

We availed ourselves of the pool, hot tub and sauna. This was probably the first time Sweeney had ever snuck into any place before. He kept looking around expecting someone to appear and throw us out, but I knew that the kids who worked at the marina weren't sticklers for the rules especially since they would all be out at the Burned Down that night.

We walked over to the Indian cemetery across the inlet with the little house-like structures for the dead. The graves there date back to when missionaries first arrived. Then we got our things ready for the gig and walked down the road past funny little cabins and older lodge-type places, past the town beach, an old church and a couple of large houses built for lawyers. We turned the corner to the right and there it was, Tom's Burned Down Café, still standing defiantly in the middle of town.

The circus tent and sails covering the place were flapping in the breeze. We walked in past the sign that read "Sorry, We're Open." The hippy music was playing loud and the tourists talking even louder. The islanders were bunched around the bar as if they were part of it. Sweeney was reluctant to sit on the stool that was carved to look like the hind end of a horse, so I found him another. The dogs were running around chasing each other and pausing now and then to lap up spilled beer.

Sweeney was trying to take it all in. There was a lot of long hair in the place on heads, chins, legs, and in armpits. Strange smoky odors that no island wind could ever blow away wafted over the scene from the fires, food, beer and bodies. I glanced at Sweeney again and it looked like his usually carefully combed hair was standing on end.

He silently pointed to a jar behind the bar. The sign on it read, "Need a prophylactic? Try one of Tom's. Free."

We got something to drink and started setting up. Sweeney kept looking over his shoulder. Just then Tommy Nelson strode around the corner of the office/musicians' quarters. This wooden structure that had been moved to Tommy's in 1994 after the first fire and been partially burned in the second. Tommy was wearing a vintage suit, white with black stripes, but no shirt. He had a tall hat perched on top of his head with his weather-beaten ponytail hanging down in back. He welcomed me and I introduced him to Tom Sweeney. There we were, three Toms, and at least two of us ready for whatever came next.

Tommy asked, "Do you guys mind waiting before you start? We have a bikini contest scheduled that was supposed to start an hour ago."

We said, "Sure," and sat on a bench that was originally part an old school bus waiting for the contest to begin. The rest of the bus had most likely been cut up and turned into art.

The contestants appeared from out of the crowd. They were all ages, shapes and sizes. Some had one piece swimsuits, some had bikinis and some, those who had not planned on participating, just wore their underwear. They each took their turn dancing to the music. One woman, who had come totally unprepared, had purchased her costume, a pair of skimpy Tommy's Burned Down panties, from behind the bar. As she took her turn, she noticed that Sweeney was looking a little lost and decided to cheer him up. She moved in Sweeney's direction wiggling her forefingers in a come on gesture trying to get him to dance. When Tom shook his head emphatically, she smiled and turned around to shake her barely covered backside at him, adorned with the message "Let's make getting in trouble fun again."

Sweeney turned bright red and I thought he might have a heart attack, but he survived. The contest ended and now it was our turn.

As soon as the music starts, the crowd at Tommy's picks up the beat. Feet begin to tap and before long someone jumps up and begins to shake, stomp or jitterbug. Soon the interpretive artistic types are inspiring the loggers and lawyers to join in. Within ten minutes, the sweat is flying and the dogs are howling. The young kids are dancing with their moms and it's on for a new night of revelry.

We linked half a dozen reels together because there is no use in stopping when everyone is dancing. Sweeney was playing for all he was worth. Even when he's happy, Sweeney's expression usually looks sad and a bunch of girls started throwing kisses his way trying to get him to smile. One fellow who looked like a cross between a punk rocker and a red neck started shouting, "SWEEENEY! SWEEENEY!"

The crowd took up the chant. The kid who started it strutted up to the stage and put his fist in front of Sweeney's face. Crossing his eyes to focus and still playing away, Tom was able to read the letters tattooed across his knuckles.

"T-U-F-F."

Sweeney looked apprehensive. Then the kid put up his other fist, giving Sweeney a good look. It read, "L-O-V-E". Sweeney finally grinned and the crowd cheered.

The Coleman sisters, wild-looking, extremely buxom women who had been born on the island emerged from the throng of dancers and cleared a spot for themselves right in front of the stage. They danced with everyone, but few could stand their pace for long. The sisters asked for Cushy Butterfield as they always did, being a couple of Cushys themselves.

The dancers gradually began to tire as the night moved towards morning. They formed a circle and any dancer who still had the energy jumped into the middle for a solo, while the others clapped and shouted encouragement.

We finished up the night and I went to get paid. We walked in silence through the dark town to the marina under a sky studded with stars. We boarded the Anna Rita and sailed back to Bayfield, arriving at about three in the morning. Before turning in Sweeney asked, "Are we going to do it all again tomorrow?"

"Oh yes," I replied.

After Sweeney's trip, I invited Larry Nugent up for a few days. The weather was hot. Larry and I sailed out of Bayfield on the Anna Rita, set up the wind vane steering and soon were playing away as we sailed around the Apostle Islands. I knew the good places to anchor and where the Lake Superior waters were shallow and warm. We would swim, cook up or stop for the night. One afternoon we tied up at the pier on Stockton and walked to the other side of the island where there was a wide open view of the big lake. The wild blueberries were ripening and we picked some and were eating them as we walked along the trail back towards the boat. Larry had gotten about twenty feet ahead of me and stopped suddenly. I became aware of a foul odor as if someone had used the side of the path as a latrine. Then I looked up and froze just as Larry had. I spotted the big black bear as it strolled across the path right in front of Larry.

As soon as it appeared to be safe, we hurried along back to the boat, laughing. I had forgotten to warn my Irish friend that there were plenty of bears on the island and that blueberries were a favorite food.

Larry, like Sweeney, played with me at the Burned Down, but unlike Sweeney, appeared to be totally in his element. In fact, the place must have seemed a little tame compared to the pubs he played in the North of Ireland, Chicago and New York. In the middle of one of Larry's rollicking flute rampages, a couple approached the stage through the dancers and shouted, "We love your music!"

Larry shouted, "What?"

"We LOVE your MUSIC!"

"What? You want to fight me?"

"WE LOVE YOUR MUSIC!"

"You want to fight me?"

"NO! WE LOVE YOUR MUSIC."

Larry happened to be on a visit home to Fermanagh the next time I was in Ireland and he travelled south to visit me in Kinvara. He hadn't seen the cottage before and after a cup of coffee he asked if I had any projects in mind.

The inside of the cottage was finished, but the outside needed a fresh coat of whitewash after all the changes to the walls for thatching. The weather was beautiful, so we found some brushes and started working. Fintan from next door dropped in for some tunes. Billy McCormick came by too and invited us to a soiree at his place.

We drove up to Kilnaboy the next Sunday where Billy and Marie fed us. Later friends and relatives dropped in. Billy and Larry told stories about Northern musicians and played tunes that only Northerners play. I dropped Larry at a bus station in the morning.

The following Wednesday I was up at Billy's again for our regular night of piping. Marie asked me, "What kind of a man was that you brought along on Sunday. He nearly blew the roof off the house with that flute." It was her way of telling me that she wanted to hear some stories about Larry.

I was never short of visits or people to visit when I was in Kinvara and I tried to see as many as I could. The old car that I bought from the Guard had been hauled away several years before and I had to rent cars for my visits now. One day Charlie Piggott came over when Tom Sweeney was visiting me again and the three of us went for a drive around the Burren on the way to Billy's. The old manor house that is used as the rectory for the Irish comedy series "Father Ted" is in the area.

As we were driving by, we decided to stop for a closer look. Charlie was wearing a black coat and with the collar turned up and a bit of help from a folded sheet of white paper, we made it look like a clerical collar. I stood next to Charlie who was posing with Father Ted's house visible over his shoulder and a suitably ecclesiastical expression on his face. Just as Sweeney took the picture around the bend roared a jeep full of Burren farm women, a mother and several daughters.

The vehicle skidded to a halt and all the faces inside turned towards Charlie with looks of amazement. They knew Charlie well, but hadn't seen him in a few years and were trying to figure out how they had missed his change in profession. All was explained in short order, much to the relief of the women.

Billy was the person that I visited most frequently. He never seemed to be annoyed at my piping such as it was, and he and Marie always made me welcome as a friend. One day when I was visiting, Marie told me that there was a great box player staying nearby on Lake Inchiquin. I asked what his name was.

“Paddy O’Brien.”

“I know Paddy,” I said, “He lives in St. Paul.”

I walked over and paid a visit. Paddy O’Brien and Erin Hart were renting a place by the lake. I told Paddy about the pipes and getting help playing them from Billy. We did some catching up and together recalled the Hill 16 days. Then I asked them what they had been doing while they were in Ireland. Paddy was playing a few concerts and Erin said she was researching bog bodies for the mystery she was writing. She now has several books in the series which I have since read, but at the time I didn’t even know she was writing. I still remembered her best as the woman with all the blond hair who sang and could handle sleeping in bars in the Bronx.

Chapter 37
April Fools

I was sitting in Big Pink one afternoon in a Barcalounger messing around with a flute that someone had given me. It was April First. The phone rang and I heard Number Three's voice, "Tom, I'm just calling to let you know I'm not coming home. I signed a lease for an apartment in Big Lake with another man and I'm moving out."

"Okay," I said. I was thinking of the date.

"I mean it. I'm not coming back."

"Okay," I repeated.

She hung up and I sat quietly for twenty minutes or so, not knowing what to think. Suddenly, I jumped up and shouted, "I'm going to be free!"

Of course it turned out to be messier that that and it definitely wasn't free. It was a rough time, but I found out that I had a lot of friends who were sympathetic. That April afternoon I called one of those friends and he offered the best advice I could have received just at the right time. He said, "Don't make it any worse than it already is. Don't do anything that you can't look back on in ten years and say 'I did the right thing'."

Number Three never did come back and the next seven years were a legal nightmare, but in the grand scheme of the cosmos, none of it really mattered in the long run. A few months after separating we went to marriage counselling. It didn't work. Then we tried mediation, but that didn't work either.

*****

There was a session in Molly Quinn's on Monday nights where I played whenever I was back in St. Paul. About a year after the separation, I returned from one of my trips to Ireland with a new chanter for my pipes made by Mickey Dunne in Limerick and headed straight to the session. I was still jet lagged and hadn't even bothered to unpack. I sat down at the table and started playing.

It was a fairly big session. Two chairs over from me was a bodhran player that I had never seen before. He was loud, persistent and oblivious to everything around him, including the other musicians. And his playing had all the rhythm of the proverbial tennis shoes being tumbled in a drier.

We were trying to play a march when I leaned across the new girl playing the tin whistle in the chair next to me and yelled at the bodhran player, as politely as possible, "You're effing us all up!" I settled back into my chair.

We continued to play. My comment had no positive effect. I was feeling a bit cranky after the long plane ride, jet lag and no sleep. I'm sure the legal limbo I was in was playing a part as well.

I leaned across the whistle player again to address the would-be drummer. "Do you want to take it outside? I'm ready."

Ginny Johnson

The man packed up and left, and I never saw him again. I did see the whistle player again. Little did I know that I had just met, and frightened, my future girlfriend.

It wasn't until about six months later that I really started noticing Ginny. She was a step dancer who had taken up the whistle and was interested in the pipes. I told her about a cheap practice set that could be ordered from a catalog. It had a plastic chanter with a plastic reed, a bright yellow vinyl bag, and a set of bellows made for blowing up rubber rafts, that looked like it was fashoined from the leftovers from the chanter and bag.

She ordered a set and brought it to The Dubliner one afternoon. I found a good reed in my supply that worked in the chanter. Ginny went to the Great Northern Pipers Tionól that spring with the plastic set and took a few beginner classes. Later she talked about going to the Willie Clancy Summer School in Miltown Malbay and I encouraged her to go.

Ginny did fly to Ireland for Willie Week along with a few other musicians from St. Paul and took a tin whistle course. On the first night of the summer school, I picked them up and drove them around to meet some musician friends.

Since they were all taking classes, I decided, just for the fun of it, to sign up for the piping course. Trying to keep up with the eight- and ten-year olds on the pipes was nearly too much for me. I would drive to Miltown in the morning, take classes until noon, attend more classes after lunch, take in the afternoon piping concert and then stop by Billy's on the way home to be debriefed and consoled. Back at the cottage I would practice for the next day's classes.

The weather was windy and raw most of the week and I wasn't sleeping much. I developed a fever, but I was determined to stick it out. My bag arm was starting to get sore, so I wrapped it up with an ace bandage and soldiered on.

One night I told Billy and Marie about my interest in Ginny and Marie looked me over and warned, "If you are thinking of asking her out, you better take a shower and start changing your shirt."

I finished out the week and Ginny went home. I had another month in Ireland. My arm was still sore and I was suffering from the occasional chill, but when Billy invited me to go up to the peat bog above Liscannor to collect turf, I decided to go.

Billy McCormick and a neighboring goat

From the mountain that we were on you could see Spanish Point, the bay at Lahinch, the Cliffs of Moher, Liscannor and O'Brien's Tower. That would be on a clear day. On the day we went for the turf we could only see about a hundred feet in front of us through the cold, damp fog. Somehow, while we were working I pulled a muscle in my right leg. The arm, leg and fever just worsened and soon Billy and I decided that I had a fully developed case of Bag Arm and Bog Leg.

The time came to return to St. Paul and the first gig I had was at the Minnesota Irish Fair on Harriet Island. A few days before the festival, I woke up and looked in the mirror to see that there was something wrong with the right side of my face. I tried to smile and the result was grotesque. I tried to whistle as I do on some of my songs, but all that came out was a stream of spit and hot air. I tried winking my right eye, and absolutely nothing happened. I was in trouble. It took a lot of concentration just to keep from drooling.

I limped over to the bed on my bad leg and sat down. I wasn't sure what to do next. I twisted around with my sore arm to fish my phone from my pocket and called Eamon Tunney. His wife, Manuela, is a doctor and after hearing my symptoms and taking a look, she kindly prescribed some antibiotics.

I hoped that things would return to normal before I had to play, but they didn't. I played my shows as best as I could. I turned in slightly to the right, so as not to shock anyone with my gruesome visage and did my best to forget to smile, just the opposite of what Marie Eason told me to do way back in the seventies. It was about ninety degrees out and humid, so I didn't have to worry about looking any more feverish than anyone else. I looked out over the crowd and saw Ginny sitting in the audience with her step dancing friends. I did have on a clean shirt.

To my relief, the right side of my face started working again about a month later. I was able to do my full pub repertoire without worrying about my whistling. My arm and leg were feeling better as well. I started bringing my pipes to gigs and playing them on stage.

The Friday and Monday sessions at Molly Quinn's ended when the pub closed that fall and I didn't see much of Ginny. Then she walked into the Dubliner with some friends one Friday night. I asked her if she wanted to come up and play. She sat on the edge of the stage with her whistle that first time and I told her that she could sit in any time. It wasn't long before I gave her a chair, and then a mic. If I played a song or tune that she didn't know, she would play away from the microphone until she learned it.

Ginny was willing to take any help with the music so I gave her some CDs and started going over to her house to play tunes and work on songs. I taught her a half dozen chords on the guitar, and with her guitar backing, I was able to sing while playing the pipes.

*****

The mediation wasn't working and eventually I had to file for divorce in an effort to end things. The boat was sold by this time. When we finally got to court, the judge ordered us to go to .... mediation.

*****

One cold early November day I went over to Ginny's to play some music and she announced that we were driving to the West Side to get some free kittens. She had to put her last cat down just before going to Willie Week the year before and said that being catless for a whole year and a half was all she could stand.

I was worried. A few years before my brother Danny had given us a little dog named Teddy. As far as I remember during the entire time we had the dog, Number Three never addressed me directly although she had long conversations with Teddy. We had the dog for two years.

Ginny brought home two kittens, brothers that she named Finbar and Eddie Furry. Not only were my fears that I would be demoted unfounded, Ginny's cats were the only cats I'd ever met that actually seemed to like the pipes. Finbar was particularly fond of piping and would lounge beside me on the table whenever I played. Eddie preferred the accordion. I later told Ginny about my worry the day we picked up the cats. She decided that I was suffering from PTMD, post traumatic marriage disorder.

*****

Mediation ended eventually and the divorce moved ahead in earnest. Two more years of delays, depositions and postponements followed. Finally the judge, not believing that either of us was truthful about where our money came from, and I'm sure thoroughly sick of the sight of us, granted our divorce and ordered me to sell the cottage splitting the proceeds. I had thought the cottage was safe since I had owned it for several years before the marriage, but that was not the case. It had taken seven years to progress from the original April phone call to the divorce decree.

Selling the cottage ate up another year, but I finally found a buyer. At the time of that long ago April phone call the Celtic Tiger was still roaring loudly. The value put on the cottage by the realtors was over $400,000. By the time it was sold, it fetched about a hundred thousand.

I had to return to Ireland to take care of the sale. I knew that I wasn't the first to lose property in Ireland by court order and somehow that thought made me feel a little better. I wouldn't have let it go for any other reason. It had not turned out as I expected, but, as John Curtin from Kinvara used to say, "And that's good, too."

My half of the proceeds went to pay off credit cards that I had used for my attorney fees. What was left bought a nice little foreclosure by the Mississippi in St. Paul near Pig's Eye cave. I'd had the cottage for twenty years and was satisfied that I had made the best of it.

The day came when it was time to move out of the cottage. My books, tools, and a few instruments were stored at Fintan's. I jumped in my rental car and started off towards Doolin for one more night at Gussie O'Connor's playing with Billy and Declan.

The car had a different layout than most of the cars I had rented. The windshield wiper and turn signal controls seemed to be reversed. The volume for the radio was on the steering wheel. I was fiddling with the controls as I drove towards Kinvara and had managed to turn the volume up way too high on the radio. Then I tried to adjust the lights and turned on the windshield wipers. I tried to turn off the wipers and switched on the high beams. I tried to turn off the brights, and only managed to turn on the windshield washer. Spray was flying into the open driver's side window as I careened around the curve by the post office. There were three women standing just outside the building and through the open window I heard one of them comment to the others, "He must be a Yank."

I thought about it and repeated grimly, "I must be a Yank."

As I left town I had finally regained control of the windshield wipers.

"I've been married three times. I must be a Yank."

My mood lightened a bit as I headed West along Galway Bay. I took a left on the road up to the Burren and found myself driving on the right for a moment.

"I must be a Yank."

I came over the mountain near Bell Harbor and was overwhelmed by the beauty of the vista that opened before me.

"Oh, I'm definitely a Yank."

I started laughing and was still laughing as I parked outside of O'Connor's.

Epilogue
St. Paul, Minnesota
2014

"Welcome to the Great Hall of the O'Gara's."

Ginny and I are up on stage. We have been playing every day of the twelve days of the Minnesota State Fair for the past five years. Today isn't quite as hot and muggy as it can be in August in St. Paul.

We launch into a jig. It's a tune that I learned from Pat Flanagan many years ago, "The Rose in the Heather". I am playing Paddy Hill's fiddle and Ginny is wailing away on the concertina much the same way Cuz Teahan used to play.

We are just inside the main gate of the Fairgrounds off of Snelling Avenue where Greg LeClaire sped past the ticket takers and cops in 1967 driving our band to the Teenage Fair area for a gig.

Pat Hill's great, great grandchildren, also great, great grandchildren of Dominick Caulfield, a girl and a boy, are listening to the fiddle. They were brought here by their mother. The boy is dancing a jig that no one had to teach him. His parents are delighted.

Pat Devaney's grandson, Martin, a musician, strides through past the Kivels, Malones and McDonaghs who are seated at the big wooden tables that empty and fill as the crowds pass through O'Gara's.

The talent show is taking place in the band shell down the street. It is not as loud as when the electric bands play. The din of the fair is always there. Thousands of people, eating and drinking, heading for the Midway rides and games, making their ways to the grandstand shows or the livestock barns.

Young Jack O'Gara, all of twenty-one, pulls a pint for the piper Patrick McCormick of the Brian Boru. If we suddenly flew back in time seventy years, we would still see an O'Gara pulling a pint for a McCormick.

Patrick's mother, Teresa, born a Daly, is acting out "Cushy Butterfield" and inciting the crowd to greater mirth. She soon has all but the crankiest clapping and singing along.

A man approaches. He asks for "The Connemara Rose." He says he heard me sing it when he and his future wife met at MacCafferty's. He was in the seminary and his wife was a nun. They would meet to play scrabble and listen to Irish music. He says they named their daughter Rose after the song.

As Ginny picks up her concertina to play, I make the announcement into the microphone, "We got a late start today folks, so we have to knock off early. This is our last song. It's a song we had a special request for. 'The Connemara Rose.' It is a very special request...but no money."

The man reaches into his pocket. "Just kidding sir" says I.

"No he's not" says Ginny. He puts some money in the jar. I lean to the microphone again.

"I want to thank you all for coming out and entertaining us tonight."

Acknowledgements

I would like to thank Matt Dahl and all the others who encouraged me to take up the pen.

Thanks to readers of earlier drafts including (in no particular order) Josh Dunson, John Nielson, Tim Johnson, Tom Sweeney, John McCormick, Eileen and Brad Johnson, Terry Maroney, Edward Forde Hickey, Mark Sutherland, Gary Brueggemann, Daithi O'Neill, Jan and Mike Casey, John Concannon, Billy and Marie McCormick, Fintan Sheehan, Angie and Richie Racine, Bobbie Scott, Joe Belde, Patty Suess, Franz Diego DaHinton, Kevin Creamer, Justin O'Brien, Mike Garry, Dave the Finn II and others who laughed in mostly the right places, provided photos and caught mistakes.

Paddy O'Brien, Sean and Mary O'Driscoll, Kevin McElroy, Chuck and Ann Heymann, Sean Tyrrell, Tom Nelson, Charlie Piggott and Larry Nugent all provided clarification of facts as well as corrections.

Special thanks goes to Mary Cavin who, while busy taking care of a difficult patient, still found the time to do a careful reading of what I had at one time thought was the final draft. Mary, you got the gets out.

Also thanks to Teresa McCormick for supplying intensive technical assistance in layout and design while providing sustenance in the form of treats from Mississippi Market.

John Dingley, Mike Faricy, Dan Sexton, and Tracie Loeffler provided support and expertise that was sorely needed.

However most of the credit for help on this book goes to Ginny Johnson whose perseverance and mostly unflappable patience allowed this story to be told in a coherent way, one that would not cause whiplash in the readers.

Sincere thanks to everyone who listens to, and loves, Irish Music.

You are the reason we play!

******

Made in the USA
Lexington, KY
13 June 2017